Praise for *New York Times* bestselling author B.J. Daniels

"*Cowboy Accomplice*…is a masterful blend of humor and suspense."
—*RT Book Reviews*

"Strong familial ties and several compelling secondary stories make B.J. Daniels' *Shotgun Surrender* (4) a heartwarming tale… with fast-paced Western intrigue and lots of cowboy action."
—*RT Book Reviews*

"Daniels will have you on the edge of your seat as you become completely engrossed in *Crime Scene at Cardwell Ranch*."
—Candy Cay, *Coffee Time Romance*

New York Times bestselling author **B.J. Daniels** wrote her first book after a career as an award-winning newspaper journalist and author of thirty-seven published short stories. Since then she has won numerous awards, including a career achievement award for romantic suspense and many nominations and awards for best book.

Daniels lives in Montana with her husband, Parker, and two springer spaniels, Spot and Jem. When she isn't writing, she snowboards, camps, boats and plays tennis. To contact her, write to B.J. Daniels, P.O. Box 1173, Malta, MT 59538 or email her at bjdaniels@mtintouch.net. Check out her website at www.bjdaniels.com.

New York Times Bestselling Author

B.J. DANIELS

Double Target

ISBN-13: 978-0-373-60600-9

This edition published by arrangement with Harlequin Books S.A.

For questions and comments about the quality of this book, please contact us at CustomerService@Harlequin.com.

Printed in U.S.A.

CONTENTS

This book is for my cousin Sandra Johnson Olinger.
Last summer she came to Montana, bringing with her
all the memories of a summer we spent camped on
Hebgen Lake so many years ago.
Thank you, Sandy.
And thanks for listening to the stories I wrote
in the tent beside the lake when we were kids
and encouraging me to follow my dream.
There is nothing like family.
Thanks for reminding me of that.

COWBOY ACCOMPLICE

PROLOGUE

Outside Mexico City

He sat on the edge of the bed in the dim mirrorless room, his face swathed in bandages, his mind several thousand miles away. He'd been waiting more years, through more surgeries and more pain than his mind could stand. When he closed his eyes he could still hear the crackle of the flames, feel the intense heat, smell his searing flesh.

"Señor Smith?"

He turned to see Dr. Ramon, a small, nervous white-cloaked figure, framed in the doorway.

"Are you ready?" the doctor asked in Spanish as he stepped in, the door closing behind him.

Ready? He'd been ready for years. He said nothing as the plastic surgeon pulled back the curtain. Sunlight streamed into the room, momentarily blinding him. He closed his eyes as Dr. Ramon put down a black medical bag on the edge of the bed beside him.

Slowly, carefully, the doctor began to peel away the bandages, his fingers trembling. They both knew what was at stake here.

Señor Smith as he was called here closed his eyes, having given up hope a long time ago that his face might ever be normal again.

A cool breeze caressed his cheek as the last bandage fell away. With a pain far greater than any physical one he'd ever known, he opened his eyes.

The doctor had stepped back and was now studying his handiwork, his face expressionless. "You are a new man," he said finally, his gaze skittering away at the intensity of his patient's look.

Señor Smith had heard such words before. He didn't want or need false hope. False hope had gotten other even more prestigious surgeons killed.

He reached his hand out for the mirror he knew the doctor had brought in his bag. His hand was steady as he took it. Hope made a person tremble. He had nothing but fear at what monstrous visage he would now see in the glass.

Slowly he held up the hand mirror and stared into the face of the new stranger he found there. To his surprise, this stranger wasn't hideous. Nor was he handsome. He was…average. The face of a man no one would look at twice on a street corner or across a crowded room.

He could feel the doctor waiting for his reaction, perhaps by now having heard what had happened to the other surgeons.

"It is perfect," he said, looking from the mirror to Dr. Ramon.

The doctor breathed a ragged sigh of relief. "Bueno, bueno. You are free to leave, Señor." He picked up his bag from the bed. "Vaya con dias." Go with God.

Señor Smith nodded and looked in the mirror again at his new face. He would go all right, only he wouldn't be going with God. He'd been to hell and right now he'd sell his soul just to go home again.

Except he'd sold his soul years ago, he thought with

a rueful smile. He was going home. And with a face no one would ever recognize, a body that had become hard and lean.

Like the Phoenix rising from the ashes, he had survived it all with only one dream in mind. Vengeance.

He couldn't wait to see the look of surprise on J. T. McCall's face. J.T. wouldn't see him coming. Until it was too late.

CHAPTER ONE

Outside Antelope Flats, Montana

Regina Holland glared down the empty two-lane highway, wishing a car would appear. Wishing anything would appear. Even a horse-drawn wagon. She was beyond being picky at this point.

But of course there wasn't any traffic now. She kicked the flat tire on her rented red convertible with the toe of her high heel and instantly regretted it when she saw the dark smudge of black on her expensive red shoe. She cursed her luck as she bent down to thumb at the smudge.

She'd been in the state for three days and her luck had gone from bad to worse. It had seemed such a simple task in the beginning. How hard could it be to find a cowboy in Montana? She had two weeks to find him. If she failed, she could kiss her dream goodbye. Everything was riding on this. Her entire future.

Regina knew exactly what she wanted and as was her character, she wasn't about to quit until she got it. Somewhere in Montana was her cowboy. All she had to do was find him.

Straightening, she tugged down the skirt of her expensive designer suit and scowled at the tire. Oh, she'd found her share of cowboys all right. Men of every size, shape and disposition but definitely not "The One."

But right now she swore she'd take the first cowboy who drove up with a jack and the wherewithal to change her tire. Unfortunately, it didn't look like any were going to come riding up. No John Wayne on the horizon. Not even a rodeo clown. The highway was empty and she could see both ways for miles.

A pickup had come by but hadn't stopped even when she'd tried to wave down the man behind the wheel. He'd acted as if he hadn't seen her. So much for western hospitality.

A few miles away, she thought she could make out a couple of buildings, possibly a town. Not much of one from what she could see, but at least it looked like something.

She could walk in this heat and these heels or—she glanced at the bag of tools she'd found in the trunk—or she could try to change the tire herself.

She looked down the highway again. Heat rose off the blacktop and an intense sun beat down from an all-too-expansive clear blue sky. She knew the moment she started to walk in these heels, vultures would begin to circle.

She picked up the bag of tools with two well-manicured fingers, spilling an assortment of metal objects onto the ground. How hard could it be to change a tire? She had degrees in business and advertising from Berkeley, for crying out loud.

Twenty minutes, and two chipped nails later, Regina knew how hard it could be. Impossible. She was squatting by the tire, trying to figure out how to get the stupid bolts off, when she heard the sound of a truck coming up the road. It appeared like a mirage, a large dirty brown shape floating on the highway's heat waves.

Regina didn't know how long she'd been squatting by the flat tire, but she found that her muscles had permanently locked in that pitiful crouched position. She could only lift an arm and wave frantically as the vehicle bore down on her.

The truck roared past and she thought for one horrible moment, that the driver wouldn't stop. To her relief, she heard the screech of brakes, heard the truck pull over a dozen yards in front of her car. She was bent over assessing a run in her silk stockings when she heard the driver approach.

A pair of boots and the bottom of a pair of jeans stepped into her line of vision. Both the boots and the jeans were worn and muddy. At least she hoped that was mud. The boots stopped before they reached her, then turned away. For one awful moment she thought he was leaving. Instead he called to someone she assumed was back at his truck.

"I told you to stay there, Jennie," he ordered gruffly. "Do as I tell you for once or next time I'm leaving you at home."

Her gaze and her eyebrow came up at the same time. She'd heard some Montana men still bossed their wives but he should be ashamed, talking to a woman like that.

She thought about telling him so in no uncertain terms. Then she remembered her flat tire and bit her glossed lower lip as the man swiveled back around to her.

"Need some help?" he asked in a soft western drawl.

Great voice. Regina took in the cowboy with a trained eye starting at his boots, noting with professional detachment the way he filled out his jeans. Muscled thighs. Long legs. She let her gaze travel up those legs past the slim hips, the narrow waist, to the man's wide chest. Nice. Real nice. His broad shoulders beneath the western shirt literally blocked out the sun.

His face was in shadow under his battered black cowboy hat. Didn't the good guys always wear white hats?

"Oh, I could definitely use some help," Regina said, a little breathless, trying not to flutter her lashes. How far would she go to get this tire changed? She hated to think.

He shoved back his hat. Handsome too, if you liked that rough around the edges type. Such a waste since it wasn't his strong masculine jaw, his spacious shoulders or his seductively low voice that she was looking for.

"If you've got air in your spare, it shouldn't take but a few minutes," he said and stepped past her to bend over to inspect her tire.

Regina sucked in a breath as she eyed the man's posterior. It was positively perfect. "I can't tell you how much this means to me." She practically shouted in glee, amazed at her change of luck. She'd found him. The One.

J. T. McCall went to work changing the tire and trying to hide his amusement. He'd been having a bad day, actually a bad couple of months, but he had to admit this little distraction was definitely elevating his mood.

He hadn't believed it when he'd first seen her dressed all in red, wearing the loftiest pair of high heels he'd ever seen, standing beside a matching red convertible in the middle of nowhere.

What was a woman dressed like that doing just outside Antelope Flats, Montana? Boy was she lost.

He flicked a look at her over his shoulder, mentally

shaking his head. Wait until he told Buck, his elderly ranch foreman, about this. Buck wasn't going to believe it.

He felt her gaze on him as he made short work of changing the tire. "Where ya headed?" he asked, unable to curb his curiosity.

"Antelope Flats."

"Really?" He couldn't imagine what business this woman could possibly have in the tiny ranching town up the road. It was so small it didn't even have cable TV. For J.T., after weeks on the ranch, it was the big city but for this woman— "All done."

He loaded the flat tire and the tools into the trunk and slammed the lid, then took another good look at her as he wiped his dirty hands on his jeans. She was definitely easy on the eyes.

"I can't tell you how much I appreciate this," she gushed.

"My pleasure." He figured she'd try to slip him money but he'd be darned if he'd take even the price of a cold beer at the Mello Dee. No, just seeing her the way she looked right now was plenty thanks. Standing there, teetering on her heels in the middle of the highway, a lock of her dark hair fleeing from her tight little no-nonsense French roll or whatever women called those things, and a smudge of dirt on that perfectly made-up face.

"I'd like to do something for you," she said.

He shook his head. "Consider it your welcome to Antelope Flats."

"You're from here?" she asked, eyeing him speculatively.

"Ranch just back up the road. Name's J. T. McCall," he said, not sure he liked the way she was looking at him. He started to step around her.

"Really, I must insist. You've been so kind," she said quickly, blocking his exit. "In fact, I have something in mind."

He raised a brow and grinned, telling himself this wasn't happening and if it was, *no one* would believe it.

"Of course, I'd have to see you in the saddle," she added.

"I beg your pardon?"

Her eyes widened. "You do ride a horse, don't you?"

Torn between feeling insulted and curious about where she was headed with this, he said, "I guess you could say I ride."

"Good." She looked pleased. "Because I'm in Montana looking for a cowboy." She flashed him a flawless smile, all teeth, all perfect. "And I think *you're* that cowboy."

If she thought he'd be thrilled to hear this, she was sadly mistaken. He'd already encountered one city girl who'd come to Montana looking for a real-life cowboy. Once was plenty enough.

"I appreciate the thought," he said more politely than he felt, "But, I'm not your cowboy." He started past her.

She caught his arm with one of those well-manicured hands, the nails the same red as her outfit. The hand was white as new snow, the skin soft-looking. This woman hadn't done one day of hard manual labor in her life.

"Wait," she cried. "You don't know what I'm offering you."

"I'm afraid I do," he said, carefully removing her hand from his arm. "No offense, but I'm just not interested."

"No!" she cried. "*That's* not it." Frowning, she brushed back a lock of hair and put another dark smudge on her cheek. The imperfection made her more appealing somehow.

"I'm looking for a cowboy to do a television commercial

for my jeans company, not—" She waved a hand through the air, her cheeks flushed.

She wanted him for a blue jeans commercial?

"You understand that you'd have to audition," she explained. "I can't promise that you'd make the cut but—"

"Audition?"

"To see how you look on a horse." She narrowed her gaze at him as if she was worried he wasn't getting it.

Oh, he was getting it all right.

"You see, it would be a close-up shot," she said, hurrying on. "Your face wouldn't show, just your—" She glanced below his elk horn belt buckle.

He followed her gaze, shocked. "My *what?*"

"Your…backside. It would be a close-up of it in the jeans on the horse. Your posterior, which I might add, is perfect. For the commercial," she quickly amended.

Well, now he really was insulted. He'd never had a woman proposition him before. Well, at least not like this. And he realized he didn't like it. She was sizing him up like a piece of beef on the hoof. Or maybe he just didn't like the fact that she was only interested in his "southend."

"Thanks just the same," he said as he tipped his hat. He and his perfect posterior were leaving.

She seemed surprised. "But the commercial will be shown on *national* television," she said trotting unsteadily along beside him toward his truck. "You'd be paid, of course, and you'd get to keep the jeans."

"Get paid *and* get to keep the jeans?" he asked sarcastically.

"Yes," she said smiling. "And if it worked out, this could lead to all kinds of opportunities. This could open the door for a whole new career for you, Mr. McCall."

He almost stopped walking to tell her what he thought, but he was trying to be a gentleman. That's why he'd pulled his truck over to help her in the first place.

"Wait," she cried. "At least let me give you my card."

"Lady, I hate to be rude, but I really don't have time for this," he said turning back to her, but she'd already trotted back to get her card for him.

He waited at the rear of his muddy flatbed truck, shaking his head in wonder. "I'm not going to change my mind," he called to her, not sure if the woman heard him, but doubting she would listen anyway.

He watched her lean into the car, providing him with a nice view of her tight-skirted bottom. Now *that* backside would make a wonderful commercial, he thought, momentarily distracted.

Before he could stop her, she'd rushed back to thrust her card into his hand. "I really think you should reconsider. This commercial pays more than you probably make in a year chasing cows," she said taking in his attire—and his truck.

That did it. He glanced down at the card, just long enough to see her name. Regina Holland. Regina? What kind of name was that? And her address. Los Angeles. He should have known.

"Listen up, Reggie, I happen to *like* chasing cows. And right now I have six hundred head to chase down from summer pasture, my camp cook is out with a broken leg and I don't want my butt anywhere but in a saddle heading into the high country before dark. Is that clear enough for you?"

He shoved the card—now slightly crumpled from being

balled in his fist—back into her hand and went to his truck, jerking open the door.

"Reggie?" he heard her mutter behind him. Then she called after him: "Perhaps you should discuss it with your wife Jenny."

His wife? He shook his head. "Good girl, Jennie," he said, patting the mutt before pushing her over to her side of the pickup seat. "What would make the woman think I was married to a mongrel dog?" He had a feeling he should be even more insulted.

Glancing back as he pulled out onto the highway, he saw that Regina Holland was standing in the middle of the road, looking as lost as when he'd found her. His irritation dissolved and he chuckled to himself as he shifted into second and put some distance between him and the red sports car.

No, he thought shaking his head, no one was going to believe this. Not that anyone would ever hear about it. He sure had no intention of ever telling a living soul now that he realized what the woman wanted. Perfect behind, his butt. He'd never live down the razzing he'd get. Never in a million years.

He topped a rise in the road and Regina Holland disappeared from his rearview mirror. Gone, if not forgotten.

All morning he'd been trying not to stew and he had a hell of a lot to stew over. Something was going on at the ranch and had been even before his mother returned. For almost all of his thirty-six years, he'd been led to believe that his mother was dead. Hell, he and his brother Cash, the only two of the McCall kids who actually remembered their mother, had been putting flowers on her grave every Sunday.

Then out of the blue, Shelby McCall shows up at the ranch and announces she's not only alive, but that she and Asa cooked up her demise because they couldn't live with each other and yet didn't want the kids to have the stigma of divorce hanging over them.

J.T. had never heard such bull in his life. On top of that, he and his three brothers had always thought that their little sister Dusty was the result of an affair their father had had years ago.

Turned out, Dusty was the result of Asa and Shelby getting together to "discuss" things.

Well, now Shelby was back at the ranch, tongues were waggling in three counties, his brother Cash, the sheriff, was trying to keep them both from going to prison for fraud, Dusty wasn't speaking to either of their parents and something was up between Shelby and Asa.

J.T. hadn't been able to put his finger on it. But he'd seen the looks that passed between them. He had a bad feeling they had another secret that would make the first pale in comparison.

If all of that wasn't bad enough, his brother Rourke had gotten out of prison a few months ago, come home, stirred things up good when he not only fell in love, but also cleared his name by finding the real killer who'd helped send him to prison eleven years ago.

The McCalls had always been the talk at the Longhorn Café in town. J.T. knew it was one of the reasons his brother Cash had become sheriff. He was tired of being one of the "wild" McCalls.

Of the bunch, J.T. looked like a saint. Probably because he'd had to take over the running of the ranch after Asa's heart attack. Rourke had been in prison, Cash was sheriff and his little brother Brandon was too busy sowing his oats.

Some days, J.T. resented the hell out of the family's reputation because everyone still painted all the McCalls with the same brush. The McCalls were the cowboys that fathers warned their daughters about. Western born and bred, they were a rough-and-tumble bunch, no doubt about that. Always fighting amongst themselves like a den of wildcats, but joining together in times of trouble.

And J.T. had a bad feeling this was a time of trouble as he drove toward Antelope Flats.

This morning a neighboring rancher had told him he'd seen something "odd" on their adjoining summer range in the Bighorn Mountains a week ago.

"It was one of your cows," Bob Humphries said after the two of them were seated in the Sundown Ranch office, the door closed. "Something had killed it."

Losing cattle to mountain lions, grizzlies or wolves wasn't that uncommon. He wondered why Bob had driven all the way out to the ranch to tell him this.

Bob met his gaze. "An animal didn't kill that cow," he said as if he could tell what J.T. was thinking. "It had been burned."

J.T. sucked in a breath, pulse pounding, the weight on his chest like a Mac truck.

"It reminded me of what happened about ten years ago," Bob said, worry furrowing his brow. "But those fellows are dead, right?"

J.T. could only nod.

"I suppose it could have been lightning," Bob said, still looking worried. "But I thought I should tell you since you're headed up there today."

Now as he neared town, J.T. glanced toward the Bighorns. The long range of mountains glistened against the cloudless blue sky.

He'd always loved this time of the year and looked forward to leaving the heat of the valley for the cool of the cow camp miles from a road. He liked the hard work of gathering the cattle and driving them back down to the ranch, but it was the camp's isolation that always appealed to him the most. No phone. No electricity. Nothing but the peace and quiet of the mountains, long hours in the saddle, sacking out at night in the line shack while the men slept in wall tents. The sound of the campfire, men talking cattle, the quiet that a man could find in the darkness of night up there.

But as he looked at the mountains where he would be spending the next few days, an icy chill skittered up his spine.

He shook it off and thought instead of the woman in red who'd wanted his butt. Much better than thinking about the dead men who had haunted his dreams for the past nine years.

REGINA STOOD in the middle of the blacktop, her face as red as her outfit. Jenny was a *dog!* The first time she'd glanced toward the truck, all she'd caught was a glimpse of red hair in the front seat. The back window was so muddy—

She felt sick. She knew she shouldn't have tried to do business in the middle of the highway. But the cowboy was perfect and she'd just wanted to get him before he got away.

If he looked as good in a saddle as he did bent over her flat tire, he would launch the jeans line and she could write her own ticket. She'd known she wanted a real cowboy. Not one of those Hollywood models. No, she needed the real thing, shot in his environment with panoramic views of the real west, cattle and all, behind his perfect behind.

And she'd found just the man for the job.

And she'd just let him walk away.

Not a chance, she thought as she looked after the truck. She'd never backed down from a challenge in her life. And her life had been rife with challenges, she thought. Getting this man to do the commercial was child's play given the other obstacles in her life that she'd overcome.

She'd been too confident that he'd accept her offer, she thought as she walked back to the rental car. She fought the urge to chase him down and set him straight on a few things. His rejection stung, especially when he'd thought she was offering herself. But she'd been rejected before. Not quite so offhandedly though.

She climbed in, dropped the visor and looked in the mirror, shocked at her appearance. Wiping furiously she tried to get the greasy smudges off her cheek with a tissue. Her clothing was wrinkled, her makeup a mess, her hair in disarray.

He must have thought she was a nutcase. That's why he'd turned down her offer. The way she looked, she didn't blame him for not believing her. And she'd probably come on a little strong. But she'd been so grateful to him for changing her tire—and his posterior *had* been so perfect….

She tucked a wayward strand of hair back behind her ear. Maybe she shouldn't have told him he had to audition. But she'd only said that so he wouldn't know how much she wanted him. She was pretty sure she could get this guy for a song. Coming in way under budget wouldn't hurt. Everything was riding on this.

Reaching into her purse, she pulled out her cell phone and dialed Way Out West Jeans. No service. What kind of place was this?

She started the car and looked down the highway, barely able to make out the rear end of the man's truck disappearing into the distance. What were her chances of finding another one like him?

She knew the answer to that. Whereas finding him again wouldn't be a problem. She'd seen the logo on the side of the muddy truck. Sundown Ranch. And he'd told her where he was headed. A cattle roundup in the mountains. Could she have asked for anything more ideal?

After he knew that her offer was legit, he'd be grateful that she'd tracked him down. Only a fool would turn down a chance like the one she was giving him.

She smiled as she headed toward Antelope Flats. Even if he still thought he didn't want to be the new "look" of Way Out West Jeans, she'd change his mind. The man had no idea what lengths she would go to—especially when she was desperate—to get what she wanted.

But he was about to find out, she thought, as she drove into the small western town and spotted a phone booth. She couldn't remember the last time she'd seen one of those.

Getting out of the car, she stepped into the glass-sided booth and dialed the company's 800-number.

"I found the perfect butt," she said when Anthony answered.

"Gina, darling, you know what that kind of talk does to me," he joked. Anthony was gay, her best friend and the best head of advertising she'd ever known. "So when do I get to meet him?"

"He's a bit rough around the edges," she hedged.

"You are making my mouth water."

She laughed. "He's straight. As an arrow."

"You're sure?"

She couldn't say how she knew, but yes, "I'm sure. There is one tiny little problem."

"I don't like the sound of this. You know what a tight deadline we're under here, darling."

"He needs a little convincing."

"Oh, well, then I'm not worried," he said, sounding relieved. "No man can turn you down."

She hoped he was right about that. "I'll call again as soon as I have the contract in hand," she told him. "It might take a couple of days. Also there is no cell phone service here."

"Ta-ta, darling. Call when you have the contract in hand."

She smiled as she hung up and looked down the street. Parked not a block away was a newer pickup with the same Sundown Ranch logo on the side. Getting back into her rental car she drove down the block and parked next to the truck. It sat in front of what appeared to be the only restaurant in town, the Longhorn Café.

Regina put the top up on the convertible and after locking it, headed toward the café entrance. Just as she started to open the door, a man came out, startling her.

Their gazes met. Something about him seemed familiar. He pushed past her, skipping out onto the sidewalk without even an "excuse me."

She stared after him, trying to remember where she'd seen him before, and then it hit her. He was the man who'd driven right past her on the highway, the one she'd tried to flag down to help her with her flat tire. He hadn't paid any more attention to her then than he did now as he disappeared into the general mercantile next door. How rude.

Fortunately not all Montana men were like him, she thought, as she stepped into the café and glanced around for the man she imagined would be driving the Sundown Ranch pickup outside.

The café was nearly empty except for one large round table at the back. Its half-dozen occupants had looked up as she'd entered and were still watching her with interest as she started toward the older man in western wear and a white cowboy hat sitting at the table with the younger cowboys.

"Am I correct in my presumption that you are the gentleman driving that vehicle?" Regina inquired.

He was a large man, strong-looking, his face weathered, heavy gray brow over kind brown eyes and his western clothing freshly laundered and ironed, distinguishing him from the other men at the table. He had a thick gray mustache that drooped at each end. He looked like someone's grandfather.

He pushed back his cowboy hat and blinked at her before glancing out the window at the Sundown Ranch pickup. When he looked at her again, he blushed. "Ah… um that's my truck if that's what you're asking, miss."

The younger cowboys at the table were nudging each other and grinning as if they hadn't seen a woman for a while.

She ignored them as she held out her hand to the distinguished elderly cowboy. "I'm Regina Holland and you're…?"

"Buck Brannigan," he stammered. "Foreman of the Sundown Ranch."

She flashed him a smile. "Just the man I was looking for."

CHAPTER TWO

Later that evening as J.T. rode his horse up to the cow camp high in the Bighorn Mountains, he decided to check out the dead cow Bob Humphries had told him about. Mostly, he hoped to put his mind to rest.

He'd left his new puppy Jennie at home. The other two older ranch dogs had gone with his sister Dusty and his dad to round up the smaller herd of longhorn cattle they kept on another range. He missed having at least one dog with him on the roundup but the new puppy wasn't trained to round up cattle and he'd have had to be watching Jennie all the time to make sure she didn't get into trouble.

He had enough to worry about. He'd had to leave the hiring of the roundup cow hands and cook up to ranch foreman Buck Brannigan.

Buck had assured him he had it covered. J.T. should have been relieved to hear this but something in Buck's tone had caused him concern. Finding good hands this late in the fall was tough and finding a good cook was next to impossible, especially around Antelope Flats.

J.T. hated to think what men Buck had come up with given that most of the hands he normally used for roundup from summer range had already moved on by now.

He should have had the cattle down weeks ago. But his brother Rourke hadn't just fallen in love with Longhorn

Café owner Cassidy Miller. The two had gotten married. If it hadn't been for the wedding, J.T. would have gotten the cattle down from the high country earlier. But Rourke had asked him to be his best man and the wedding had been only last week.

As he rode higher into the mountains, he saw his breath and swore he could almost smell snow in the air. In this country, the weather could change in a heartbeat and often did. Once the snow started in the fall, it often stayed in the high mountains until spring. With luck he could get the six hundred head of cattle rounded up and down before winter set in.

But as he neared the spot where Bob had seen the dead cow, J.T. wasn't feeling particularly lucky.

The late-afternoon sun felt warm on his back as it bled through the pines. He caught the scent of burned grass on the breeze before he saw the edge of the charred area.

He drew his horse up and dismounted. Over the years, there'd been days he had pushed what had happened that fall at the cow camp out of his mind. Murder was hard to forget. But this had been more horrifying than murder. Much more.

And it had started with one dead cow.

He ground tied his horse and walked through the deep golden grass. On the ride up, he'd convinced himself that lightning had killed the cow. Although rare, it happened sometimes, especially in an open area like this high on a mountainside. Much better to believe it was just a freak occurrence of nature than the work of some deranged man.

But as he neared the burned grass, he saw that the cow was gone. There were tracks where it had been dragged off. He shuddered, remembering the burned man who had also been dragged off into the woods and the grizzly tracks they'd found nearby.

J.T. glanced toward the dense pines. It was too late to go looking for the cow, even if he'd been so inclined. He turned and walked back to his horse, anxious to get to the line camp before dark.

As he rode deeper into the Bighorns, he couldn't shake the feeling that something—or someone—was watching him. Maybe even tracking him. An animal? Or a man?

He didn't relax until he glimpsed the light of the campfire through the pines. The men had built a fire in the pit in an open area between the wall tents and the line shack. Shadows pooled black under the cool dark pines and the familiar scent of the crackling fire drifted on the breeze, beckoning him with warmth and light.

Everything looked just as it had for years. The two wall tents were pitched a good distance to the right of the fire pit. The cook's cabin, a log structure almost hidden by the pines, sat back some off to the right. The ranch hands slept on cots in the tents. The boss and foreman took the bunks in the cabin with the cook.

Past the campfire and down the hillside sat the hulking outline of the old stock truck. He was glad to see that the truck had made it up the rough trail. It would probably be its last year. He'd put off buying another truck because this one had been doing roundups almost as long as he had and there was something about that that he liked.

As he turned his horse toward the corrals, he felt his earlier unease settle over him like a chill. Something was very wrong. The camp was too quiet. Usually the hands would be standing around the campfire, talking about cattle or horses, telling tales and arguing about something.

And typically, his foreman would be right in the middle of it, Buck's big deep bellow carrying out over the pines like a welcoming greeting.

Instead, the men were whispering among themselves and Buck was nowhere to be seen.

Riding over to the corral, he dismounted. Something had happened and whatever it was, it must not be good. The cowhands' horses milled in the corral. Eight horses, six the hands had ridden up individually during the day from the trailhead. The two extra horses Buck had brought up in the stock truck.

As J.T. began to unsaddle his horse, Buck came out of the line shack and headed toward him as if he'd been waiting anxiously for his arrival. Not a good sign. J.T. tried to read the look on the elderly foreman's weathered face. Worry? Guilt? Or a little of both? Whatever it was, J.T. feared it spelled trouble.

He waited for his foreman to bring him the bad news as he busied himself unsaddling his horse. His first thought was that Buck had lied about finding a camp cook. Their regular one had broken his leg riding some fool mechanical bull. Without a camp cook, they'd be forced to eat Buck's cooking, which was no option at all. Ranch hands worked better on a full stomach and there was a lot less grumbling.

Buck's cooking was so bad that the men would want to lynch J.T. from the nearest tree within a day, so Buck damned sure better have gotten them a cook.

"Okay, what's wrong?" he asked as Buck sidled up to the corral fence.

A mountain of a man, large, gruff and more capable than any hand J.T. had ever known, Buck had been with the Sundown Ranch since before J.T. was born. Buck was family and family meant everything to a McCall.

But J.T. swore that if Buck hadn't found a cook he'd shoot him.

"What makes you think somethin's wrong?" Buck asked, taking the defensive, another bad sign.

J.T. wished he didn't know Buck so well as he studied the older man in the dim light that spilled through the trees from the campfire. He would have sworn that the men over by the fire were straining to hear what was being said. Oh yeah, J.T. didn't like this at all.

He stepped closer to Buck, not wanting to be overheard, and realized he'd been mistaken. The look on the foreman's face wasn't worry. Nor guilt. Buck looked sheepish.

J.T. swore. He couldn't help but remember Buck's cockiness a few days earlier: "I'll find you a camp cook or eat my hat."

"Tell me you found a cook," J.T. demanded, trying to keep his voice down.

"Well, I need to talk to you about that," Buck said.

If it came down to a choice, *he'd* rather eat Buck's hat than Buck's cooking. "What's to talk about? You either hired a cook or you didn't."

"Have I *ever* not done something I said I would?" Buck demanded.

J.T. shot him a let's-not-go-there look and counted heads around the campfire. Six men sitting on upended logs around the fire, all as silent as falling snow. An owl hooted in a treetop close by. Behind him, one of the horses in the corral whinnied in answer.

"Do I know any of the men you hired?" he asked Buck,

that earlier uneasiness turning to dread as he let his horse loose in the corral with the others.

"A couple. I was lucky to find *any.* Hell, I had one lined up but he got hurt in a bar fight and another one—"

"I wish I hadn't asked." He could tell by the foreman's excuses that he'd had to scrape the bottom of the barrel to get six hands together for this roundup. He hated to think how bad the six might be.

"Let's get this over with," he said, hefting his saddle and saddlebag with his gear in it, as he headed for the campfire.

The men all got to their feet as J.T. approached with Buck trailing along behind him.

"Evenin'," he said to the assortment of men standing around the campfire resting his saddle and saddlebag on a log by the fire. "I'm J. T. McCall." At a glance, he'd seen the men ranged from late twenties to late thirties. They seemed to study him with interest.

"Luke Adams." A thirty-something, slim cowboy held out his hand.

J.T. took it, feeling that he knew the man. At thirty-six, J.T. had been doing roundups for thirty years so the faces of past cowhands sometimes blurred in his memory as did most of the cattle drives. But something about this man.... "You worked for us before?"

Luke seemed surprised he would remember. "Almost ten years ago."

The memory fell into place, dropping like his heart in his chest. Luke Adams had been one of the cowhands who'd left camp after the first trouble nine years ago. Luke had been one of the smart ones.

While J.T. had never been superstitious, it still gave him

an odd feeling that one of the cowhands from that tragic cattle roundup had signed on for this year's.

"I haven't seen you around Antelope Flats," J.T. said, wondering where Luke had been all these years.

Luke shook his head. "Went down to New Mexico for a while."

He nodded, feeling uneasy as he studied him in the firelight before moving to the next man.

"Roy Shields," the man next to Luke said quietly, then awkwardly pulled off his hat before sticking out his hand. Roy was slim and wiry-looking with thin red hair, early to late thirties, one of those people it was hard to tell his age.

His grip was strong but not callused. He looked like a cowhand, one of the quiet ones that seldom gave him any trouble. But how did the saying go, still waters run deep? Roy could have been familiar. The man hurriedly shook his hand, keeping his eyes downcast. J.T. made a note to watch him.

"Cotton Heywood," the next man said eagerly reaching to shake J.T.'s hand. He was one of the local ranch hands who worked in the area. He had a full head of white-blond hair, which explained his nickname.

"Good to see you again, Cotton," J.T. said, trying to remember the latest scuttlebutt he'd heard about the man. Cotton had gotten into some kind of trouble at another rancher's cow camp, but for the life of him, J.T. couldn't remember what. He seldom paid any attention to rancher gossip, but now he wished he had.

J.T. looked to the next man.

"Nevada Black," said a strong-looking man with dark hair and eyes. His hand wasn't callused either. He gave J.T.

a knowing smirk. "That's my real name. I was born at a blackjack table."

"You have any experience on cattle roundups?" J.T. asked.

"I took a few years off, but I've been rounding up cattle since I was a boy," Nevada said. He rattled off a series of ranches in Nevada and northern California where he'd worked.

J.T. nodded and looked to the next man.

"Slim Walker," said the gangly cowboy. He held out his hand and when J.T. took it, he couldn't stop himself from pulling back. Slim nodded, then stretched out both hands in the firelight for everyone to see. "Burned them. Got knocked into a campfire at a kegger." He shrugged. "Gave up drinking after that."

J.T. barely heard the man over his thundering pulse. He tried to hide his embarrassment and quickly looked to the last man.

The sixth cowhand stood back a little from the fire as if he'd been watching J.T. make his way around to him and waiting.

"Will Jarvis," he said slowly stepping forward, removing his hat. He had thin brown hair and was the oldest of the bunch, late thirties like J.T. himself.

J.T. studied the man's face as he shook his hand. Something about him was familiar but he couldn't put his finger on it. The man's hand was smooth and cool. He was no ranch hand. Buck really *had* been desperate.

"Glad you're all here," J.T. said, not sure of that at all as he tried to shake the bad feeling that had been with him from the moment Bob Humphries told him about the dead, burned cow. "We have a lot of cattle to round up over the next few days. I suggest you turn in right after supper. We start at first light."

As he glanced toward the cabin, he realized he didn't smell food cooking, just smoke, and shot a look at Buck before picking up his saddle and gear and heading in that direction.

Behind him, he had the strangest feeling that the men around the fire were not only watching him, but also waiting for something to happen.

"Maybe we should talk for a minute before you go into the cabin," Buck said as he caught up to him.

"Why is that, Buck?" he asked without slowing his stride. J.T. had always liked to get whatever was waiting for him over with as quickly as possible. "If you got a cook, then what—" The rest of his words died on his lips as he saw the camp cook through the cabin window. "What the—"

"Now, boss—"

J.T. shoved his saddle and gear at Buck without a word and, with long purposeful strides, stormed across the porch and into the line shack. "What are *you* doing here?"

It was a stupid question since Reggie whatever-her-name-was stood at the cookstove with a pan in her hand. She was dressed in fancy western wear, all spanking new and all in that same shade of red that had blinded him on the road earlier today.

"You know each other?" Buck asked in surprise from the doorway.

J.T. swung around long enough to slam the door—with Buck on the other side of it. Slowly, trying to control his temper, he turned back to the woman standing in his line shack. "What *are* you doing here?"

"Isn't it obvious?" she asked. "I wanted to give you another chance to reconsider my offer so I hired on as your camp cook." She held out her hand. "Regina Holland. I wasn't sure you remembered from my card."

He ignored her hand. He could not believe the woman's nerve. Had she no sense at all? Coming up to his cow camp after him? And worse, signing on as the cook. Women didn't belong in a cow camp. He was going to kill Buck.

"Listen, lady, it is one thing to be cute on the highway but not in my line camp," he snapped. She really had no idea what she'd done. Or who she was dealing with.

"I'm not being cute," she said, frowning as she lowered her hand. "I'm *very* serious."

She couldn't have looked less serious in that urban cowboy getup if she'd tried. "I already turned down your offer flat," he ground out from between gritted teeth as he tried to keep his voice down. "*All* of your offers. How much more plain can I be?"

He knew the men outside were straining to hear what was going on. A *woman* in cow camp? Worse, a woman who looked like this? A woman with designs that had nothing to do with cooking. A recipe for disaster if there ever was one.

She lifted her chin, standing her ground as she looked up at him. Without her high heels, he towered over her. He also outweighed her by almost a hundred pounds. But she didn't seem to notice—or care.

"You didn't give me a chance back on the highway today," she said, seemingly unconcerned by the ferocious angry scowl he was giving her. "If you'd just listen to what I'm willing to give you—"

"You listen to me, *Reggie,*" he said, biting off each word as he stepped closer. "I told you I'm—"

"This is an opportunity—"

"…not interested and I'm not going to—"

"…that doesn't come—"

"…change my mind and I don't want to hear—"

"…along every day—"

"Reggie!" he shouted, forgetting how important it was to keep their conversation private.

She flinched but still had the audacity to mutter, "…of the year. And it's Regina," she snapped. "*Not* Reggie, *McCall.*"

McCall? He swore under his breath.

She took a breath. "Couldn't we just start over?" She gave him a breathtaking smile and spoke in a soft seductive tone. "I feel like we got off on the wrong foot."

He recalled how odd the men had been acting around the campfire. A knife of alarm buried itself in his chest. Had she already announced what she was doing here? He told himself he wouldn't be responsible for what he did to her.

"Did you say anything to the men about…" He couldn't bring himself to say the words given that Buck probably had his ear to the door not to even mention the cowhands eavesdropping around the fire. He needed these men to look up to him over the next few days, to respect him and follow his orders without fail. He didn't need them checking out his butt and laughing behind his back.

"About my offer?" she asked with wide-eyed innocence.

He'd wring her pretty little neck. "So help me, if you said one word—"

"I haven't told *anyone.*"

"Not even Buck?"

She shook her head.

He hated to think what story she'd concocted to get Buck to give her the cook job. His instant relief that she hadn't told everyone was short-lived. She hadn't told anyone *yet.* "Get your things. You're going back to town. *Now.*"

"At least give me a chance to apologize," she said touching his sleeve. He pulled free, stepping back to ward her off. "I'm sorry. When I heard you talking to Jenny, I just assumed she was your wife."

He groaned, remembering telling his new puppy Jennie to stay in the pickup or be left at home. That's why Reggie thought Jennie was his wife? And just when he thought she couldn't insult him further.

"I also want to apologize for assuming by your attire and truck that you were a poor cowhand—"

"Stop while you're *behind,*" J.T. snapped, instantly regretting his unfortunate choice of word.

She flushed. She was trying so hard he almost felt sorry for her. Almost. "I don't see why you're so upset," she said, actually sounding puzzled. "I'm offering you *fame.*"

Just what he always wanted. A famous butt. "And I'm offering you a chance to clear out of here before—"

"If I could just make you realize what an asset you have in your—"

"All right, Ms. Holland!" There was no getting through to this woman. "The answer is no. I accept all of your… apologies. But the answer is still *no.* So since there is nothing else for you here—"

He was so close to her that he could smell her perfume. Something expensive and unforgettable. Her eyes were the color of the Montana sky. He dragged his gaze away to the floor and noticed that even her boots were red! She had "dude" written all over her and looked as out of place as a fancy skyscraper on this mountaintop. But what really graveled him was that she looked as sexy in this getup as she had in the expensive suit earlier.

"What's with you and red?" he had to ask.

She looked down at her outfit. She really did fit the western shirt nicely. "It's my signature color."

He should have known.

"Well, unless you want your signature color to be dirt-brown I suggest you step away from that cookstove."

She didn't move. "You don't like red?"

How had he gotten sidetracked from the real issue here to red? He didn't care if the woman wore nothing at all. He groaned as his imagination flashed on *that* image.

"I want you to just get back in your—" He looked out the window to the pines below the line shack suddenly realizing he had no idea how she'd gotten here. No way could she drive here in her sports car. It took one hell of a four-wheel drive truck to make it up the rough trail to the camp—and only in good weather. Once it rained or snowed—

"How did you get up here?" he asked, his heart in his throat.

"I rode up in the supply truck with Buck."

She could have told him Martians had dropped her off at the camp and he would have been less skeptical. "Buck brought you up?" Had Buck lost his mind? The only way to get rid of her would be to send her down on horseback or drive all the way back down the mountain in the supply truck. J.T. swore under his breath.

Well, at least no harm had really been done, he told himself. He would lose Buck for half a day but this situation could be resolved.

"Buck?" he called. The door to the cabin instantly opened and Buck stuck his head in the door. "Go start the truck. You're taking Ms. Holland back to town."

Buck shot a sympathetic glance to Reggie, but had the good sense not to argue before he ducked back out the door.

"I don't think you realize how important this is. Can't we please discuss it like rational adults?"

"No. Get your stuff. You're out of here."

"What will you do for a camp cook?" she asked.

"We'll manage."

She studied him for a moment, fire in her eyes, then turned and went to the set of bunk beds in the corner. A huge expensive suitcase was open on one of the lower bunks. He caught sight of a bunch of frilly lingerie. He groaned inwardly. A woman like this in a cow camp? He was going to kill Buck.

"I wish you would reconsider," she said, looking close to tears. "This could open all kinds of doors for you. It could very well make you famous. Everyone wants fifteen minutes of fame."

"Not this man. Or his butt." He moved beside her, closed the suitcase and picked it up. "Shall we?" he said, motioning toward the door.

Before she could move, Buck opened the cabin door. "Boss?" His face was pale and drawn as he motioned J.T. over. Worse, Buck only called him boss when there was trouble.

Now what?

"The truck won't start," Buck said. "When I looked under the hood—"

J.T. didn't wait for the rest. He shoved past the foreman and headed down the hillside to the old stock truck. That truck had never let him down even when it was forty below zero and blizzarding outside. He could hear Buck behind him, muttering to himself.

Buck had left the hood up, a flashlight lay across the top of the radiator. J.T. picked it up and shone it at the engine and swore.

"That's what I was trying to tell you," Buck said. "Someone took the distributor cap."

Was it possible someone had taken the part as a joke? This sort of thing was definitely not funny. Any fool knew there could be an emergency that would prevent one of them from riding out of here on horseback and they would need the truck to get out.

J.T. turned slowly to look at Buck. "You don't know anything about this?"

Buck looked shocked by the question. "Why would I do something this stupid?"

To help that woman in my line shack. But he knew Buck was right. He wouldn't do anything this dangerous. Not even for a beautiful woman.

"I was thinking about the last time something like this happened," Buck said quietly, glancing toward the campfire. "The truck had been disabled that time too, right?" Buck hadn't been on that roundup nine years ago. But like everyone else in four states, he'd heard about it.

"The tires were slashed," J.T. said. The method used was different, but the end result was the same. "And the hands involved are all dead." One crazy, two greedy fools. All dying horrible deaths. And for what? He glanced toward the line shack. "This has to be that woman's doing. She's the only one who benefits from this—and the only one who doesn't realize how dangerous it is." She'd already proved how low she would stoop to get what she wanted. She'd done this to prevent him from sending her packing.

"You're right," Buck said, sounding relieved.

This had to be her doing. But he couldn't stop thinking about the cow Bob Humphries had found. Also Reggie didn't look like the kind of woman who would know a distributor cap from a hubcap, he thought, remembering how she hadn't even been able to change her own tire. But in hindsight, that had probably just been a ruse to get him to stop and help her.

Had to be Reggie's doing, J.T. told himself as he slammed the hood. He refused to think something else was going on here and that she wasn't the only one who didn't want any of them leaving here.

But as he headed for the cabin, he felt his skin crawl as he glanced past the camp into the darkness of the pines and imagined someone hiding out there watching them, waiting to pick them off one by one. Just like last time.

CHAPTER THREE

Buck caught up to him just before he reached the line shack and stopped him. "You won't be too hard on her, will you?"

J.T. stared at the older man in astonishment. Either Buck Brannigan was getting soft in the head or that woman had gotten to him. Either was unbelievable having known Buck all his life.

"Did you just temporarily lose your mind or were you drunk when you hired her?" J.T. demanded, more upset than he would have been under normal circumstances. He couldn't shake the uneasy feeling that had settled in his gut after seeing where the cow had been burned and dragged off into the woods. A missing distributor cap and a disabled truck. A crew he didn't know—or necessarily trust. Hell, he had more than enough to worry about without having a woman in camp. Especially *that* woman.

"You said, find a cook," Buck said stubbornly. "I found a cook. And let me tell you, I had one heck of a time but I knew better than to show up without one so when Regina walked into the Longhorn and begged me for the job..."

J.T. swore. There was only one way she had known about the job opening. J.T. had opened his big mouth and told her. But Buck still shouldn't have hired her.

"Any man with even one good eye can see that that

woman doesn't belong off concrete sidewalks, let alone in a cow camp," J.T. snapped.

Buck rubbed his grizzled jaw with a large paw of a hand, then grinned. "Heck, J.T., she was such a determined little thing and cuter than a white-faced heifer. She talked me into hiring her before I knew what had happened. She said she was desperate for the job and we *do* need a cook. I thought, what could it hurt?"

They both looked back toward the truck.

"Sorry, boss," Buck said again.

J.T. just shook his head. "I want you to ride out at first light. Come back with the other four-wheel drive truck. When you get back, you take Ms. Holland to town and find us another cook if you can. Either way I want you back here by early afternoon."

Buck nodded looking contrite. "You didn't mention how you knew her."

"No, I didn't," J.T. said and glanced toward the fire. The men were all pretending not to be watching—or listening—to what was going on. None of them had complained that they hadn't had dinner yet. Under normal circumstances there would be some powerful bellyaching going on. Nothing about this roundup was normal.

He thought about the warm bunk beds waiting in the cabin as he glanced over at the wall tents where he would be sleeping instead. Damn this woman.

Reggie begged to be a camp cook? Well, J.T. would oblige. She could cook supper over the woodstove, then they'd see how she felt about being a camp cook.

He leveled his gaze at Buck. "You'd better hope she's the best darned cook this side of Miles City, starting with supper tonight."

"She was just so desperate," Buck said again.

"Yeah," J.T. said, "but desperate to do what?" He was wondering if her story about the TV commercial was even true. Maybe there was something else she was after. Something even worse than his perfect posterior.

Buck chewed at the end of his thick mustache. "I might be a fool but I can't imagine that woman in there taking the truck part."

"*Might* be a fool?" J.T. let out a snort. Buck was no pushover, quite the contrary, except somehow Reggie had the old cowboy wrapped around her finger. But he had to agree with Buck, even if she'd faked her incompetence when it came to tire changing, he still couldn't see her stealing the truck's distributor cap—not with seven men in camp watching her every move.

"If she's really behind this," Buck said, "then someone must be helping her. I suppose it could be someone who followed us up here and camped nearby. Or someone in camp."

"My thought exactly," J.T. said as he looked from the campfire back to Buck. "No one in this camp better be trying to help her, Buck. I'm warning you and you better warn the men."

"I can't believe the men wouldn't know how dangerous this is," Buck said. Without the truck, the only way off this mountain was on horseback. A twenty-mile ride to the ranch. If anyone got sick or hurt—

Maybe someone had followed them up here and was camped nearby. "I'll ride out and take a look in the morning, if I can't talk her out of the distributor cap tonight." He glanced toward the cabin. "You have no idea what that woman is capable of."

Buck lifted a heavy gray brow. “But you do?”

He ignored the question and Buck’s curiosity. “Let me handle this. If she’s behind taking that distributor cap—”

“Just don’t be too tough on her, okay?”

J.T. shot the foreman a warning look and stomped to the cabin.

Reggie had rolled her suitcase as far as the door.

“The truck doesn’t run,” he said.

She looked alarmed. “How do we get out of here?”

“I could have Buck saddle up a horse for you.”

Her eyes widened in even more alarm. “You would send me off this mountain in the dark on a *horse?*”

“In a heartbeat. All you have to do is follow the trail fifteen miles down to the county road. From there just go east. You shouldn’t have any trouble finding the ranch. One of my brothers will give you a ride into town to your car from there.”

She looked at him as if she couldn’t believe he was serious.

He wasn’t. He was angry and upset but there was no way this woman could find her way back to the ranch even in broad daylight with street signs to follow. She’d sooner fall off a cliff or stumble into the river and drown herself and one of his horses. For the horse’s sake, he couldn’t do it.

But it was tempting. Especially if she was responsible for the disabled truck. And if she wasn’t? Well, then he wanted to get her out of here and as quickly as possible because he didn’t have a clue what was going on.

“You can’t send me off this mountain on a horse,” she said again.

He thought he saw tears in her eyes. Had she finally realized that she'd gotten herself into something she couldn't handle?

Her voice dropped to a whisper. "I don't know how to ride a horse."

J.T. looked at her. Of course she didn't ride. Any fool could have guessed that. "You do know how to walk though, don't you? It's probably only twenty miles to the ranch as the crow flies."

She practically gasped.

Fighting the urge to throttle the woman *and* Buck, he said, "You can stay here tonight." As if he had a choice. He was tempted to throw her to the wolves. Not literally, but at least make her sleep in one of the wall tents tonight on a cot instead of the warm cabin where *he* should have been sleeping, he thought with a curse.

"Buck is riding down in the morning," he said. "He'll bring back a truck and take you to town. In the meantime, you're the camp cook. Buck?" he called.

Buck was waiting outside the door listening, of course. "Yes, Boss?"

The words were almost impossible to get out, knowing that Buck and Reggie cooking together could be lethal. But he wasn't going to stay in here with her. No way.

"Help Ms. Holland with dinner," he ordered.

Buck grinned. "You got it, boss."

"She can stay in the cabin. You and I will take one of the wall tents."

"I'm sorry to put you out of your cabin," Reggie said sweetly enough to give a man a toothache. "I can sleep in the tent."

Like she had ever slept in a tent on a cot in her life, J.T. thought.

"I don't mind staying in the tent," Buck said quickly.

All J.T. could do was shake his head in wonder. There was nothing worse than a sentimental old fool.

Except for a young one, he thought with disgust as he left the cabin. Buck must be getting old. There'd been a time when even a woman like Reggie Holland couldn't have conned a man like Buck Brannigan. What was the world coming to?

J.T. marched over to the fire, apologized that supper was running late and explained the new sleeping arrangements. He'd expected the men to complain and loudly.

"No problem, boss," Cotton said grinning as he glanced toward the cabin. "Let me know if there is anything I can do to help Ms. Holland."

This was why women didn't belong in a cow camp.

Slim and Luke quickly offered their assistance as well.

J.T. groaned under his breath and reminded himself that she would be gone by tomorrow. But he couldn't help but worry that she hadn't given up. What would she try next? He hated to think. Especially if she had an accomplice in one of his men.

Well, before the night was over, J.T. figured he could talk Reggie into handing over the distributor cap and the name of her accomplice. Both would be out of here at first light.

As BUCK EXPLAINED cooking over a woodstove, Reggie tried to tell herself that she'd won round one.

So she had to cook supper. A slight drawback. Maybe she would wow J.T. McCall. True, she had never cooked anything in her life other than taking something out of a container and popping it into the microwave. She'd never had time to learn. But she *was* fearless. And determined not to leave this camp until she had McCall signed to the commercial. Her future depended on it.

Not just her future, she reminded herself. A lot of people were depending on her to pull this off. This entire advertising campaign was her idea, a desperate last-ditch effort to save the company—and her job.

If the campaign succeeded, Way Out West Jeans would go public and no longer just be a tiny obscure family-owned company. Regina's future would be secure.

If it failed, the employees would be without jobs and Way Out West Jeans would have to close its doors, the hundred-year-old company bankrupt.

She was determined that wasn't going to happen. No matter what she had to do.

She needed authenticity and J. T. McCall and his Sundown Ranch were it. She'd been flabbergasted when Buck had shown her the ranch before they'd come up the mountain. Thank goodness for Buck.

She'd overheard just enough of the conversation outside the cabin between McCall and Buck to know that without Buck she'd be on her way down the mountain in the dark either on the back of one of those horses in the corral or on foot.

How lucky that the truck hadn't started. And how lucky that Buck Brannigan had been sympathetic to her story about needing this job. He'd probably heard the real desperation in her voice. She *did* need this. Just not the job she'd been hired on to do.

She felt a little guilty for putting Buck in what was obviously an awkward situation with his boss. But she got the feeling that Buck was one of the few people who wasn't afraid of J. T. McCall.

She found Buck's bashfulness cute, along with his "Aw shucks ma'am," hat-in-hand protective politeness. For a moment, she wondered what her life would have been like if she'd had a father like Buck.

Shoving that thought away, she concentrated on the task at hand, cooking over the woodstove and assuring Buck she could handle this while he moved his stuff out of the cabin and into the tent.

"You *can* cook, right?" Buck had asked her earlier at the Longhorn Café.

She'd known all she had to do was answer the man's question correctly. "I'm a woman, aren't I?"

That seemed to appease him, just as she knew it would. A lot of men thought all women were born being able to cook and clean. Not in her family, that was for sure.

No, her talents lay somewhere else. That's why, given time, she had no doubt that she could persuade even a man as mulish as J. T. McCall that he'd be a fool to just sit on his assets.

But she didn't have much time. Only until tomorrow when Buck returned. Shoot, she'd closed impossible deals in a lot less time than that, she told herself. Whether she liked it or not, she was her mother's daughter.

In the meantime, she would cook supper following the instructions Buck had given her. She just hoped cooking proved easier than changing a flat tire.

WHEN J.T. WALKED into the line shack cabin for supper, the air reeked of smoke even though all the windows were open and a stiff breeze was blowing through the place.

He didn't have to ask how the new cook had done. As he settled into the chair at the head of the table, he spotted a large platter of incinerated steaks, black and shrunken and no longer resembling anything edible.

The cowhands who'd earlier seemed overjoyed to have a pretty female cook in camp were now eyeing the burnt steaks warily.

"You want to pass the steaks around?" Buck asked, sounding as if he had a sore throat.

J.T. noticed how Buck avoided his gaze as J.T. picked up the platter of cremated meat. Silence filled the cabin. He sensed the men around the table watching him as if waiting to see what his response would be. He knew if the cook had been a male, everyone in this room would be complaining, J.T. at the top of the list. Yet another reason a woman didn't belong in a cow camp.

J.T. looked from the platter to Reggie. She stood in the corner not far from the woodstove, hanging back in the shadows as if trying to make herself smaller. Loose hair hung in limp tendrils around her face, a large dark smudge of charcoal graced her cheek and her new duds looked as if she'd been in a mud wrestling match—and lost. So much for her signature color. All in all, she appeared exhausted. And close to tears.

But it was the expression on her face that was his undoing. She looked downright contrite. He watched her inspect a red, inflamed fingertip, then bring it to her mouth to suck on the burn, and he felt a rush of sympathy for her.

Earlier he'd threatened to throw her to the wolves, but he realized now that that's exactly what he'd done by allowing her to pretend to be the camp cook. He doubted she'd ever cooked in her life, let alone over a woodstove.

Cursing himself, he looked down at the ruined meat on the platter. "Steaks huh, great," he said between gritted teeth as he slid one of the charred chunks of once grade A beef onto his plate before passing the platter to the man next to him, Cotton Heywood.

Cotton quickly helped himself to a steak. "Looks good! Boy am I hungry."

The spell broken, each man complimented Reggie as the meat made its way around the table, each man except for Will Jarvis. He stared at the steak remains, then let his gaze lift to J.T.'s for a long moment before finally stabbing one and dropping it to his plate.

J.T. watched him, still fighting the feeling that there was something familiar about the man.

When J.T. glanced up, he found Reggie's gaze on him. While she still looked duly chastened, he glimpsed gratitude in her blue eyes. He wanted to tell her that he was only keeping peace in his camp, not saving her, but he doubted she'd believe it any more than he did.

He mentally shook his head. This woman had the ability to make a man want to wring her neck one minute and take her in his arms and comfort her the next. Women like her were damned dangerous.

"You *are* going to join us, aren't you, Ms. Holland?" he asked, reminding himself that this was her doing. She'd gotten herself into this. And if she thought she was going to get out of eating what she'd cooked, she was sadly mistaken. He wouldn't force his men to eat anything the cook wouldn't also be required to eat.

"I'm not very hungry," she said in a quiet, almost timid voice.

He'd just bet she wasn't considering what she'd done

to this food. He studied her. Was she ready to give up? He could only hope. "I insist you have something to eat."

Luke Adams got up to pull out a chair for her. Even though the men had to know this woman was going to ruin their food as long as she was here, they all smiled over at her as she sat down. But how could they not feel sympathy for her? She looked as pathetic as a rain-drenched stray kitten. He wondered which of the men had taken the distributor cap for her. The woman was persuasive enough, she could have talked any one of them into it, J.T. realized—even Will Jarvis, the most cantankerous of the bunch it seemed.

Buck passed a bowl full of something small, shriveled and crispy brown. J.T. frowned down at them, trying to figure out what food they'd originally been. The brown nuggets resembled large hard nuts.

"Do you want some butter on your baked potato?" Buck asked with more pleasantness than J.T. had ever heard in the big man's tone.

So that's what they'd once been? He would never have thought it possible to make a potato look like this. He wondered what she'd done to them. And decided he didn't want to know.

He was almost afraid to take the large bowl Buck offered him next, but was relieved to see that he recognized the food in it. Baked beans. He scooped a healthy serving onto his plate, glad at least something would be edible. How much damage could Reggie do to a can of pork and beans?

He started to take a bite, but stopped, disturbed to realize what else Reggie's presence had done. Cow camps revolved around male custom. The conversation at the table should have been about critters, who'd be riding the draws looking for strays tomorrow, who'd be wrangling the horses. Instead the men ate in silence.

Nor were they wolfing down their food, though who could blame them. Still some of them were actually using napkins and employing the utensils in the way they were designed.

J.T. shook his head. Reggie was destroying century-old rituals, making grown men behave against their nature, and he didn't like it.

He sawed off a piece of steak and took a bite. It tasted like charred cheap shoe leather. He chewed and chewed and finally forced the bite down with beans. Big mistake. Fire shot through his mouth and down his throat. Choking, he grabbed his water glass, his wild-eyed murderous gaze leaping to Buck.

Buck kept his head down as if intent on his food. Everyone else at the table also seemed unduly interested in their plates.

He downed his water, then glared across the table at Reggie, fire in his eyes as well as his mouth. The woman was going to kill them all. Any woman who could do this much damage to food wouldn't even blink when it came to disabling a truck.

Was all of this just a plot to get him to change his mind and do the commercial? My God, the woman would stoop to anything.

She appeared busy pushing her food around her plate. Smart not to eat it. She glanced up as if she felt his gaze on her. She stared at him in concern. Was she worried that he might leap across the table and throttle her or that he might die right before her eyes? He knew his face must be bright red, his eyes were running water and he could not stop choking.

"Buck said you liked a lot of green pepper in your beans," she said into the strained silence. No doubt the men were quietly choking to death as well. "So I found a bag of chopped peppers and put them all in. I think they might have been the wrong peppers."

No kidding.

Buck let out an uncharacteristic little laugh. "There were two different bags of peppers in the cooler. I should have shown her which ones to use. I think she used the jalapenos."

"Yeah," J.T. said, narrowing his gaze at her. Was it an honest mistake? Or had she purposely done this? No one would be *that* cruel, would she?

Well, she'd underestimated him. There was nothing she could do to get him to change his mind. Not poison him. Not kill his taste buds. Not starve him. Nothing. He would get her out of here tomorrow and Buck would bring back a real cook. Now that J.T. knew what she was capable of, he wasn't letting her near the stove again. He would cook breakfast himself.

"I like my beans hot," Cotton piped up. "They're spicy but real good." He smiled at Reggie.

Luke and Slim jumped to Reggie's defense as well. J.T. watched them eat the beans, their eyes tearing with each bite, lies on their lips, their politeness costing them dearly.

He would have felt sorry for them except for one thing. Reggie was losing that chastened look. Their compassion and polite compliments seemed to be giving her renewed strength. When J.T. looked down the table at her, he saw that spark of determination, still fairly dim, but burning again in her eyes.

It was the last thing he wanted to see burning there.

"Here, Luke, have some more beans," J.T. said, passing him the bowl. "There's enough for all of you to have seconds." He watched each man take his share as the bowl was passed around the table. How could they not without hurting Reggie's tender feelings?

Everyone except Will Jarvis and Nevada Black helped themselves to more beans.

"I've never been a big fan of beans," Nevada said. Nor burnt steak and potatoes, it seemed. His plate looked untouched.

Same with Will, only he didn't bother to say anything as he passed on the beans.

J.T. didn't blame the men. He was feeling a little guilty about making the others eat more of the horribly hot beans. It wasn't their fault that they'd gotten caught in the middle of this war between him and Reggie and they didn't even know what was really at stake. J.T. wasn't even sure he did. He just couldn't let them get too taken with this woman before he could get her out of here.

He felt her reproachful gaze on him as the beans reached her and she scraped the last of them onto her plate. Defiantly, she ate them, her gaze fixed on him. He watched her, knowing how much each forkful cost her, and yet, other than unshed tears swimming in her big blue eyes, she didn't let it show. She ate every bite.

The men did the same.

If Reggie had wanted to make him feel like a heel, she'd succeeded. Worse yet, her defiant act had only managed to do just what he'd feared. It had allied the men to her.

Even Will and Nevada were watching her with a look of something like respect. Damn this woman was impossible! She already had Buck on her side, now she had them all eating out of her hand, so to speak.

Earlier he'd thought her beaten, close to crying, ready to cave in. He saw now that Reggie Holland didn't fall to defeat easily. He'd not only underestimated her tenacity, he found himself admiring it and at the same time fearing it. How far would the woman go to get what she wanted? And how many of his men would she use to do it?

The disabled truck nagged at him. He looked around the table, trying to imagine what any of the cowhands had to gain by taking the distributor cap. Cotton, Slim and Luke weren't paying attention to anyone but Reggie.

Will Jarvis seemed to be watching everyone at the table while picking at his food with distaste. Roy, head down, was eating quietly, but then Roy did everything quietly, it seemed. Nevada Black was eating what he could salvage of the meal, but he didn't look happy about it.

Of the men, Nevada Black looked like the one who had probably done some time. He seemed the most likely to have disabled the truck. But for what possible motive? J.T. wouldn't be surprised if Nevada Black was gone in the morning. He didn't look like a man who put up with much.

Neither did Will Jarvis. Both men were older and no doubt less tolerant. Unless they needed this job desperately, they would hit the road if the conditions didn't improve.

Luke, Slim and Cotton were a whole other story. Any of the three could have come to Reggie's rescue and disabled the truck.

J.T. let his gaze come back to Reggie. She had to have

known he would send her packing as soon as he found her at the line shack. She'd gotten to stay here tonight only because of the missing distributor cap. And she was the one person who supposedly didn't ride a horse.

She looked up at him, resolve burning again in those eyes like a hot blue flame. He shouldn't be surprised by anything this woman did, but he found himself surprised over and over again. He'd never met anyone like her and hoped he never did again.

He cursed under his breath as he watched each of the men take his plate and utensils over to the large galvanized tub full of hot dishwater on the stove, something they would never have done for a male cook. Several tipped their hats to Reggie and actually thanked her for cooking, then hung around as if not wanting to leave.

She bestowed one of her drop-a-man-to-his-knees smiles on each of them. Even Will Jarvis who had hardly touched his meal returned her smile, though grudgingly.

J.T. couldn't blame them. Reggie looked like a waif. You wanted to take her in your arms and tell her everything was going to be all right. She seemed so tired that he had to wonder what was keeping her on her feet as she got ready to do the dishes. She meant to finish the job she'd started, even if it killed her. And for a moment, he thought about seeing if it would.

"Cotton, why don't you and Slim clean up the dishes tonight," J.T. suggested. "Luke, you can see to the horses." Everyone but Reggie knew it was an order. "I need to talk to Ms. Holland and I think she's done quite enough for one day."

If the men were surprised by his irregular order or resented it, they didn't show it. Doing dishes in a cow camp was strictly the cook's domain, but Reggie had already destroyed most of the established codes of the west, why not break a few more?

J.T. saw Cotton and Slim exchange knowing smirks as they set about their work. They thought something was going on between him and Reggie! He wanted to deny it. Well, at least tell them that what they thought was going on wasn't.

But he knew better than to open his mouth. Protesting would only dig the hole he was in deeper.

He was just thankful that Buck would be leaving early in the morning and Reggie would be history by afternoon. Even if her cooking didn't kill them all, he couldn't have her here. Pretty soon, she'd have the men fighting over her. Or worse.

Sending Buck into town would put the roundup behind a little, but it would be worth it. Things could get back to normal. Even if Buck didn't find a cook, J.T. would rather hear the men complain about Buck's cooking than put up with this.

Buck looked worried as J.T. ushered Reggie out the door of the line shack. What did the old coot think he was going to do to her? Take her out and shoot her? Let Buck think the worst since he was the one who'd gotten them into this mess.

No, J.T. thought, he couldn't blame it all on Buck. He should have made it clearer to her on the highway this afternoon that he was never going to change his mind. And he should never have mentioned to her that he needed a camp cook. Nor should he have let Reggie cook tonight.

Discouraging this woman wasn't easy but he had to try. He couldn't let her continue with this charade. She was wasting her time and his. He would make her see that. Somehow.

He'd convince her to return the distributor cap and send her back to town with Buck tonight in the truck. The sooner she was out of the camp the better. Especially since he had a bad feeling about this roundup.

The last time he'd had that feeling, five men had died.

CHAPTER FOUR

Regina shivered as she stepped out into the night. The cute little western jacket she'd bought at the Antelope Flats general store did little to chase away the cold. She had never known such darkness as she moved through the trees away from the light of the cabin. She stumbled and would have fallen headlong if J.T. hadn't caught her arm and righted her.

"It's just so dark," she said and realized he was standing only inches from her.

"Your eyes will adjust," he said softly, his voice sending a different kind of chill through her.

She could feel his gaze on her face. She hugged herself and gulped the cold night air, feeling like an alien who'd landed in a strange, hostile environment. Nothing looked familiar: not the terrain, not the men, not the clothing and certainly not the food, especially after she'd finished cooking it.

She hadn't eaten red meat in years—until tonight. But she would have choked on it before she'd have let J.T. think she wasn't going to eat it because it was burned to a crisp.

Not even the atmosphere of this place agreed with her. Air she couldn't see made her suspicious. The high altitude left her dizzy. And the boots hurt her feet. She didn't even want to think about the accommodations.

J.T. had announced she could sleep in the cabin as if he was doing her a favor. Now that she'd had a good look at it, she would beg to differ.

On top of that, she ached all over. Her fingers were burned. And she feared she'd never get rid of the smell of smoke and grease on her skin, especially as she hadn't seen a place to bathe. Or relieve herself other than what appeared to be an outhouse a couple dozen yards off the hillside in the pines. Like she was going out there in the dark.

But she'd asked for this. True, it was the most drastic thing she'd ever done, but it would be worth it. Once she had McCall under contract.

"We need to talk," he said.

She could see his face more clearly as her eyes adjusted to the darkness. A sliver of moon hung in the dark velvet sky above the lofty pines. A splattering of bright glittering stars twinkled across the vast skyscape. She'd never seen anything like it before and she found everything about this place too intense. Especially J. T. McCall.

Regina couldn't remember a time she'd felt so inept. Or so lost. But she wouldn't quit. Nor would she admit defeat, although she could see he was hoping for just that.

"I'm sorry about dinner," she said quickly. "I'll do better in the morning."

He stared at her, clearly surprised. "You'd actually put yourself through that again?" So he *had* thought she'd given up.

Not that there hadn't been a few moments when it had crossed her mind. Like when Buck had pointed to the woodstove and told her she was to cook on that fire-breathing, smoke-belching dragon in the corner.

Cook what? He'd outlined the meal and how the woodstove worked. It had sounded simple enough. Although, so had the microwave the first time she'd used it. Thanks to modern technology, she'd managed to turn grated cheddar cheese into orange plastic at the touch of a button.

The woodstove was far from modern technology, but about the time the steaks caught fire, she realized she could do a lot more damage with a woodstove.

"I hired on as camp cook," she said firmly. "I'll finish the job."

"Over my dead body—and I suspect if I ate any more of your cooking that would be the case."

"What are you trying to say?"

"You can't cook."

She couldn't argue that. "I can learn."

"Not fast enough."

She lifted her chin and met his gaze. "You'd be amazed what I am capable of when I set my mind to it."

"That's what I'm worried about." He sighed. "Look, until Buck returns with a truck, I don't want you going near the cookstove."

She started to open her mouth.

"No arguments. I'm sorry you wasted your time coming up here in the first place. Once back in Antelope Flats you can continue your search for your…cowboy."

"I've found the only cowboy I want."

He shook his head.

"I'm risking everything for this advertising campaign," she said, surprised by her candor and the slight break in her voice. "If this doesn't work out, I'm finished and a lot of other people will lose their jobs."

He eyed her as if this was just another ploy. "I'm sorry

to hear that. You just found the wrong cowboy. Cut your losses. The sooner you get out of here, the sooner you can find someone else for the commercial." He held up his hand to ward off her next argument. "This is a battle you can't win. You're leaving. Either by truck, on horseback or on foot. Your choice. You won't change my mind and as far as the camp cook job, you're fired."

She'd known this might happen, especially after he'd experienced her cooking. She'd just hoped it wouldn't come to this. She glanced back toward the cabin. "Maybe you're right." Was that a sigh of relief she heard? "But perhaps one of your men might know of a cowboy who would be interested in the job after hearing that you turned down the offer."

"You aren't trying to blackmail me, are you?"

She could tell from his tone that blackmailing J. T. McCall wouldn't be a good idea. He might be surprised if he knew just how desperate she was. Or maybe he wouldn't.

He stood immobile, pale as the moon, jaw clenched, a deadly look in his eyes.

A sliver of guilt pricked her conscience. She did her best to ignore it. After he made the commercial, he'd be glad she'd been so determined. They would both be. Okay, at least she would be for sure.

"I would not take kindly to being blackmailed," he said in a tone that was soft like a silk glove with a fist in it.

His warning tone sent a chill through her, but she couldn't back down. "Think of it as incentive."

"I should turn you over my knee and—" He stepped toward her menacingly.

She drew back. Surely he wouldn't actually do such a thing? But what did she know about Montana cowboys?

"You try to blackmail me and I swear I will personally take you down this mountain tonight if I have to drag you every step of the way."

She nodded, trusting he meant it. "Fine, then I guess I'll be leaving tomorrow after Buck gets back."

"If you're smart, you'll go tonight."

"I thought the truck wasn't running."

"Reggie, if you know where the distributor cap is, now would be a good time to cough it up."

She stared at him. "You think *I* took it?"

"You or one of the cowhands you conned into it. You're the only person ignorant enough to pull a stunt like that and the only one who has gained by it."

She felt as if he'd slapped her. "What kind of person do you think I am?"

"Scheming, manipulative, devious, conniving and underhanded," he said.

She felt her cheeks flame, surprised that his opinion of her was so low—worse that it bothered her. "You forgot uncompromising."

He sighed again. "What can I do to make you stop this?"

"Give my offer some serious thought." She held up her hand. "Just tell me you will think about it. If you still don't want to do the commercial by the time Buck returns tomorrow, then I will leave and you will never see me again. I give you my word."

"Your word?" He let out a laugh. "I have a better idea. You give me the truck part, I pay you a week's wages and I won't make you walk out of here. I'll drive you myself tonight."

She cocked her head at him. "You're afraid you'll change your mind about my offer if I stay the night?"

A muscle in his jaw jumped. His eyes, a paler blue than her own, turned as hard and cold as ice. "Ms. Holland, this is a cow camp. I have six hundred cattle to get out of these mountains before the snow falls, which could be tomorrow. I have men who need to keep their minds on their jobs. In order to do that, they need a dry place to sleep, food they can actually eat and no distractions. You are a distraction."

She smiled. Maybe she *was* getting to him. "Thank you."

"That wasn't a compliment. Please, just give me the truck part. Even if you were to stay up here the rest of the week you would never convince me to do your commercial."

He actually sounded as if he meant it.

"I wish I had this distributor cap thingy," she said honestly. She could feel his gaze on her. He didn't believe her.

"Fine," he said, sounding even angrier. "You want to keep up this charade, you got it. As long as you stay, you're the camp cook. Breakfast is at daybreak."

She shuddered involuntarily. Daybreak? What time was that? "You're rehiring me?"

"We generally have ham, bacon, pancakes, eggs and hashbrowns."

Holy cow. She should have known a continental breakfast would be too much to hope for. "Anything else?"

"Make the eggs fried, over easy."

"Why not."

He raised a brow. "You think you're up to frying an egg on a woodstove, Reggie?"

"I'm ready for whatever you throw at me, McCall." She didn't want to even think about *seeing* an egg that early in the morning let alone *cooking* one. "Anyway, Buck says it's possible to cook *anything* on a woodstove. It's just all a matter of getting the heat adjusted."

"Is that what Buck says?" He muttered something under his breath she couldn't hear and was glad of it. He pulled off his hat and raked a hand through his hair in obvious frustration. "Dammit, woman, don't you know you're in over your head?"

She said nothing. If this evening were any indication, she had a pretty good idea of what she'd gotten herself into.

He shoved his hat back on his head. "You're making a very big mistake and so is your accomplice." With that, he turned and stalked toward the camp.

As she watched McCall's perfect posterior walk away from her, she felt a stab of real doubt. Was he right? Was she wasting her time? Would he *ever* agree to the commercial?

She tried hard not to think about daybreak or eggs or this accomplice he suspected. But if she hadn't taken his stupid distributor cap he kept talking about, then someone had. But who? Buck? Was he trying to help her?

Or was there someone else in the camp who didn't want her or anyone else leaving tonight?

She shivered as she hurried back toward the lights of the cabin, afraid she really had gotten in over her head this time.

IN THE WEE HOURS of the morning, J.T. woke to the sound of someone walking around outside his tent. He slipped quietly from his sleeping bag, pulled on his jeans and boots and stepped out of the wall tent. Clouds hung low over the pines, making the night even darker, as if someone had dropped a blanket over the mountaintop. The last embers of the campfire cast an orange glow between the tents and the cabin. Beyond was blackness.

The horses whinnied softly in the corral. He looked in the direction of the line shack, suddenly worried about Reggie. Was it possible that she and one of the cowhands were in this together? But she hadn't known any of the ranch hands before yesterday. Or had she?

He'd just assumed that she'd conned one of them into helping her once she got to the cow camp. But what if the plan had nothing to do with a TV jeans commercial? Then what? Rustling? That had been the plan nine years ago.

J.T. heard the creak of a porch floorboard and worked his way through the pines to the opposite side of the structure.

The darkness was complete, the air heavy and cold. He could see his breath as he worked his way along the side of the cabin.

He'd just reached the porch railing along the side when he spotted a ghostlike figure at the edge of the trees. He froze, pretty sure he couldn't be seen from where he stood in the darkness.

The figure took a few tentative steps deeper into the woods. There was no mistaking the size, shape or the way she moved. Reggie. She leaned forward into the pines as if looking for something. Someone?

As she stepped deeper into the darkness and trees, he lost sight of her, but he could hear her whispering to someone.

He cursed himself. Who was she talking to? The person who had disabled the truck? He let out a silent oath as he realized this might have been a setup from the get-go. Had she known he'd be going into town yesterday and been waiting for him with that flat tire? No man could have driven past her, not the way she looked. But why go to so much trouble? So she could end up at his line shack. Her and her accomplice.

He told himself he was being paranoid, but then was reminded of the dead cow, the missing distributor cap, the feeling he couldn't shake that the incidents were just the tip of the iceberg.

She came back out of the pines, barefoot, tiptoeing, holding up the hem of her long white nightgown. The fabric hugging her curves, leaving little to the imagination.

He cursed the effect it had on him as he watched her run back inside the line shack and quietly close the door and lock it, and hated to think what effect she had on whoever she'd been meeting in the woods.

He stayed hidden for a long while, waiting to see who came out of the trees. No one did. But the person she'd been talking to could have sneaked back around to his wall tent easily enough without being seen.

"Everything all right?" Buck whispered drowsily as J.T. reentered into the wall tent.

J.T. hoped so. "Just checking things," he said, slipping into his sleeping bag on the cot. He lay there staring up into the darkness, listening to the soft whinny of the horses, the whisper of the night breeze in the pines, the occasional pop of the dying campfire, wondering who the hell Reggie was and what she really wanted with him. Also who she'd roped into helping her.

He had no way to check out her story—or her. Nor could he find out more about the men Buck had hired. Not until he returned to the ranch and that would be days from now.

Too late. Even if he owned a cell phone, it didn't work up here. There was no service even in Antelope Flats.

As he lay there, he couldn't help but think about the cattle roundup nine years ago. That one had been cursed, Buck used to say. "Weren't nobody's fault what happened up at that line shack. Sometimes things just happen and no one on this earth can stop it."

J.T. didn't believe that any more than he believed in curses. But he did believe there was evil in the world, evil in some men, and he knew only too well what could happen when you put a handful of strangers in an isolated place miles from civilization and that evil showed up with a grudge and a knife.

He closed his eyes and tried to get some sleep. In the dream, a woman in a bright red dress danced while behind her the line shack burned, flames shooting into the black night sky and a man stood in the darkness watching her, waiting.

J.T. WOKE to the smell of smoke. Through the canvas of the wall tent, he heard the crackle of flames and saw the glow. Fire!

He rolled over. Buck's cot was empty. He must have already gotten up and left for town.

Heart racing, J.T. pulled on his jeans and boots and lunged out the tent door headlong into the steel-gray morning, convinced one of the wall tents or the line shack was on fire.

Will Jarvis looked up in surprise beside the campfire.

J.T. stumbled to a stop, his pulse thundering in his ears as he tried to calm himself. The line shack wasn't on fire nor the other wall tent. History wasn't repeating itself.

"Everything all right?" Will asked, his tone almost mocking.

J.T. knew he must have looked like a fool the way he'd come barreling out of his tent. He glanced toward the line shack. Dark.

He pulled on his jacket as he walked over to the fire, needing the warmth and taking the opportunity to find out what he could about Will Jarvis.

"Smells like snow," Will said, sniffing the breeze before turning to warm his hands over the fire.

"Let's hope not," J.T. said, his mood not improving. He was tired and cranky. What little sleep he'd gotten had been haunted with nightmares. He hadn't been able to get Reggie off his mind, especially after seeing her sneaking out to talk to someone in the middle of the night.

Obviously there was more going on than he knew. The sooner he got her off this mountain, the better.

With luck, Buck would be back before noon. J.T. had told Reggie last night that she had to cook breakfast. Fortunately, it was only a threat. He'd make breakfast and by the time he got back in the evening for supper, the new cook Buck found would have dinner ready and Regina Holland would be history.

So why did he feel so disagreeable this morning? Because he couldn't forget that someone had helped Reggie. Possibly someone in this very camp. He couldn't forget that Reggie had been talking to someone in the woods last night. An accomplice. But an accomplice to what?

He took a deep breath of the morning air. Will was right. The weather was changing. It wouldn't be long and snow would blanket these mountains and stay for the long winter months to come.

"You been on a lot of cattle roundups?" J.T. asked Will, trying not to sound suspicious. But he was suspicious of all the cowhands now and there was something about Will....

"I've been on my share."

"What ranches?"

Will looked over at him and shook his head. "Some in Colorado and Wyoming. None you would know."

J.T. wanted to be the judge of that. He waited.

"The Pine Butte, the Triple Bar Three, Big Spring Station."

All ranches J.T. had heard of. All ranches pretty much anyone would have heard of. Which meant Will could be lying through his teeth, knowing there was no way to check....

J.T. heard a rustle from the second wall tent and Slim Walker and Cotton Heywood came out, followed by Roy Shields and Nevada Black. After a few minutes of standing around the campfire, J.T. asked about Luke Adams.

"Haven't seen him," Slim said. "He was already up and gone when I woke." Roy and Cotton nodded in agreement and everyone looked to Will Jarvis.

"His cot was empty when I got up and made the fire," Will said.

J.T. took a look in the wall tent. Luke's gear was gone and when he walked over to the corral, he wasn't surprised to find Luke Adams's horse gone as well. What the hell?

Maybe after last night's dinner Luke decided he didn't need any more of this. Luke just hadn't seemed like the type to leave in the middle of the night.

Now J.T. was a man short. Worse, he didn't like the way Luke had left—without a word. Was it a coincidence that Luke Adams was gone and Reggie had been talking to someone in the woods in the middle of the night? J.T. highly doubted it as he headed for the line shack.

Shafts of pearl-gray shot down through the tops of the pines, turning the early morning dew to diamonds.

As he neared the cabin, he found himself getting angrier by the minute. The woman had lied and somehow disabled his truck and even tried to blackmail him! She was definitely after his ass all right. But he doubted it had anything to do with a TV commercial. She was trying to sabotage his cattle roundup. Had already done a pretty good job of it. He'd had to send Buck back to the ranch and now he was short another hand with Luke gone.

What the hell was J.T. going to do with her? He knew what he'd like to do with her—and it wasn't let her cook.

He just couldn't let her get to him. Look what she'd done to poor unsuspecting Buck. All that delicate softness, curvaceous sweetness and apparent defenselessness sucked a man in. He remembered the way she'd been last night after that awful meal, all doe-eyed and apologetic. It still annoyed him that she'd made him feel guilty as if all of this was his fault.

As he stepped up onto the porch, he wondered what devious plots she'd been hatching last night. He paused just outside the door. He didn't need to announce his entrance. After all, it was *his* cabin. But he still scooped up an armload of firewood before noisily stomping his feet on the porch. He didn't want to catch her naked, that was for damned sure.

He started to open the door, but stopped himself. Irritated, he knocked.

When he didn't get an answer, he opened the door a crack. "Ms. Holland?"

To his surprise, the fire in the stove crackled warmly, casting a faint glow over the room. He took a couple of steps into the room, reminded that he was walking into her bedroom. "Ms. Holland?"

Still not a sound. He cleared his throat and called out again wondering if it was possible that she'd taken off with Luke Adams.

No hint of daybreak bled through the windows and he realized that she'd draped towels over them for curtains. As his eyes adjusted to the semidarkness, he could make out a lump burrowed under a pile of covers on the first bottom bunk. He figured she'd be dead to the world after last night—no doubt her first real manual labor.

He stomped over to the woodstove, making enough racket to raise the dead—if not a Los Angeles talent agent. If that really was what she was.

She didn't stir—not until he stumbled over something out in the middle of the floor. A series of objects thudded loudly and something rolled across the floor.

Cursing under his breath, he worked his way around the far edge of the floor to the woodstove, dropped his armload of wood unceremoniously and felt around for a match. From the bunk came a loud groan.

He lit the lantern. Reggie was completely covered by blankets, not even her head visible.

"Buck?" came a faint sleepy voice from deep in the bunk.

"No," J.T. snapped, sounding as irascible as he felt. Buck was on his way to Antelope Flats because of her. Reggie was on her own. And look what had happened last night when Buck had *helped* her cook.

"Oh, McCall," she said from under the blankets, not sounding in the least pleased that it was him.

He held up the lantern to see what he'd tripped over. All of the canned goods and food supplies Buck had brought up were now stacked in a semicircle around Reggie's bunk on the floor.

"What in the—?" J.T. shook his head as he stepped closer. Why in the world would she literally surround herself with groceries?

He swung the lantern around to shine it on the bottom bunk. All he could see of her was one bare arm sticking out of the mountain of blankets. The arm was curled around a ten-pound bag of flour. J.T. frowned in nothing short of true bewilderment.

"Why is all the food on the floor?" he asked patiently.

Reggie's head poked out from under the blankets, she blinked as if blinded by the firelight—or him, then she ducked back under with a louder groan.

He smiled, cheered immensely that he'd woken her from her beauty sleep. The fact that he was the last person she wanted to see this morning made it all the better.

She looked out at him, blinking away sleep, seeming to find it hard to focus on him.

In the lantern light she looked a lot better than he felt. It annoyed him greatly.

"How were your accommodations?" he asked, hoping she'd gotten less sleep than he had, especially since she'd had that late-night secret summit in the woods. He wanted to demand who she'd been talking to out in the woods last night but he decided to keep that piece of information to himself a little longer. First he would watch her with the cowhands. Better to let her think she had gotten away with her late-night rendezvous. "Sleep well?"

"Like a baby." She blinked those big blue eyes at him, clearly lying through her teeth. "What time is it?"

"Time to start breakfast."

Her gaze went to the window. "It's still dark outside."

He didn't tell her that normally the cook got up way before daybreak to start the fire. It took an hour before the fire was ready to cook on.

Fortunately, she'd kept the fire going so breakfast wouldn't be as late as he'd figured.

"As camp cook," he said, "you have to get up earlier than anyone else and usually go to bed later."

She tried to sit up and then seemed to realize she still had her arm around the bag of flour. She sneaked a quick look at him, then haughtily freed her arm and glaring at him, sat up, banging her head on the overhead bunk. "Ouch." She rubbed her forehead and eyed him as if this too were his fault. "Well, aren't you going to say something smart?"

He tried not to laugh. Served her right. If she hadn't been glaring at him—

"If you will just go away and let me get up and dressed…."

"Not so fast." The more he looked at the semicircle of staples, the more curious—and concerned—he'd become. "You haven't told me what the food is doing around your bed. I'm sure there is a simple explanation." He highly doubted it since it was Reggie. He wasn't sure what exasperated him more about her, the fact that she looked so good in the morning or that she really thought she could evade his question.

She glanced at the supplies on the floor and chewed for a moment on her lower lip. "Have it your way—" She threw back the covers, swung her legs over the side of the bed and stood up.

Just the sight of her killed every coherent thought except one: Wow.

The white silken gown fell over her curves like melting butter on flapjacks, making it hard to tell where the gown began and skin ended. To make matters worse, there was her hair. Yesterday it had been wrapped in a tight little bun or whatever at the nape of her neck. Now it floated around her pale shoulders, dark and luxurious.

He turned his back to her, going to the woodstove to stoke the fire, a fire of his own burning hot inside him. He was about to excuse himself and give her a chance to get dressed when she padded barefoot over to where he stood by the woodstove.

She had pulled another garment over the gown, something in the same thought-stealing silk that did little to hide her own assets. He tried to keep his gaze on her face. It was soft and cute as a newborn calf and just as harmless looking. Appearances could be *so* deceiving. Her fragrance floated around him. Perfume and—he frowned—dish soap? "What are you doing?"

She shot him a look as she picked up one of the skillets from the counter behind her. "I'm getting breakfast."

"Not dressed like *that!*" It was the pure impracticality of the ensemble that infuriated him, not the effect it had on him. Worse, he feared she knew exactly what she was doing to him and she was enjoying it a lot more than he was. "Anyway, I fired you."

She seemed to ignore him as she dropped the skillet on

the back of the woodstove and went to dig in the cooler. "Then you rehired me. Is it always this cold up here?"

Cold? The cabin felt suffocatingly hot. "Maybe if you were dressed appropriately—"

She shivered and went back to the bunk to get her socks and boots. He watched her wince as she pulled them on. They looked ridiculous with the expensive peignoir. And as ridiculous and out of place as Reggie herself had looked in the red suit yesterday on the roadside. The same way she didn't fit in here at the line camp.

Getting to her feet again, she looked like the only thing keeping her upright was pure stubbornness alone. Why didn't she have the good sense to give up now? Why didn't he?

He watched her draw one fingertip into her mouth, the same one he'd noticed she'd burned the night before. He felt himself weaken.

"I have some balm for your burns," he heard himself say. "You can put it on your boot blisters as well."

She looked over at him in surprise. The gratitude in her gaze grabbed hold of him in a death grip. She bit her lip as if she might feel a little guilty for putting him through this. Or maybe it was just him who was feeling guilty. Could he be wrong about her motives?

J.T. stepped to one of the smaller coolers just off the porch and came back with a chunk of cheese. He held it out to her. "Eat this."

Regina took the cheese and did as she was told before she even thought to question him. As she chewed, she looked up at him, realizing that people just did what J. T. McCall told them to do and he expected nothing less. He wasn't used to anyone not following his orders. No wonder he'd been so angry with her.

The cheese helped, she felt more awake, not quite so tired. She figured that was his intention. "Thank you."

He wasn't like anyone she'd ever known. His looks alone made him stand out. A blond, blue-eyed handsome cowboy. The real thing. Just what she needed.

And yet he was nothing like she'd originally thought she wanted. He drove an old dirty pickup, wore worn clothing, often had mud and manure on his boots and jeans and smelled of sweat and horseflesh, leather and dust. And she'd never met a sexier man in her life.

No man had ever stirred the desires in her that McCall did. When this was over, she knew she would look back on it and wonder if she'd lost her mind in Montana. She could just imagine what her mother would say if she knew that her daughter was having such thoughts about a man like J. T. McCall.

Not that she would ever let a sexual desire make her stray from her purpose. Too much was at stake for a roll in the hay—literally—with such a man. But she couldn't help but wonder what it would be like.

And he was attracted to her. He'd just about died when she'd gotten out of bed in her nightgown. She smiled to herself at the memory.

If everything in her life wasn't riding on this advertising campaign....

She could just hear Anthony. "Gina, baby, what could it hurt? You can't work all the time."

But looking at McCall, she knew it could hurt. He wasn't the kind of man you just bedded and walked away from unscathed. Not that she'd ever just bedded a man.

She hardly had time even to date. Her grandmother was always telling her she'd be an old maid if she didn't forget about work for a moment and think about a man.

Well, she was thinking about a man right now. And her thoughts would have shocked her grandmother. Maybe not. But they definitely shocked Regina.

J.T. DIDN'T LIKE that look in her eyes. "I'll go get that balm," he said as he retreated backward until he felt the doorknob digging into his behind. "Get dressed. Don't touch that stove. I'll make breakfast." He felt much too heroic.

That's why her next words floored him.

"I'd really like to see you ride today," she said. "Do you think that would be possible?"

Her words stunned him. She couldn't be serious. The guilt he'd felt just an instant before took off like a wild stallion on open range. It took any sympathy he'd felt for her with it as well.

"You just don't know when to quit, do you?" He stepped to her, forgetting for the moment how she was dressed. Or not dressed, as the case was. "I'm going to tell you this one more time. I don't know what you're really up to, but I want you out of my cow camp."

"What I'm up to? I told you what I want. All you have to do is agree to the commercial and you won't ever have to see me again."

So she was sticking to that story. "I thought you had to see me ride first before you could make me the offer?"

She seemed to realize her mistake. "I do. Why else would I want to see you ride?"

"My question exactly." She looked so innocent standing there in her negligee and cowboy boots—"Whatever it is you're really after, give it up, Reggie. I told you, no one can be more stubborn or determined than me. Not even you."

She smiled, baby blues twinkling. "I guess that's the one thing we have in common, McCall. We're both tenacious to a fault."

"Wrong, Reggie," he said as he towered over her. "With you, it's a fault. With me, it's my best quality." He tipped his hat and headed for the door.

But as usual, Reggie got in the last word.

"Believe me, McCall, your pigheadedness isn't your greatest asset. If it were, I wouldn't be here."

CHAPTER FIVE

Blurry-eyed, Regina sat down slowly on the lower bunk and pulled off her boots so she could get her jeans on. She ached all over. A faint blush of light sifted down through the pines beyond a gap in her makeshift towel curtains at the window. She felt like the walking dead, her boot-blistered feet aching, her eyes sandpapery, her fingers burned and red.

But she'd done her best not to let McCall see it. She looked at the bunk, wanting sleep, but not even tempted to get back into that hard bunk. Even if her pride would have let her. She was going to make pancakes. Come hell or high water.

She dressed in her new cowboy clothes, not that they looked new anymore. She wished now that she'd just bought a plain western shirt, a pair of her own jeans and some brown boots so she fit in more. The thought surprised her. What was happening to her? She was a Holland. Their whole goal in life was to stand out.

Dressed, she picked up all the food supplies she'd left on the floor. As she began to mix the ingredients for pancakes she felt like she was having a recurring nightmare. She'd stayed up most of the night practicing making pancakes, one batch after another. She'd been determined to show J. T. McCall that she wasn't as helpless as he thought.

Part of her wanted to shock him. The other part wanted to please him. That was the part that worried her.

Before last night she'd never made pancakes in her life, but fortunately she'd discovered a recipe on the back of the flour sack and other recipes on boxes and cans of food and she *could* read.

After she was sure everyone had gone to bed, she'd gotten up, covered the windows with towels and, working by flashlight, had practiced making pancakes. One batch after another. She hated to think how many mistakes she'd made and had to dispose of before she finally got a pancake that looked like the one on the flour sack.

Now she put more wood on the fire and looked down at her pancake batter and smiled. Her only concern was the amount of supplies she'd used. She hoped they didn't run out of food. But there seemed to be enough for an army and Buck would be bringing back a truck so they could go get more, right?

She tried not to think about Buck's arrival—and her forced departure. She didn't have much time and she was rather at a loss as to how to proceed. J. T. McCall didn't need the money, didn't want the fame and wasn't even flattered by the offer. She would never have believed such a man existed if she hadn't met him.

What McCall was, she realized, was incredibly stubborn. It would take dynamite to dislodge him once he'd made up his mind. And according to him, his mind was as set as cement.

There was the thump of boots on the porch, a step she recognized, then a soft knock at the door. She reached up to tuck an errant lock of hair behind her ear. "Come in, McCall."

J.T. OPENED THE DOOR, another armload of firewood and the balm for her blisters, expecting he would need to get Reggie out of bed. Again.

To his surprise, she was dressed and standing at the cookstove. Nothing appeared to be on fire. In fact, she seemed to have breakfast almost ready.

He'd taken a little extra time to give her a chance to get up and dressed. After saddling his horse, he rode the perimeter of the camp looking for any sign that he and his crew might not be alone up here.

He found none. No tracks. No sign of a newly used campfire ring. No sign of a spot where a tent might have been erected. He hadn't realized how long he'd been gone.

Since he'd planned to cook something simple when he returned, he hadn't worried. He never expected to see Reggie cooking. Especially over a stove where there was no flaming food.

Cooking was supposed to have been punishment for Reggie. The last thing he wanted was to see her looking competent at that cookstove, to see her looking as if she belonged here.

He checked out the pancakes she had going on the griddle. They actually looked like pancakes. She also had some ham and bacon fried up on the back of the stove. It wasn't even burned.

He glanced at the lower bunk. She'd picked up all the canned goods and supplies around it.

She followed his gaze and seemed to blush. "I was practice-cooking, all right?"

"Practice-cooking?" he echoed.

"I read the recipes off the backs of the bags, cans and

boxes of food. Then I practiced preparing a few dishes. That's all."

That's all? In the lantern light, he could see an array of freshly cleaned pots and pans on the counter in the kitchen. That's why she smelled of dish soap this morning. He couldn't help but smile.

"What's so funny?"

He shook his head. He knew he must be looking at her as if she'd just single-handedly forged a mission to Mars. He couldn't help it. Nor would he have been more surprised.

Why would she stay up half the night reading recipes off the backs of containers and practice-cooking when he'd fired her and by lunchtime she was out of here? He sobered. This woman's persistence knew no boundaries.

He felt his dread deepening and told himself that Buck would return by early afternoon at the latest and Reggie would just be a memory. One he wouldn't soon forget.

"Do you mind if we didn't have eggs this morning?" she asked.

All he could do was shake his head. Earlier he'd thought of things he wanted to say to her but they'd all flown right out of his head. He just stood looking at her, overwhelmed by the woman's doggedness, but grudgingly impressed. She was truly a babe in the woods but she was trying so hard, he had to admire her grit.

"Here, I brought you this," he said holding out the balm.

She took it with a look of such gratitude that he had to look away so she didn't see how guilty he felt.

"What do you have against city girls?" she asked as she flipped one of the pancakes. It was a beautiful golden brown and smelled wonderful. Almost as good as Reggie, dish soap and all.

For a moment he was taken aback by her question though. He was going to tell her it was none of her business but then she looked at him, those big blue eyes drawing him in.

"I…I almost married a woman from the city."

Reggie lifted a brow. "You were in love with her."

He thought about lying, but nodded. "She wanted a cowboy and the fantasy, but she soon realized what she didn't want—the reality of my lifestyle." He turned away and saw that she'd set the table already. Or had she set it last night when she was practice-cooking and he just hadn't noticed?

"She broke your heart."

He wished he had told her it was none of her business and left it at that. "She just made me realize that the last thing I needed was a city girl on a Montana cattle ranch."

To his surprise Reggie was silent. For that he was grateful. She flipped the pancakes and looked up at him, the spatula in her hand. He knew he must be staring at her, but he couldn't help himself.

He was hoping to hell she didn't have anything to do with Luke Adams's disappearance. And he was also trying to understand what it was about this woman….

REGINA MET his gaze and suddenly felt like giggling. It was his baffled expression, her own lack of sleep, the ridiculousness of her situation and the fact that she'd stayed up all night teaching herself to make *pancakes* to get a cowboy's perfect posterior in a pair of her jeans. If her grandmother could see her now.

She tried to hold back the giggle but it escaped.

"Reggie?"

To her horror, she started giggling and couldn't stop. Tears ran down her face and her body shook with laughter.

McCall was staring at her as if she'd lost her mind and then he did the strangest damned thing, he laughed. J. T. McCall laughing.

It came as such a surprise, the sound of it, the rich lyrical depth of it, she stopped giggling and looked at him and then to her shock, began to cry, huge sobs that racked her body.

He moved to her. "Finally sunk in, huh."

She nodded, crying and laughing until she took a breath and was sane again.

He reached over to thumb a tear from her cheek.

"You must think I'm the biggest idiot you've ever met," she said.

He shook his head. "But you are the most determined *woman* I've ever met." He thumbed away another tear. "And one of the bravest."

She smiled and he stood there just looking at her.

"Want to tell me anything before I call the men in for breakfast?" he asked, his voice sounding hoarse.

Tell him something? Like the fact that she wished he'd kiss her. Is that what he meant? Or was he still thinking she had the truck part?

She saw that was more what he had in mind. And to think that a second ago she'd thought he might want to kiss her as much as she had wanted him to. She really had lost her mind.

He edged backward to the door, never taking his eyes

from her as if he feared what she might do next. Then turning, he left.

Men. She would never understand them.

She stopped long enough to hurriedly apply the balm to her blistered feet and fingers. It helped, giving her hope that after breakfast her feet would feel good enough that she could sneak off and watch him ride. She already knew he would look great in the saddle. But she wasn't just doing it for the commercial.

The truth was the more she was around McCall, the more curious she became about the man. Not that she wasn't still determined to have him for her commercial. What would it hurt to learn more about him? She was curious about his life—a life he wouldn't even trade for fame and fortune.

She shook off the exhaustion and poured the last of the not-bad-looking pancake batter onto the griddle as if born to do it, then stood back and watched the cakes bubble. She could make pancakes!

Even after all her practicing, it still amazed her. Might not mean much to some people, but to her it was nothing short of a miracle.

She flipped the pancakes with an expertise born of practice and pain the night before. The pancakes had cooked to a rich golden brown. She smiled to herself again, feeling as if she'd really accomplished something, feeling good in spite of the burned fingers, blistered feet and sore back and legs.

The only thing that could make this day any better would be for J. T. McCall to agree to do the commercial before Buck got back. She realized that was probably the only reason J.T. was being even civil to her. He knew he would be rid of her soon.

Well, she wasn't down and out yet. Somehow she would change his mind before Buck's return. Going at it head-on hadn't worked. Perhaps there was another way. Although it wasn't her nature but it just might work.

The cowhands came in slowly, as if afraid of what they'd find. Who could blame them after last night's meal. It had frightened her more than them. She'd been the one who'd had to extinguish the flaming food.

She watched the men file in. There was the tall blond, Cotton, then Slim, the lanky cowboy with the scarred hands. Burns? She had an acquaintance who'd burned himself with chemicals while working at a meth lab. He had scars like that.

Then there was Roy, the quiet one and Nevada, the one who looked like an ex-con to her. Not his face, but something about the way he carried himself. And then there was Will. Will Jarvis. If J.T. wanted to know who had taken his stupid distributor cap he should look to Will. The man had passed her on the highway yesterday. She distrusted a man who wouldn't help a damsel in distress.

The men all seemed to brighten when they were able to recognize the food on the table. The men all took their places. All except for Luke Adams, the shy one.

As J.T. joined the men at the table, she put the plate with pancakes next to him, took her chair and waited. J.T. filled his plate and passed the food.

She wondered where Luke was, but was relieved to see the men filling their plates without McCall having to hold a gun to their heads.

But the true test would be McCall. She stole a look at him, anxious for him to take a bite of the pancakes.

Instead, he looked pointedly at her empty plate. She couldn't possibly eat at this ridiculous hour of the morning, could she? With his gaze still on her, she took two small pancakes and a strip of bacon.

Foregoing butter or syrup, she took a tiny bite of the pancake, feeling like a monarch's official food taster. She blinked in surprise. She took another bite, a larger one, and then quickly finished off the pancake. It was *delicious.*

She helped herself to a couple more and decided a little butter wouldn't hurt her. She'd work off the calories before the day was over, she was sure of that. She drizzled some of the huckleberry syrup over the top of her short stack, amazed at just the thought that *she'd* made these.

She took a bite, closed her eyes and let out a moan of delight. When was the last time she'd had pancakes, let alone *butter* and *syrup* on them? Breakfast in L.A. was usually a cup of coffee on the run. She would swear that she'd never had pancakes that tasted this good.

She opened her eyes and realized that J.T. was staring at her, an amused expression on his face. She quickly wiped away her look of ecstasy then the buttery syrup from her lips with her tongue.

She waited, her heart in her throat, annoyed at how much she wanted him to say he liked them.

J.T. took a bite of his pancake, chewed, stopped, looked up at her in surprise. "Not bad." He gave her a slight nod, then a smile.

She looked down, trying to hide how pleased she was.

J.T. LOOKED AROUND the table, worried. Over the years he'd had cowhands leave. Some missed girlfriends, others didn't like the work. Some got into fights with one of the other cowhands and left. Some just couldn't take all the quiet.

None of those reasons seemed to fit Luke Adams, but J.T. knew he could be wrong. He hoped to hell he was wrong about a lot of things he suspected.

"Luke didn't say anything about leaving last night?" J.T. asked as he cut a bite of ham with his knife.

He looked around the table, carefully avoiding looking at Reggie. All he got from the men were head shakes or shrugs in answer to his question.

"He get into a fight or argument with anyone?"

Head shakes, shrugs.

"Luke left?" Reggie asked, sounding surprised.

"So it seems," he said.

She glanced around the table, then asked Slim to pass her the pancakes.

"No one heard him leave the tent?" J.T. asked. Apparently not. He let his gaze light on Reggie. She had her head down, seeming more interested in her pancakes then Luke's departure.

"You know where Luke might have gone, Ms. Holland?"

Her head jerked up. She blinked. "How would *I* know?" She had a dab of syrup on her lower lip.

"I thought you might have heard or seen him leave since you were up late?"

She shook her head, her tongue coming out to lick away the syrup.

She might have been the last person to see him, he wanted to say, but didn't pursue it in front of the others. He'd been watching her with the cowhands and he hadn't seen anything pass between them, not even a suspicious look.

Luke's disappearance seemed to indicate he'd been the

person she'd met in the woods last night; the person who'd disabled the truck for her. If so, they were obviously in this together. Whatever *this* was. Was it possible she wanted him to make a jeans commercial *that* badly? It had to be something else.

"Maybe he just got up early and went for a ride," Reggie suggested. "Or maybe he went with Buck."

"Buck would have said something if he'd known Luke was leaving. Doesn't it seem odd to you that Luke would take off without a word to anyone?" he asked her.

Her eyes widened. She shrugged. "Everything here seems odd to me."

His gaze killed the splattering of laughter that erupted around the table from her comment. "Well, I don't want anyone else leaving here without me knowing about it." He looked to the men. "I want you to work closely, keeping the others in sight today. Also keep a look out for Luke in case he just wandered off. I don't want anyone else getting lost."

J.T. saw Will Jarvis glance over at Slim. Slim was busy eating and didn't seem to notice, but J.T. did. "Luke didn't mention anything about leaving to you, did he Slim?"

Slim looked up in obvious surprise. His Adam's apple worked for a moment. "I might have heard someone get up last night, but whoever it was came back a little while later."

It seemed no one had heard Luke leave. The six men had all been sleeping in the same tent. He wondered how Luke had been able to leave, gear, horse and all, without anyone being the wiser.

His gaze settled on Reggie. He also wondered what she and presumably Luke Adams might have had to discuss in the middle of the night in the woods. Maybe she was just thanking him for helping her. Because if Luke was the man she'd been whispering to in the dark, J.T. would lay odds Luke had also been the man to take the distributor cap.

REGINA COULD FEEL McCall's gaze on her. He thought she had something to do with Luke leaving? She'd never laid eyes on Luke Adams or any of the rest of them before yesterday. But she could see trying to convince McCall otherwise would be futile.

What exactly was he accusing her of, anyway? He already thought she'd done something to the truck to keep it from running so she could stay the night. Now he thought she'd done something to Luke?

She excused herself and got up to start the dishes. She had a pretty good idea that J.T. wasn't going to have the men help her. She was right. As soon as they all finished their breakfasts, he told everyone to get saddled up.

Chairs scraped and boots thumped across the floor to the door. She didn't bother to turn as they all left.

"I would suggest you stay in the cabin until Buck returns with a truck," J.T. said behind her, startling her. She thought he'd left with the others.

She nodded and kept washing the dishes. Stay in the cabin. He must be kidding. She had no intention of missing the chance to see him ride. She had pictured it in her mind given the way he carried himself, all that confidence and competence, all that arrogance.

But in order to see him in the saddle, she'd have to get out of this cabin soon after the men left. She wished now that she'd paid more attention to how far away the cattle were when Buck was explaining how the cowboys rounded them up.

"I don't want you wandering off and getting lost," J.T. was saying.

He was still here? She nodded again and when she still felt him waiting behind her, she gave up and turned to look at him.

He handed her a dirty plate from the table. As she reached for it, her fingers brushed his.

They both released the plate. It clattered to the floor but didn't break. Regina jumped back, startled, her gaze going to his. Other than the color, she'd never really noticed his eyes before. Probably because she'd only been interested in his butt.

Now she saw that part of what made him so handsome was his eyes. They were a pale deep blue, but with flecks of gold. The eyes alone could have held her attention. But something in his gaze—

Suddenly the cabin seemed ridiculously hot. She swallowed, unable to take her eyes from his, although it felt as if all the heat in the room was being generated by his gaze.

Her insides seemed to soften, while at the same time, she felt as if she couldn't catch her breath. Then over the erratic thudding of her heart, she heard the room grow painfully still.

It all happened in an instant. So quickly that Regina wasn't really sure she hadn't imagined it.

J.T. jerked his gaze away, cleared his throat and stooped to pick up the plate as one of his men appeared in the doorway to ask something about riding the ridgeline.

J.T. barked out the answer, his sumptuous, deep voice a little hoarse sounding.

The man—she saw out of the corner of her eye it was the young blonde Cotton—drew back in surprise, then seemed to leave quickly so J.T. didn't see his knowing grin.

J.T. dropped the plate into the hot sudsy dishwater.

Regina began to wash the plate as if nothing had happened. Nothing *had* happened, had it? Then why did her face feel flushed and her hands seem to shake as she washed the plate? All because a man had *looked* at her?

When she finally did turn around she found McCall long gone. She set to washing the pans and skillets, keeping hot water going on with the fire so she could finish her job as quickly as possible and catch J.T. in the saddle.

Through the window she could see that it was growing light out, the sun coming up, the pines shimmering like green silk in the early morning light. The last time she'd seen the sun come up, she'd been out all night.

She stood staring out the window, surprised by how breathtaking the view was, then shook herself. What was she thinking? If she hoped to see J.T. ride— She quickly dried her hands.

But as she started toward the door, she heard a thud like something hitting the side of the cabin. Her gaze flew to the window but she saw nothing through the glass. Could it have been one of the men? Not likely. She'd heard them ride out a while ago. It had probably just been a tree limb blowing in the breeze.

Cautiously, she opened the door. The porch was empty. She stared out at the trees. But there was no breeze. It hadn't been a limb hitting the side of the cabin. Whatever she'd heard was nowhere to be seen.

She looked out toward the corral. Only two horses remained. No cowboys. She stood at the porch railing listening. She heard no sign of the men or the cows. She realized she didn't even know which direction they'd ridden off in or how far away they had gone. Mostly, she realized, she didn't like the idea of going out there alone.

It wasn't like her to be afraid, but it was as if she sensed something waiting in the woods, something more dangerous than anything she'd ever encountered in L.A.

Not that she would let that stop her. Buck would be back soon. She didn't have much time and she wanted to see McCall ride. She knew once she saw him in the saddle nothing on this earth could keep her from talking him into doing the commercial.

But as she pushed wide the cabin door, she saw a large dark shadow fall across the porch. J.T.? Had he been waiting outside, knowing she wouldn't do as he'd told her?

Or had he come back because of earlier and what had happened between them. *Had* something happened? He must have thought so for him to come back.

Her heart did a little flutter at the thought as she leaned around the edge of the door expecting to see him standing just off the porch, the sun behind him.

At first it didn't register what she saw—or heard.

She let out a shriek of alarm. A huge bear rummaged in the dirt just off the end of the tiny porch—just feet from her.

She stumbled back into the cabin, slamming the door behind her. She could hear the bear snorting and scraping at the earth next to the porch.

What if it decided to come into the cabin?

She glanced around, looking for a way out. The windows didn't open and there was only the one door—the one with the bear just outside. She was trapped!

Frantically she looked around for a weapon, then let out an oath. What was she thinking? Even if she'd found a rifle she didn't have the faintest idea how to shoot one. Nor was she apt to shoot the bear even if she did.

Belatedly, she remembered something Buck had told her when she'd asked if there were any bears in the mountains.

CHAPTER SIX

J.T. had sent the cowhands off to start rounding up the cattle. He wanted a few minutes alone to cuss and fuss and mentally kick himself—and to take a look around their tent.

What the hell had happened back in the cabin? One minute he was looking at Reggie and the next—

He swore under his breath, shaking his head at his own foolishness. One minute he'd just been looking at her, thinking what a handful the woman was, remembering the way she'd enjoyed her pancakes, and the next minute—hell, he didn't know what he'd been thinking the next minute.

He couldn't have been thinking at all to be thinking anything about a woman like her. A fool city girl. Worse, one with designs on him. At least this one had been honest from the get-go. All she wanted were his…assets.

So she'd stayed up most of the night and taught herself how to make pancakes and hadn't burned breakfast to a crisp. So what? No reason to go all soft on her.

She was a damned fine-looking woman so who could blame him for being attracted to her if that's what it had been for that split second when their fingers had touched?

Whatever it had been, it wasn't going to happen again. He needed to keep his distance from her. Who knew what womanly wiles she would use on him if he weakened even the slightest. He already knew what lengths she would go to. At least he thought he did.

What really ticked him off was that she'd made him forget all about her late-night rendezvous. He had meant to ask her, not that he thought she would tell him the truth.

But as he led his horse over to the second wall tent, he couldn't help worrying that she hadn't been behind taking the distributor cap. So how did he explain her wandering around in the night whispering to someone in the trees?

He started to open the tent and stopped, thinking he heard a noise. He glanced toward the cabin. He was tempted to check on her and make sure she was all right. Uh-uh. He wasn't going near that cabin or Reggie. It didn't matter what she was doing out in the dark last night or who she was talking to. Buck would return and take her to town. By the time he and the men came in for supper, she would be gone.

So what was his problem? He knew it was the idea of leaving her alone even for a few hours. Who knew what kind of trouble she could get into?

He glanced around, feeling as if someone was watching him. He knew he couldn't be seen through the pines from the cabin. Reggie would probably still be doing the dishes anyway. Taking another glance around, seeing no one, he entered the tent. The cowhands should all be out rounding up cattle, trying to keep each other in sight. So no one could sneak back for any reason, right?

He knew what was nagging at him. Luke Adams. He was surprised that the cowhand would leave in the middle of the night without a word. Especially if Luke was the person Reggie had been whispering to out in the woods.

Luke's disappearance on top of the disabled truck left him feeling all the more uneasy.

He'd already checked and knew Luke's gear was gone. But still he wanted to have a look around the tent.

He checked each man's gear but didn't find anything out of the ordinary. He straightened, hitting his shoulder on the tent frame. He thought he heard a sound, a soft rustle, like something shifting over his head. He looked up and noticed something odd—an object had been stuck between the layers of canvas in the frame. He wouldn't have noticed it at all if he hadn't hit his shoulder and dislodged it.

He reached up and sliding his hand into the space touched cold metal. His heart leaped to his throat as he pulled out the 9 mm pistol.

J.T. knew that each man had a rifle or pistol on him when he was gathering cattle. Sometimes a man had to put down an injured cow. Or scare off a bear or mountain lion. Even put down a horse with a broken leg.

His camp rule, which he was sure Buck had shared with the men, was no alcohol. And no firearms in the tent or cabin. He'd heard too many stories from his father and grandfather about cowhands getting drunk and having shootouts in the middle of cow camp.

So why had one of the cowhands *hidden* a gun in the tent? As he stared at the gun he wondered not only who it belonged to but also what the owner was planning to do with it.

Sticking the pistol into his coat pocket, he stepped from the tent, glanced around and saw no one, then went to his own tent and hid the pistol beneath his cot for the time being.

As he exited his tent and started toward his horse, he

heard a noise come from the cabin. He told himself he was just imagining the banging sound, looking for an excuse to go back to the cabin and Reggie.

As he looked toward the cabin, he realized he half-expected to see it on fire. It was that damned nightmare he'd had last night.

Through the trees he could see a portion of the building and the only smoke rising out of it was through the chimney. But the memory of the nightmare coupled with everything else left him anxious.

The banging sound seemed to be getting louder.

He stared at the cabin, telling himself not to go back there. He had six hundred head of cattle to get out of these mountains before the snow hit and the sooner the better, all things considered.

But it was impossible to ignore this much racket. And there was no doubt that the incessant banging was coming from the cabin.

He shook his head and headed toward the sound. What in the devil was she up to now?

REGINA HAD RUSHED to the kitchen, grabbed the largest pan she could find and a good-sized spoon. Out on the porch, she heard the creak of a floorboard groan under the weight of the bear. It was on the porch!

She began to pound the bottom of the pan with the spoon like a mad woman. To her horror, the ear-splitting banging didn't seem to phase the bear. She beat the pan harder and realized she would have to open the door. Obviously, the bear couldn't hear it well enough.

Hadn't she read somewhere that bears ate people in Montana? Grizzly bears. Was this a grizzly? Probably, with her luck. From the size of the bear, it looked as if it could get into the cabin without any problem and she had no doubt that it would break in if she didn't scare it away.

She beat the pan as hard as she could, her heart pounding louder than the spoon on the bottom of the pan. Moving quietly to the door, she opened it a crack and looked out. She couldn't see its shadow on the porch anymore. Maybe she'd chased it off.

She stepped farther out on the porch. No sign of the bear but she kept beating the pan just in case as she inched along the porch to the side of the cabin.

The bear reared up in surprise to see her. Not half as surprised as she was to see it. She turned and ran, afraid to slow down to make the ninety-degree turn back into the cabin let alone to get the door closed and locked before the bear burst into the cabin.

Her feet barely touched the porch as she flew across it expecting to feel the bear's breath on her neck any moment.

Climb a tree! She was looking for a tree she could climb, pounding the pan as hard as she could as she ran, afraid to look back—

Something clawed at her shoulder with enough force to spin her around. She shrieked, and instinctively closed her eyes and swung the pan. She heard the pan thump off something solid and swung again.

J.T. LET OUT AN OATH and grabbed for her, but she nailed him again with the pan, knocking his hat into the dust. "Dammit, Reggie! What in the hell is wrong with you?"

She opened her eyes. They were bigger and bluer than ever in her pale, frightened face. "I thought—" She seemed to be trying to catch her breath, her substantial chest moving up and down with the effort.

He rubbed the knot rising on his forehead with one hand and leaned down to pick up his hat from the dirt with the other. "Are you nuts?"

She grimaced as her gaze went to his bruised forehead. "Sorry."

"Yeah." He gingerly settled his hat back on his head and took the pan and spoon from her. The woman had beat huge craters into the bottom of the aluminum pan. He frowned at her. "Why in the world were you—"

"Buck told me to do it."

He eyed her. "Are you sure you got the directions right? What exactly were you trying to cook?"

She mugged an unamused face at him and stepped around him to point back toward the cabin. "I was trying to scare the bear away."

He turned. "What bear?"

"It must have gone into the cabin."

He shot her a disbelieving look. "You're sure it was a bear?"

"I know a bear when I see one. I think it's a grizzly."

He nodded, skeptical on all counts. "Come on," he said impatiently as he started toward the cabin.

At the porch, Reggie hung back. He shook his head as he crossed the porch. The woman was going to be the death of him. As he peered around the doorjamb, he was relieved to see that there was no bear in the cabin but he heard something around the corner.

Moving to the end of the porch, he looked around the corner and spotted a small black bear rummaging in something along the side of the cabin. He turned to find Reggie had joined him, hiding behind him for protection.

"Buck told you to bang on a pan if you saw a bear?" he asked incredulously. He hated to think what she'd have done if he'd given her a real weapon.

"It's a grizzly, isn't it," she whispered.

"No, it's just a young black bear."

"Just?"

He stomped his boots on the flooring. "Go on, get!" he called out to the bear.

The bear lifted its head. J.T. could feel Reggie's body pressed against his back, her fingers digging into his ribs as she held on.

"I said, get!" he hollered again and tossed the battered pot at the bear's rump. It startled the young bear. He loped off into the pines.

"It's gone," J.T. said to Reggie, but he wondered what the bear had been so interested in beside the cabin.

Reggie loosened her hold on him and he stepped off the porch to investigate. He hadn't gone far when he saw what the bear had been in to. It looked as if a hen house had exploded, there were so many eggshells on the ground. With a groan, he turned to look back at Reggie. She was standing at the edge of the porch, still looking scared.

"You didn't throw food out here, did you?" he asked, knowing full well that she had.

"Food?" she repeated.

He watched her wet her lips, calling more attention to her mouth than he really needed her to do. She glanced after the bear, then at the eggshells on the ground and the marks where the bear had torn up the earth. For a moment, she only chewed at that soft-looking plump lower lip.

"I wouldn't exactly call what I tossed out *food,*" she said slowly. "Just some practice pancakes and a…few eggshells."

He shook his head at her. "Reggie…" He took a breath, trying to control his temper. "This is bear country. You put out food and you're going to attract bears and I don't think that's what you want to do."

Her eyes came up to meet his. For a moment, he almost lost himself in all that sky-blue.

"Not only that, having bears in camp is real hard on pans," he said, no longer able to hide a grin.

"Very funny." She did not look amused.

He reminded himself that she was a city girl and as out of her element as she could get. If he went to L.A., there would probably be things that would scare him and make him look foolish.

He handed her the spoon and went to pick up the pan and clean up the garbage to keep the bear from coming back. As he did, he found himself fighting back a grin at just the memory of her charging through the woods, banging that pan. The woman was something, he'd give her that.

Men often underestimated women. Not that he thought any man was prepared for a woman like Reggie. Look what she'd done to poor unsuspecting Buck. Look what she'd done to him. He remembered the way she'd looked last night in the cabin, all doe-eyed and apologetic. It still annoyed him how she'd made him feel guilty as if it were his fault she was here.

He heard her behind him and turned to hand her the battered pan.

She glanced again in the direction where the bear had disappeared. "What do I do if the bear comes back?"

He heard the worry in her voice. "He shouldn't unless you cook up something for him again."

She mugged a face at J.T. The color had come back into her cheeks and she no longer looked frightened, but her eyes were still large and bottomless and clear as a high mountain lake. It was hard not to take a dip in them.

He realized that the bear had been a blessing of sorts. "But if I were you, I'd stay in the cabin just in case," he said, knowing that's exactly what a city girl would do after seeing a bear. And at least with her locked in the cabin, he shouldn't have to worry about her. Unless she really did set the cabin on fire or tried to cook or— Best not to think about it.

"Just try to stay out of trouble," he said, then turned and headed for his horse. His head hurt from where she'd hit him and he still had cattle to round up. He hoped to hell Buck hurried back.

REGINA STOOD on the porch, torn between doing exactly what he'd said—locking herself in the cabin until he returned—and seeing him in the saddle.

She hurried to the edge of the porch, peered around the corner and watched as he strode back to where he'd left his huge horse. She watched him swing up into the saddle. If she'd had any doubts how his buns would look on a horse, she didn't anymore. He was perfect. The consummate cowboy keister.

Now all she had to do was find a way to get him to do the commercial, she thought as she watched him ride away. For the first time, she realized that might not happen. She might fail. She shoved the thought away. Over her dead body!

She stood at the edge of the porch watching him ride up the hillside, mentally willing him to turn, to look back. If he didn't turn, there was no way he was going to do the commercial. If he did—

He was almost to a stand of white-barked trees, the golden leaves flickering in the morning breeze, when he looked back.

She quickly ducked behind the corner of the cabin, smiling. J.T. McCall wasn't as immune to her as he pretended. She was getting to him.

Feeling better, she turned, glad to see that there was no bear at the end of the porch. But as she started to take a step, she heard a sound. The crack of a twig off in the trees, then another. Something was out there. Something big enough to break a stick.

Heart pounding, she glanced over her shoulder, expecting to see the bear behind her. Or something worse, although she couldn't imagine what that would be.

Hearing the crack of another limb breaking, she turned, thinking it might be one of the men who'd come back for something.

She looked toward the tents, the trees blocking her view, then up the hillside toward the corrals. Nothing.

Listening, she waited, thinking that if it was one of the men he would say something to her. She heard no sounds of the men or the cows. She didn't know which direction they'd ridden off in or how far away they'd gone. Mostly, she realized, she was vulnerable out there for whatever might be in the woods.

She hurried back inside the cabin and locked the door.

J.T. hadn't said when they'd be back. She tossed another log on the woodstove and eyed the lower bunk. It was the best she was going to do.

J.T. RODE TOWARD the sound of lowing cattle. As he came up over a rise, he saw the undulating herd below him in the wide pasture and stopped to get his feet back under him. This was what he had been born to do. Be a rancher. He loved the sight and sound of the herd, preferred to be on a horse than in a pickup and would fight any man—or woman—who tried to take it from him. And had.

He knew that was what was worrying him. That history was starting to repeat itself. The dead cow. Truck trouble. One cowhand already gone. It hadn't happened in the same way nine years ago but the similarity was enough to scare him. On top of that, there was Reggie. Maybe that worried him the most because he felt protective toward her. Hell, someone had to protect the woman.

Nevada rode toward him and J.T. knew at once that something was wrong. "I found a dead cow I thought you might want to take a look at."

J.T. nodded and followed Nevada back through the towering pines. It was cool and dark under the dense green boughs where the morning sun hadn't reached yet. He breathed in the pine scent, filling his nostrils with it, knowing that soon he would be smelling burned hide.

The cow lay on its side at the edge of a small ravine. It had been killed, its side slit open, its innards removed and then a fire built in the carcass.

"Have you ever seen anything like this?" Nevada asked, sounding spooked.

Unfortunately J.T. had. "It's someone's idea of a prank."

Nevada looked at him as if he had to be insane. "This isn't a prank. This is a warning."

J.T. nodded and looked Nevada in the eyes. "I think someone's trying to sabotage my roundup. Or at least make me think they are."

"Rustlers?"

That would be anyone's first thought. "Possibly. Could just be someone messing with me. I would prefer you didn't mention this to the others."

Nevada held his gaze for a long moment, then nodded.

"I would also understand if you wanted to draw your pay and get the hell out of here," J.T. said.

Nevada seemed surprised. He laughed. "Not a chance. I wouldn't mind meeting up with the fellow who did this."

"Me, too," J.T. said and listened for sounds of the other men. "That's one reason I want everyone to keep an eye out for the other men."

Nevada pushed back his hat and looked back through the pines toward the herd. "You think it's one of your men."

"I hope to hell not, but I haven't seen any sign of anyone else around," J.T. said, wondering if he was telling Nevada because he trusted him. Or because he didn't.

"I'll watch my back," Nevada said and rode off to join the others.

J.T. sat on his horse for a moment, fighting the urge to go back and check on Reggie and listening for the sound of a truck engine coming up the mountain. Then he spotted a half-dozen strays down in a ravine and past them, what looked like a rope noose hanging from a tree.

CHAPTER SEVEN

Regina woke cramped in a ball beneath the blankets. The fire in the stove had died and the cabin felt chilly. What time was it anyway? The sun was now shining low in the window on the opposite side of the cabin.

She sat up, careful not to bang her head again, and listened, wondering if a sound had awakened her. Or just the numbing silence.

Getting up, she put more of the balm on her blisters, then pulled on her boots and went to the door. Shouldn't Buck be here by now? She'd expected McCall to come back by now. Maybe she wasn't getting to him as much as she'd hoped.

She ventured out onto the porch, remembering that awful feeling earlier. There had been something out there, she was sure of that. But now, she heard a comforting sound. Cows mooing.

J.T. would be where the cows were, right? She had to admit, she knew nothing about gathering cattle but she knew she wanted to see what he did and the mooing didn't sound that far away. And there was no sign of the bear.

She promised herself she wouldn't go far, although the cool air felt good and the balm he'd given her and the Band-Aids she'd found in a first-aid kit made walking possible.

The landscape felt less threatening with the sun coming through the branches to splash the bed of dried needles below in pale gold. The pine boughs shimmered, a silken soft green, and a light breeze flapped playfully at the hem of her western shirt. Overhead, large white cumulus clouds bobbed along in a sea of infinite blue.

As she wound her way through the pines, she took deep breaths of the clear mountain air, surprised that it seemed a little less alien. In fact, even the countryside felt less hostile.

She followed the sound of the cows, weaving in and out of the trees and around huge rocks, thinking about how different it was from Los Angeles, how different the men were in Montana.

She'd reached the edge of a ravine when she suddenly realized she had no idea where she was. Behind her all she could see was trees and rocks and they all looked alike. No cabin.

In front of her there was nothing but more trees and rocks. No street signs. No taxi cabs. No other cabins. And nobody around to ask.

Worse yet, she was having trouble pinpointing exactly where the sound of the cattle was coming from. The mooing seemed to echo through the pines and she had the frightening feeling that the mooing might carry for miles.

Fighting panic, she wondered how anyone would ever find her. Would J.T. even look? Should she try to find her way back? Or keep going in hopes of finding the cattle and help?

Suddenly her blisters were killing her. Why hadn't she paid more attention to where she was going?

Close to tears, she walked over to a rock at the edge of a clearing. From here she could see a stand of white-barked trees, the leaves golden. She could hear their soft rattle in the breeze, like thin gold coins.

She tried to calm herself. She couldn't have gone very far. Of course she'd be able to find her way back. Anyone who would drive in L.A. could handle this.

But she did wonder how long it would take before someone came looking for her if she couldn't. She wished she'd thought to leave a trail of bread crumbs, but then, that would probably have just led a bear to her.

She heard a noise. Something large crashing through the trees on the other side of the clearing. A large dark object came running out of the pines, kicking up the fallen gold leaves. She let out a cry as she saw that it was a horse, its mouth foaming, its eyes wild. It ran at her.

Her heart in her throat, she stumbled to her feet and tried to get out of the horse's path. In her hurry, she didn't see the tree root. The next thing she knew she was face down on the ground—and in pain.

"Oh." She'd hit the ground hard but it was her ankle that hurt. She'd twisted it badly as she'd fallen. As she lay in the dirt she wondered if this was where McCall would find her body come spring.

She sat up. She'd be damned if she would just lie in the dirt and wait for someone to find her. Using the tree trunk for support, she worked her way to standing on her good ankle. She tried her other ankle and groaned.

One thing was clear, she wasn't going far.

This had been a fool thing to do. Following McCall out here. She looked around, trying to decide which direction to try to walk in. The last thing she wanted was to run into that horse again. She didn't know there were wild horses out here. What was she saying? She didn't have any idea what was out here in the wild.

She turned, startled again as a half-dozen brown-and-white faced cows trotted past to drop out of sight.

The cows brought tears of relief to her eyes but nothing like the voice she heard behind them. Limping, she followed the cows to the edge of the clearing and saw that they had dropped down into a small rocky ravine.

Bracing herself against a small pine, she stood on the edge in the pines as the cowboy's voice floated up to her.

"Go on, get up there," J.T. called softly to the cows as he rode into sight below her.

At first all she saw was his worn black hat and a glimpse of his yellow-checked western shirt and blue jean jacket through the brush.

She could hear other cattle now and saw through the pine boughs dozens of cows in a wide open meadow farther down the mountain—in the direction J.T. was headed. Her gaze quickly returned to him as he came into full view below her.

She had planned to call out to him but instead she stayed unmoving in the shelter of the pine, watching him herd the cows through the bottom of the ravine. There seemed to be little wasted motion and she wondered how many times he'd done this particular task before.

"Get up there," he called almost affectionately to the cows.

He was directly below her now. She watched, taken aback by how commanding he looked in the saddle. Bigger than life. And yet so natural, as if he and the horse were one.

She felt a pull inside her so strong that at first it felt as alien as everything else in Montana.

AN EERIE FEELING raised the fine hairs on the nape of J.T.'s neck. The feeling was so strong he actually reached back to rub his neck. For a moment there he thought he'd felt Reggie's gaze on his fanny the way he could sense a bad storm or trouble coming. With storms and trouble though, he was seldom wrong. With this, he hoped to heaven he was mistaken.

Reggie was back at the cabin. For once she would do as he asked. Hell, she'd be scared to death to wander out by herself after that bear incident.

But he turned anyway, unable to resist the power of the feeling that he was being watched. No, not watched, scrutinized. And by a pair of big blue eyes.

He brought his horse up short at the sight of her standing under the pine just above him, his first reaction pleasure. His second, worry and anger.

She was smiling a self-satisfied, knowing smile. It took him a moment to fully comprehend the extent of that smile, the flush of her cheeks, the glow in her gaze.

"Damned woman," he muttered under his breath. She'd come out here to see how he sat the saddle. What had made him think she'd behave sensibly? "I thought I told you to stay in the cabin?"

Her smile deepened. "I wanted to see you work."

He hadn't felt even a little self-conscious under a woman's gaze in years. Until now. She had a look he'd seen often enough on coyotes. He didn't particularly like the predatory way she was considering him or the way it made him feel. Especially since he was damned sure her scrutiny was aimed at his south-end.

"It was a fool thing to do," he snapped. "It's a wonder you didn't get lost, fall off a cliff, drown in the creek, twist an—"

"I *am* lost and I did twist my ankle," she interrupted. "That's why I'm so glad to see you."

He swore under his breath. She seemed way too happy to see him—even for a lost city girl. This had been his "audition" for the TV jeans commercial he wasn't going to do. Not that that made any difference to Reggie. Not even the arduous job of camp cook could dissuade this woman. And from the radiance of her smile, he'd lay odds that he'd passed her screen test.

So why did he get the feeling she wanted more than him in a commercial? His cattle? He couldn't see her throwing her lot in with rustlers, but what did he know. If not his cattle, then what?

"Stay here," he ordered her. "Don't move until I come back. Do you think you can do that?"

"I wouldn't know where to go and my blisters hurt too much to move and I can barely walk on my ankle."

"Great." He drove the cattle on down to the herd in the pasture. When he rode back, he was surprised to find her sitting where he'd left her, as good as her word, and he'd realized he'd ordered her just as he had his dog Jennie. His face burned in shame that he'd been insulted because she'd originally thought Jennie was his wife and he'd ordered her to stay in the truck.

Her conception of Montana cowboys would be based on him. He groaned inwardly at the thought and wondered what to do with her now. He'd thought things couldn't get worse but Reggie was proof they could.

As he dismounted, he noticed that her face was flushed. She'd never looked so beautiful sitting there in the sunlight. He saw a fire burning in her eyes. Damn. She hadn't given up on him doing her commercial. If anything she looked all the more determined, he thought as he joined her under the wide sweeping arms of the pine.

The day was hot, the sun nearly at its apex. Rays of heat cut through the not yet bare aspens, making the fallen leaves shimmer beneath their feet. The leaves overhead rattled like dry paper.

She started to get up. "McCall, I need to tell you—"

He nodded, reached down and pulled her to her feet. Determined not to let her get in another word about that damned commercial or whatever she was after, he pulled her to her feet and kissed her, successfully shutting her up.

And being a man who liked to finish what he'd started…

It wasn't until he'd thoroughly kissed her that he realized the folly of his actions. By then he'd completely lost himself in the sweet, soft pliant warmth of her lips, in the deep, dark, wet secrets of her mouth.

All he knew was that it felt good and right and, if he was being honest, something he'd wanted to do since he'd seen her on the highway.

When he finally came to his senses, he jerked back. What had he been thinking? Had he lost his mind?

He had to hold her to keep her from slumping to the ground, having forgotten about her twisted ankle. She reached up to touch a finger to her lips and took a ragged breath that made her chest rise, her body tremble. Then ever so slowly, she smiled.

Damn, he thought. He'd just done the worse thing he could have.

REGINA HAD ALWAYS prided herself on her quick recovery rate. But it took a moment to get her feet back under her after *that* kiss even without a sprained ankle.

"What was that about, McCall?" Not that she was complaining, mind you. It was just such a surprise. The kiss. Even more surprising, its effect on her.

Her heart still pounded fiercely and her limbs felt like running water. Good thing he was still hold-ing her. What had he put into that kiss? She felt almost…intoxicated as she met his equally stunned gaze.

"It was just a kiss," he snapped, as if the kiss had had no effect on him.

"You just keep telling yourself that, McCall." She'd like a replay just to see if it had been as amazing as she thought. But then another kiss like that would only lead to trouble. "Unless that kiss was your way of saying yes."

"What?" J.T. said, letting go of her and stepping back.

"Your way of saying yes to the commercial." She laughed so he'd know she was just trying to lighten the mood between them.

He didn't seem to get the joke. "How could you possibly get that out of one silly little meaningless kiss?"

"I was *joking*." Silly, little, meaningless kiss? He was starting to irritate her, but she knew she was more upset with herself than him. She didn't fraternize with blue jeans models. Even those who hadn't given in yet.

"I would think a woman like you would have kissed

enough men to know that was just a kiss, nothing more," he said, shoving back his hat in obvious frustration.

She'd been kissed by a fair amount of men. But none of them had kissed her like *that.* Nor had she kissed them back like *that.* Maybe she'd been dating the wrong men. Wait a minute. *A woman like you?* What was that supposed to mean?

"In my experience, McCall, a kiss, no matter how small, means *something,*" she snarled, now clearly more irritated with him than herself. She brushed past him and headed off through the trees in what she hoped was the direction of the cabin, limping and in pain, but determined to walk all the way back without his help. He could just stuff his forgettable kiss.

She took a couple of steps and stumbled. Unfortunately, her legs hadn't forgotten that damned kiss either.

"You can't walk all the way back to the cabin with a sprained ankle and blisters," he said and cursed as he grabbed her to keep her from falling. "Come on."

She barely had time to cry in protest before he swept her up into his arms. At first she thought he planned to carry her back to the cabin. But then she realized what he had in mind was much worse.

He whistled and his horse trotted over to them. "You can't walk so you have to ride."

The beast looked even larger close up. "Not a *horse.*"

"A horse is your *only* option. I'm not going to carry you. Anyway, Killer isn't just any horse."

Killer? "Really, I can walk. I'll just—" Before she could say more, he tossed her up into the saddle like a sack of potatoes. She grabbed the saddle horn, afraid she'd go right on off the other side. “His name is Killer? Why would you name him killer unless—”

“You’ll be fine,” J.T. said, humor back in his voice.

She looked down at the man as she teetered precariously, miles from the ground, straddling a wild brute named Killer on the slipperiest saddle on earth. J.T. was enjoying her discomfort. The bastard.

If she’d felt weak at his kiss, it was nothing compared to being on his horse. “You forget,” she said a little breathlessly. “I don’t know how to ride.” Did she dare mention her fear of large animals?

“Do you know how to sit?” he inquired. “Because that’s all you have to do.”

Before she could answer, he swung up behind her on the horse. The horse shuddered under them and took a step. She let out a shriek.

Killer seemed to roll his eyes at her. He obviously wasn’t any happier about this than she was.

“How did…Killer get his name?” she asked.

“You don’t want to know,” J.T. said and nudged the horse with his heels.

The horse began to move. Regina felt as if she was going to slide off. She clamped her legs tight around the beast. Killer jumped forward.

“Easy,” J.T. said, wrapping an arm around her as he worked the reins and the horse settled back down. “Unless you’d like to get us both bucked off I’d suggest you not do that again.”

She barely heard him over the pounding of her heart.

“Maybe now you’ll have the good sense to stay at the cabin until Buck comes back for you,” he said.

She would have sworn she heard him chuckle to himself. Well at least someone was enjoying this, she thought, as she clung to the saddle horn and tried not to look down.

She had better luck with that than trying not to think about the man behind her.

Good sense? If she had good sense she wouldn't have come up with this last-ditch ad campaign, she wouldn't have set her sights on J. T. McCall's perfect posterior, she wouldn't have hired on as his camp cook, and she certainly would have never let him kiss her—let alone throw her on his horse.

She tried to relax, leaning back a little into him, feeling tired and resigned to whatever her fate might be on the back of Killer. She'd made so many mistakes with the man, including kissing him back the way she had, even death didn't look so bad.

"Sit still," he ordered, his voice sounding strange to her.

She ran her tongue over her lips, not surprised to find his kiss branded there. She felt suddenly soft and vulnerable and…so female it hurt.

McCall was angry with her. She'd no doubt destroyed any hope of getting him to model the jeans. She didn't even want to think what would happen if she returned to California without the perfect cowboy butt contract in hand.

Worse, she'd probably get bucked or fall off this horse and be killed and never get out of the mountains, let alone Montana, the way things were going.

She was fighting the urge to cry when the horse rocked. She shifted her weight, and with a start felt McCall's arm tighten around her. He pulled her back against him and heard the change in his breathing.

Silly little meaningless kiss indeed.

She was smiling to herself when she looked up and saw the horse that had almost run her down.

"What the hell," she heard McCall say behind her.

"That's what I was trying to tell you back there before you kissed me," she said. "That wild horse almost ran me down. That's how I twisted my ankle."

"That's not a wild horse," he said behind her and she heard fear in his voice. "That's Luke Adams's horse."

CHAPTER EIGHT

J.T. slipped quietly off his horse and reached up to lift Reggie down. He motioned for her to be quiet and stay back as he approached Luke's mount.

The horse's coat was lathered. He moved slowly toward it. "Easy, boy. Easy."

The horse rolled his eyes and backed away. J.T. carefully opened the corral gate, then began to work his way around to the other side of the horse.

As he did, he tried to make sense of what he was seeing. Luke's horse. No saddle. The horse had come back here, had been standing next to the corral when they'd ridden up. J.T. could only assume that Luke hadn't gotten far from camp. But if he'd been riding the horse, it would have had a saddle on it.

With the corral gate open, J.T. stood back. One of the horses in the corral whinnied, catching Luke's horse's attention. J.T. worked his way closer to the horse, then slipped off his hat and shooed it toward the open corral.

The horse shied, then trotted into the corral.

He closed the corral gate.

Where was Luke and what had happened? And the big question: where was Luke's saddle? It should have been on the horse if Luke had been thrown or the horse spooked for some reason.

He glanced toward an old tack box at the back of the cabin. The lid wasn't quite closed. He walked to it and lifted the lid. Luke's saddle and gear were inside. He closed the lid and stood, trying to make sense of it.

Luke hadn't really left? He'd just wanted everyone to think he had? Or someone else wanted them to believe it.

"Why would Luke's horse come back here?" Reggie asked when he walked back over to where he'd left her.

He shook his head as he began to unsaddle his horse. Fear vibrated through him like a low frequency hum. Buck should have been back by now.

As he released his horse into the corral with the others, he saw Reggie glance down the hill where the old truck was still parked. No newer four-wheel-drive rig. No Buck. He was relieved to see that she seemed as surprised by that as he was.

What could have happened that Buck was running this late? The foreman knew how important it was that he get right back here. Buck was no fool. He would have high-tailed it back to the camp. Unless something had kept him from it. Or someone.

"I would kill for a bath," Reggie said behind him.

Her choice of words jarred him out of his thoughts. He turned to look at her as he picked up his saddle. The afternoon sun had sunk into the pines. Long shadows spilled across the camp. They had plenty of time before the others would be back for dinner.

She looked tired, her clothes filthy. He'd bet they were the only ones she'd brought that were even close to appropriate in that big suitcase of hers. He met her blue eyes and, even though he fought it, felt sorry for her. She'd really had no idea what she was getting herself into and she'd held up pretty well, all things considered.

Hell, she was a city girl. Stronger and with more courage than the other one he'd known, that was for sure.

She looked up at him. Her lips parted slightly and right then he would have given her anything—short of agreeing to do her commercial. Was that really all she wanted from him?

"There's a creek not far from here," he said. "But you can't go alone."

She lifted a brow in question.

He shook his head. "I've already got Luke missing. From now on I don't want anyone leaving this camp alone. Especially you."

She smiled, giving him a look he didn't like. She'd already figured out that he would always be paired with her. He would have trusted her safety with Buck—but Buck hadn't come back. And now J.T. didn't trust Reggie with anyone but himself. He was bound and determined to get this woman off this mountain and back to civilization in one piece.

"How badly do you want a bath?" he asked.

Her brow shot up again.

"I need some straight answers out of you," he said.

"For a bath? I'll get my stuff."

"I'll dump my saddle and meet you on the porch." As he was passing the cowhands' tent, he saw that the door was untied. Through the breech, he could see something on the floor just inside.

His heart began to race. Like a sleepwalker he moved toward the tent and what looked like a body lying on the tent floor.

Clothes. A bundle of clothing lay on the floor. Past it more clothes had been strewn around the tent, but to his relief there were no bodies. He stared at the mess. It appeared that someone had gone through all of the cowhands' belongings. Who? And maybe more important, why? Was the person looking for the gun? Or something else?

He moved to his own tent and opened the flap that acted as a door. His and Buck's possessions were just as they'd left them. He dropped his saddle inside the tent and took the 9 mm pistol from where he'd hidden it. Checking to make sure it was loaded, he stuck it into his jacket pocket, then closing the flap, turned back to the cowhands' tent.

Whoever had ransacked the tent had been looking for something. If not the gun, then possibly money? Not likely since where would a cowhand spend cash up here?

No, it must have been something else, although he couldn't imagine what, other than the gun, as he closed the tent flap and walked toward the cabin. If his hired hands had done as he'd told them, they'd spent the day keeping the others within sight. That would narrow down the suspects.

But he knew that a cowhand could disappear down a gully chasing cows and the others could lose track of time while doing their own work. Any one of them could have sneaked back here and that's what scared him. Reggie had been here alone. Until she decided to take a walk.

Had her walk been a blessing in disguise?

He glanced at his watch, wanting to hear the whine of a truck engine coming up the mountain. Worry settled like a heavy dark blanket over him as he tried to imagine what kind of trouble Buck might have run into.

Reggie came out on the porch as he approached. Her

step seemed a little lighter. No doubt due to just the thought of a bath. He was glad to see that the bear didn't appear to have come back.

"Here, let me help you," he said, taking the bag with who knew what in it from her and slipping her arm around his waist to take the weight off her sprained ankle.

They moved slowly through the thick green canopy of pines in companionable silence, the sound of the creek growing louder and louder.

WATER. Regina could hear the rush of it, smell it in the air. She practically ran when, through the trees, she spotted the stream pooling in the rocks.

She heard McCall chuckle next to her. Her excitement at even the prospect of a bath must show. She hadn't even tried to talk to him about the commercial on their walk through the woods. True, she was almost too tired to argue about it.

"There's a nice pool the right depth through there," he said when they reached the river. "I'll wait for you over here. Do you know how to sing?"

The question took her by surprise. "What?"

"Sing. If you sing, I promise not to look. That way I'll know you're all right."

He actually looked serious.

She nodded, more intent on the bath than anything else. If she had to sing, she'd sing. She limped toward the spot where he'd indicated and began to sing, "My home's in Montana, I wear a bandana, my spurs are of silver, my pony is gray." Those were the only words she knew. She hummed loudly, turning to see what he was doing.

He had sat down under a large pine, arms folded, his back against the trunk, his hat over his eyes.

She stripped down, the retreating sun warm on her back. She knew the water would be cold.

She kept humming, wavering only a little when she stuck her foot in the water and felt how cold it was. Wading out into the water to where a circle of rocks formed a deep pool in the stream, she lowered herself in slowly.

It wasn't bad once you were all in. She breathed in the damp, pine-scented air and dunked below the surface to wet her hair.

J.T. PUSHED BACK his hat at the sound of the sudden silence. He sat up and looked toward the pool.

She surfaced just then, coming up in a shower of water, her hair a dark wave, her back slim and pale.

"Hum," he called to her and leaned back, pulling the hat down over his eyes.

This had been a terrible idea, he thought, listening to her hum, sounding happy. After that one glimpse he could imagine her sudsing her hair, chest deep in the creek.

The ache he felt surprised him. It was pure sexual. Hell, he was a normal, red-blooded male. But the desire to protect her was even stronger.

"Stopping humming to rinse hair," she called.

He counted to ten and was getting nervous, when he heard a splash. He waited for her to hum. Hum, dammit, woman.

"My home's in Montana," she sang and he realized she was closer than she'd been. She was no longer in the creek, but standing on the rocks directly in front of him.

He didn't dare move, listening as she sang softly, her voice growing nearer and nearer until he could smell her clean scent. Her damp hair brushed across his hand resting on his knee.

Still he didn't move, didn't breathe.

He felt her fingers on the brim of his hat, felt her shove back the brim.

He opened his eyes.

She had knelt down, and was leaning toward him so her hair hung down on each side of her face.

Her gaze was on his, bluer than his own eyes.

He let out the breath he'd been holding slowly, still not moving.

"Thank you," she whispered.

He let himself smile. "You're welcome," he whispered, afraid she would kiss him, afraid she wouldn't.

He sat up, determined not to let her distract him again. He had to have answers. Especially after the noose he'd found in the woods today.

"Reggie, I need you to be honest with me."

She leaned back, looking disappointed that he hadn't kissed her again.

"I have been honest—"

"Listen to me. We're a long way from the ranch, even farther from town, we don't have a way to get out of here except on horseback because the truck won't run." He paused, his gaze holding hers. "This is very dangerous, Regina."

Regina? She could hear the fear in his voice. It echoed in her chest and she had the feeling that something else had happened. "I thought Buck was bringing a truck back?"

His gaze bored into hers. "I'm afraid something has happened to him."

She swallowed, tears stinging her eyes at the thought.

She liked Buck. He'd been kind to her. If something really had happened to him, it was her fault. He would never have left the mountain alone except for her. She felt sick.

"Regina, if you know what's going on here, I need you to tell me now," he said quietly.

She realized she liked it better when he called her Reggie. "You think I had something to do with Buck's disappearance, too?" She shook her head. "How is that possible?"

"You tell me. Is this really about a TV commercial?"

"Yes. What else?"

"That's what I was hoping you would tell me." Clearly he didn't believe a word she said. "Who did you meet in the woods last night?"

She blinked. "What?"

"I saw you meet someone in the trees outside the cabin last night," he said, sounding angry. "I heard you talking to him."

She was shaking her head. "Last night?" She remembered the only time she'd ventured past the porch. "I went to the bathroom."

"The outhouse is back the other way."

She felt her cheeks warm. "The outhouse was too far away. I went into the trees."

"Who were you talking to?"

She stared at him. "No one."

"I *heard* you."

She thought for a moment, remembering walking around out there barefooted, stepping on prickly pine needles and twigs, muttering to herself.… "I was talking to myself."

"You weren't talking to Luke?"

"Luke?" she echoed. "I wasn't talking to Luke or anyone else."

He glanced toward the creek. "Did you happen to go in the men's tent for any reason?"

She couldn't believe this questioning. "No. Why would I?"

"I don't know. Someone ransacked the tent."

She stared at him in shock. First someone fixed the truck so it wouldn't run and now someone went through the cowhands' tent? Worse, J.T. was acting as if he didn't believe that Luke just quit without notice and rode out of camp before anyone else got up.

"You're worried because his horse came back," she said.

He nodded. "I found his saddle, tack and gear in the box at the back of the cabin. I think he just wanted us to believe he left. Or someone else did."

She stared at him. "Why would anyone do that?"

He shook his head.

"If something is going on here, it has nothing to do with me," she said, wishing he would believe that.

"All you want from me is a TV commercial?" he said.

She hesitated only a moment. "That's it."

J.T. had seen her hesitate. She wanted something else but he still didn't think it had anything to do with his cattle or this roundup. The way she was looking at him… "You promised you'd be honest. You want something else from me. What is it?"

"I want to learn to ride a horse."

"What?"

"I want to learn to ride a horse."

"I thought you were afraid of horses?"

She nodded, rocking back a little on her heels as she

flashed him a knock-you-to-your-knees smile. "I was but after riding with you, I've changed my mind."

"If this is some new plot—"

"Isn't it possible that I might want to learn to ride a horse and it has nothing to do with the commercial?"

"No." He felt a chill. Dark shadows pooled under the pines, the sun gone. "We need to get back to camp and start supper."

Her disappointment was so acute and so clear in her face that he almost weakened. Rising, he helped her to her feet, wrapped one of her arms around his waist as he helped her back to the cabin.

"I think you underestimate me," she said as they neared the porch.

He hoped not. "You can take riding lessons when you get back to L.A.," he said, realizing that he liked thinking of her as a city girl who didn't fit in here, could never fit in here. It distanced him from her and he wanted that distance between them. She *was* a city girl and she *didn't* fit in here. It was that simple. And even if she did learn to ride, what would that change? Nothing.

"But what would be the point once you're back in L.A.?" he added.

"I watched you ride and I want to be able to feel that confident in the saddle," she said seeming to ignore his jibe.

He could tell she was still afraid of horses. Why the sudden interest in learning to ride? "I've been riding a horse since I was a toddler," he said, waiting for her to bring up the commercial. That was where she was going with this, wasn't it?

But she didn't.

Nothing about this woman should surprise him and yet it did.

"I could start learning to ride here in Montana and then continue with classes in Los Angeles."

"Do they have horses in California, let alone enough open space to ride them?" he asked facetiously as he wove his way through the pines.

"Have you ever been to California?"

"I've never felt the need to leave Montana."

"Well, you might want to someday," she said smoothly.

He didn't have to look to know she was arching one brow. He could feel the heat of her look and hear the invitation in her voice as clearly as if it had been engraved and hand delivered. And he cursed himself silently for kissing her earlier. Who knew what he'd gotten this woman thinking now.

"In the meantime, would you teach me to ride?" she asked.

"What?" He knew he must sound like a moron but keeping up with this woman was giving him whiplash. Would he teach her to ride? He helped her up on the porch and looked into her face. Her eyes were that deep bottomless blue he was so fond of. "Hell, no. What do I look like? An equestrian center?" But even as he said it, he realized it wasn't such a bad idea. She might have to ride out of here. And soon.

What would he do if Buck didn't return? He shoved the thought away. He knew Buck. If there was any way in hell, the old foreman would be back.

"Did you forget that I have six hundred head of cattle to round up and get out of these mountains before the snow falls?" he demanded.

"Sorry, I just thought when you weren't rounding up cows..."

"I need to get dinner going," he said over his shoulder. "The men will be coming in hungry."

She still didn't say anything as she went inside. He heard the rattle of pots and pans as he gathered an armload of firewood.

He could hear the lo of the cattle just over the hill and knew the men wouldn't be far behind. He just hoped to hell no more of them went missing. He wondered which one had hidden the gun in the tent fold. More important, why.

REGGIE LOOKED UP as J.T. came through the door. She had a fire going in the woodstove and was peeling potatoes. He looked worried. "What's wrong?" she asked.

He shook his head and took the peeler from her and showed her how to use it correctly.

"Thanks," she said. It worked much better the way it was supposed to be used.

He sat down at the table across from her and leaned toward her before glancing toward the lower bunk bed. "You have some sort of identification with you?"

She told herself she shouldn't be surprised. But it bothered her that he didn't trust her. Okay, maybe she could understand his lack of faith, all things considered. But since when did going after what you wanted automatically make you a liar and a thief and whatever else he thought of her?

She got up and went to the bunk, found her red leather purse in her suitcase and took out her wallet. She handed it to him without opening it.

He held the wallet in his hand for a moment, his eyes on

her. She stood, feeling like a child before the principal as he slowly unzipped the small leather wallet. She watched him flip through it, stop on her California driver's license, then continue flipping through the plastic photo holders.

She felt as if he were going through her underwear drawer. Her whole life was in that wallet.

"You work for Way Out West Jeans," he said. "You never told me the company's name."

"You never gave me the chance."

He was still holding the wallet. "Who is this?"

She stepped closer to glance at the photograph of an attractive woman standing next to an amazingly handsome man. The photo was old, the edges worn and wrinkled. "My mother and father."

"Nice-looking people."

"My dad died when I was two. I was raised by my mother and grandmother." Why had she told him that?

"I'm sorry." He flipped back to her other photographs, glancing from each then to her as if he was looking for a resemblance.

"Friends," she said and reached for the wallet. "I was an only child."

He looked embarrassed for going through her things as he handed back the wallet. "I'm sorry I didn't believe you about the jeans."

She turned and went back to the bed to put her wallet away. He hadn't moved. She could practically hear him struggling to come up with something to say to her. No matter what he thought, she hadn't really lied to get this job, but she could see where he might think she had.

"I talked Buck into giving me the cook job and led him to believe I could cook, but I had nothing to do with the truck not running or anything else," she said as she looked over her shoulder at him.

He had turned and was taking a package of meat from the cooler.

She stared at his broad back realizing what he thought of her. That she was a cold-blooded bitch who used people to get what she wanted no matter the cost. Why should she care what he thought of her? Tears stung her eyes.

Worse, his opinion of her hit a little too close to home. "You have no idea how competitive the jeans market is or what it's like being a woman in that world."

He said nothing as he put the potatoes she'd peeled on to boil.

"This advertising campaign means everything," she said, surprised she was close to crying.

He turned then to look at her. *"Everything?"*

She swallowed. "It's critical to the future of the company and to my future." She stopped as she realized how desperate she sounded. "I thought a man like you could understand working hard for something you believe in."

"A man like me? You don't know me at all if you think I would use any means to get what I wanted," he snapped.

"I've had to work hard for everything I've ever gotten. You, McCall, know nothing about me or my life or what I've been through to get to where I—"

A tree limb brushed against the window. They both turned at the sound. Outside the wind had come up. Pine boughs now swayed. One thumped softly against the window.

J.T. went back to his cooking. She turned away and wiped hastily at her tears, angry with herself for crying, angry at him for thinking so little of her.

He was wrong. She did know who he was. Not just the eldest son of Asa McCall and the man who ran the Sundown Ranch. She'd seen his kindness, his compassion, his strength and his determination. She'd seen how the men respected him. He inspired loyalty. The man could even cook.

She'd spent the years since college creating the Wild West to sell jeans. But now that she was *in* the Wild West, she saw that it was nothing like she'd thought. She'd fantasized about a cowboy's life for her jeans. But J. T. McCall was nothing like it and now she found herself fantasizing about the man.

She wanted to know this man better and it didn't have anything to do with the kiss earlier. Well, hardly anything.

But she also realized that by going after what she wanted—J. T. McCall's backside—she might have jeopardized his cattle roundup, not to mention ruined any chance of getting him for the commercial and made a lasting bad impression on him. She might also be responsible for whatever had happened to Buck.

She wanted a chance to make things right and gain J.T.'s respect, to show him she wasn't as inept as he thought she was. If she hoped to win his respect she'd have to show him that she could survive in his world and that meant being able to ride a horse. The mere thought terrified her. The only thing she had loved about being on his horse had been having J.T. behind her holding her. She tried not to think about riding alone, without J.T. not only behind her, but not even holding the reins.

J.T. would teach her to ride, she was pretty sure of that, and she was a quick study.

Of course, once she could ride a horse, he would send

her down the mountain and she would lose any chance—as if she hadn't already—of changing his mind about the commercial.

But she had to prove to him that he was wrong about her. She would overcome her fears. Even if it killed her.

J.T. STUDIED each cowhand as he came into the cabin for supper.

Nevada Black stormed in first. "Someone ransacked our tent." He sounded angry as he took his chair.

J.T. nodded. "It was like that when I got back." He sat down at the table and began to pass the platters of food around. "Any idea what they were looking for?"

Nevada looked surprised by the question. "I guess that would depend on what was in the tent." He glanced at the other men.

Will Jarvis didn't even bother to look up. Roy glanced at J.T., then took the bowl of potatoes and began to dish up his plate. Slim and Cotton exchanged shrugs.

"Was there anything of value left in the tent?" J.T. asked and watched for a reaction. After his trip to the creek with Reggie, he'd hidden the 9 mm pistol in the cabin.

All the men shook their heads as they served their plates and began eating.

He'd hoped that one of them would admit to hiding the gun in the tent. The fact that no one did made him all the more worried that the danger was coming from inside not outside the camp.

"I asked you to keep in sight of each other," he said, but could see before anyone said anything that there had been times when the men had lost sight of each other. He could almost feel the suspicion, which alone could drive a wedge between the men and make matters worse. If that were possible.

"I was thinking it might have been a bear who messed up our tent," Roy Shields offered, his face coloring. It was the first time Roy had said that many words since J.T. had met him. "I saw prints on the way back to camp."

Cotton groaned. "I did have some cookies my girlfriend sent and they're gone."

"It wouldn't be the first time we had a bear in camp," Slim chimed in, the group seeming to relax a little.

"You all know this is bear country and we need to keep a clean camp," J.T. said and looked pointedly at Reggie.

"Sorry, Mr. McCall," Cotton said.

The talk around the table turned to cows and how many had been rounded up. Tomorrow they would begin gathering the rest of the strays. With luck they could be out of here the next morning.

J.T. noticed that the men all seemed tired while Reggie appeared to be getting her second wind. He didn't see that as a good sign.

He felt a little guilty for what he'd said to her earlier. He hadn't meant to come down so hard on her. Maybe she wasn't responsible for the disabled truck, or for whatever had happened to Luke Adams, or Buck not returning yet. But he had a bad feeling that someone in this camp was and he feared it was the owner of the gun he'd found.

CHAPTER NINE

All the men cleared out right after dinner, including J.T. Regina could hear some of the men standing around the fire, a couple of them talking quietly. She could see the flicker of the campfire through the window and their silhouettes.

J.T. wasn't one of the men standing around the fire. She wondered where he'd gone. She wished he'd stuck around. She'd hoped to talk to him. It dawned on her that if he continued to be suspicious that she was behind the things that had been going on in the camp, he wouldn't be looking for the real culprit.

She'd seen how worried he was about Buck. She hoped he was wrong and that the elderly foreman was just running late for some reason. She couldn't bear it if anything happened to Buck because of her.

She finished the dishes and stepped out on the porch, needing a breath of fresh air. The bath in the creek had been wonderful. She felt like a new woman and smiled, remembering J.T. under that tree. His eyes were the palest blue she'd ever seen in a face that was rugged and so sexy it made her knees weak. J.T. had insisted on wrapping her sprained ankle, which felt much better.

She heard someone approach from the darkness of the pines and knew without looking that it was him.

"Come on," J.T. said and motioned for her to follow him.

She didn't question where they were going, just stepped off the porch, glad for his company tonight. She followed him along the dark edge of the cabin on the side away from the campfire, away from the men. Her ankle ached, but she wasn't about to complain.

He stopped at the edge of the corral. She saw that he'd moved the other horses into the corral next to it.

Stars popped out in the clear midnight-blue sky over the tops of the pines. Tonight the sky seemed even bigger, the stars brighter. Or was it just being here with McCall? She felt awed, humbled under such a sky, everything that had motivated her to this point in her life seeming insignificant.

"The first thing you need to learn is how to saddle a horse," he said quietly as he picked up his saddle, which was straddling the corral fence, and shoved it at her.

Her knees practically buckled. The saddle was heavy, much heavier than she'd expected. She could feel his look of disdain and hurriedly righted herself, hefting the saddle a little higher, getting under it. She'd be damned if she'd drop it.

She followed him over to where he had his horse tied to the corral railing.

"It takes a little effort to get the saddle on," he said.

She imagined so given that she was way down here and the horse's back was way up there. She took a breath and tried to lift the saddle up and onto the horse's back. The saddle went over the top, almost taking her with it.

He retrieved the saddle and handed it to her without a word. This time she got the saddle in the right place and practically swelled with pride at her accomplishment.

He straightened the saddle and proceeded to show her how to cinch it down and put on the bridle.

The horse, of course, moved away, snorting and giving her a look that said, over his dead body. She grabbed the rope Killer was tied to and pulled the beast closer. She refused to groan. At least out loud.

"Good job. You're stronger than you look," J.T. said, with maybe a little admiration in his tone, when she'd finished. "Okay, let's adjust the stirrups. It's time to get on the horse."

Her heart was thundering in her chest, her hands shaking as she took the reins he handed her.

"Don't drop these. This is how you control the horse, okay?"

She nodded, staring at the horse, remembering that feeling of being out of control when she was astride the monstrous thing. She swallowed and repeated her resolve to learn to ride.

Reaching up to grab the saddle horn, she put her foot into one of the stirrups and pulled herself up, swinging her leg over, grinning in surprise to find herself astride the horse.

McCall smiled.

The horse shuddered and hopped over a few feet to the side. She quickly dropped the reins and hunched over the saddle horn, gripping it with white knuckles.

She heard J.T. groan.

"What did I tell you about the reins?" he asked handing them to her again.

"Don't drop them."

He nodded and looked up at her, shaking his head as if she were hopeless.

He got the horse moving and showed her how to hold the reins in one hand and lay them to one side of the horse's neck. To her amazement the horse turned.

"Good," he said.

She tried turning the horse the other way. Shoot, it was like driving a car. Kinda.

"Okay, walk him around the corral." McCall climbed up on the corral to watch.

She rode around the corral and even let go of the breath she'd been holding when she didn't immediately slide off. Or get bucked off.

After a dozen laps, she brought the horse to a stop next to J.T. She couldn't see his face in the darkness but she could feel his gaze.

"Good job. How's the ankle?"

"Fine," she lied.

"Right. Better call it a night."

A twig cracked off in the woods behind them. The horse shuddered. J.T. brushed her leg as he steadied the horse.

"Okay, let's see you get off by yourself," he said quietly as if he was listening to something beyond them. "Think you can get down and unsaddle him?"

She nodded. The horse felt warm against her calves. She reached down to run her hand over his neck. Nice boy. It surprised her. She didn't want to get down yet. The truth was, she didn't want this time with J.T. to end.

"You never told me how he got the name Killer," she said, remembering just what she was sitting on.

J.T. drew his attention back to her. "His full name is *Lady* Killer."

"Why would you— You were just trying to scare me?"

"I was angry with you for taking off by yourself. I was trying to teach you a lesson."

"I'm sorry." She really meant it. "I didn't realize when I talked Buck into hiring me as your camp cook the trouble I was causing."

"I know."

"I know you're worried about Buck," she said. "Can't you ride down and check on him?"

J.T. shook his head. "I can't leave here."

"But don't the men know what to do while you're gone?" She could feel his gaze on her. She knew what she was suggesting. If he went, he'd come back with a four-wheel-drive truck and insist she leave. Any chance she had of talking him into the commercial would be over. "I'm worried about Buck, too."

J.T. THOUGHT she couldn't surprise him. He looked up at her. She didn't look afraid of the horse anymore. She seemed to have forgotten that she was even on it. But he feared there was much worse in the night to be afraid of.

She swung down out of the saddle and reached for the ground with her foot, the one attached to the sprained ankle. The moment it touched earth, she fell backward.

He caught her, his hands curling around her waist, keeping her close. Past her, he could see the campfire through the pines but no one around it. Earlier all five men had been standing around it. The fire had burned down to glowing coals now. Everyone had gone to bed. Maybe.

"If I left and came back with a truck you'd be free to go search for another jeans model," he said quietly as she turned in his hands to face him.

She shook her head and smiled ruefully. “Anyone else would just be settling.”

“I thought this was your big chance, that it meant everything to you.”

“There’ll be other commercials,” she said, her voice wavering a little.

He wanted to believe her. “This cowboy thing was your idea?”

She nodded. “Most of our models are professionals who look like…models.”

He knew without asking. “You have a deadline coming up soon?”

“It doesn’t matter.”

Of course it mattered. He got the feeling that if she blew this assignment, it would have very bad consequences on her career and he knew how much her career meant to her. Everything, she’d said.

“Ride out in the morning,” she said now. “I can make breakfast for the men. Hey, I might surprise you.”

He could count on that. He laughed softly and pulled her closer. “I can’t leave you here,” he whispered against her mouth. “It’s too dangerous.”

REGINA THOUGHT she heard a noise in the darkness over the trees. It sounded like the crack of a twig, only this time it was closer. Much closer.

He must have heard it, too. He drew back. “Go to the cabin.” He dropped his voice. “Keep the door locked.”

If he was trying to scare her, he was doing a darned good job of it. She hurried back to the cabin, taking the path on the campfire side this time, her ankle aching badly now. She heard the murmur of voices in the cowhands' wall tent, but saw no one.

The porch side of the cabin was dark. She hurried along the worn boards to the door. She'd left the lantern on in the cabin and was welcomed by its warm glow as she rushed inside. Because the cabin was small and only one room, she saw at a glance that it was empty. Hurriedly, she locked the door behind her and stood for a moment trying to catch her breath.

J.T. said he couldn't leave because of her. Because it was too *dangerous.* What did he mean by that? Surely he wasn't just trying to scare her into giving him the distributor cap from the truck. She wouldn't put it past him. After all, he'd told her his horse's name was *Killer.*

But they'd both heard something out in the woods. And Luke's horse had come back, his saddle and gear stuffed in a box outside the cabin to make it look as if he'd left. Had that been Luke out there spying on them? Listening?

She touched her tongue to her lips and hugged herself, still excited by the horseback ride and the kiss. She must be losing her mind. But then so must McCall. How else could she explain the kiss? How did she explain any of J.T.'s kisses, she thought with a sigh.

With only towels on the windows, she felt too vulnerable with the lantern on. She went to the bunk, found her small flashlight and extinguished the lantern. For a few minutes, she stood in the dark, watching the gap between the window frame and the towel. Nothing but tree limbs moved beyond the glass.

She turned on her flashlight and put more wood in the stove. She wasn't tired at all—not after that long nap she'd had.

Was she really resigned to finding another model for her jeans commercial? If she was trapped up here much longer it wouldn't make any difference. Unless she had a model by the end of the month, she could just kiss the promotion goodbye. But so much more had been riding on this advertising plan. She tried not to think about it.

She couldn't search for another cowboy posterior until she could get off this mountain. But she knew what she'd told McCall was true. She'd just be settling if she chose another cowboy. She would always know that she'd gone for second best—and that had never been her style.

So why wasn't she in a complete panic? She told herself it was because there was nothing she could do, but she knew there was a lot more to it. McCall had changed everything. The six-foot-four man with blond hair and blue eyes and the best behind she'd ever seen had spoiled her for another cowboy. Or another man.

She listened, hoping she would hear his footfalls on the porch soon. She was worried about him. If Buck didn't return soon, what would J.T. do? She knew he was trying to get as many cattle rounded up as possible but he seemed…scared. Not for himself but for her and his cowhands. And she knew him well enough to know that J. T. McCall wouldn't scare easily.

She thought about everything that had happened at the cow camp. None of the incidents should have had him that frightened. There had to be more going on than he'd told her.

J.T. WALKED the perimeter of the camp, telling himself the sound he'd heard was a deer or an elk. He circled back to the corral, the camp quiet, and unsaddled his horse and carried the saddle to the big tent.

On the way, he looked in on the cowhands.

All five cots appeared to be occupied. He closed the tent door, sure at least one of men had seen him checking on them. Will Jarvis. Was he awake because he'd just climbed into his sleeping bag?

The campfire had burned down. No light burned in the cabin. Maybe Reggie's walk had been good for her, made her too tired to do any roaming tonight.

But still he had to go check on her. He left his saddle in the tent and walked toward the cabin feeling strangely vulnerable because of her. She was his Achilles' heel. He wanted desperately to go look for Buck, but he couldn't leave her. Nor was he sure he could protect her.

The men would take care of themselves as best they could if they had to. They'd known what they were getting into when they'd signed on. There was always some danger involved whenever you were this far up in the mountains. And they could all ride. Any one of them could get out of here in a matter of hours by horse.

But Reggie… He hated to think how ill-equipped she was to survive here. Especially since she didn't ride a horse and he could tell that her ankle was hurting her more than she wanted him to know.

He reached the cabin and tapped softly on a windowpane, waited and tapped again. He wasn't about to go to the door. The last thing he could trust himself not to do would be to go inside where it was warm, where Reggie would be possibly wearing that heart-stopping negligee—

Her face appeared in the window, startling him. She looked pale.

"Are you all right?" he mouthed.

She nodded and gave him a smile. "You?"

He had to smile. "I'm fine. Did you bolt the door?"

She nodded again and motioned did he want to come in?

He shook his head a little too vigorously because she laughed. "Good night."

"Good night," she mouthed back. She did have a great mouth.

He quickly turned and walked toward the tent, smiling to himself.

Now if Buck and Luke Adams would just show up. But he knew he wouldn't stop worrying until this roundup was over, until Reggie was safe, until he knew who had sabotaged the truck and killed the cows.

He wished a cell phone did work up here. He would call the ranch and see what had happened to Buck.

But a phone call wouldn't solve the mystery of what had happened to Luke. J.T. thought the cowhand had left in the middle of the night because he'd realized he'd made a mistake by coming back here, the memory of what had happened nine years ago too much for him.

But with Luke's horse returning, his saddle and gear stuffed in the box behind the cabin, J.T. was worried that Luke hadn't left running scared. Luke hadn't even left under his own power.

J.T. stopped to listen to the night. Hearing nothing unusual, he stepped into his tent and tied the canvas door closed. He pulled off his boots and jeans and crawled into his sleeping bag, knowing he wouldn't get much sleep tonight.

As he closed his eyes, he listened for the sound of a

truck coming up the mountainside. Prayed for it. What he wouldn't give to see Buck's weathered old face right now and know he was safe.

Just before daylight, J.T. heard a sound that bolted him upright in bed. A terrified shriek.

J.T. pulled on his boots and dove from the tent wearing only his long underwear. It took him a moment to realize the sound hadn't come from the cabin where he'd expected it had.

The wall tent door next to his flew open, the air filling with cries and cussing as the men lunged out into the darkness half-dressed.

"What is it?" J.T. demanded as everyone circled, Roy snapping on a flashlight and shining it on Cotton.

"Rattlesnake," Cotton said from between gritted teeth and leaned down to pull up the leg of his long underwear. "The son of a bitch got me."

J.T. stared at the bite mark in the glow of the flashlight. There weren't any rattlesnakes up this high in the mountains. Especially in October. He could feel everyone looking at him, no doubt thinking the same thing.

"What's wrong?" Reggie called from the cabin porch, sounding scared. "McCall?"

"Go back in the cabin! I'll be there in a minute," J.T. hollered back. He swore as he turned to go out into the trees. He picked up a limb and returned. Roy handed him the flashlight without a word. Carefully, he stepped into the tent.

The flashlight beam illuminated only a small circle of golden light. He quickly shined the light around the tent, the beam skittering over the canvas floor. No snake.

Gingerly, he moved along the cots, shaking out each

sleeping bag. He hadn't gone far when he heard the distinctive rattle and froze.

Leaning down slowly, he shined the light under the cots. He could hear the men outside, talking among themselves, still sounding scared, high on adrenaline, all but Cotton glad it hadn't been them.

The light picked up a pair of eyes, prehistoric looking. The large greenish-colored snake was coiled in the corner behind a duffel bag.

He stepped closer, shoving the cot and the bag aside. The tent filled with the sound of the deadly rattle as he moved nearer, the limb ready.

The snake struck, lunging its long thick-scaled body at him. He dodged to the side and trapped the snake against the side of the wall tent with the limb.

After several attempts, he was able to pin the snake's head so he could reach down and grasp it behind the head.

It was a big heavy prairie rattler, a good five feet long. Lifting it, he carried the snake out of the tent. The men all stepped back, giving him a wide berth as he took the snake deep into the woods. The beam of the flashlight bobbed ahead through the darkness, the snake growing heavy, his fingers fatigued from the pressure needed to keep the reptile from biting him.

In the quiet darkness away from the camp, he finally released the snake. Someone had to have brought this snake up the mountain, kept it hidden outside of camp and then put it in the tent tonight. To what? Scare the men? Or scare him?

J.T. swore. Well, he was scared and angry. He watched the snake slither away into the trees, following it with the flashlight beam, trying to understand what the hell was happening in his camp.

Then slowly, he turned back, studying the ground in the thin light, looking for a sign that anyone was camped nearby. Any sign that they weren't alone up here.

But the only tracks in the soft earth were his own. When he'd ridden the perimeter of the camp, he hadn't found anything either. All of which led him to believe the one thing he had feared from the beginning, that the trouble was coming from *within* his camp. One of his own men was doing this.

He told himself that so far it had just been pranks. No one had been killed. At least as far as he knew. The men had ridden up separately to the line shack. Any one of them could have brought the snake, kept it hidden out in the woods in a container and then let it loose in the tent tonight. But if that was the case, the fool had taken the chance that he might be the one who was bitten. Only a crazy person would take a chance like that.

J.T. thought of the only man he'd considered truly crazy. That man had died on this very mountain nine years ago. Killed by his own madness. Just the thought of Claude Ryan chilled J.T. to his marrow.

Was that what this was about? Someone wanted him to relive that cattle roundup of nine years ago, re-creating it not exactly but just close enough that J.T. wouldn't know what was going to happen next? That he couldn't be sure it was really happening—until it was too late?

Nevada was inspecting Cotton's bite in the glow of the lantern inside the wall tent when J.T. returned. It was obvious the men had thoroughly searched the tent to make sure there were no more snakes, but no one was going back to sleep in the hours until daylight.

"He needs to get to a doctor," Nevada said, looking up as J.T. ducked in through the tent doorway.

Isn't this what J.T. had feared when the truck hadn't run? The men were looking at him, waiting for him to tell him which one of them could drive Cotton to the hospital.

"The truck doesn't run," he said. "Buck went down yesterday morning to get a part for the truck and bring back another vehicle."

Slim looked up in surprise. "What's wrong with it?"

J.T. sighed. "Someone took the distributor cap."

The men all looked at each other.

"When is Buck coming back?" Will asked.

Good question. "He should have been back by now," J.T. said. He had to be straight with them. If he was right, they were in danger. No cattle roundup was worth getting men killed.

"Any of you who want to leave, I understand," he said. "We'll round up what cattle we can this morning and then herd them down this afternoon for anyone who wants to stay."

"What about the strays?" Nevada asked. "There must be a good fifty head out there."

"We'll have to leave them," J.T. said, his mind made up. "We head out by ten. That way we can reach the ranch by early afternoon." Unless someone tried to stop them. He just prayed that nothing else happened between now and then.

Reggie would have to ride down. With her sprained ankle, it would make it difficult—and painful, but there was no other way. He just wished he had a horse up here that was more suitable for a rank beginner. But they would be trailing the cattle out, moving slow. And the woman had grit.

He looked at Cotton. "You think you can ride out now?"

Cotton nodded. Clearly he just wanted away from here—and to get medical attention, even though few people died of snakebites. But J.T. knew they were painful and could make a man really sick. He didn't want to take any chances. He had a first-aid kit in the cabin, but nothing for rattlesnake bites. He hadn't thought snakes would be a problem since there weren't any poisonous snakes at this altitude.

"I'll go with him," Slim said, sounding upset and scared.

"What about the rest of you?" J.T. asked, studying the men's faces in the lantern light. The rattlesnake hadn't been an accident. Like him, they were probably wondering who'd put it in the tent and why. Was Cotton the intended victim or one of them?

Will, Roy and Nevada looked at each other, suspicion in their expressions, but no one else appeared to be leaving.

J.T. tried to hide his relief. Part of him wanted to send them all out with Cotton, but he suspected that whoever was doing this would just be waiting up the road for him. And then there was Reggie. She had no idea what she'd blundered into. These men would have at least heard about what had happened up here nine years ago and maybe suspect it was happening again. Reggie didn't have a clue.

"Make sure Cotton gets to the ranch," he said to Slim. "One of my brothers will take him to the hospital from there and see that you are both paid."

Slim nodded and glanced around the tent, his fear almost palpable. J.T. understood a healthy fear of snakes, but clearly Slim was more afraid of the men with whom he'd been sharing the tent.

J.T. watched Slim pick up both his gear and Cotton's, then duck out the tent door to go saddle their horses. Slim was practically running to get out of camp.

Is that what had happened to Luke? Had something scared him away as well? Something that reminded him of nine years ago and what had happened? But a man wouldn't leave his gear or his saddle or his horse.

J.T. glanced at his watch. "I'll get breakfast going." It would be light in a couple of hours and none of them would be able to get any sleep anyway. "Thanks for staying on."

He ducked out the tent door and walked to his own to finish getting dressed. He could hear the men rustling about in the other tent. No conversation now. They would all be leery of each other. Probably for the best, he thought. They would be watching each other like hawks, making it hard for one of them to pull another stunt like the snake.

Outside again, J.T. walked up to the corral as Cotton and Slim were getting ready to leave. He pulled Cotton aside, the one cowhand he knew and thought he could trust. "When you get to the ranch, would you ask my father to send Cash up?"

Cotton's eyes widened a little at the mention of the sheriff's name. He nodded and glanced warily over at Slim.

"Good luck," J.T. said, hoping neither of them needed it. As they rode away into the darkness, he fought the fear that neither of them would ever reach the ranch.

If Buck had made it that far, even if he was injured, one of J.T.'s brothers would have driven up to make sure everyone was all right and give him the news about Buck.

That meant Buck had never reached the ranch.

With growing dread, J.T. headed for the cabin. Lantern light bled from the small paned windows. He moved toward the light and Reggie, anxious to see her. He couldn't help but think about what would have happened if the snake had been put in the cabin instead of the men's wall tent.

CHAPTER TEN

Regina had the fire going in the stove when she heard J.T.'s footfalls on the porch. "Come in," she said at his soft knock. He looked horrible. Her heart lurched at the sight of him. "What's happened?"

"There was an accident. Cotton was bit by a rattlesnake."

A rattlesnake? She shivered.

"Slim is riding out with him." He moved to the stove, warmed his hands. She could see that his hands were steady but he was obviously shaken. It had been one thing after another. First the truck not running, then Luke disappearing and Buck not returning. Now Cotton and Slim were leaving?

"Someone put the snake in the tent," he said, his voice so low she had to lean toward him to hear it.

"Why would someone do that?" she asked horrified.

"Maybe as a prank," he said. "Maybe to sabotage the cattle roundup." He shrugged. "I've decided to move the cattle down today."

"You'll have them rounded up by then?"

"Enough of them," he said. He sounded weary. And worried. "I'm sorry about your ankle, but you're going to have to ride a horse out of here, Regina."

Regina? He must be serious. She nodded. “I’ll do whatever you need me to do.”

He smiled at that as if he wished she’d done that in the beginning. So did she. Coming up here had been a mistake. McCall was right about that. She was no closer to signing him to the advertising contract than she’d been on the highway days ago.

She would have to ride all fifteen miles down this mountain on a horse. She would have to return to L.A. defeated. She would never find another cowboy like J. T. MacCall even if she had the time to look. She’d failed. But right now she was even more worried about Buck. “Maybe Buck will get back before we leave,” she said, praying that would be the case.

J.T.’s look said she shouldn’t count on that.

Her heart fell. Unexpected tears blurred her vision. “What do you think happened to him?”

McCall shook his head.

What was going on? “Are the rest of the men staying?” she asked, wondering how J.T. would get the cattle down if they all left.

“For the time being.”

She reached for one of the large cast-iron skillets on the stove. “Should we start breakfast?” It wasn’t light out and, according to her watch, it wouldn’t be for several hours.

He nodded. “We’ll get an early start, right at daybreak,” he said almost to himself. “I want you to be ready to ride as soon as I return,” he said to her.

She looked around the cabin. “What about my suitcase, my clothes?”

He shook his head. “I’ll come back for everything once you’re safe.”

Safe.

He took off his coat, hung it by the door and set about making breakfast. She helped, working beside him, trying hard not to think about Buck. What had happened to him? What was going to happen to all of them before they got out of here? Worse, would whoever was doing this let them leave?

Will, Nevada and Roy came in and took their places at the table with barely a nod in her direction. They all ate, heads down, a jittery silence filling the room even though the food wasn't burned. But she knew just the sight of the four empty chairs made them all solemn. That and the fear that more of them would be missing if they didn't get out of here soon.

"You want me to try to get some of the other strays we saw down in that ravine?" Nevada asked. "I can catch up if you move the herd out before I get back."

J.T. shook his head. "Once we get the main herd down, I can come back for the others."

Will was shaking his head. "In a day's time you aren't going to be able to get back up into this country." He nodded at their surprised looks and motioned to his left leg, his hand going to his thigh. "A snowstorm is coming in. A big one. I have a bad leg. It's never wrong. The weather's about to change."

"Let's just hope we can get the cattle out before it hits," J.T. said.

Roy was quiet as usual, but when he did look up, Regina thought he looked worried.

She broke the awkward silence that followed by getting up to do the dishes. After a moment, the men all pushed back their chairs, brought their dishes over to her, then filed out. All except J.T.

"I want you to stay here. Keep the door locked," he said behind her.

She nodded, scared by the fear she heard in his tone. She kept washing the dishes so he didn't see that her hands were trembling. He'd warned her she was in over her head.

"I'll be back for you soon," he said but seemed to hesitate. "Will you be all right until then?"

"If you're trying to scare me—"

"I didn't mean to." He sighed and raked a hand through his hair. "You just need to be careful." He studied her face, looking worried that she might become hysterical at any moment. Not that she didn't have the potential.

"I'll be fine." But even as she said the words, she worried that she might be wrong about that. She wanted to throw herself into his arms. Just to be held for a moment and then she really would be fine. For the time she was wrapped in his arms anyway.

"Regina?"

Why didn't he call her Reggie? That would have made her mad, made her not want to cry.

He leaned in to look at her, his expression puzzled. He must have seen her trying hard not to cry. He made a face. "Don't..."

He put his arm around her awkwardly as if this man who could run a ranch, round up six hundred head of cattle and boss grown men around didn't have a clue what to do with one five-foot-six-inch woman.

She leaned into him, pressing against his broad solid chest. His arms came around her, pulling her to him with obvious reluctance.

She didn't care. She didn't even like him most of the time but right now it felt wonderful just being held, being sheltered in all that warmth and strength, feeling safe, no longer feeling alone and scared.

He seemed to soften, his arms molding her to him.

He bent his head and she felt his breath in her hair. "Oh, Reggie," he whispered. "What am I going to do with you?"

He seemed to breathe her in, dropping his head to hers, his cheek against the top of her head. She was completely enclosed by his arms, his body, cocooned in his protective embrace. She couldn't remember ever feeling so safe. She would have stayed there forever.

But boots thumped across the porch outside. McCall opened his arms, took her shoulders in his big hands and held her in front of him at arm's length.

"Ready when you are," Nevada called.

"Give me a few minutes," J.T. called back, then seemed to wait until he heard Nevada's boots retreat back down the porch.

His expression softened as he looked at her. "Sit down. *Please,*" he added. "I need to tell you something. I'm not trying to frighten you. But I think you should know this."

She nodded as she sat down, even more afraid of what he was going to tell her.

"Nine years ago three men came up with a plan to rustle my cattle," J.T. began, his jaw tight, his face pale. "The plan was to get rid of as many of my men as possible to make the odds better once we had the cattle down the mountain where they had semitrailers waiting."

She stared at him. This roundup had started with six men and was now down to three. "They killed them?"

He shook his head. "Only the ones they couldn't get rid

of other ways. They camped nearby and hit us at night, taking out the men one at a time, scaring some off, killing several. I didn't know what was happening. At first I thought the cowhands had just left." Like Luke, he didn't say but she heard it anyway. "The things that happened seemed like accidents," he continued. "Until I realized they'd disabled the truck. I set up a trap, caught them in an old cabin down by the truck where we used to keep supplies."

She held her breath.

"During the gunfight that ensued, a kerosene lantern inside the cabin was knocked over. The fire burned quickly, the cabin was old, the timbers dry. The men could have gotten out. But they wouldn't give themselves up."

"They burned to death?" she asked, aghast at the thought of being trapped in a cabin that was on fire.

"We found two bodies inside. The third man got away but we knew he was badly burned. We knew he couldn't have made it off the mountain alone."

"You never found his body?"

J.T. shook his head. "But we found some of his clothing and marks in the dirt where he'd been dragged off."

She grimaced. "By what?"

"A bear. A grizzly. There were prints in the dirt near the scraps of clothing we found."

She thought she might be sick. "I thought you said there weren't any grizzlies up here."

He shook his head. "I said the bear you fed pancakes to wasn't a grizzly." He stepped over to the woodstove to throw on another log. "There was an investigation nine years ago. My brother Cash was and still is sheriff so the state held the inquest. Legally, the case was closed because the three men were dead. There were semitrailers found near the county road on the way out of here where they'd planned to load the cattle."

She stared at his broad back. "Steal the cattle?"

He nodded.

"You think it's happening *again,*" she said, shocked to realize that's exactly what he had to be thinking—and with good reason.

"The incidents are similar enough."

"But how, if the men are dead?"

He turned to look at her. "Someone connected to that old incident could be trying to get revenge. It's the only thing that makes any sense."

"But it wasn't your fault."

"It was my roundup. I'm responsible for everyone under my hire."

Like her. Except he hadn't hired her exactly and certainly didn't want her up here. She was beginning to understand why he was so upset, so worried. This was no place for a woman.

"If it really is about revenge, why has it taken them nine years?" she asked, not wanting to think about the spot she'd put J.T. in by being here, complicating things. And no wonder he'd thought she had something to do with what was going on. She shows up and look what happens.

"The time frame bothers me too," he said. "Why wait? Maybe because I wouldn't be expecting it, not after all this time." He shrugged. "I hope I'm wrong about what's going on up here. But in case I'm not, I wanted you to know."

She nodded, not sure how knowing this helped her. She'd been scared before. Now she was terrified. "You think they're hiding out in the woods like last time?" If he was trying to keep her in the cabin, he didn't have to worry.

To her surprise, he shook his head. "I think the person doing this is here in camp."

She stared at him in shock. "There are only three men left."

He nodded and walked over to a cabinet in the corner. Opening it, he fished around in back.

To her amazement, he took out a gun.

"Have you ever fired a 9 mm pistol?" he asked, sounding hopeful.

She shook her head, hating to see the disappointment on his face.

"I'm not planning on you ever having to use it, okay? But I want you to know how—just in case."

She nodded as he pressed the gun into her hand. She listened as he instructed her on how to fire it. She wasn't sure what frightened her most. That he feared she would need it. Or that she might have to shoot someone.

AS J.T. RODE OUT of camp with the three men, he couldn't shake the feeling that he shouldn't be leaving Reggie alone. Maybe especially with a gun. But he couldn't leave her unarmed and he had to get ready to move the cattle down.

He had thought about taking her with him but they had a long ride ahead of them later this afternoon and with her ankle, the ride would be painful enough without making her ride this morning as well.

The only way he could be sure she was all right would have been to stay with her. Since he couldn't do that, he hoped that by keeping an eye on the last three cowhands she would be safe. As long as he was right about the trouble he was having coming from within the ranks—not from the outside, then all he had to do was keep track of the men.

He had his rifle in the scabbard on his saddle. He noticed that the other men had their weapons as well as they rode out of camp.

He'd considered sending Reggie down the mountain with Cotton and Slim, but he knew he couldn't do that. Cotton was hurt and would be suffering the effects of the snakebite. Slim had been acting too scared. J.T. couldn't even be sure that Slim would stay with Cotton and get him to the ranch and medical help. And the truth was he didn't trust anyone.

At this point, he just hoped that with any luck, he would meet up with his brother Sheriff Cash McCall on the way down the mountain this afternoon. That is, if Cotton made it to the ranch with the message.

He tried not to think about the alternative. Just as he tried not to dwell on getting Reggie off this mountain. He couldn't ride double with her. Not twenty miles. She would have to ride her own horse and no matter what she said about wanting to learn to ride, he had seen how afraid she was of horses. As long as she didn't do anything foolish—

He groaned. What could have been more foolish than following him up here in the first place? At least with everything going on, she'd given up on the commercial. He supposed that was something.

Ahead, Slim and Will cut into the trees to pick up three stray cows. He looked around for Roy. He didn't want to lose any more men. Nor did he want any of the three to double back to the cabin. With relief, he saw Roy through the trees, rounding up several more cows.

On the mountain below him, the main herd milled in the large meadow where he and the men had left them yesterday. Their coats shone in the sun, a dark rich brown and stark white. He'd been around cattle all his life but right now they were as beautiful as anything he'd ever seen. He loved this way of life. Anger boiled up in him at the thought that someone was trying to take it away from him—and using his men to do it. Just like last time.

He told himself that by this afternoon he would have the cattle and the crew back at the ranch. If he could just hold things together until then. He headed into the trees to cut a couple of strays back toward the herd, anxious to get back to Reggie and head down the mountain to the ranch.

He couldn't wait to see the ranch house where he'd been born and raised. Only a few days ago, he'd been glad to leave. With his father Asa McCall acting strangely, his mother Shelby back from the dead, Dusty mad and pouting, Brandon stuck on the ranch working to pay off some gambling debts, Rourke away on his honeymoon, Cash living in town and keeping busy being sheriff, J.T. had wanted as far away from the ranch as he could get.

But even with the craziness at the ranch, J.T. would give anything to be riding up to it right now. He had half a million dollars worth of beef to get off this mountain. The Sundown Ranch was a working ranch that depended on the sale of the cattle each year to keep going.

He had to get the cattle down. And, he reminded himself, maybe whoever was behind the incidents would quit now that they were moving the cattle down. No one had been seriously hurt. This time. So far.

Right. He thought about Buck. He couldn't be sure that was true. Worse, as he watched the cattle milling below him, he couldn't shake the feeling that the incidents hadn't been random, that they were leading up to something bigger. He hoped to hell he was wrong.

The one thing he couldn't ignore was the chance that whoever was doing this had the same plan Billy Joe Duncan, Leroy Johnson and Claude Ryan had had nine years ago.

The only one he'd known was Claude Ryan. Clearly, it had been Claude's plan and he'd found two men to help pull it off. With Claude it had been personal. Claude had been nurturing his grudge against J.T. since they were kids.

He'd died trying to even some score that J.T. had never even understood. It was Claude's face J.T. saw in his nightmares. Claude on fire, his face melting in the flames at the window, his gaze filled with hate as he screamed that he would kill J.T.

That kind of hate scared J.T. more than he wanted to admit. Fueled by that hate and madness, was it any wonder that Claude had been the one who'd escaped the burning cabin and had dragged himself partway down the mountain?

J.T. couldn't imagine the last hours of Claude's life. Had he still been alive when his body had been dragged off into the trees by the bear to be devoured?

Not even Claude deserved that.

REGGIE HAD just finished the dishes and packed the necessities for the ride down the mountain. She glanced at her watch, anxious for J.T. to return. It seemed like weeks since she'd seen J.T. kneeling beside her rental car, changing her tire. Changing her life, she thought.

Her head snapped up as she smelled it. She had gotten

one of the windows open a crack earlier when she was doing the dishes. Now she wasn't surprised to see smoke blowing in. She could hear the flames licking at the dry wood. Her heart leaped to her throat. The cabin was on fire!

Fire had killed the three rustlers and now the line shack was on fire. Her mind raced. Was it possible she could put the fire out? With what though?

She could hear the crackling of the flames. Smoke billowed past the window and began to bleed through the cracks along the back wall. Her eyes and throat burned as the cabin began to fill with smoke. The whole place could go up in flames at any moment. She had to get out of here!

She limped to the bed, grabbed her jacket and saw the gun where she'd left it on the mattress. As she reached for it, she knew the fire was no accident. Someone was trying to scare her. Or kill her.

Scooping up the gun, she tried to remember everything J.T. had told her about firing it. Her hand shook and she hurried to the door, her ankle throbbing, but nothing like even the thought of being burned alive in this cabin.

She unlocked the door and tried to push it open. The door wouldn't budge. What was wrong? The door had always opened easily. Fear paralyzed her. She threw herself against the door. It still didn't move. Rational thought intervened. Someone had barricaded the door.

Smoke moved like fog around her waist-deep and quickly climbing. She had to get out. The windows were small and paned and her only way out. She hoped she could squeeze out that way. Otherwise, she was trapped in the burning cabin.

Regina rushed to the window farthest from the burning

part of the building and began to break out the glass and wooden panes with the butt of the pistol. The glass was old and brittle, the wooden panes weathered.

The cabin was full of smoke now, her eyes blurred, she could barely breathe. Covering her mouth, she dropped the pistol out the window and then climbed after it. The space was tight. She was half out when she heard something inside the cabin fall with a crash as the fire spread.

Her hips stuck in the small window. With all the strength she could muster, she pushed against the side of the cabin, forcing the rest of her body from the window.

She tumbled headfirst into the dirt and lay there for a moment, the breath knocked out of her, coughing and crying. Her hips were scraped and cut from the broken glass. Her hands were scraped and bleeding.

But she was alive. She sucked in the fresh air as she picked up the pistol and scrambled to her feet. The cabin was ablaze, the heat and smoke forcing her back. She stared at the flames for a moment, then turned and looked around the camp, sensing that she wasn't alone.

She couldn't see him but she could feel him watching her. He hadn't expected her to escape. Or had he?

The air felt colder than it had earlier. She moved through the trees, keeping the pistol in front of her, wanting him to see it, wanting him to know she would kill him, praying she would have the courage to pull the trigger.

She stumbled and almost fell. Ignoring the pain that shot up from her ankle, the ache in her chest that made her cough and the tears that blurred her eyes, she ran for her life.

CHAPTER ELEVEN

J.T. spotted the fourth dead cow not far from the line shack. As he approached he caught the smell of charred fur. His heart dropped at the sight of the burned cow lying in the open meadow.

"Bastard," he breathed and dismounted. He'd seen this same work before so he wasn't surprised that the cow had been bludgeoned to death, then set on fire. He could still smell the accelerant used to start it. What a waste. And for what? Just to frighten him? Or to warn him? Either way, the person behind this had already succeeded at both.

He remembered a run-in he'd had with Claude Ryan years ago. Claude had been drunk and looking for a fight. He'd always had a chip on his shoulder when it came to J.T. They were the same age, had been in the same class all the way through grade school and high school.

But while J.T. had gone away to college, Claude had stayed and become a bouncer at the Cowboy Bar. In the years before that, Claude and his father had lived in an old house on the edge of town that always smelled of skunks. His mother had run off with a trucker when he was nine and his father had been killed in an accident at the sawmill where he'd worked when Claude was nineteen. Claude had blown what little money he'd gotten from the insurance company.

Claude had never made it a secret that he resented J.T. and felt everything had been handed to him while Claude had had to scrape and scrap for everything he got.

"Life isn't fair," he'd told J.T. that night their paths had crossed. "Why is it that you were born into a ranch and I was born into crap?" Claude asked him.

J.T. hadn't wanted to get into a fight so he'd tried to walk past Claude, but Claude had grabbed his arm.

"You don't deserve it," Claude blubbered. "Someday I'm going to take it all away from you." He'd let go of him then and stumbled back. "My kind of existence breeds killers. Did you know that? I have nothing to lose and you have everything. That scare you, J.T.? It ought to."

It hadn't then because he'd thought it was just the booze talking. Claude had been in his face numerous times over the years for little slights. If J.T. got better grades or made the football team and Claude didn't, Claude blamed his life circumstance—and he blamed J.T. as if he measured himself by J.T. and always found himself wanting.

As he looked down at the dead cow, J.T. wondered if stalkers didn't have this same type of obsession. They fixated on one person, blaming them for everything wrong in their lives.

But Claude was dead, he reminded himself. He'd seen the spot where the body had been dragged through the dirt and dead pine needles. He'd seen the grizzly tracks.

He'd looked for Claude's remains, planning to at least bury the man at the cemetery outside of town. But he'd never found them. Not unusual in a country this vast. The bear could have carried the carcass miles away.

He turned his horse away from the desecration and rode

back toward the herd. This would be the last of the cattle rounded up. It was time to leave.

But he wasn't foolish enough to think that it was over. He feared what would be waiting for them on the trip down. The county dirt road was about fifteen miles away. That's where Claude and his cohorts in crime had had the rented cattle trucks waiting to be loaded with the stolen beef nine years ago.

What would be waiting for him this time?

THE WIND TORE at her as Regina struggled up the hillside. She thought this was the direction she'd gone the day she'd found the cattle herd, the day she'd found J.T. She prayed she wasn't going in the wrong direction.

At the top of the hill, she let herself look back at the cabin. The flames had almost entirely consumed it. Smoke billowed up, the wind tugging at the rancid dark cloud, stretching it, distorting it.

She fought to catch her breath, taking the weight off her ankle for a moment, easing the pain, as she searched for any movement, any sign that whoever had started the fire was chasing after her.

The wind whipped her hair around her face. She brushed it back, holding it, her eyes watering from the wind and the smoke. She didn't see him. But that didn't mean he wasn't there, hiding in the pines.

Turning, she began to run again. Her lungs ached and she knew she wouldn't be able to go much farther on her ankle. She didn't dare look back, stopping only when she couldn't run any farther and only then to lean against the large trunk of a tree, hidden. She hoped.

Her chest ached from the smoke, the fear, the running.

She fought to catch her breath, trying hard not to think about who was behind her or what he would do if he caught her.

Right now all she wanted was to see J.T.'s face. To hear him come riding up. To be safe in his arms.

She tried to quiet her breathing, the pounding of her pulse, so she could hear if someone was coming after her. A hawk cried overhead, making her jump.

She knew she couldn't stop for long. He was probably tracking her. She had to keep moving. She peered around the tree, saw no one, and turned, stumbling as she caught movement in a stand of the white-barked trees nearby. Her heart leaped to her throat in that instant before she saw that it was just the wind picking up the leaves, sending them sailing in a golden whirl.

She stared at the stand of trees. They looked familiar. If she was right, the ravine was just on the other side and beyond that the large meadow where the cattle were gathered.

Catching her breath, she stumbled toward the golden leafed trees, praying she was right. The wind whipped at her hair, the cold air biting her cheeks. She could see the dark clouds through the tops of the trees, feel the temperature dropping.

The first snowflakes seemed flung from the sky overhead as the black clouds snuffed out the sun. She slowed, the day suddenly darker and colder and more ominous. She stopped, that feeling that someone was watching her so strong—

Through the stark-white branches of the trees, something blue fluttered beyond the golden leaves. The wind whirled snowflakes and leaves around her, but she could see that what she'd seen was a piece of blue cloth. J.T.?

He'd been wearing a blue shirt today.

She couldn't run anymore. Her ankle felt as if it wouldn't hold her weight.

"McCall!" she called, the wind sucking the name away. "McCall?" Only the wind answered with a groan as it thrashed the limbs of the pines and sent the last of the aspen leaves hurling into the air.

What if it wasn't McCall?

The snow began to fall harder. Holding the gun in front of her, Regina inched forward, catching fleeting glimpses of the blue fabric through the trees as the wind whirled leaves and snowflakes around her.

Her fingers ached from the cold and holding the pistol so tightly, but she didn't dare lower it, didn't dare take her finger off the trigger.

What if it was a trap? She caught the sound of cows mooing on the wind. Her heart began to race. It had to be J.T.

But why wasn't he moving? She stumbled closer, suddenly afraid of what she would find.

J.T. REINED IN his horse as he neared the herd. The wind had picked up. He felt the cold on his face and knew even before he turned that Will Jarvis had been right. A storm had blown in.

The sky was almost black as the snow squall scudded across the treetops toward him. It came on so fast, that one moment the sun was out, the day mild, and the next snowflakes began to fall. He'd seen storms like this come in before, without warning, often the snow falling while the sun was still shining.

But today the dark clouds swept over the sun, extinguishing it and the light. The snow began to fall harder as the day darkened, the landscape quickly changing.

J.T. looked around for his men. He'd seen Roy earlier cutting some cows into the herd. Through the snow, he saw Will Jarvis dismount and bend down as if to check one of the horse's shoes. Nevada Black was nowhere in sight. But he'd been near just moments before J.T. had spotted the dead cow and ridden over to it.

As he lifted his face to the wind, he smelled the smoke. At first he thought it was coming from the dead cow but the wind was blowing the wrong direction. He caught a strong whiff of it, his gut tightening at the horrible memory of the scent of burned flesh.

In an instant, the snow obliterated everything. He called to the men, his voice swept away by the wind and the whirling snow. He lost sight of them, of the cattle herd below him. But he could smell the smoke now, even stronger than before.

He turned his horse back toward the cabin, riding as fast as he could with the visibility quickly dropping to nothing.

The snow whirled around him, huge smothering flakes of ice and cold that turned his world white, making him quickly lose his sense of direction.

He'd heard stories all his life about ranchers who'd gone out to feed the cows, got lost in their own pastures and froze to death.

Some ranchers had a rope that stretched from their barn

to their house so they could get back that short distance in a blizzard.

Often times the only thing that would save a man was his horse—if his horse could find his way home even in a blizzard. Many a cowboy credited his horse for saving his life in a freak snowstorm.

Lady Killer had gotten J.T. out of some tight spots over the years. He hoped to hell he did now as he gave the horse his rein. The smell of smoke teased him through the whirling snow. Not the smoke of a woodstove or a campfire. This was the smell of destruction, of burned belongings, of destroyed lives.

He pulled the brim of his hat down against the storm and rode blindly toward what he hoped was the cabin—and Reggie.

THE SNOWFLAKES were so thick, Regina lost sight of the blue fabric through the trees for a moment.

She could hear the cows mooing on the wind, but something else, something closer. She stopped. Over the roar of her pulse, she heard a creaking sound. She waited, heard the creak again.

Just a branch creaking in the wind. She took a few more steps and caught another glimpse of the blue fabric again through the snowstorm. If she was right, this was where she'd seen Luke's horse when it had almost run her down. That image of the terrified horse burned itself into her mind, frightening her even more as if this spot held some evil. An evil a horse would sense. And a city girl would not.

"McCall!" She moved like a sleepwalker through the falling snow, the dead wet aspen leaves sticking to her boots, her gaze locked on the spot of blue, a prayer on her lips.

The aspens gave way to large old pines. She rounded one of the ponderosas and froze. She'd been right about the piece of blue cloth. It was a shirt. The same color as the one J.T. had worn this morning.

The cloth flapped in the wind. A sleeve. She stepped around the pine tree, her scream lost in the storm as she saw what was making the creaking sound. A rope bit into the bark of a wide limb. From the rope hung Luke Adams, his feet dangling just inches from the ground, the noose tied tight around his neck, the rope over the limb creaking as his body swayed in the wind.

CHAPTER TWELVE

She came out of the snowstorm in a blur of red. Just moments before, the wind had seemed to shriek and suddenly there she was, the gun clutched in her hand.

J.T. drew his horse up short, but Reggie still stumbled into the two of them. He had to grab her to keep her from falling, swinging down from his horse to hold her upright and gently take the pistol from her ice-cold fingers.

Her eyes were wide with terror, her face as white as the snow and twisted in a mask of horror. She was crying and shaking, her words making no sense to him as they tumbled out all over each other.

"It's all right, Reggie," he said softly, pulling her into his arms. She slumped against him and he pressed his face into her wet hair. Her hair smelled of smoke. "What happened?"

She leaned into him, taking huge gulping breaths, her body jerking with each sob, her words incoherent and lost in the storm. He strained to see past her into the snow, fearing what might be coming after them.

Two words registered. "He's dead."

J.T. felt his skin crawl. "Who's dead, Reggie?"

She took a shuddering breath. "Luke. I saw him. He was—" She choked on a sob. "The cabin. He burned it down."

"Luke burned down the cabin?"

She shook her head. "Someone burned down the cabin. I ran. I was looking for you when I found—" Her eyes teared up again, she bit her lower lip. "Luke. He's in a tree." She pointed behind her.

Luke in a tree?

Her blue eyes were wide with fear as she pulled back. "He had a rope around his neck and he was—" She started crying again. "His eyes were bulging and his tongue—"

"Okay." He drew her back into his arms. "I need you to show me where."

She nodded against his chest. He brushed the snow from her hair with his hand and took off his coat and put it on her. He had to get her out of the weather and if he'd understood her, someone had burned down the cabin. That would explain the smoke he'd smelled earlier, the same scent as in her hair.

She brushed away her tears with the heel of her palm. Her lower lip trembled. Snowflakes caught in her lashes. But she straightened and started limping back the way she'd come. He needed her to be strong now and was for once thankful that she was the kind of woman who didn't let anything stop her.

He caught her hand, turned her to face him and lifted her up into the saddle. She didn't protest. Adrenaline pumping, he slipped his rifle from the scabbard and led the horse. Reggie's tracks hadn't quite filled in. He followed them into the stand of aspens, the same area where Reggie said she had first seen Luke's horse the day before.

The wind wasn't as strong back here in the trees, but still the falling snow whirled around him as they walked through the stand of now nearly bare aspens. Reggie sat on the horse, gripping the pommel, her gaze riveted to a spot beyond the grove.

The wind had torn the last of the leaves from the limbs. The white branches were dark against the snow, looking sinister as if reaching out at them as they passed.

As the aspen grove gave way to the dense pines, he saw Reggie glance over her shoulder, shudder, then straighten, shoulders back, stilling the trembling in her lower lip as she bit down on it.

He stepped into the pines, the rifle in the crook of his arm, the reins in his other hand. It was darker in here, more protected from the storm. The snow fell silently. Cold shadows hunkered under the wide pine boughs. Past the quiet, he heard a creaking sound. Reggie must have heard it, too. She tensed, making the horse shudder beneath her.

Still following her tracks, he moved through the pines until he saw something through the branches. A blue shirt. His heart leaped to his throat. He'd been hoping that Reggie was mistaken, that in her fear she'd only imagined that it was Luke. That he would find a noose like he had earlier; a tree branch with nothing hanging from it but the rope.

That hope evaporated the moment he stepped around the last pine and saw Luke. He turned away, sick to his stomach. What monster would do something like this?

The rope creaked on the limb and he saw something on the body.... "Stay here," he said to Reggie and walked the few yards to where someone had thrown the rope over the limb and hung Luke Adams. As the body turned in the wind, J.T. saw that something had been written on the blue shirt.

Stepping closer, he squinted in the falling snow to read

the scrawled word. The ink had run but he could still make out the word "Traitor."

A chill, colder than the day, rattled up his spine. He stepped back wanting to distance himself from this horror, from the mind that conceived this type of retribution. He wanted to cut Luke down, but he knew the body would be safer where it was. It was high enough off the ground that most animals wouldn't bother it. There was no cabin to take it to. Luke would have to remain here until he could get back with help.

He turned and hurried back to Reggie. She no longer looked terrified, just numb, eyes glazed. He handed her the rifle. She took it, blinking as if coming awake. He swung up behind her on the horse and retrieved the rifle and reins from her.

Even if someone had burned the cabin to the ground, the wall tents might still be standing. He had to get her into some dry clothing. He had some for both of them in his tent.

As he rode back toward camp, the wind died down. Snow fell around them in a cocoon of dense cold white, but the visibility was better. He knew where he was and where he was going. But still he wouldn't be able to see anyone come out of the storm until it was too late.

He tried not to think past getting to the camp. He couldn't even be sure the tents would be standing, but if they were, he and Reggie would get changed into some dry, warmer clothing. And then what?

He couldn't think that far ahead, afraid they wouldn't even reach the camp. He expected a surprise attack, someone coming out of the storm. Whoever had killed Luke was out there somewhere. All of this was just leading up to something more horrible. He felt it as clearly as the cold. It was only a matter of time before he crossed paths with the killer. J.T. was sure of that.

And J.T. had several huge disadvantages. He had no way of knowing what the killer looked like. And he also had Reggie. J.T. had no doubt that the killer planned to use both against him.

The killer had to be either Will, Nevada or Roy. Or all three of them. He wouldn't know who was innocent or who was guilty until it was too late.

He smelled the smoke first, then what was left of the cabin took shape through the falling snow. Only the hulking dark shape of the old woodstove stood in the ashes of what had been the line shack.

The smell reminded him of another burned cabin nine years ago. Except there were no bodies in the ruins this time. At least he hoped not.

As he and Reggie neared the camp, no one appeared from out of the falling snow. Wisps of smoke spiraled up from the ruins of the cabin, disappearing into the falling snow.

Fortunately, no trees near the cabin had caught fire and burned. Through the pines he saw with relief that both wall tents were still standing.

As he rode into camp, he noted that the corrals were empty, the gate open, the extra horses gone. Someone had let them loose. Before setting the fire? Or after Reggie had taken off?

No sign of the men. No fresh tracks in the snow. He rode up to the tents, heard a horse whinny and raised the rifle. One of the extra horses came out of the snow toward him, head down, walking slowly.

He handed the rifle to Reggie and slipped off the back of his horse. Taking the lasso he kept on his saddle, he moved toward the horse.

It was a horse named Silver, the gentlest of the bunch. Silver eyed him, no doubt afraid after the cabin fire. J.T. got close enough that he could loop the end over the horse's neck. He spoke softly, rubbing the horse's neck to soothe it, then tied the end of the lasso to a limb of a nearby tree.

Going back to his own horse, he helped Reggie down. She stood hugging herself, fear back in her eyes. He handed her the pistol and motioned for her to wait by the horse as he took a look in the tents.

She nodded, her fingers closing over the grip.

He took the rifle and looked in the cowhands' tent first, expecting to find their gear gone and them as well. Their gear was still there. Someone was lying on a cot in the far corner, Nevada Black's cot, his back to the door.

"Nevada?" he called.

No answer.

He stepped closer, reached out to touch the man's shoulder and saw the knife buried to the hilt in the man's chest. One hand was over the knife handle as if he had tried to pull it out.

The skin on top of the hand was scarred from where it had been burned.

J.T. jerked back his own hand, his breath coming hard, as he stared down at Slim Walker.

What was Slim doing here? And where was Cotton? J.T. stumbled back toward the door, sure now that neither of them had reached the ranch. That meant his brother Cash wasn't on his way up here.

He and Reggie were on their own.

J.T. scrambled out of the tent, afraid he would find Reggie gone. But she stood next to the horse, still hugging herself, still looking scared.

"What is it?" she asked, obviously seeing how upset he was.

He didn't answer as he checked his own tent, afraid he would find another body inside it. The tent was empty except for the two cots and his and Buck's gear.

J.T. ducked back out to take Reggie's hand and pull her inside, out of the snow and cold. He took the pistol from her and laid it on the cot.

"McCall." Her eyes shone. "What did you find in the tent?"

He wanted to lie to her, to protect her, but she had a right to know how much danger they were in. He also needed her to be strong and not fall apart on him. Better now though than later when they could be in a worse situation. "I found Slim. He's dead. Someone stabbed him."

"Slim? But Slim left with Cotton…." Tears spilled down her cheeks. "Cotton?"

J.T. shook his head, and putting down the rifle, stepped to her. Gently, he thumbed away the tears on her cheeks, then pulled her to him, wrapping his arms around her. "We have to get dressed in dry, warm clothing. We have to get out of here, Reggie."

She nodded against his chest, then pulled back.

He gave her a reassuring smile. "That's my girl." He found some dry clothing, handed it to her, and turned his back so she could dress as he put on a dry shirt and a heavy coat of Buck's. He would give Reggie his winter coat, a heavier one than he'd been wearing earlier.

He could hear her behind him dressing quickly as he

picked up the rifle. She put on the coat he handed her over the flannel shirt and long underwear and wool pants. All were huge on her, but at least she was warm and dry now.

"Here," he said, handing her a pair of lined boots. "They're Buck's. His feet are smaller than mine. I think with a couple pairs of socks…"

She pulled on the socks, then the boots. He noticed that her hands were steady. He knelt in front of her and laced them. Feeling her hand on his cheek, he looked up at her. He met her gaze. In that moment, he couldn't be sure what either of them might say. She had to know that the killer probably wasn't going to let them get out of these mountains. Not without a fight.

He'd die trying to save her. He figured if she knew anything about him, she'd know that. "I'll go saddle the other horse," he said quickly and stood. "I'll be right outside."

"No, I'm going with you."

He started to tell her that she would be warmer in the tent, not to mention drier, but he could see by her expression that she didn't want to stay alone any more than he wanted to leave her.

She got to her feet. The high boots seemed to help her ankle.

He picked up Luke's saddle and tack from where he'd put it in his tent last night. She followed him outside. The snow wasn't falling as hard now. The wind had died and the silence was heavy and close. He kept his rifle within reach as he saddled Silver for Reggie.

She swung up into the saddle and he handed her the reins. She winced as she put weight on her bad ankle in the stirrups but said nothing as she watched the forest and the falling snow. He didn't have to ask what she was looking for.

There was one thing he had to check before they started down the mountain, although he knew what he would find.

The snow stopped falling almost as quickly as it had begun. Low clouds hung over the tops of the trees. The air was cold and wet and stung his eyes.

As he topped a rise, the wide open meadow stretched below him. The snow had been trampled, the dirt kicked up.

The herd was gone, just as he knew it would be.

REGINA STARED down at the meadow where hundreds of cattle had been yesterday. The only sign that they'd ever been there was the disturbed earth and trodden snow.

"Where are the cows?" she whispered as her horse edged up beside his.

"Headed for the black market, I would imagine," he said and looked over at her. "I guess that's what they've been after all along."

"They killed Luke and Slim for cows?" she asked.

"Half a million dollars worth," he said.

She blinked in surprise. "I had no idea—"

He nodded as if he suspected she didn't.

"You have to go after them and stop them," she said with a fierceness that surprised her.

It must have surprised him, too. He smiled. "The only thing I have to do is get you to the ranch where you will be safe."

"But if they have your property—" She saw by his expression that he feared whoever had stolen the cattle wanted more than the cattle and ultimately the money. "If I wasn't with you, you'd go after them, wouldn't you."

He laughed softly. "Probably and it would be the stupidest thing I could do. I don't even know how many of them there are. I'd probably get myself killed."

She doubted that. J. T. McCall was a man who could take care of himself.

"Come on." He spurred his horse and started back the way they'd come, then cut through the trees away from the trail where the cattle had gone.

Her horse followed without her having to do anything and she was grateful. Her ankle ached and she felt chilled from earlier. She stared at McCall's broad back, thankful that he was with her. Another man might have abandoned her to go after his cattle. Actually, most men she'd known. A half million was a lot of money. She doubted McCall could spare it and she feared she was at least partly responsible for its loss. If he hadn't had to take care of her...

The rocking motion of the horse put her to sleep.

She woke with a start, almost falling off the horse. McCall had stopped. She stared into the pines, surprised how dark it had gotten.

Her rump hurt from the saddle and her ankle felt as if it were ten sizes larger than normal, the boot too tight now and cutting into her flesh. She was tired and hungry, thirsty and her hair stunk of smoke, reminding her of the fire, her skin grimy.

But none of that mattered in an instant as she watched McCall motion for her to keep silent as he dismounted and, raising the rifle, disappeared into the pines.

J.T. HAD BEEN following a trail through the snow for the last quarter mile. Now he caught a whiff of campfire smoke on the breeze. A moment later, he heard a horse whinny ahead of him.

He moved silently through the fallen snow with the rifle ready, stopping behind one of the pine trees to listen. A horse whinnied just beyond a small clearing.

The moment he stepped around the wide branches of the pine tree, he saw a figure crouched over a small fire in a heavy coat with a hood, a coat he didn't recognize.

J.T. edged silently up behind the man. Snowflakes danced in the air drifting restlessly on a slight breeze. The ground around the fire was dark with footprints but beyond it everything was covered in a blanket of icy white.

He pressed the barrel of the rifle to the back of the man's head. "Move and I will kill you."

The man froze.

Slowly, J.T. stepped to the side until he could see the man's face.

"Take it easy," Will Jarvis said. "This isn't what you think."

"You know what I'm thinking?" J.T. asked, shifting the rifle barrel to aim it at Will's chest, his finger on the trigger.

"I'm FBI," Will said his voice sounding a little strained. "You probably don't remember me but I was on the case nine years ago."

J.T. couldn't hide his surprise. Something about the man had been familiar, something that reminded him of the horror of that unforgettable cattle roundup. He couldn't remember any of the FBI agents, who'd been called in because of a federal warrant on one of the men, Leroy Johnson.

He didn't remember Will Jarvis, but that didn't really

mean anything given the condition he'd been in after what had happened nine years ago. "You have some sort of ID?" He kept the rifle on him.

"If you'll let me reach into my coat pocket," Will said.

"I can pull the trigger on this rifle before you can pull a gun," J.T. warned.

"I'm no fool." He reached slowly into his coat pocket and brought out his identification. He flipped it open. FBI. William Robert Jarvis. Special agent.

"So it was your gun I found hidden in the tent."

Jarvis smiled. "We all know agents don't carry a 9 mm, but yes, it was one of several I had hidden around the camp. I like to have back ups, plus this." He pulled out a knife and met J.T.'s gaze. "As I recall, this was Claude Ryan's weapon of choice."

J.T. shuddered at the memory and lowered the rifle as Jarvis slid the knife back into a sheath under his pant leg. "What the hell is going on?" Out of the corner of his eye, he could see Reggie waiting in the darkness of the pines, watching. She had the pistol in her hands, her gaze on Jarvis's back.

"I think you know what's going on," Will said. "Someone's been killing off your cowhands, getting rid of them one by one. I would imagine your cattle are gone as well." He nodded, seeing that none of that was news to J.T. "I can tell you don't want to believe who's behind it. You don't even like saying his name, do you?"

"Claude Ryan is dead."

"Is he?" Will said and chuckled.

J.T. stared at Jarvis, surprised how much he wanted it to be true. "Are you telling me he's not?"

The FBI agent shrugged. "*Someone* from that cattle

roundup is alive. He's left a trail of dead plastic surgeons across Mexico. I followed that trail to your cow camp."

J.T. was shaking his head. "A grizzly got Claude."

"Something got him all right," Will said. "I would imagine it was one of his gang."

"The other two were dead inside the cabin."

Jarvis smiled. "You think it was just the three of them in it together?" He shook his head. "There were five of them, maybe more. The ones I know about are Claude Ryan, Leroy Johnson, Billy Joe Brady, Slim Walker and Luke Adams."

J.T. had known the last two names were coming as sure as sunrise. "You're telling me that Claude killed Luke and Slim."

"I didn't know they were dead for sure, but I figured he'd get them," Will said. "Even though Slim risked his life to save Claude—got his hands burned—Claude considered them both traitors because they didn't kill you when they had the chance."

J.T. looked to the pines where he'd left Reggie. "How do you know all this?"

"Some of it I've figured out over the past nine years. That first night in camp I heard Luke leave the tent. Him and Slim. I followed them, overheard them talking about Claude, both scared."

J.T. studied Will, having trouble believing what he was hearing and not sure why. "Why would Slim and Luke agree to work for me after what happened up here?"

"I suspect Claude was behind it somehow. I heard Luke say he knew they shouldn't have come back up into the Bighorns. Said it wasn't worth what they were being paid.

Don't think they were talking about cowhand wages, do you?"

"No," J.T. said and looked over at Reggie.

"Why don't you invite her over to the fire?" Will suggested and smiled. He hadn't turned around but he'd known she was back there.

"We're not staying," J.T. said. Reggie was safer in the shadow of the pines with the horses. "If Claude is alive, why wait so long to come back?"

Will picked up a stick and stirred the dying embers of the fire. "He was badly burned, horribly disfigured. Took years of surgeries, most of them unsuccessful."

"Are you telling me the last one was successful?"

Will looked up at him. "You didn't recognize him, did you."

J.T. felt something stir inside him as he thought of the six men who'd been in camp.

"It seems all these years he's been planning to come back here and steal your cattle—only make it work this time," Will said.

"You think that's all he wants?"

Will Jarvis shook his head. "I think not. The man obviously has a hell of a lot of patience. Nine years. That's a long time to hold a grudge."

"Not for Claude. It's an obsession with him," J.T. said. "He's sick. He's wasted his life hating me. He's a pathetic coward. Look how many people he's killed and for what?"

Will said nothing, just stared into the flames.

Something about Will Jarvis made him uneasy, had from the beginning. "I would think if you hoped to catch him, you'd be following the herd."

Will smiled at that. "Then you don't know Claude very

well. He's not interested in the herd." He looked up then, meeting J.T.'s eyes. Claude had gray eyes. None of the six cowhands had gray eyes, including Will Jarvis, but with today's colored contact lenses…

"He'll be following you," Will Jarvis said. "But first he'll come for me. I've been dogging him for years. He knows he has to kill me or I won't stop."

"So Claude will come down this way?" This was the shortest route to the ranch. Claude would know that, too. He knew these mountains maybe better than J.T. did because Claude was often unemployed, camping out all summer, living off the land and some of the Sundown Ranch herd, while J.T. was working.

"I followed a set of tracks down here yesterday," Will said. "Obviously he knows you, figured you would come down this way. He thinks he knows what you're going to do before you do it. If I wait right here, I'll see him."

J.T. shook his head. "You're a sitting duck."

Will smiled. "I've been waiting for this day for more years than I want to count. You and the woman had better get moving. You can still make the ranch before dark if you hurry."

J.T. studied Will Jarvis in the firelight. "Don't underestimate Claude Ryan. It will get you killed."

Will grunted and stirred the fire with the stick for a moment before throwing it into the flames. "You just worry about your own neck and your girlfriend's." He reached down to touch the knife in the sheath at his ankle. "And hope that Claude finds me before he does you."

CHAPTER THIRTEEN

J.T. turned and walked back to where Reggie waited in the trees. He should have been relieved that there was an FBI agent here.

"I don't trust him," Reggie said after they'd gotten out of earshot.

"Neither do I," J.T. said quietly. If Jarvis was right, Claude had ridden the shortcut the day before. For what reason? Looking for a place to attack? And when had Will Jarvis gotten away to follow him?

They could reach the ranch before dark if they continued down the mountain the way they were headed. But with the storm and the low clouds, they were losing light fast. They would be easy pickings. And if Will Jarvis was right, Claude had already anticipated that this was the way they would come.

Not to mention that Jarvis could be behind them right now, following them, tracking them.

Not too far down the mountain, they ran out of snow. In good light, J.T. knew they could still be tracked even without the snow. He was counting on it getting dark before anyone would find them. He couldn't risk going for the ranch as badly as he wanted to.

He rode along the side of the mountain, weaving

through the trees, keeping just below the snow line to hide their tracks before he turned toward the rock rim high above them.

REGINA LOOKED UP at the band of red rock and realized that was where they were headed. Not the ranch. She'd been turned around since she got to Montana. Without an ocean nearby or any distinguishing buildings, she couldn't tell east from west.

But she was smart enough to know they weren't headed for the ranch. The ranch was down the mountain and they were headed up.

As J.T. dismounted at the foot of the wall of rock, she lost all hope of a hot bath and a real bed.

"We aren't going to the ranch," Reggie said as he lifted her down.

"Sorry. Too dangerous. We'll leave before it gets light. Don't worry, by tomorrow morning you'll see civilization again."

She nodded. She ached all over and realized she could sleep anywhere. As long as she didn't have to ride a horse anymore today.

"Come on." He led her and the horses along the edge of the rock face.

The boots were too large and she stumbled several times and almost fell. Her ankle ached and she was limping badly.

"Here, take my hand," he said, removing her glove and enclosing her hand in his large one. His hand was warm and strong and she wished he would do the same with her entire body. She felt cold and so tired that picking up her feet took every ounce of her energy.

Finally, he stopped. In the last of the light, she could

see that they were high above the valley. Lights glittered in the far distance. Her chest ached from the climb and sudden longing to be down there away from the cold and horses and killers.

"This way," McCall said, as if sensing her yearning for the city and everything she'd left behind. He led her and the horses through a narrow slit in the rocks. The space opened, a tree towering over their heads. J.T. shoved one of the branches aside, and leaving the horses, pulled her into what she realized was a cave.

Once through the small opening, he snapped on a flashlight and she saw that she could stand up. It was cold and dark in here but the floor was dirt and soft.

"Here," he said handing her the flashlight. "I'll tend to the horses and be right back."

He was good to his word. He returned with firewood and built a small fire in a corner near a crack in the rock. The smoke rose and disappeared out through the crack.

"Still cold?" he asked as she curled around the fire, unable to keep her eyes open.

"A little." The side of her body exposed to the fire was warm but her other side was cold. She kept turning like a chicken on a rotisserie but still couldn't get everything warmed.

"Here, lie down," he said.

She curled around the fire and felt him lie down behind her, curling his warm body around hers.

"Better?"

"Hmmm," she said and closed her eyes, the fire flickering on her face, the crackling of the flames lulling her.

"You did really well today," he whispered. "You're okay, Regina Holland."

She opened her eyes and smiled to herself before closing them again and falling into a deep sleep. She didn't hear the scream that awakened J.T.

J.T. GOT UP, careful not to wake Reggie and, picking up the rifle, went out of the cave to the edge of the cliff.

The night was cold and clear. He wished to hell he was at the ranch and that Reggie was upstairs asleep in the guest bedroom, safe. But he knew he'd made the right decision to wait.

He let his gaze travel down the mountainside to where Will Jarvis had camped, not sure what he thought he might be able to see. Maybe the trees around the clearing on fire.

There was nothing but darkness. Nor did he hear another sound. He told himself that the scream he'd heard could have been a mountain lion. Men didn't usually scream like that. Unless they were in a lot of pain.

He shivered, thinking of Claude Ryan. If Will Jarvis was right, Claude would kill as many people as it took to get to him.

Back inside the cave, the fire had burned down to coals. He covered Reggie with his coat, then went to sit in the shadows at the cave entrance to wait. They would ride out at first light, going down a way that Claude would least expect—straight down to the county road.

A DARK SHADOW moved over her. Startled, Regina jerked back.

"It's just me," McCall whispered. "Sorry to scare you."

She blinked, trying to wake up, the dream still with her, a dark weight that pulled at her. "I was having this horrible dream…."

"It was just a dream," he said and sat down across from her, the fire between them.

She sat up, letting herself drift as she stared into the flames of the fire and soaked up the heat. She could tell it was the middle of the night, still dark outside.

"Wishing you had just gone with a model?"

She looked up at him over the top of the fire and shook her head.

He chuckled softly. "You still haven't given up."

"Have you given up getting back to the ranch, getting away from this madman?"

He shook his head, licked his thumb and reached across the fire to wipe a smudge of dirt from her cheek.

She froze, her gaze locking with his. He seemed to hold his breath. The fire popped softly. He drew back his hand to rest it on his thigh.

She reached out to touch his fingers. Her hand was cool on his but it sent a shaft of heat through him.

He shook his head. "You don't want to do this, Reggie."

She smiled a little at that. "I'm a big girl, McCall. I know what I want." Tears shone in her eyes. "Hold me?"

He moved around the fire to her. She melted into his arms. The flames flared, sparks rising into the darkness of the cave.

She felt soft and warm and he wanted to envelop himself in her, to feel the pounding of her pulse, to hear the drum of her heart, to assure himself that she was alive. That he was alive as well.

He tried to think of tomorrow, how they would both feel if he did the one thing he wanted, make love to her. But right now it didn't feel as if there would be a tomorrow. There was only now. The two of them in this cave. A crazy homicidal maniac or two out in the darkness.

Her kiss was soft, a gentle kiss, tentative, questioning.

His answering kiss was fire and heat, all consuming.

She had known that it would be all or nothing with him. Like the first kiss, McCall didn't do anything halfway. He wrapped her in his arms, in his kiss.

Her pulse jumped at his gentle touch, his big hands stroking her body until she was the fire, burning hot inside the cave. His mouth moved over her, warm and wet, sparking fissures of pleasure, stripping her bare beneath her clothing until he possessed every inch of her body.

Wrapped in his arms, he took her as she cried out in pleasure and release, her body pressed hot against his damp flesh, his mouth stealing her cries as the fire flamed, shadows flickering on the cave walls.

"IT'S TIME."

Regina opened her eyes. He still held her, his face inches from her own, their bodies melded together, clothes pushed aside, sleeping bare skin to bare skin.

She didn't want to move. Didn't want to leave this cave. Or his arms. But she feared they couldn't stay here for long. Just as she feared what waited for them outside.

He moved away from her, getting up to dress. Cold air skittered over her exposed flesh. She could feel his eyes on her as she sat up and covered herself.

When she read his expression, she saw that he wanted to make love to her again almost as badly as she wanted him to. But faint light bled into the cave. They had to leave, had to try to get to the ranch. She tried not to think about all the miles. Or the darkness of the trees. The shadows that could be death.

She rose and stumbled ahead of him to the cave entrance, her ankle aching along with the rest of her muscles. She clung to their lovemaking, to the memory of McCall's gentle hands, and tried not to look into the shadows as she stepped outside.

A slice of moon still hung in the dark sky high over the valley, a few stars, a shimmer of light low on the horizon the only hint of the coming day.

Regina shivered in spite of herself. The horses were saddled. McCall must have slipped away to do that, then returned to lie next to her. She couldn't remember ever being this tired. Her whole body ached and she felt cold all the way to her bones.

Just the thought of getting back in the saddle made her want to cry. He helped her up onto the horse as if sensing her resistance.

He walked the horses down the mountainside. She had to lean way back to keep from going over the horse's head, the terrain was so steep. Finally they reached flatter ground and he stepped into his saddle, motioning for her to keep quiet.

She nodded. It wasn't like she had anything to say this time of the day anyway. It was too late to be out on the town, even in L.A., and too early to be getting up. She would have been sleeping in her warm bed, worrying about work, not worrying about dying.

The dream she'd had earlier in the night came back to her. She could feel it around her, hanging over her like a dense awful shroud. She couldn't remember a lot of it, just that horrible feeling of being grabbed by the man. She never even saw his face. He'd come at her from behind, covering her mouth, then her eyes, then binding her so she couldn't move, couldn't scream.

She shuddered at the memory and let the horse lull her, drifting in and out of sleep, her mind like thick fog.

Regina heard the sound first, a noise off to her right. She

opened her eyes, startled as she caught movement coming at her from the side.

The man came out of a thick stand of pines, running low, reaching for her, one bloody hand outstretched, the other clutching a knife. The blade glistened in the dull light of the day where the blood hadn't completely dried.

She screamed and tried to get off the horse, but her boot was stuck in the stirrup. Riding in front of her, McCall spun his horse around and was already leaping down as the man grabbed her calf with his free hand.

McCall lunged at the man, knocking him to the ground with the butt of the rifle.

Regina's horse reared and suddenly she was falling through the air. She landed on the ground hard, all the air knocked from her lungs.

When she looked up she saw McCall standing over Will Jarvis, the rifle pointed at the man's head.

"Are you all right?" McCall cried, moving to her side, while keeping the rifle aimed at Jarvis.

She could only nod.

"Can you move?"

She nodded again. But she didn't want to move. She wanted to lie here. She promised herself she would never get back on a horse.

"Help me," Jarvis whispered.

She could see the blood across the front of his coat, on his hands and the knife, and realized it was his blood he had all over him.

He released the knife, dropping it as his fingers opened and his eyes closed.

She heard another noise. McCall turned to listen. It sounded like a vehicle coming slowly up the mountain. As she turned her head, she thought she saw what looked like a dirt track down the hillside through the trees. A road?

J.T. motioned her to silence as a truck came around a bend in the road below them.

She saw the Sundown Ranch logo on the side and began to cry. There was no way the driver would be able to see them up here on the hillside. He would drive right past.

McCall raised the rifle, the barrel pointed to the sky and fired three shots. They boomed in the morning air.

The driver of the truck hit his brakes. Dust boiled up. McCall fired another three shots and the driver was out of the car, looking up the hillside.

Regina closed her eyes, tears spilling down her cheeks. When she opened them, two men with blond hair and blue eyes were looking at her in something close to disbelief. One of the brothers, the one J.T. was calling Cash, had on a sheriff's uniform.

Vaguely she remembered McCall lifting her from the ground, touching her forehead, his palm ice-cold and him saying, "My God, she's burning up."

He'd carried her down to the truck. She remembered leaning against him, her face buried in his chest, his arm around her, shivering, trying to say something but her lips felt so dry and her mind so filled with fog.… She thought she recalled McCall's lips against her hair whispering, "You're going to be all right, Reggie" as the truck bumped down the mountainside.

CHAPTER FOURTEEN

"Who is this woman, James Thomas?" Shelby McCall demanded of her son as she drew him aside into the empty den and motioned for him to take a seat.

J.T. was too tired to argue. He sat and scrubbed a hand over his face. He hadn't slept last night, instead spending the hours beside Reggie's bed after the doctor had left. "It's a long story."

He was anxious to hear from Cash, to find out if they'd found Claude Ryan. If Claude really was alive.

After the pickup ride down the mountain with J.T. and Reggie, FBI agent Will Jarvis had been taken to the hospital where he had been flown to Billings for immediate surgery. The last time J.T. had checked, he was still in surgery for knife wounds.

But before Cash had got him out by helicopter from the ranch, Jarvis had said he'd wounded Claude badly and that they should look for his body on the mountain.

Unfortunately, Claude had also wounded the agent. Will Jarvis was lucky to be alive. If he hadn't headed for the county road and stumbled across J.T. and Reggie…

"James Thomas?" His mother had her arms folded in front of her, waiting for his answer as if she had all the time in the world. She did.

"I'd rather hear about what's going on with you and the

old man," he said. He'd seen his mother and father with their heads together earlier, then Asa had left, taking Brandon and Dusty with him to try to find the missing cattle.

Cash had gotten a call from a bow hunter who'd seen a bunch of cattle with the Sundown Ranch brand on national forest land in the Bighorns south of the cow camp.

"Looks like your killer wasn't after the cattle," Cash had said before leaving with the state investigators.

"You and the old man seemed to be arguing about something," J.T. said, watching his mother. She had never told any of them why she'd come back here after pretending to be dead for so long.

She gave him a look that only a mother can pull off even though she hadn't been in their lives for over thirty years. "Don't call your father 'the old man.'" Were those tears in her eyes? She really did seem to love the old man. "About this woman…"

J.T. shook his head, raked a hand through his hair and sighed. "I met her on the highway. She had a flat. I fixed it. She works for a blue jeans company and she was in Montana looking for a cowboy to do a commercial." He glanced at his mother. She was still waiting. "Reggie got the idea that I was that cowboy. I told her I wasn't interested but as determined and foolhardy as she is, she conned Buck into giving her a job as our camp cook."

Shelby lifted a brow.

J.T. nodded. "You know the rest of it, at least as much as I do." He'd barely reached the ranch when the call had come in from a neighboring rancher that they'd found Buck and taken him to the hospital. He had a mild concussion and some abrasions, couldn't remember what had happened to him. He thought he'd been bucked from his horse.

But he was doing well and was expected to be released by the end of the week.

J.T. wanted to go see him, but couldn't leave Reggie. Nor could he leave the ranch until he heard from Cash.

"This Reggie sounds like quite the woman," his mother commented.

J.T. smiled. "She is something, all right."

Shelby was eyeing him intently. He still couldn't call her mother. "You obviously care about her."

"I'm just worried that she's going to be all right," he said, wanting this conversation over. The doctor had said Reggie needed bed rest. She was suffering from exhaustion and a low-grade infection from a cut on her leg.

He'd noticed the cut on her calf last night when they'd made love in the cave. She'd said she didn't remember when she'd gotten it. The past few days had been so crazy....

"It's all my fault," he said.

"Oh, stop looking so down in the mouth," his mother said. "She's going to be fine. She can stay here as long as she needs to. But what about this commercial?"

"I refused to do it."

Shelby gave him that mother look again, making him think of all the years he'd been spared it.

He got to his feet. "I need to go check on her."

"No, let me." She rose, daring him to argue. "Get that old wheelchair out of the barn. We don't want her walking on that ankle once she's up and around."

He nodded, anxious for Cash to return with news. He hoped that herd in the Bighorns really was the Sundown Ranch's missing cattle. But this wouldn't be over until

Claude Ryan was found. If it really was Claude who FBI agent Will Jarvis had wounded on the mountain.

"I think you should do the commercial," his mother said, her look speaking volumes. She thought he owed Reggie. He thought so, too. But it was more complicated than a simple debt, he thought, remembering their lovemaking in the cave.

As he headed for the barn, he saw the sheriff's four-wheel-drive SUV coming up the road. He walked out to meet his brother, afraid to hear what Cash had found up on the mountainside.

REGINA WOKE to sunshine streaming in the window. She blinked, afraid she was only dreaming. She was lying in a nice soft bed with warm covers over her. Her hair beside her head on the pillow smelled clean and fresh as the sheets.

She heard a sound at the open doorway and looked up. A beautiful blond woman stood there, her eyes the same color as J.T.'s.

"You're awake," the woman said, coming into the room. "How are you feeling?"

"Better," Regina managed.

The woman sat down on the edge of the bed and smoothed the covers as she smiled at Regina. "I'm Shelby McCall, James Thomas's mother."

James Thomas. She'd wondered what the J.T. stood for. "Regina Holland."

Shelby's smile broadened. "Oh, I've heard all about you."

"Really?" She wondered what J.T. had told her. Her face flushed at the knowing look in the pale blue eyes.

"You must be starved," Shelby said.

Regina's stomach growled on cue. She laughed. "I guess I am."

"Good, there is nothing wrong with a healthy appetite," J.T.'s mother said, her gaze intent on Regina. "I have Cook making you some breakfast. We can visit while you eat."

The phone rang. Shelby McCall picked it up. She was beautiful. Regina could see where J.T. got his looks.

"It's for you," Shelby said, her look saying, *It's a man.*

Regina didn't reach for the phone. "No one knows I'm here."

"He says his name is Anthony Grand?" Shelby said.

Anthony. Regina had completely forgotten about him, about the jeans company, the commercial, her life in Los Angeles. How was that possible?

She felt completely off-kilter. After everything that had happened, all the things that had been a matter of life or death in Los Angeles seemed silly. She really had been in a life-and-death situation.

But she knew that wasn't what had changed her priorities. It was J.T. McCall.

She took the phone. "Anthony?" She saw Shelby lift a brow and motion that she would leave. Regina nodded and smiled and waited until she disappeared before saying, "How did you find me?"

"It wasn't easy. I heard the most amazing story about you being a cow camp cook and then almost getting killed by some homicidal maniac?"

"A lot has happened," she agreed. "I got thrown from a horse."

"Oh, darling, what in heaven's name were you doing on such a beast?"

"It's a long story, but I'm fine. I just have to stay off my sprained ankle for a while." She heard a squeak in the hall.

"A while? Sweetie, you haven't got a while. We need to go into production ASAP. You have the contract, right?"

She took a breath, glancing toward the doorway. J.T. was framed in it. "I'm going to have to get back to you."

"I don't like what I hear in your voice. Your cowboy did sign the contract, right?"

"I'll call you later." She hung up before he could pressure her for more details. "A friend," she said to McCall.

He nodded, looking more than skeptical that it was a "girl" friend. He rolled an antique wheelchair into the room. "The doctor said you were not to walk on your ankle. Is everything all right?" McCall asked.

"Fine." She gave him a smile but she could see he wasn't buying it.

"How are you feeling?"

"Better."

He pushed the wheelchair over by her bed. "You want to have breakfast in bed?"

"Would you mind if I tried the chair?" She wanted to see the house. She felt like an invalid lying in the bed and she had so much she wanted to ask McCall. "So the J.T. stands for James Thomas?" Regina asked, smiling at him after he slipped his arms under her and lifted her effortlessly into the wheelchair.

"I'm named after my mother's grandfather."

She looked down and saw that she was wearing a beautiful cotton nightgown.

"My sister Dusty lent you a few clothes until I can go

to town for some," McCall said, seeing her surprise. "The two of you are about the same size fortunately."

Regina vaguely remembered being in a bathtub filled with warm water and lots of bubbles and McCall washing her hair. The memory swept over her like the warm water and McCall's soapy hands. She felt her cheeks heat. "Thank you."

He snorted. "For what?"

She touched her hair and met his gaze. "Everything."

He looked away. "I almost got you killed."

"You heard something from your brother about what happened back on the mountain," she said.

J.T. nodded and told her everything that Cash had told him. "It looks like Claude Ryan is dead. They found another body not far from where FBI agent Will Jarvis said he wounded the man who attacked him, the man he said was Claude Ryan. It was Roy. Roy Shields. He was dead."

She looked surprised. "Roy. The quiet cowboy who never said two words. And you're sure Will Jarvis is an FBI agent?"

"Cash called. Agent Will Jarvis has been working with the Mexican government on the killings of the plastic surgeons and the possible connection to Claude Ryan," he said.

She seemed to breathe a sigh of relief. "What about the others?"

He shook his head. "They found the bodies of Slim Walker, Luke Adams and Nevada Black. Cotton's body was found part way down the mountain. He'd been shot in the back of the head."

Her eyes filled with tears.

He covered her hand, still feeling sick. "It's over. Claude Ryan is dead. He won't be hurting anyone else."

She nodded and turned his hand, pressing it to her lips. He could feel her breath against his palm, warm and moist, and he thanked God that she was alive and safe. He didn't know what he would have done if Claude had gotten her.

She looked up into his eyes and he felt desire spark and begin to burn through him. Desire and something deeper, something that made him ache to take her in his arms.

"I've decided to do your commercial."

She looked so surprised, he wanted to laugh.

She shook her head. "No, you don't have to do that. I don't want you doing it because—"

"I'm not." He wasn't sure what she'd been about to say. He didn't want her thinking he was doing this because of what they'd shared in the cave. "Make the arrangements. The sooner the better."

He just wanted to get it over with. He didn't want to delve into his reasons for agreeing after swearing that nothing could change his mind. He'd been wrong about that, wrong about a lot of things.

"This isn't the way I wanted it," she said, and he thought she might cry.

"I thought you would take it any way you got it," he said, unable to hide his surprise. "You said it meant *everything* to you."

She shook her head and said nothing. He wheeled her down the hallway to the kitchen where his mother was waiting. She waved him away, saying she and Regina were going to get acquainted. He hated to think.

But as he looked out the window, he saw almost six hundred head of cattle coming across the valley toward the ranch. "I'm going to go help bring in the cattle," he said.

Neither woman seemed to notice.

As he left, he told himself he'd made the right decision about the commercial. A few years of grief over his backside was nothing. He couldn't let Reggie lose everything. He felt responsible, no matter what he said.

He tried not to think past that because he knew once the commercial was over and Reggie's ankle was healed, she'd probably be eager to get back to Los Angeles and her life there.

And that was just what he wanted too, he told himself as he went out to saddle his horse and go meet the herd.

SHELBY QUIZZED Regina over a breakfast of steak, eggs, biscuits with butter and honey, fresh fruit and juice.

Regina was surprised how hungry she was. A woman who'd never eaten breakfast in her life and she was eating like a truck driver.

"You really need to tell him," Shelby said when Regina had finished eating.

Regina looked up in surprise. "Tell who what?"

"My son James Thomas," she said. "You need to tell him how you feel about him."

Regina opened her mouth, closed it and opened it again. "I…I don't think that's a good idea. He already feels guilty enough about everything that's happened."

Shelby just smiled sadly. "He might be a little confused right now. He *is* a man. They're easily confused. He's doing the commercial, isn't he?"

Regina nodded, a little confused herself. What was it his mother thought she should tell him?

Shelby looked thoughtful for a moment. "Maybe it would be better to wait. At least until after the commercial." She got up. "Let me take you back to your room. You look as if you might fall asleep right there in that chair."

After Shelby helped her back into bed, Regina picked up the phone and dialed Anthony's number at Way Out West Jeans. "It's me."

"You don't sound good, sweetie."

"The commercial is a go. Get everyone up here."

"Your cowboy agreed to do it? Oh I knew you could pull this off." She wanted to tell him not to call McCall her cowboy. "Sweetie, why aren't you jumping up and down for joy? You did it!"

Yes, she thought. She'd done it. Unfortunately, it was a hollow victory. Her driving ambitions had changed over the past few days. Changed since she'd met J. T. McCall. But she wasn't about to tell Anthony that any more than she was McCall himself. She knew how he felt about city girls. Especially this city girl.

He'd only agreed to the commercial because he felt responsible for what had happened at the cow camp and the cave and he wanted to get rid of her. By the time the commercial was shot, her ankle would be strong enough for her to leave.

"I can have the crew there within days," Anthony was saying. "This is such great news for everyone here. You're going to pull this off, darling, so be happy."

"Yes," she said, finding herself close to tears. She'd forgotten that she wasn't the only one who was counting on this commercial's success. She had everyone at the jeans company to consider. She was doing the right thing. So why didn't it feel like it?

Because she knew the only reason McCall was doing the commercial was because he felt like he was to blame for everything that had happened.

She hung up, feeling miserable.

CHAPTER FIFTEEN

Regina watched the filming from the bedroom window. Since she couldn't see it from the wheelchair, she stood, hiding at the edge of the drapes, not wanting to be seen.

She knew McCall must be hating every moment of it. She had been getting better every day and knew there was nothing to keep her here after today. The commercial shoot would be over, the crew would leave and she would have no choice but to go back to Los Angeles.

The problem was she didn't want to leave. She'd fallen in love with McCall. She wasn't sure when it had happened exactly but the thought of leaving here, of never seeing him again, broke her heart.

She'd also fallen in love with his family. Crusty old Asa was a sweetheart under that rough exterior. He reminded her of Buck but more cantankerous. Buck was out of the hospital and convalescing in the other guest room. Shelby was an amazing woman, very perceptive and loving.

Regina had come to know eighteen-year-old Dusty McCall. Dusty had been reserved at first but now came up to talk about boys with her. Regina smiled at the memory of their "talks."

Rourke was still on his honeymoon, but she felt as if she knew him from everything she'd heard about him. Brandon was quiet around her, almost shy. Something was going on with him. He'd been sneaking out at night and meeting some woman. At least that was the family scuttlebutt. Everyone wanted to know who Brandon's secret woman was, but he wasn't talking.

She'd only seen Cash a few times. He seemed the most serious of the McCalls. Dusty had filled her in on Cash's lost love from college. Jasmine Wolfe had been on her way to Antelope Flats to meet his parents so the two could announce their engagement. But Jasmine never made it. She disappeared and was never found. Brokenhearted, Cash had stayed single all these years, pining away for her.

The McCalls were full of stories. The only McCall she hadn't seen much of was J.T. He seemed to be keeping his distance making it clear he just wanted the jeans commercial over with so the ranch could get back to normal.

Tears burned her eyes. She brushed at them, angry with herself. She'd never been a woman who cried at the drop of a hat. Until recently. She blamed the horror of what she'd been through, but knew it had more to do with her feelings for McCall. The dire situation at Way Out West Jeans. Her conflict of interests.

Through the window, she watched the film crew set up the next shot, the director signaling J.T. to ride through the scene. She hated the way the commercial romanticized his life, almost devaluing the man and his rugged, hard-earned lifestyle, which she had come to admire.

"It's just a commercial," she said to herself in the empty room. But it wasn't. This commercial would make millions of dollars for Way Out West Jeans. Hadn't that been the plan? It would launch the line, take the company national—public—and change her life.

She just hadn't figured on it changing her life this much.

The contrast between her world and McCall's was so extreme…and suddenly she didn't feel like she belonged in either. She'd changed and in ways she couldn't even comprehend yet.

She looked out across the land and felt an ache for all this space—and for that man down there on the horse. She didn't want to leave this ranch—or McCall.

J.T. COULDN'T BELIEVE Reggie had gone to all this trouble for a stupid television commercial. It wasn't bad enough that she'd almost gotten herself killed, she'd turned his ranch into a circus.

This commercial didn't reflect his life in the least. She could have gotten herself some L.A. model and saved herself a lot of money, time and trouble. Not to mention save him a lot of grief.

He knew why he was in such a bad mood. This was the last shoot. Then it was over. The commercial and Reggie. He wondered how long she'd stay once the commercial was shot. She was probably packing at this moment. He swore at the thought.

As he rode across the set, he told himself that this was how Reggie saw him and his lifestyle. As a fantasy western life straight out of the movies. She didn't want the reality in her commercial any more than she wanted it in her life.

He swore under his breath as he heard the director yell, "Cut! Let's try that one more time."

J.T. trotted back to the man. Anthony Grant. Reggie's friend. He seemed like a nice enough man but after fourteen "takes," J.T. had had it.

He rode up to him and leaned down so only Anthony

could hear. "I think you meant to say, 'That's a wrap,'" J.T. said, meeting the man's gaze.

Anthony squirmed under J.T.'s intent stare. "Yes," he said. "I see your point. I think that last one was perfect." He raised his voice. "That's a wrap."

"Thank you." J.T. rode toward the barn. He couldn't wait to get these clothes off, couldn't wait to get these people off the ranch, couldn't wait for things to get back to normal.

Normal meant Reggie leaving, he reminded himself. He couldn't believe the way his family had taken to her. But then she could be quite adorable. The thought made him ache.

He'd done his level best to keep her at a distance. At night though, he would weaken and think about going to her, holding her, making love to her, begging her not to go.

And that is exactly why he hadn't gone to her.

She couldn't stay even if she had wanted to. It was perfectly clear how much all of this meant to her. He'd seen how responsible she felt for the crew and knew she was banking on this commercial selling a lot of jeans. And that was her life. L.A. and blue jeans. Not the Sundown Ranch and cows.

He swung off his horse and kicked at a dirt clod, angry with himself for letting the woman get to him. Well, she had what she wanted. There wouldn't be anything keeping her on the ranch now that the commercial was done. Her career meant everything to her. Everything, she'd said.

Even if she'd had a change of heart—which she hadn't or she wouldn't have let him do the commercial—she would never fit in here on the ranch. The woman couldn't cook anything but pancakes! And he had no intentions of living in the main ranch house with a hired cook and housekeeper. He'd always wanted to build a place a few miles from here. There was a perfect spot in the foothills.

But he wanted it to be just the two of them. Until the kids came along. Although, knowing Reggie she could get the hang of being a ranchwoman—if she set her mind to it.

He shook himself, amazed where his mind had taken him. But damned if for a moment he hadn't imagined that log house with Reggie and a houseful of little McCalls running around in cowboy boots.

"Damn," he said under his breath. The last thing he wanted was for Reggie to go back to L.A. and that scared the hell out of him.

He thought of his own parents. All those years apart because as much chemistry as they'd had between them, they couldn't live together.

He realized that could be him and Reggie.

J.T. looked up and saw Cash driving up in his patrol car. He'd already had Brandon giving him a hard time, saying things like "nice duds" and "nice ass." He didn't need Cash getting his two cents in. J.T. was just thankful that Rourke wasn't around. That would be the last straw.

He'd managed to keep the filming of the commercial quiet. He'd take the storm once the commercial hit national television.

Cash got out, glanced at the fake western set, and shook his head.

"Don't ask," J.T. said. "What are you doing here?"

"You agreed to do the commercial?" Cash sounded more than a little surprised as he glanced from J.T. to the set, looking as if he'd suddenly been dropped into Hollywood. His speculative gaze came back to his brother. "I don't believe it. Why would you do that?"

"Don't read anything into it," J.T. snapped. "She was going to lose her job. She almost got killed up at the line shack. I owed her."

"Uh-huh," Cash said nodding.

"What?" J.T. demanded, scowling at his brother.

"I ran a check on her." He held up his hands and stepped back as if he thought J.T. would take a swing at him. "I ran a check on everyone at that line shack. It's my job. J.T. She wasn't about to lose her job. She *owns* the company."

He could only stare at Cash. Reggie owned Way Out West Jeans?

"But that's not what I came out to talk to you about," Cash said. "Can we talk in the barn for a minute?"

J.T. didn't like the sound of this. He followed his brother over to the barn, still trying to digest what Cash had told him. How was it possible that Reggie owned the company? She'd made it sound as if her career was riding on this commercial. Was it possible the woman had conned him? He almost laughed.

Reggie had won. He'd done the commercial. She must be gloating in her room at the back of the house. His mother had given her the first-floor guest room so she could get around in the wheelchair until her ankle was better. There was no doubt that she'd played on the sympathy of his family—and him as well. She knew he felt responsible for everything that had happened to her.

Well now that the commercial was in the can, her ankle would be miraculously better and she'd be on the next plane to L.A.

"I have some bad news," Cash said without preamble once inside the barn. "We just got a positive ID on the man you called Roy Shields. His real name is Roy Sanders. He's with the FBI."

J.T. felt all the air rush out of him, knowing what was coming.

"Roy Sanders was working on a case with Mexico involving the deaths of three plastic surgeons."

"If Roy was the FBI agent, then Will Jarvis—"

"An FBI agent by the name of Will Jarvis was also on the case," Cash said. "I got a photo of Will Jarvis the FBI agent faxed to me. No resemblance to the wounded man you knew as Jarvis. Sheridan, Wyoming, had Claude Ryan's DNA from a rape charge when he was about nineteen. The hospital had a blood sample of the man who called himself Will Jarvis. The DNA samples matched. The man you know as Will Jarvis is really Claude Ryan."

J.T. knew what was coming. "He isn't in the hospital in Billings anymore, is he."

Cash shook his head. "He survived surgery and had been moved to a private room to recover. After I got the news about Roy, I had the DNA samples checked and sent police to the hospital to detain Claude Ryan, but he was gone. The others found one of the doctors dead in the hospital room closet, naked. Claude had stolen the man's clothing. The doctor's car is also missing."

J.T. thought about the talk he'd had with Will Jarvis around his campfire. He hadn't been waiting for Claude Ryan to come to kill him. He'd been waiting for the FBI agent Roy Sanders. Claude had just been playing with him. He could have killed him then. So why didn't he?

"When we went back up to the line shack nine years

ago, we found drag marks and grizzly tracks. We also found boot prints but with everyone tromping around up there searching… We'd been so sure the grizzly had gotten him," Cash said.

"He had help getting away," J.T. replied, the pieces starting to fall together as he thought about what Will Jarvis had said about the burn scars on Slim's hands. J.T. remembered the fear he'd seen in Slim's eyes. Slim had known that one of the men in camp was Claude Ryan. But like J.T., he wouldn't have recognized the man's face because of all the plastic surgery Claude had been through. The only people who had seen Claude after the surgeries were the doctors and they were all dead.

J.T. felt his heart take off as he looked toward the ranch house. "Claude is alive." And he wasn't finished. He'd somehow gotten Slim and Luke to the line shack to kill them.

"I have the state police on their way down here to make sure the ranch is safe—"

But J.T. wasn't listening, he was already running toward the ranch house, afraid he was too late.

REGINA HEARD the bedroom door open behind her. She'd been so intent on her thoughts that she hadn't realized that the shooting of the commercial was over, everyone packing it in. She didn't see J.T. anywhere. Time had run out.

She turned, realizing she couldn't leave here without telling J.T. the truth. She'd fallen in love with him.

But it wasn't J.T. standing in the doorway. She stared at the man, at first too shocked to react. And then it was too late. Before she could scream or move, Will Jarvis grabbed her, pressing the tip of the knife blade into her side, the blade biting through her shirt to her skin, his hand covering her mouth as he whispered next to her ear, "Make a sound and I'll kill you."

Her mind raced. This man wasn't an FBI agent. Oh God, he was Claude Ryan. He dragged her out the back door, the same way he'd come in. She'd been given this room because it was on the first floor at the back and had easy wheelchair access.

With all the commotion of the commercial, no one noticed as he dragged her across a small patch of lawn then through the trees toward what appeared to be an old shed.

The lock on the shed door had been broken, she noticed as he pulled her inside and shoved her hard against the wall.

The shed was long and narrow, dark except for a little light sifting in through a small dirty window. It took a moment for her eyes to adjust.

He smiled, looking her over. "I saw the number you did on J.T." He laughed. "You had him where he didn't know if he was coming or going. What the hell was he thinking hiring someone like you to cook at a cow camp?"

"He didn't hire me. Buck did," she said, lifting her chin, determined not to let him see her fear. Men like him fed off fear. She seemed to know that instinctively. Just as she had never trusted him.

He drew back a little in surprise and smiled. "You're a feisty one, you are. I still can't believe you got out of the cabin before it burned to the ground."

She took a breath and tried to calm her pounding pulse as her eyes adjusted to the semidarkness inside the shed and objects began to take shape. An old stool, some garden tools against the far wall, several old wooden buckets, a few old doors leaning against the wall next to her, lots of cobwebs and dust.

She shivered at the thought of spiders and realized how ridiculous that fear was right now. She was in an old shed with a crazy man with a gun and a penchant for killing.

One thing was for certain. She didn't want to die in this shed. Not before she told McCall how she felt about him. A week ago she couldn't have imagined herself in this predicament, not in a thousand years. Not only had she never been in love, but she'd also certainly never been through what she had the past few days.

But because of both, she felt stronger, more capable and she had every reason to want to live. She took in the junk in the shed, decided what would make the best weapon. This man wasn't going to kill her without her putting up a fight.

"You tried to burn me up in the cabin?" Her voice broke, betraying her a little. "Why are you doing this?"

Meanness shone like insanity in his eyes. "You have no idea what it's like to feel your flesh on fire, to feel it melting off your face." He put the gun into his pocket and took out a knife, rotating it back and forth so the blade caught the dim light. He stared at the blade as if hypnotized by the flicker of light and dark. "I have been under the knife so many times I lost count. I knew I couldn't come back until I had a new face, one that showed no sign of the scarring."

"You wanted a new face just so you could get revenge?" she asked, unable to hide her astonishment.

He glared at her as he put the knife away and pulled a length of cord from his pocket, advancing on her. "I survived only to get my revenge. So many times I wanted to die, but then I would think about J. T. McCall, back here on his big ranch."

"What a waste of your life, revenge," she said, almost feeling sorry for the man. She couldn't imagine what demons motivated him, only that he was a tormented man, obsessed with J. T. McCall.

"Shut up," he snapped and moved toward her, just as she knew he would, anger and hate in his eyes. "I am going to set this shed on fire and watch it burn from the hills just beyond here. I will hear your cries when your flesh melts like mine did. J.T. will hear your cries but he won't be able to save you. He won't be able to save himself. I will kill you both slowly. With J.T., an inch at a time, taking from him everything, just as he did me."

He was close enough now. She grabbed the edge of the doors and pushed with all her strength as she dodged to the side. The old heavy doors toppled over, hitting him in the shoulder, making him shriek in pain just before the stack thundered to the shed floor in a cloud of dust.

She ran for the shed door but he was on her before she could reach it. She let out a scream and he slapped her, knocking her to the floor. That's when she saw the gas cans in the corner. New cans and she knew that's how he intended to burn down the shed—with her in it.

"WHAT IS IT?" his mother cried as J.T. ran through the house to the back guest room and threw open the door to Reggie's room. She was gone!

"Have you seen Reggie?" he demanded, not surprised to find his mother and sister behind him. They both shook their heads.

"She was in here packing, planning to leave as soon as

the commercial was over," Shelby said, accusingly. "She was upset."

He glanced around the room. Her suitcase was open on the bed, packed, ready to leave. But he'd seen her little red rental sports car on his way into the house. It was parked out front.

"See if she is outside with the crew," he said, glancing toward the back door. "I'm going to check out back. If you find her, keep her with you."

"James Thomas, what is going on?" his mother demanded.

"The killer could have her." And then he was gone out the back door. He hadn't gone but a few feet into the trees when he saw the fresh tracks.

His mother had insisted on an area of lawn behind the house and Asa had had sod put in and a sprinkler system that came on every few hours during the summer.

The grass was wet now from early frost. So was the ground at the edge of the lawn. Boot tracks. And another track where someone had been dragged, heels digging into the wet earth.

He looked up and saw the old shed in the distance and began to run toward it. He hadn't gone far when he heard something heavy crash to the floor and then a scream.

REGINA TRIED to fight Claude off but he was too strong for her. He held her down while he began to bind her wrists in front of her with the cord.

She kicked and screamed until he hit her again, making her see stars. He bound her ankles, holding her down where she couldn't kick out at him. The shed floor was rough against her back as he pressed her into the wood a dust. She struggled to breathe, the pressure of his body on her heavy and painful. And then he released her.

She futilely fought the cords he'd put around her wrists and ankles, as she heard the splash of liquid against the walls and smelled the gasoline.

J.T. HIT THE SHED DOOR, bursting into the shed in time to see Claude Ryan dumping gasoline on the floor of the shed.

Claude stopped when he saw J.T., dropping the can to pull the knife. He smiled. "You're a little early. The party hasn't started." Claude had a lighter in his other hand, his thumb poised over it, ready to flick the flame to life.

J.T. saw Reggie on the floor behind Claude. She was bound, eyes wide in the dim darkness. If Claude ignited the shed from where he stood, he wouldn't be able to get out. But then neither would J.T. be able to get to Reggie in time.

"You do that and you will burn up in this shed," J.T. said, looking at the lighter. He thought about rushing the man but knew Claude would set the shed on fire if he did. "I'm not letting you past me. I'll die first."

Claude Ryan laughed. "You'll die first all right." His expression turned mean. "Do you know how long I've waited for this day, J. T. McCall?" He glanced over his shoulder for just an instant at Reggie. "I have something you want for a change and there is nothing you can do about it."

"You would burn up in this shed to even some score between us?" J.T. saw the insanity in Claude's gaze, knew this had never really been about him. It was something in- [illegible] Claude Ryan, something sick that had only gotten [illegible] lignant over the years.

[illegible] d Claude, J.T. saw Reggie. She had pushed herself against the wall and managed to get to her feet. Balancing precariously, ankles and wrists still bound, she worked her way over to the shovels leaning against the wall. Did she hope to cut the cord on the dull blade of the shovel? He knew it was futile. No way was Claude going to give either of them that much time.

"I know you," Claude said smiling again. "You won't be able to live with yourself if you can't save the damsel in distress." He flicked on the lighter. The flame flared, catching a light in Claude Ryan's eyes that chilled J.T. to his soul. Claude tossed the lighter toward the wall he'd just soaked with gasoline.

But only an instant before, Reggie had gripped the shovel handle and throwing her body into it, managed to swing the shovel as she fell.

The shovel blade caught Claude in the center of the back. Off balance and not expecting the attack from behind, Claude was knocked against the wall as the lighter dropped, the flame licking at the gasoline and the air suddenly whooshed in a bright loud boom—Claude right at the center.

Flames leapt on him, setting his clothing on fire in an instant. He shrieked, arms and legs flailing in a dance of horror as his body went up in a blaze.

J.T. dove for Reggie, sweeping her up in his arms and lunging out the door of the shed an instant before it exploded.

EPILOGUE

J.T. CAME OUT of the barn, swearing under his breath as he looked toward the ranch house. Christmas lights blinked through the falling snow. His mother's doing. She had announced that they were going to have an old-fashioned Christmas this year.

He'd caught her crying just this morning as she was wrapping presents.

"I'm just feeling a little sentimental," she'd said when he asked her if something was wrong. "This is my first Christmas with all of you."

He hadn't pointed out that it had been her choice—and his father's. He'd just nodded and left the room, running into Rourke and Cassidy. They'd come back from their honeymoon and had taken over one wing of the house until they could break ground on their place in the spring.

He'd never seen Rourke so content or happy. Even Dusty was getting along better with Shelby, although like the rest of them she wasn't calling her Mother yet. Brandon was obviously still seeing his mystery girlfriend and actually seemed to be enjoying working on the ranch. He was to start law school next fall.

Cash had come out to help their mother decorate and put up strings and strings of lights. Asa had insisted on getting the Christmas tree, riding up into the hills to bring back a huge tree that was now glittering in the living room.

It was as if his entire family had been transformed into a Christmas special. Everyone seemed to be in good spirits except him.

He still had nightmares about fires. Only this time Claude died in the shed fire. Cash and the state investigators found his body and made a positive identification based on the DNA samples. Claude Ryan was dead. J.T. paid to have him buried at the local cemetery. He'd even bought him a stone that read May He Rest In Peace under his name and dates.

He and Reggie had talked before she left for Los Angeles. She'd admitted that she owned the jeans company. It had been passed down to her by her mother and grandmother, but it was in trouble financially. She had to make one last-ditch attempt to change the company's image. Her mother and grandmother were depending on her.

She'd never wanted the company, never wanted that life to be hers but hadn't known anything different because she'd been raised in the garment industry.

But neither her mother or grandmother had realized the need to change the company's image until it was too late. Both were broke. It had been left up to Reggie to save the company and take care of her mother and grandmother.

She was sure this new commercial promotion would do it. Then she had intended to take the company public, set up a trust fund for her mother and grandmother and finally get a chance to decide what she wanted out of life.

J.T. had listened to how she had to return to Los Angeles to finish what she'd started.

"I want to come back," she'd said. "Back here, that is if..."

He'd been so surprised he hadn't said anything for a moment. And he certainly hadn't said what was in his heart. He believed that once she got back to Los Angeles, she would never want to return to Montana. Not to a ranch in the middle of nowhere. Not to this life. Once she'd gotten the jeans company back on its feet and sold it, she'd have enough money to do whatever she wanted. He couldn't imagine she would want Montana ranch life or him.

"You know you're always welcome here," he'd said.

She nodded, biting down on her lower lip, tears in her eyes. "I'm sorry I didn't tell you everything from the beginning."

"It wouldn't have made any difference," he said. The commercial had come out. He was now known as Hollywood McCall in town. It hadn't been as bad as he'd thought it would be. He tried not to catch the commercial when it came on TV. It only reminded him of Reggie. He just hoped the promotion turned her jeans company around and that she was happy.

As he walked through the snowstorm toward the house, he realized he would do the commercial over in a heartbeat just to have Reggie back here. His whole family had missed her after she'd left but not half as much as he did.

Hell, he'd fallen for her against every ounce of common sense he'd ever had. And his heart broke to think that he would probably never see her again.

As he neared the house, he heard laughter over the sound of Christmas music and started to turn around and go back to the barn. He had no Christmas spirit this year, wasn't sure he would ever again.

"McCall?"

He looked up at the sound of her voice, caught half-turning back toward the barn.

She was standing at the end of the porch, her dark hair floating around her shoulders. She had on a sheepskin coat, jeans and boots and she looked so right standing next to the ranch house that his heart just stopped.

"Reggie?" He thought he must be seeing things.

"I told you I'd be back." The snow fell around her as she stepped off the porch and came toward him. "The commercial promotion worked. I don't have to worry about my mother and grandmother anymore. I'm free."

He just stared at her. Was she saying what he hoped she was?

"I love you, James Thomas McCall. I had to come back and tell you."

"Reggie." His voice broke and his feet were moving and she was smiling at him, crying, running toward him now. He threw his arms around her. Nothing had felt more right than holding her.

Snowflakes drifted down around them. She snuggled against him. "Merry Christmas, McCall."

He pulled back to look down into her face. "Oh Reggie, I love *you.* Merry Christmas." He kissed her, lifting her into his arms. He would have carried her away but the Christmas music seemed to grow louder and when he raised his lips from hers, he saw his entire family on the porch. They began to applaud.

And he realized how much he loved them and needed them. This was going to be the best Christmas he'd ever had. But it was only the first of many. He put his arm around Reggie and they walked back toward the ranch house and his family.

* * * * *

SHOTGUN SURRENDER

This one is for Kayley Mendenhall.
A ray of sunshine for everyone who has had the honor of knowing her. Best wishes for a bright, fun and romantic future!

PROLOGUE

The moment the pickup rolled to a stop, Clayton T. Brooks knew he should have put this off until morning. The night was darker than the inside of an outhouse, he was half-drunk and he couldn't see two feet in front of him.

Hell, maybe he was more than half-drunk since he was still seriously considering climbing the nearby fence and getting into a pasture with a bull that had almost killed its rider at a rodeo just a few days ago in Billings, Montana.

To make matters worse, Clayton knew he was too old for this sort of thing, not to mention physically shot from years of trying to ride the meanest, toughest bulls in the rodeo circuit.

But he'd never had the good sense to quit—until a bull messed him up so bad he was forced to. Just like now. He couldn't quit because he'd come this far and, damn, he needed to find out if he was losing his mind. Quietly he opened his pickup door and stepped out.

He'd coasted down the last hill with his headlights out, stopping far enough from Monte Edgewood's ranch house that he figured his truck wouldn't be heard when he left. There was no sign of life at the Edgewood Roughstock Company ranch at this hour of the night, but he wasn't taking any chances as he shut the pickup door as quietly as possible and headed for the pasture.

If he was right, he didn't want to get caught out here. The whole thing had been nagging him for days. Finally tonight, he'd left the bar when it closed, climbed into his pickup and headed out of Antelope Flats. It wasn't far to the ranch but he'd had to make a stop to get a six-pack of beer for the road.

Tonight he was going to prove himself wrong—or right—he thought as he awkwardly climbed the fence and eased down the other side. His eyes hadn't quite adjusted to the dark. Wisps of clouds drifted low across the black canvas stretched on the horizon. A few stars twinkled millions of miles away, and a slim silver crescent moon peeked in and out.

Clayton started across the small pasture, picking his way. Just over the rise, he froze as he made out the shape of the bull dead ahead.

Devil's Tornado was a Braford brindle-horned, one-ton bull—a breeder's Molotov cocktail of Brahma and Hereford. The mix didn't always turn out good bucking bulls, but it often did. The breed had ended more than a few cowboys' careers, his included.

He stared at the huge dark shape standing just yards from him, remembering how the bull had damn near killed the rider at the Billings rodeo a few days before.

The problem was, Clayton thought he recognized the bull, not from Billings but from a town in Texas some years before. Thought he not only recognized the bull, but knew it intimately—the way only a bull rider gets to know a bull.

Unless he was losing his mind, he'd ridden this brindle down in Texas four years ago. It had been one of his last rides.

Only back then, the bull had been called Little Joe. And Little Joe had been less than an exciting ride. No tricks. Too nice to place deep on and make any prize money on.

The other bulls in the roughstock contractor's bag hadn't had any magic, either—the kiss of death for the roughstock contractor. Last Clayton had heard the roughstock outfit had gone belly-up.

Earlier tonight, he'd finally remembered the roughstock contractor's name. Rasmussen. The same last name as the young man who'd showed up a few weeks ago with a handful of bulls he was subcontracting out to Monte Edgewood.

If Clayton was right—and that was what he was here to find out—then Little Joe and Devil's Tornado were one and the same.

Except that the bull at the Billings rodeo had been a hot-tempered son-of-a-bucker who stood on its nose, hopped, skipped and spun like a top, quickly unseating the rider and nearly killing him. Nothing like the bull he'd ridden in Texas.

But Clayton was convinced this bull was Little Joe. Only with a definite personality change.

"Hey, boy," he called softly as he advanced. "Easy, boy."

The bull didn't move, seemed almost mesmerized as Clayton drew closer and closer until he could see the whites of the bull's enormous eyes.

"Hello, Little Joe." Clayton chuckled. Damned if he hadn't been right. Same notched ears, same crook in the tail, same brindle pattern. Little Joe was Devil's Tornado.

Clayton stared at the docile bull, trying to make sense of it. How could one bull be so different, not only from years ago but also from just days ago?

A sliver of worry burrowed under Clayton's skull. He

definitely didn't like what he was thinking because if he was right…

He reached back to rub his neck only an instant before he realized he was no longer alone. He hadn't heard anyone approach from behind him, didn't even sense the presence until it was too late.

The first blow to the back of his head stunned him, dropping him to his knees next to the bull.

He flopped over onto his back and looked up. All he could make out was a dark shape standing over him and something long and black in a gloved hand.

Clayton didn't even get a chance to raise an arm to ward off the second blow with the tire iron. The last thing he saw was the bull standing over him, the silver sickle moon reflected in the bull's dull eyes.

CHAPTER ONE

Antelope Flats, Montana
County Rodeo Grounds

As the last cowboy picked himself up from the dirt, Dusty McCall climbed the side of the bucking horse chute.

"I want to ride," she said quietly to the elderly cowboy running this morning's bucking horse clinic.

Lou Whitman lifted a brow as he glanced down at the only horse left in the chute, a huge saddle bronc called The Undertaker, then back up at her.

He looked as if he was about to mention that she wasn't signed up for this clinic. Or that The Undertaker was his rankest bucking bronc. Or that her father, Asa McCall, or one of her four brothers, would have his behind if they found out he'd let her ride. Not when she was supposed to be helping "teach" this clinic—not ride.

But he must have seen something in her expression, heard it in her tone, that changed his mind.

He smiled and, nodding slowly, handed her the chest protector and helmet. "We got one more," he called to his crew.

She smiled her thanks at Lou as she took off her western straw hat and tossed it to one of the cowboys nearby.

Slipping into the vest, she snugged down the helmet as Lou readied The Undertaker.

Swallowing any second thoughts, she lowered herself onto the saddle bronc in the chute.

None of the cowboys today had gone the required eight seconds for what was considered a legal rodeo ride.

She knew there was little chance of her being the first. Especially on the biggest, buckingest horse of the day.

She just hoped she could stay on long enough so that she wouldn't embarrass herself. Even better, that she wouldn't get killed!

"What's Dusty doing in there?" one of the cowboys along the corral fence wanted to know. "Dammit, she's just trying to show us up."

She ignored the men hanging on the fence as she readied herself. Bucking horses were big, often part draft horse and raised to buck. This one was huge, and she knew she was in for the ride of her life.

Not that she hadn't ridden saddle broncs before. She'd secretly taken Lou Whitman's clinic and ridden several saddle broncs just to show her brothers. Being the youngest McCall—and a girl on top of it—she'd spent her first twenty-one years proving she could do anything her brothers could—and oftentimes ended up in the dirt.

She doubted today would be any different. While she no longer felt the need to prove anything to herself and could care less about what her four older brothers thought, she had to do this.

And for all the wrong reasons.

"Easy, boy," she said as the horse banged around in the chute. She'd seen this horse throw some darned good cowboys in the past.

But she was going to ride him. One way or another. At least for a little while.

The horse shook his big head and snorted as he looked back at her. She could see her reflection in his eyes.

She leaned down to whisper in his ear, asking him to let her ride him, telling him how she needed this, explaining how much was at stake.

She could hear the cowboys, a low hum of voices on the corral fence. She didn't look, but imagined in her mind one in particular on the fence watching her, his dark eyes intrigued, his interest piqued.

Her body quaking with anticipation—and a healthy dose of apprehension—she gave Lou a nod to open the gate.

In that split second as the gate swung out, she felt the horse lunge and knew The Undertaker didn't give a damn that she was trying to impress some cowboy. This horse had his own agenda.

He shot straight up, jumped forward and came down bucking. He was big and strong and didn't feel like being ridden—maybe especially by her. Dust churned as he bucked and twisted, kicking and lunging as he set about unseating her.

But she stayed, remembering everything she'd been taught, everything she'd been teaching this morning along with Lou. Mostly, she stuck more out of stubborn determination than anything else.

She vaguely heard the sound of cheers and jeers over the pounding of hooves—and her heart.

When she heard the eight-second horn signaling she'd completed a legal rodeo ride, she couldn't believe it.

Too late, she remembered something her father always warned her about: pride goeth before the fall.

More than pleased with herself, she'd lost her focus for just an instant at the sound of the horn and glanced toward the fence, looking for that one cowboy. The horse made one huge lunging buck, and Dusty found herself airborne.

She hit the ground hard, the air knocked out of her. Dust rose around her in a cloud. Through it, she saw a couple cowboys jump down into the corral, one going after the horse, the other running to her.

Blinking through the dust, she tried to catch her breath as she looked up hoping to see the one cowboy she'd do just about anything to see leaning over her—Boone Rasmussen.

"You all right?" asked a deep male voice.

She focused on the man leaning over her and groaned. Ty Coltrane. The *last* cowboy she wanted to see right now.

"Fine," she managed to get out, unsure of that but not about to let him know if she wasn't.

She managed to sit up, looking around for Boone but didn't see him. The disappointment hurt more than the hard landing. Just before she'd decided to ride the horse, she'd seen Boone drive up. She'd just assumed he would join the others on the corral fence, that for once and for all, he would actually take notice of her.

"That was really something," Ty Coltrane commented sarcastically as he scowled down at her. Ty had been the bane of her existence since she'd been born. He raised Appaloosa horses on a ranch near her family's Sundown Ranch and every time she turned around, he seemed to be there, witnessing some of her most embarrassing moments—and causing more than a few.

And here he was again. It never failed.

She took off the helmet, her long blond braid falling

free. Ty took the helmet and motioned to the cowboy on the fence, who tossed her western straw hat he'd been holding for her. It sailed through the air, landing short.

Ty picked it up from the dirt and slapped the dust off against his jeaned thigh. "Yep, that one could go down in the record book as one of the dumber things I've seen you do, Slim." He handed her the hat, shaking his head at her.

As a kid, she'd been a beanpole, all elbows and knees, and she'd taken a lot of teasing about it. It had made her self-conscious. Even when she began to develop and actually had curves, she'd kept them hidden under her brothers' too large hand-me-down western shirts.

"Don't call me that," she snapped, glaring at him as she shoved the hat down on her blond head, tucking the single long braid up under it as she did.

He shook his head as if she mystified him. "What possessed you to ride The Undertaker? Have you lost all sense?"

The truth was, maybe she had. She didn't know what had gotten into her lately. Not that as a kid she hadn't always tried to be one of the boys and ride animals she shouldn't have. It came with being raised on an isolated ranch with four older brothers and their dumb friends.

That, and the fact that for most of her life, she'd just wanted to fit in, be one of the boys—not have them make fun of her, but treat her like one of their own.

All that had changed a few weeks ago when she'd first laid eyes on Boone Rasmussen. Suddenly, she didn't want to blend in anymore. She didn't want to be one of the boys. She felt things she'd only read about.

Now all she wanted was to be noticed by Boone Rasmussen.

And apparently there was no chance in hell of that ever happening.

"Here," Ty said extending a hand to help her up.

She ignored it as she got to her feet on her own and tried not to groan as she did. She'd be sore tomorrow if she could move at all. That *had* been a fool thing to do, but not for the reason Ty thought. She'd only done it to get Boone's attention. She couldn't believe she'd been so desperate, she thought as she took off the protective vest. Ty took it as well and handed both vest and helmet to one of the cowboys along the fence.

She hated feeling desperate.

Being that desperate made her mad and disgusted with herself. But the problem was, even being raised with four older brothers, she knew nothing about men. She hadn't dated much in high school, just a few dances or a movie. The boys she'd gone out with were like her, from God-fearing ranch families. None had been like Boone Rasmussen.

She realized that might be the problem. Boone was a *man.* And Boone had a reckless air about him that promised he was like no man *she'd* ever known.

"Nice ride," one of the cowboys told her as she limped out of the corral.

"Don't encourage her," Ty said beside her.

There was a time she would have been busting with pride. She'd ridden The Undertaker. She'd stayed on the eight seconds for the horn.

But today wasn't one of those days. The one cowboy she'd hoped to impress hadn't even seen her ride.

"You don't have to go telling my brothers about this," she warned Ty.

He grunted. "I have better things to do than go running to your brothers with stories about you," he said. "Anyway, the way you behave, it would be a full-time job."

She shot him a narrow-eyed look, then surreptitiously glanced around for Boone Rasmussen, spotting him over by the bull corrals talking to the big burly cowboy who worked with him, Lamar something or other.

Boone didn't even glance in her direction and obviously hadn't seen her ride or cared. Suddenly, she felt close to tears and was spitting mad at herself.

"You sure you're all right?" Ty asked as he reached to open her pickup door for her.

She could feel his gaze on her. "I told you I'm fine," she snapped, fighting tears. What was wrong with her? She normally would rather swallow tacks than cry in front of him or one of her brothers.

"You're sure you're up to driving back to the ranch by yourself?" he asked, only making her feel worse.

She fought a swell of emotion as she climbed into the pickup seat and started to close the door.

Ty stopped her by covering her hand on the door handle with his. "Okay, Slim, that was one hell of a ride. You stayed on longer than any of those cowboys. And you rode The Undertaker. Feel better?"

She looked at him, tears welling in her eyes. He thought she was mad at *him* because he'd chewed her out for riding today?

She half smiled at him, filled with a sudden stab of affection. Funny, but since Boone, she even felt differently about Ty.

Unlike Boone though, Ty had blue eyes like her own. There was no mystery about Ty. She'd known him her whole life. Boone on the other hand, had dark eyes, mysterious eyes, and everything about him felt…dangerous.

"You wouldn't understand even if I could explain it," she said.

Ty smiled ruefully and reached out to pluck a piece of straw from a stray strand of her blond hair. "Probably not, Slim, but maybe it's time you grew up before you break your fool neck." He let go of her hand and she slammed the pickup door. So much for the stab of affection she'd felt for him.

Grow up? Without looking at him, she started the truck and fought the urge to roll down her window and tell him what she thought. But when she glanced over, Ty had already walked away.

She sat for a moment in a stew of her own emotions. The worst part was, Ty was right. It was definitely time for her to grow up. Too bad she didn't have the first clue how to do that.

She shifted the pickup into gear. Boone Rasmussen was still talking to Lamar by the chutes. He didn't look up as she pulled away.

TY MENTALLY KICKED HIMSELF all the way to his truck. He'd only come by the rodeo grounds this morning to see if Clayton T. Brooks was around. The old bull rider hadn't shown up for work.

Everyone said Ty was a fool for hiring him. Even part-time. But Clayton was a good worker and Ty knew Clayton needed the money. Sometimes he showed up late, but he always showed for work. Until today.

"Any of you seen Clayton today?" he called to the handful of men on the corral fence. Several of the cowboys were trying to get Lou to let them ride again. Couldn't let some little gal like Dusty McCall show them up.

"Saw him at the bar *last night,*" one of them called back. "He was three sheets to the wind and going on about some bull." The cowboy shook his head. "You know Clayton. Haven't seen him since, though." The rest shook their heads in agreement.

"Thanks." Ty *did* know Clayton. For most of his life, Clayton had ridden bulls. Now that he couldn't ride anymore, he "talked" bulls. Or talked "bull," as some said.

Still, Ty was worried about him. He decided to swing by Clayton's trailer on the opposite side of town before returning to the ranch.

Dusty McCall drove past as Ty climbed into his truck. He let out a sigh as he watched her leave. All he'd done was make her mad. But the fool girl could have gotten herself killed. What had been going on with her lately?

Not your business, Coltrane.

Didn't he know it.

In spite of himself, he smiled at the memory of her riding that saddle bronc. She was something, he thought with a shake of his head. Unfortunately, she saw him at best as the cowboy next door. At worst, as another older brother, as if she needed another one.

He shook off that train of thought like a dog shaking off water and considered what might have happened to Clayton as he started his pickup and drove into town.

Antelope Flats was a small western town with little more than a café, motel, gas station and general store. The main business was coal or coal-bed methane gas. Those who worked either in the open-pit coal mine or for the gas companies lived twenty-plus miles away in Sheridan,

Wyoming, where there was a movie theater, pizza parlors, clothing stores and real grocery stores.

Between Antelope Flats and Sheridan there was nothing but sagebrush-studded hills and river bottom, and with deer, antelope, geese, ducks and a few wild turkeys along the way.

Antelope Flats had grown some with the discovery of coal-bed methane gas in the land around town. There was now a drive-in burger joint on the far edge of town, a minimall coming in and talk of a real grocery store.

Ty hoped to hell the town didn't change too much in the coming years. This was home. He'd been born and raised just outside of here, and he didn't want the lifestyle to change because of progress. He knew he sounded like his father, rest his soul. But family ranches were a dying breed and Ty wanted to raise his children on the Coltrane Appaloosa Ranch just as he'd been raised.

Clayton T. Brooks had bought a piece of ground out past town and put a small travel trailer on it. The trailer had seen better days. So had the dated old pickup the bull rider drove. The truck wasn't out front, but Ty parked in front of the trailer and got out anyway.

The sun was high in a cloudless blue sky. He could smell the cottonwoods and the river and felt the early spring heat on his back as he knocked on the trailer.

No answer.

He tried the door.

It opened. "Clayton?" he called as he stepped into the cool darkness. The inside was neater than Ty had expected it would be. Clayton's bed at the back looked as if he'd made it before he left this morning. Or hadn't slept in it last night. No dishes in the sink. No sign that Clayton had been here.

As Ty left, he couldn't shake the bad feeling that had settled over him. Yesterday, Clayton had been all worked up over some bull ride he'd seen the weekend before at the Billings rodeo.

Ty hated to admit he hadn't been listening that closely. Clayton was often worked up about something and almost always it had to do with bulls or riders or rodeo.

Was it possible Clayton had taken off to Billings because of some damn bull?

TEXAS-BORN BOONE RASMUSSEN had been cursed from birth. It was the only thing that explained why he'd been broke and down on his luck all twenty-seven years.

He left the rodeo grounds and drove the twenty miles north of town turning onto the road to the Edgewood Roughstock Company ranch. The road wound back in a good five more miles, a narrow dirt track that dropped down a series of hills and over a creek before coming to a dead end at the ranch house.

Boone could forgive those first twenty-seven years if he had some promise that the next fifty were going to be better. He was certainly due for some luck. But he'd been disappointed a few too many times to put much stock in hope. Not that his latest scheme wasn't a damned good one.

He didn't see Monte's truck as he parked in the shade of the barn and glanced toward the rambling old two-story ranch house. A curtain moved on the lower floor. She'd seen him come back, was no doubt waiting for him.

He swore and tried to ignore the quickened beat of his

heart or the stirring below his belt. At least he was smart enough not to get out of the truck. He glanced over at the bulls in a nearby pasture, worry gnawing at his insides, eating away at his confidence.

So far he'd done two things right—buying back a few of his father's rodeo bulls after the old man's death and hooking up with Monte Edgewood.

But Boone worried he would screw this up, just like he did everything else. If he hadn't already.

He heard someone beside the truck and feared for a moment she had come out of the house after him.

With a start, he turned to find Monte Edgewood standing at the side window. Monte had been frowning, but now smiled. "You goin' to just sit in your pickup all day?"

Boone tried to rid himself of the bitter taste in his mouth as he gave the older man what would pass for a smile and rolled down his window. Better Monte never know why Boone had been avoiding the house in his absence.

"You all right, son?" Monte asked.

Monte Edgewood had called him son since the first time they'd met behind falling-down rodeo stands in some hot, two-bit town in Texas. Boone had been all of twelve at the time. His father was kicking the crap out of him when Monte Edgewood had come along, hauled G. O. Rasmussen off and probably saved Boone's life.

In that way, Boone supposed he owed him. But what Boone hadn't been able to stand was the pity he'd seen in Monte's eyes. He'd scrambled up from the dirt and run at Monte, fists flying, humiliation and anger like rocket fuel in his blood.

A huge man, Monte Edgewood had grabbed him in a bear hug, pinning his skinny flailing arms as Boone struggled furiously to hurt someone the way he'd been hurt. But Monte was having none of it.

Boone fought him, but Monte refused to let go. Finally spent, Boone collapsed in the older man's arms. Monte released him, reached down and picked up Boone's straw hat from the dust and handed it to him.

Then, without a word, Monte just turned and walked away. Later Boone heard that someone jumped his old man in an alley after the rodeo and kicked the living hell out of him. Boone had always suspected it had been Monte, the most nonviolent man he'd ever met.

Unfortunately, Boone had never been able to forget the pity he'd seen in Monte's eyes that day. Nor the sour taste of humiliation. He associated both with the man because of it. Kindness was sometimes the worse cut of all, he thought.

Monte stepped back as Boone opened his door and got out. Middle age hadn't diminished Monte's size, nor had it slowed him down. His hair under his western hat was thick and peppered with gray, his face rugged. At fifty, Monte Edgewood was in his prime.

He owned some decent enough roughstock and quite a lot of land. Monte Edgewood seemed to have everything he needed or wanted. Unlike Boone.

But what made Monte unique was that he was without doubt the most trusting man Boone had ever met.

And that, he thought with little remorse, would be Monte's downfall. And Boone's good fortune.

"How's Devil's Tornado today?" Boone asked as they walked toward the ranch house where Monte had given him a room. He saw the curtain move and caught a glimpse of dyed blond hair.

"Son, you've got yourself one hell of a bull there," Monte said, laying a hand on Boone's shoulder as they mounted the steps.

Didn't Boone know it.

Monte opened the screen and they stepped into the cool dimness of the house and the heady scent of perfume.

"Is that you, Monte?" Sierra Edgewood called an instant before she appeared in the kitchen doorway, a sexy silhouette as she leaned lazily against the jamb and smiled at them. "Hey, Boone."

He nodded in greeting. Sierra wore a cropped top and painted-on jeans, a healthy width of firm sun-bronzed skin exposed between the two. She was pinup-girl pretty and was at least twenty years younger than her husband.

"It will be interesting to see how he does in Bozeman," Monte continued as he slipped past his wife, planting a kiss on her neck as he headed for the fridge. He didn't seem to notice that Sierra was still blocking the kitchen doorway as he took out two cold beers and offered one to Boone.

After a moment, Sierra moved to let Boone pass, an amused smile on her face.

"He's already getting a reputation among the cowboys," Monte said heading for the kitchen table with the beers as if he hadn't noticed what Sierra was up to. He never seemed to. "Everyone's looking for a high-scoring bull and one hell of a ride."

Boone sat down at the table across from Monte and took the cold beer, trying to ignore Sierra.

"Are you talking about that stupid bull again?" she asked as she opened the fridge and took out a cola. She popped the cap off noisily, pushing out her lower lip and giving Boone the big eyes as she sat down across from him.

A moment later, he felt her bare toes run from the top of his boot up the inside seam of his jeans. He shifted, turning to stretch his legs out far enough away that she couldn't touch him as he took a deep drink of his beer. He heard Sierra sigh, a chuckle just under the surface.

He knew he didn't fool her. She seemed only too aware of what she did to him. His blood running hot, he focused on the pasture out the window and Devil's Tornado, his ticket out, telling himself all the Sierra Edgewoods in the world couldn't tempt him. There was no greater lure than success. And failure, especially this time, would land him in jail—if not six feet under.

Devil's Tornado could be the beginning of the life Boone had always dreamed of—as long as he didn't blow it, he thought, stealing a sidelong glance at Sierra.

"Everyone's talking about your bull, son," Monte said with pride in his voice but also a note of sadness.

Boone looked over at him, saw the furrowed thick brows and hoped Monte was worried about Devil's Tornado—not Boone and his wife.

There was a fine line between a bull a rider could score on and one who killed cowboys. And Devil's Tornado had stomped all over that line at the Billings rodeo. Boone couldn't let that happen again.

Sierra tucked a lock of dyed-blond hair behind her ear and slipped her lips over the top of the cola bottle, taking a long cool drink before saying, "So what's the problem?"

Monte smiled at her the way a father might at his young child. "There's no problem."

But that wasn't what his gaze said when he settled it back on Boone.

"The bull can be *too* dangerous," Boone told her, making

a point he knew Monte had been trying to make. "It's one thing to throw cowboys—even hurt a few. But if he can't be ridden and he starts killing cowboys, then I'd have to take him off the circuit." He shrugged as if that would be all right. "He'd be worth some in stud fees or an artificial insemination breeding program at this point. But nothing like he would be if, say, he was selected for the National Finals Rodeo in Las Vegas. It would be too bad to put him out to pasture now, though. We'd never know just how far he might have gone."

A shot at having a bull in the National Finals in Las Vegas meant fifty thousand easy, not to mention the bulls he would sire. Everyone would want a piece of that bull. A man could make a living for years off one star bull.

That's why every roughstock producer's dream was a bull like that. Even Monte Edgewood, Boone was beginning to suspect. But only the top-scoring bulls in the country made it. Devil's Tornado seemed to have what it took to get there.

"I wouldn't pull him yet," Monte said quickly, making Boone smile to himself. Monte had needed a bull like Devil's Tornado.

And Boone needed Monte's status as one of the reputable roughstock producers.

After more rodeos, more incredible performances, everyone on the circuit would be talking about Devil's Tornado. That's when Boone would pull him and start collecting breeding fees, because it wouldn't matter if the bull could make the National Finals. Boone could never allow Devil's Tornado to go to Vegas.

But in the meantime, Devil's Tornado would continue to cause talk, his value going up with each rodeo.

If the bull didn't kill his next rider.

Or flip out again like he did in Billings, causing so much trouble in the chute that he'd almost been pulled.

Devil's Tornado was just the first. If this actually worked, Boone could make other bulls stars. He could write his own ticket after that.

But he could also crash and burn if he got too greedy, if his bulls were so dangerous that people got suspicious.

Monte finished his beer and stared at the empty bottle. "I don't have to tell you what a competitive business this is. You've got to have good bulls that a cowboy can make pay for them. But at the same time you don't want PETA coming down on you or those Buck the Rodeo people."

Boone had seen the ads—Buck the Rodeo: Nobody likes an eight-second ride!

Monte looked over at him. "When I got into this business, I promised myself that the integrity of the rodeo and the safety of the competitors would always come first. You know what I'm saying, son?"

Boone knew *exactly* what he was saying. He looked out the window to where Devil's Tornado stood in his own small pasture flicking his tail, the sun gleaming off his horns, then back across the table at Sierra Edgewood. Boone had better be careful. More careful than he had been.

CHAPTER TWO

Sundown Ranch

Asa McCall heard the creak of a floorboard. He turned to find his wife standing in the tack room doorway. His wife. After so many years of being apart, the words sounded strange.

"What do you think you're doing?" Shelby asked, worry making her eyes dark.

"I'm saddling my horse," he said as he hefted the saddle and walked over to the horse. The motion took more effort than it had even a few weeks ago. He hoped she hadn't noticed, but then Shelby noticed everything.

"I can see that," she said, irritation in her tone as she followed him.

Shelby Ward McCall was as beautiful as the day he'd met her forty-four years ago. She was tall and slim, blond and blue-eyed, but her looks had never impressed him as much as her strength. They both knew she'd always been stronger than he was, even though he was twice her size—a large, powerfully built man with more weaknesses than she would ever have.

He wondered now if that—and the fact that they both knew it—had been one of the reasons she'd left him thirty years ago. He knew damn well it was the reason she had come back.

"I'm going for a ride," he said, his back to her as he cinched the saddle in place, already winded by the physical exertion. He was instantly angry at himself. He despised frailty, especially in himself. He'd always been strong, virile, his word the last. He'd never been physically weak before, and he found that nearly impossible to live with.

"Asa—" Her voice broke.

"Don't," he said shaking his head slightly, but even that small movement made him nauseous. "I need to do this." He hated the emotion in his voice. Hated that she'd come back to see him like this.

Shelby looked away. She knew he wouldn't want her to see how pathetic he'd become. He wished he could hide not only his weakness but his feelings from her, but that was impossible. Shelby knew him with an intimacy that had scared him. As if she could see into his black soul and still find hope for him. Still love him.

"I could come with you," she said without looking at him.

"No, thank you," he added, relieved when she didn't argue the point. He didn't need a lecture on how dangerous it was for him to go riding alone. He had hoped to die in the saddle. He should be so lucky.

He swung awkwardly up onto the horse, giving her a final look, realizing how final it would soon be. He never tired of looking at her and just the thought of how many years he'd pushed her away from him brought tears to his eyes. He'd become a doddering sentimental old fool on top of everything else. He spurred the horse and rode past her and out of the barn, despising himself.

At the gate, something stronger than even his will forced him to turn and look back. She was slumped against the barn wall, shoulders hunched, head down.

He cursed her for coming back after all the years they'd lived apart and spurred his horse. Cursed himself. As he rode up through the foothills of the ranch his father had started from nothing more than a scrawny herd of longhorn cattle over a hundred years ago, he was stricken with a pain far greater than any he had yet endured.

His agony was about to end, but it had only begun for his family. He would have to tell them everything.

He tried not to think about what his sons and daughter would say when he told them that years ago, he'd sold his soul to the devil, and the devil was now at his door, ready to collect in more ways than one.

J.T., his oldest, would be furious; Rourke would be disappointed; Cash would try to help, as always; and Brandon possibly would be relieved to find that his father was human after all. Dusty, his precious daughter, the heart of his heart… Asa closed his eyes at the thought of what it would do to her.

He would have to tell them soon. He might be weak in body and often spirit, but he refused to be a coward. He couldn't let them find out everything after he was gone. Not when what he'd done would put an end to the Sundown Ranch as they all knew it.

Sheridan, Wyoming, rodeo

IT WAS FULL DARK and the rodeo was almost over by the time Ty Coltrane made his way along the packed grandstands.

He'd timed it so he could catch the bull riding. No one he'd talked to had seen Clayton, nor had there been any word. But Ty knew that if Clayton was anywhere within a hundred-mile radius, he wouldn't miss tonight's rodeo.

Glancing around before the event started, though, he didn't see the old bull rider. He did, however, see Dusty McCall and her friend, Leticia Arnold, sitting close to the arena fence.

Dusty didn't look the worse for wear after her bucking bronc performance earlier today. He shook his head at the memory, telling himself he was tired of playing nursemaid to her. She wasn't his responsibility. He couldn't keep picking her up from the dirt. What if one day he wasn't around to save her skinny behind?

"Now in chute three, we've got a bull that's been making a stir across the country," the announcer bellowed over the sound system. "He's called Devil's Tornado and for a darned good reason. Only a few cowboys have been able to ride him, and those who have scored big. Tonight, Huck Kramer out of Cheyenne is going to give it a try."

Ty felt a start. Devil's Tornado. *That* was the bull that Clayton had been so worked up over. Ty was sure of it. He angled his way through the crowd so he could see the bull chutes as he tried to recall what exactly Clayton had said about the bull.

Devil's Tornado banged around inside the chute as Huck lowered himself onto it to the jangle of the cowbell attached to his rosin-coated bull rope. The cowbell acted as a weight, allowing the rope to safely fall off the bull when the ride was over. Riders used rosin, a sticky substance that increased the grip on their ropes, to make sure they were secured to the bull in hopes of hanging on for the eight-second horn.

Huck wrapped the end of the bull rope tightly around his gloved hand, securing himself to the one-ton bull. Around the bull was a bucking rigging, a padded strap that was designed to make the bull buck.

A hush fell over the crowd as the bull snorted and kicked at the chute, growing more agitated. Huck gave a nod of his head and the chute door flew open with a bang and Devil's Tornado came bursting out in a blur of movement.

Instantly, Ty knew this was not just any bull.

So did the crowd. A breath-stealing silence fell over the rodeo arena as Devil's Tornado slammed into the fence, then spun in a tight bucking cyclone of dust and hooves.

Devil's Tornado pounded the earth in bucking lunges, hammering Huck with each jarring slam. Ty watched, his heart in his throat as the two-thousand pound bull's frantic movements intensified in a blur of rider and bull.

The crowd found its voice as the eight-second horn sounded and bullfighters dressed like clowns rushed out.

With his hand still tethered to the monstrous bull, Huck's body suddenly began to flop from side to side, as lifeless as a dummy's, as Devil's Tornado continued bucking.

The bullfighters ran to the bull and rider, one working frantically to free the bucking rigging from around the bull and the other to free Huck's arm from the thickly braided rope that bound bull and rider.

Devil's Tornado whirled, tossing Huck from side to side, charging at the bullfighters who tried desperately to free the rider. One freed the rigging strap designed to make the bull buck. It fell to the dirt, but Huck's bull rope wouldn't come loose. The cowbell jangled at the end of the rope as Huck flopped on the bull's broad back as the bull continued to buck and spin in a nauseating whir of motion.

Other cowboys had jumped into the arena, all fighting to free Huck. It seemed to go on forever, although it had only been a matter of seconds before one of the bullfighters pulled a knife, severing Huck from Devil's Tornado.

Huck's lifeless body rose one last time into the air over the bull, suspended like a bag of rags for a heart-stopping moment before it crumpled to the dirt.

The crowd swelled to its feet in a collective gasp of horror as the rider lay motionless.

Devil's Tornado made a run for the body. A bullfighter leapt in front of the charging bull and was almost gored. He managed to distract the bull away from Huck, but only for a few moments.

The bull started to charge one of the pickup riders on horseback, but stumbled and fell. He staggered to his feet in a clear rage, tongue out, eyes rolling.

Cowboys jumped off the fence to run to where Huck lay crumpled in the dirt. A leg moved. Then an arm. Miraculously, Huck Kramer sat up, signally he was all right.

A roar of applause erupted from the grandstands.

"That was some ride," the announcer said over the loudspeaker. "Let's give that cowboy another round of applause."

Ty sagged a little with relief. He hated to see cowboys get hurt, let alone killed. Huck had been lucky.

Ty's gaze returned to Devil's Tornado. The bull ran wild-eyed around the other end of the arena, charging at anything that moved, sending cowboys clambering up the fence. Ty had seen this many times during bull rides at rodeos.

Devil's Tornado was big and strong, fast out of the chute and one hell of a bucker, but those were attributes, nothing that would have gotten Clayton worked up.

"Whew," the announcer boomed. "Folks, you aren't going to believe this. The judges have given Huck a whopping ninety-two!"

The crowd cheered as Huck was helped out of the arena. He seemed to be limping but, other than that, okay.

Had Clayton just been impressed by Devil's Tornado? No. Ty distinctly remembered that Clayton had been upset, seemingly worried about something he'd seen at the Billings rodeo involving Devil's Tornado. But what?

The pickup riders finally cornered the bull, one getting a rope around the head and a horn and worked him toward the exit chute. Devil's Tornado pawed the earth, shaking his head, fighting them.

Ty worked his way in the direction of the exit chute, hoping to get a closer look. As Devil's Tornado was being herded out, he seemed disoriented and confused, shying away from anything that moved.

Usually, by the time a bull got to the exit chute, he recognized that it was over and became more docile. Not Devil's Tornado. He still seemed worked up, maybe a little high-strung, stopping when he saw the waiting semitrailer, looking scared and unsure. Still, not that unusual for a bull that had just scored that high a ride.

Ty wouldn't have thought anything more about the bull if he hadn't seen Boone Rasmussen rush up to the exit chute and reach through the fence to touch the still aggravated Devil's Tornado. What the hell? Ty couldn't see what Boone had done, but whatever it was made the bull stumble back, almost falling again. Rasmussen reached again for the bull, then quickly withdrew his hand, thrusting it deep into his jacket pocket.

How strange, Ty thought. Devil's Tornado was frothing at the mouth, his head lolling. Ty saw the bull's eyes. Wide and filled with…panic? Devil's Tornado looked around crazily as if unable to focus.

Ty tried to remember where he'd seen that look on a bull before and it finally came to him. It had been years ago in a Mexican bull ring. He was just a kid at the time, but he would never forget that crazed look in the bull's eyes.

Is this what Clayton had witnessed? Is this what had him so upset? Had Clayton suspected something was wrong with Devil's Tornado, just as Ty did? But what would Clayton have done about it?

Ty wasn't even sure what he'd just witnessed. All he knew was: something was wrong with that bull. And Boone Rasmussen was at the heart of it.

"DID YOU SEE THAT?" Letty asked, sitting next to her friend.

Dusty stared through the arena fence toward the chutes and Boone Rasmussen, not sure what she'd seen or what she was feeling right now. "See what?"

Letty let out an impatient sigh. "Don't tell me you missed the entire bull ride because you were gawking at Boone Rasmussen."

Dusty looked over at her friend, surprised how off balance she felt. She let out a little chuckle and pretended she wasn't shaking inside. "Some ride, huh."

But it wasn't the ride that had her hugging herself to ward off a chill on such a warm spring night. She wasn't sure what she'd seen. Letty, like everyone else, had been watching Huck Kramer once the bull had gone into the chutes.

Dusty had been watching Boone. That's why she'd seen the expression on his face when he reached through the fence and hit Devil's Tornado with something. Not a cattle prod but something else. The bull had been in her line of sight, so she couldn't be sure what it had been.

Boone Rasmussen's expression had been so…cold. It all happened so fast—the movement, Boone's expression. But there was that moment when she wondered if she'd made a mistake when it came to him. Maybe he wasn't what she was looking for at all.

TY MOVED ALONG the corrals to the exit chute where Devil's Tornado now stood, head down, unmoving. Rasmussen stood next to the fence as if watching the bull, waiting. Waiting for what?

A chill ran the length of his spine as Ty stared at Devil's Tornado. This had to be what Clayton had seen. The look in that bull's eyes and Rasmussen acting just as strangely as the bull.

"Where do you think you're going?" Lamar Nichols stepped in front of him, blocking his view of the bull and Rasmussen.

Ty looked past the big burly cowboy to where Rasmussen prodded the bull and Devil's Tornado stumbled up into the trailer. Rasmussen closed the door behind it with a loud clank.

A shudder went through Ty at the sound. "That's some bull you got there."

"He don't like people." Lamar stepped in front of him,

blocking his view again. "Unless you're authorized to be back here, I suggest you go back into the stands with the rest of the audience."

Ty looked past Lamar and saw Rasmussen over by the semitrailer. "Sure," Ty said to the barrel-chested cowboy blocking his way. No chance of getting a closer look now.

He knew if he tried, Lamar would call security or take a swing at him. Ty didn't want to create that much attention.

As Ty headed back toward the grandstand, he searched the crowd for Clayton T. Brooks with growing concern. Now more than ever, he wanted to talk to the old bull rider about Devil's Tornado and what had happened at the Billings rodeo that had riled Clayton.

But Ty didn't see him in the crowd or along the fence with the other cowboys. Where was Clayton anyway? He never missed a rodeo this close to home.

"THANKS FOR HANGING AROUND with me," Dusty McCall said as she and her best friend, Leticia Arnold, walked past the empty dark grandstands after the rodeo.

The crowd had gone home. But Dusty had waited around, coming up with lame excuses to keep her friend there because she hadn't wanted to stay alone—and yet she'd been determined not to leave until she saw Boone.

But she never got the chance. Either he'd left or she just hadn't seen him among the other cowboys loading stock.

"I'm pathetic," Dusty said with another groan.

Letty laughed. "No, you're not."

"It's just..." She waved her hand through the air unable to explain all the feelings that had bombarded her from the first time she'd laid eyes on Boone a few weeks before. He was the first man who'd ever made her feel like this, and it confused and frustrated her to no end.

"Are you limping?" Letty asked, frowning at her.

"It's nothing. Just a little accident I had earlier today," Dusty said, not wanting to admit she'd ridden a saddle bronc just to impress Boone and he hadn't even seen her ride. She hated to admit even to herself how stupidly she'd been behaving.

"Are you sure Boone's worth it?" Letty asked.

Right at that moment, no.

"He just doesn't seem like your type," her friend said.

Dusty had heard all of this before. She didn't want to hear it tonight. Especially since Letty was right. She didn't understand this attraction to Boone any more than Letty did. "He's just so different from any man I've ever met," she tried to explain.

"That could be a clue right there."

Dusty gave her friend a pointed look. "You have to admit he *is* good-looking."

"In a dark and dangerous kind of way, I suppose," Letty agreed.

Dark and dangerous. Wasn't that the great attraction, Dusty thought, glancing back over her shoulder toward the rodeo arena. She felt a small shiver as she remembered the look on his face when he'd reached through the fence toward the bull. She frowned, realizing that she'd seen something drop to the ground as Boone pulled back his hand. Something that had caught the light. Something shiny. Like metal. Right after that Monte had picked whatever it was up from the ground and pocketed it.

"You're sure he told you to meet him after the rodeo?" Letty asked, not for the first time.

Dusty had told a small fib in her zeal to see Boone tonight. On her way back from getting a soda, she'd seen Boone, heard him say, "Meet me after the rodeo." No way was he talking to her. He didn't know she existed. But when she'd related the story to Letty, she'd let on that she thought Boone had been talking to her.

"Maybe I got it wrong," Dusty said now.

Maybe she'd gotten everything wrong. But that didn't explain these feelings she'd been having lately. If she hadn't been raised in a male-dominated family out in the boonies and hadn't spent most of her twenty-one years up before the sun mending fence, riding range and slopping out horse stalls, she might know what to do with these alien yearnings. More to the point, what to do about these conflicting emotions when it came to Boone Rasmussen.

Instead, she felt inept, something she wasn't used to. She'd always been pretty good at everything she tried. She could ride and rope and round up cattle with the best of them, and she'd been helping run the ranch for the past few years since her father's heart attack.

But even with four older brothers, she knew squat about men. Well, one man in particular, Boone Rasmussen. And after tonight, she felt even more confused. She wasn't even sure that once she got his attention, talked to him, that she would even like him. Worse, she couldn't get that one instant, when he'd reached through the fence, out of her mind. What had fallen on the ground?

"Dusty?" Letty was a few yards ahead, looking back at her.

Dusty hadn't realized that she'd stopped walking.

But then again, she was a McCall. She'd been raised to go after what she wanted. And anyway, she couldn't wait around for Boone to make the first move. Heck, she could be ninety before that happened. She was also curious about what Boone had dropped. Stubborn determination and unbridled curiosity, a deadly combination.

"Oh, shoot, I forgot something," Dusty said, already walking backward toward the arena. "I'll talk to you later, okay?"

Letty started to argue with her, but then just nodded with a look that said she knew only too well what Dusty was up to.

She thought again about the look she'd seen on Boone's face earlier and felt a shiver as she wandered back through the dark arena.

The outdoor arena looked alien with all the lights off, no crowds cheering from the empty stands, no bulls banging around in the chutes or cowboys hanging on the fences. Even the concession stands were locked up.

As Dusty headed toward the chutes, stars glittered in the dark sky overhead. The scent of dust, manure and fried grease still hung in the air. She felt a low hum in her body that seemed to grow stronger as she neared the chutes, as if the night were filled with electricity.

The same excited feeling she'd had the first time she'd seen Boone Rasmussen a few weeks before. He'd been sitting on a fence by the bull chutes, his cowboy hat pulled low over his dark eyes. He'd taken her breath away and set something off inside her. Since then, Dusty hadn't been able to think straight.

Like now. If she had a lick of sense, she'd turn around and hightail it out of here. She heard the scuffle of feet in the dirt behind the chutes, a restless whisper of movement and saw a dozen large shapes milling inside a corral. The bucking horses.

The roughstock contractor hadn't finished loading up. That meant Boone could still be here since he had been working with Monte Edgewood, who provided the stock for the rodeo. Maybe Boone had stayed behind to help load the horses.

She climbed over the gate into the chutes. It was dark, but the stars and distant lights of the city cast a faint glow over the rodeo grounds. She moved along the chutes, stopping when she heard voices.

She looked past the empty corral and the one with the bucking horses and saw what appeared to be several cowboys. All she could really see were their hats etched against the darkness. Boone? She couldn't be sure unless she got a little closer.

Climbing over the fence, she dropped into an empty corral next to the one with the bucking horses. On the cool night breeze came the low murmur of voices. She felt her stomach roil as she tried to think of what she would say to Boone if that was him back there.

Unfortunately, she found herself tongue-tied whenever she saw him. She'd never had trouble speaking her mind. Quite the opposite. What the devil was wrong with her?

She knew she couldn't keep trying to get his attention the way she would have when she was ten. She had a flash of memory of her bucking horse ride earlier and Boone completely missing it. She still hurt from the landing. And the humiliation of her desperation.

Through the milling horses, she caught sight of the dark silhouette of three cowboy hats on the far side of the corrals. She couldn't see enough of the men to tell if one of them was Boone. It was too dark, and the horses blocked all but the men's heads and shoulders.

She stepped on one rung of the fence and tried to peer over the horses, surprised to hear the men's voices rise in anger. She couldn't catch the words, but the tone made it clear they were in a dispute over something.

She recognized Boone's voice and could almost feel the anger in it. Suddenly, it stopped. Eerie silence dropped over the arena.

Hurriedly she dropped back down into the corral, hoping he hadn't seen her, but knowing he must have. She felt her face flush with embarrassment. What if he thought she was spying on him? Or even worse, stalking him?

BOONE CAUGHT MOVEMENT beyond the horses in the corral and held up his hand to silence the other two.

A light shone near the rodeo grounds exit, but the arena and corrals lay in darkness. He stared past the horses, wondering if his eyes had been playing tricks on him. Through a break in the horses, he saw a figure crouch down.

"Go on, get out of here," he whispered.

Lamar nodded and headed for the semitruck and trailer with Devil's Tornado inside.

Boone glanced at Waylon Dobbs. The rodeo veterinarian looked scared and ready to run, but he hadn't moved.

"Who is it?" Waylon whispered.

Boone motioned with an impatient shake of his head that he didn't know and for Waylon to leave. "I'll take care of it. Go. We're finished here anyway."

Slipping through the fence into the corral with the bucking horses, Boone used the horses to conceal himself as he worked his way to the far gate—the gate that would send the massive horses back into the corral where he'd just seen someone spying on them.

Had the person heard what they'd been saying? He couldn't take the chance. Everyone knew accidents happened all the time when nosy people got caught where they didn't belong.

The horses began to move restlessly around the corral, nervous with him among them. His jaw tightened as he thought about who was just beyond the horses. He couldn't see anyone, but he knew the person was still there.

Carefully, he unlocked the gate and stepped back in the shadows out of the way of the horses. Whoever had been spying on him was in for a surprise.

CHAPTER THREE

Ty Coltrane cupped his hands around his eyes and tried to see into the dark semitrailer. He could smell the bull, hear him breathing, but he couldn't see anything.

Unfortunately, there didn't seem to be anything to see. Devil's Tornado was so calm now that the bull had him doubting he'd seen anything unusual earlier.

Rodeo roughstock were raised to be as rank as possible. No one—not the bull rider, nor the audience—wanted a bull that didn't buck, that didn't put on show, that let the rider score big.

Devil's Tornado had done that and more.

So why had Ty stayed until the rodeo was over to sneak back here and get another peek at that bull? Because he couldn't forget what he'd seen in that bull's eyes. Or quit wondering what Rasmussen had done to the bull as it came down the exit chute.

But he wasn't going to find out anything tonight.

Earlier, he thought he'd heard voices over by the corrals, but hadn't been close enough to recognize them. When he'd been looking into the back of the semitrailer, he'd heard what sounded like the voices escalate into an argument.

But suddenly he realized that he couldn't hear them anymore. A sliver of worry burrowed itself under his skin. He didn't want to be caught back here snooping around the trailer. If he had reason to be suspicious, he didn't want Rasmussen or his cowboy thug getting wind of it.

He moved along the side of the trailer in time to see a short, squat figure moving toward a shiny black Lincoln. Veterinarian Waylon Dobbs.

The sound of the semitruck door opening made Ty jump. He peered between trailer and cab and caught a glimpse of Lamar Nichols a moment before the springs on the cab seat groaned under the big cowboy's weight. The semi's engine roared to life. Ty realized he'd be in clear view once the truck pulled away.

He glanced toward the horses in the corral and caught a glimpse of someone over by the gate. Boone Rasmussen.

In that instant, Ty felt a wave of apprehension as he realized that the voices he'd heard raised in argument had to have been those of veterinarian Waylon Dobbs, Boone Rasmussen and his employee, Lamar Nichols.

What the hell had they been arguing about? Devil's Tornado? Had the veterinarian seen what Ty had and confronted Rasmussen?

As Ty stared through the darkness past the horses, he heard the faint squeak of a gate and realized Rasmussen had just opened the gate to let the large bucking horses back through toward the arena.

Now why would he do that?

The semitruck pulled away and Ty made a run for the corrals hoping Lamar wouldn't glance back.

Ty hadn't gone two feet when he saw Lamar's face reflected in the side mirror. The cowboy slammed on the semi's brakes as Ty slipped through the corral fence, disappearing into the dark.

DUSTY LISTENED, afraid to move. She heard the sound of the semitruck engine and what could have been another vehicle starting to leave. She waited, crouched in the darkness just inside the empty corral.

She felt like a fool. Could her timing be any worse?

The bucking horses in the next corral began to mill nervously, as if they were also aware of her presence.

She really needed to get out of here—hopefully, without being seen again. She tucked her long blond braid up under her western straw hat and tried to see through the moving horses. Dust rose around them. Her legs were starting to cramp. She leaned forward, one hand holding on to her leather-fringed shoulder bag, the other dropping to the soft earth. Her fingers felt something cold and hard in the dirt.

Dusty squinted down, shocked to see a used syringe lying in the dirt. What if one of the horses had stepped on it? Or one of the cows had eaten it? Carefully, she picked it up with two fingers and dropped it into her shoulder bag, planning to throw it away as soon as she reached the trash cans. She forgot about it almost at once as she heard a sound behind her.

She didn't dare turn and look. Straightening, she took a breath, rose and started back across the empty corral as if she weren't dying of embarrassment. Several of the horses snorted, and suddenly the whole bunch began to lap the adjacent corral behind her.

She winced, realizing she must have spooked them. Leticia had been right. She shouldn't have come back here looking for Boone. What had happened to her common sense?

She was halfway across the corral when she heard a

gate groan open behind her. She turned, foolishly thinking all might not be lost. Maybe Boone had seen her and come after her. She tried to come up with a good excuse for being there.

But what she saw was the herd of huge bucking horses pour through the now open corral gate in a stream of pounding hooves, headed right for her.

Dusty started to run for the fence, her boots sinking in the soft turned earth. But she realized she wouldn't be able to reach it in time. She swung around, knowing the only way to keep from being trampled was to stand her ground.

As the horses thundered toward her, she waved her arms wildly, stomped her feet and yelled. The giant horses swelled around her, towering over her, the ground trembling under their weight, dust billowing up around them.

She could feel hot breath on the back of her neck as the dark shadows of the horses blocked any light from the stars above her. She waved, stomped and yelled as she edged back toward the fence.

A hand suddenly grabbed the back of her jean jacket and hauled her roughly up onto the rails as the horses circled the dark corral in a dusty stew.

She turned to face the man who'd just hauled her up on the fence, expecting to see Boone Rasmussen's handsome face.

"Ty?" she croaked, unable to hide her disappointment for the second time today. Ty Coltrane. "What are you doing here?" she demanded and shot a look past the corral. There was nothing but darkness where the three men had been earlier. In the distance, she heard the sound of vehicles leaving.

"How about, 'Ty, thank you for saving my skinny butt and not for the first time,'" he whispered, dragging her down off the fence. "Come on, let's get out of here."

She didn't argue. She could hear the horses racing around the corral behind her, which meant Boone would have a hard time getting them loaded now. If there was a chance he hadn't seen her...

She hightailed it through the space between the grandstands, glad for the darkness as Ty led her toward the nearly empty parking area.

"What were you doing back there?" Ty demanded once they were a good distance from the arena. He sounded like he always did after bailing her out of one of her messes. He was worse than one of her brothers.

"None of your business. Don't you get tired of following me around?"

It was too dark to see his blue eyes under the brim of his western straw hat. And she was glad of it. He shook his head at her as if he didn't know what to do with her. How about leaving her *alone?*

"My pickup's parked over there." He motioned toward the street and his black truck. Her tan ranch pickup was parked in the rodeo lot in the opposite direction. "Think you can make it home without getting into any more trouble?"

"I do just fine by myself, thank you very much." She mugged a face at him.

"Right."

She turned and stomped off toward her truck. It appeared to be the only one left in the lot. And to think earlier today she felt some semblance of affection for him.

As she neared the ranch truck, she realized there was

another rig parked on the other side, all but hidden by the size of her truck. She quickened her step. Was it possible Boone had been out here waiting for her this whole time?

Rounding the front of the truck, she saw that it was only Leticia's yellow VW Beetle. Letty leaned against the car, waiting.

Dusty felt a surge of emotion to see that her friend had waited for her.

"Did you see Boone?" Letty asked.

Dusty shook her head.

"What happened? You look like you got rolled in the dirt," Letty said, straightening in alarm.

Dusty recounted her tale of woe as Ty made a circle through the empty parking lot, slowing as if he planned to follow Dusty home. But he sped up, seemingly relieved to see Letty with her.

"Was that Ty Coltrane?" Letty asked, as surprised as Dusty had been to see him earlier.

"*Yes.*" She brushed at the dirt on her jeans feeling foolish. "Just my luck, I run into Ty instead of Boone."

"What was Ty still doing there?" Letty asked as he left.

What *had* he been doing hanging around the rodeo grounds this late? Dusty shook her head, thinking instead about the men she'd heard arguing.

"You couldn't tell who the men were that Boone was arguing with?" Letty asked.

Dusty shook her head. "Boone's voice was the only one I recognized and I couldn't hear what he was saying." The sound of a large truck engine made them both turn to look toward the rodeo grounds again. A semi-truck left by the back way.

The night suddenly seemed darker. A quiet fell over

the rodeo grounds. Only a few lights from town could be seen in the distance.

"I'd better get home." Letty started to get into her car, as if she were tired and did not want to hear any more about Boone.

Dusty couldn't blame her. She touched her sleeve. "Me, too." Things were weird enough at the ranch. Dusty didn't want her father worrying about her, and as long as she still lived in the main house… "Thanks for waiting for me."

Letty nodded and seemed to hesitate. "Sorry things didn't work out the way you'd hoped. Boone will come around."

Dusty smiled at her friend. Boone, she was beginning to realize, didn't just make her heart jump or her pulse pound. He made her crazy. No, she thought, he made her reckless, which right now seemed much worse. "Talk to you tomorrow."

Letty nodded and waited as Dusty got into the truck and started the engine. They'd brought separate vehicles because Letty had had to work late. Letty followed her all the way north as far as Antelope Flats before honking goodbye as she turned into the motel her parents had left her when they had retired.

Dusty continued north toward the ranch. Her disappointment hit her the moment she and Letty parted. She'd gone to the rodeo with such high hopes tonight.

She brushed at her tears of frustration. She hated feeling like this. Worse, acting like this.

Something flashed in her rearview mirror. She glanced back to see a set of headlights as a vehicle came roaring up the highway behind her.

The headlights grew brighter, as if whoever was driving was trying to catch her. She couldn't imagine who it could be, unless Ty had been waiting to follow her home. That would be just like him.

She shook her head and sped up. Because of the hour, there were no other vehicles on the road. The lights behind her grew brighter and brighter. She glanced back in the rearview mirror, surprised how fast the vehicle was coming up on her.

The headlights were high, the rig definitely a pickup. That might have narrowed it down in any other place except the ranching town of Antelope Flats, Montana, where trucks outnumbered cars ten to one.

The truck was right behind her now. She flipped the rearview mirror up so the lights weren't blinding her. But she was still silhouetted in the glare of them.

Ahead, through her own headlights, she could see the county road turnoff. She waited, expecting the truck behind her to pass. But instead, it stayed right behind her.

She touched her brakes, hoping the driver would back off. But he didn't and she had the horrible feeling that he planned to force her off the road.

As the turnoff came up, she took the turn onto the county dirt road a little fast, fishtailing on the ruts. Behind her a wall of dust kicked up under her tires.

Forced to slow a little on the washboard dirt road, she looked back and saw nothing but dust. She tried to relax, thinking she'd lost him. It had probably just been somebody with a few too many beers under his belt.

But she kept her speed up anyway. She knew this road, had driven it since she was twelve and had conned her dad into letting her get her license early, with the stipulation that she was only to drive on the ranch. That wasn't uncommon for ranch and farm kids in the state of Montana. What was uncommon was Asa McCall allowing it.

She hadn't realized how fast she was going until the pickup started to fishtail again on the washboard. Having driven more dirt roads than paved highway, she quickly got the pickup back under control and allowed herself to slow down a little.

In the distance, she could see the lights of the McCall ranch house and the turnoff to the ranch. Behind her, nothing but dust. Maybe.

She knew she'd have to slow down to make the turn onto the road down to the ranch, but once she did, she was sure no one would follow her up to the house. No one who knew the McCall men, anyway—and how protective they were.

Behind her, dust roiled up into the darkness. The entrance to the ranch road loomed in her headlights, the log arch, the sign: Sundown Ranch. Home. Safety. She'd never felt afraid here, didn't want to now.

She hit her brakes and cranked the wheel—glancing back as she did. The rearview mirror filled with headlights.

She swung through the ranch arch and onto the road that led to the ranch house, her pulse a war drum in her ears. The other rig had been right behind her!

Racing down the quarter-mile-long road to the house, she roared into the yard, shut off the engine and jumped out, ready to run as she looked back, half expecting to see the other rig coming after her. A few more stars had popped out, and there was just a sliver of moon.

As the dust settled, she felt her breath seize in her chest. A quarter mile back on the county road by the entrance to the ranch road, she could see the dark shape of a pickup, the headlights turned out. It was too far away and too dark to see who was behind the wheel. But the driver was sitting there in the darkness as if… Her heart began to pound furiously…as if watching her.

She turned and ran to the house. Racing up the steps and across the porch, she jerked open the door.

"What in the hell?" Asa McCall demanded as he came out of his den scowling at her. "I heard you come driving in. Are you drunk or just crazy, girl?"

"Someone followed me home." She pointed toward the road, shaking with fear.

Her father stepped out onto the porch and looked toward the gate. Asa was a big man with a reputation for being hard and uncompromising. Dusty knew he had a soft spot—at least where she was concerned. Soft spot or not, he would kill to protect his family.

"What are you talking about?" he demanded.

She moved to his side and followed his gaze. The dark shape of the pickup was gone, the road empty. "But he was just there."

"He?" Asa asked looking over at her.

"I just assumed it was a man," she said. "It was a pickup. Sitting up there by the gate with the headlights off. He chased me home."

Her father was still eyeing her. Dust hung like low clouds over the county road from where she'd raced home. Her father knew her, knew she didn't scare easily; he had to believe her.

"Was this some man you met at the rodeo?"

"No. I don't know who it was."

A muscle jumped in his jaw as he looked back out at the

road. "I don't like you hanging around a rodeo this late at night."

"I was with Letty."

He glanced down at her as if sensing the truth. It was as if he could smell it on her.

"Ty Coltrane was there, too," she added quickly, knowing how much her father liked Ty.

He glanced back toward the road. "I'll take a look around in the morning."

She touched his arm as he turned to go back inside. "Thank you." She hadn't realized how much she'd needed him to believe her.

He smiled at her and cupped her cheek with one callused hand before he left her on the porch, the door closing behind him.

Dusty stood listening to the sound of his footfalls disappear down the hall as she stared at the ranch gate. The county road was empty, the pickup gone. Had he turned around and gone back to town? Or gone on up the road?

Someone had chased her home. But for what purpose?

She started out to the truck to get her shoulder bag, still unnerved. Had the driver planned to run her off the road or just follow her home? He'd definitely been trying to intimidate her.

She opened the pickup door and reached for her bag. Why would anyone follow her home unless…. Her heart thudded in her chest. Unless he wanted to see where she lived.

Clutching the leather pouch to her, she closed the truck door, telling herself that made no sense. All the person would have to do was mention her name and anyone in the county could tell him where to find the McCalls' Sundown Ranch.

McCall had always been an impossible name to live down, thanks to her four older brothers. They were to blame for how protective her father had always been with her. And the reason her teachers had warned her the first day of school that they weren't putting up with any more shenanigans from McCall kids.

She started up the front steps of the house and stumbled as a thought hit her. What if the driver of the pickup hadn't known who she was? Or where she lived?

Well, he did now, she thought with a shudder.

CHAPTER FOUR

Outside Antelope Flats

Sheriff Cash McCall slid down the steep embankment toward the partially hidden wrecked pickup lying in the bottom of the ravine. Coroner Raymond Winters waited in the shade of a chokecherry tree.

Winters was fifty-something, a quiet, mournful man who, besides being coroner for the county, owned Winters Funeral Home, just across the border in Sheridan, Wyoming.

The pickup had obviously rolled several times before coming to rest at the base of the tree. A rancher had spotted it while out on his four-wheeler checking calves and called 911.

As Cash neared the battered truck, he could see the Montana plates. Same county as Antelope Flats. He leaned into the cab, afraid he would know the driver.

He did.

"It's Clayton," Winters said behind him, sounding regretful. "Clayton T. Brooks. I saw him ride during Cheyenne Days. He was one hell of a bull rider. Damned shame. Heard he started hitting the bottle hard after he was forced to quit. That last bull broke him up good."

Cash nodded. Clayton T. Brooks was a legend in these

parts. "They don't make 'em like him anymore," he agreed. What a hell of a way to end up, though, Cash thought.

Clayton was crumpled, beaten and broken on the floorboard on the passenger side of the pickup—and he'd been there for a while.

"Takes a certain kind of man to keep climbing back up on an animal that weighs a ton and would just as soon stomp you as not, don't you think?" Winters commented.

Unlike his brothers, and even his little sister Dusty, Cash had never rodeoed. Nor had he ever really understood the attraction. But then, he'd never been that much into ranching, let alone trying to ride animals intent on stopping you.

Cash tried the pickup door on the uphill side of the cab. Jammed. He went around, yanked on the other door. A dozen empty beer cans clattered to the ground.

"I would suspect his blood alcohol level was over the legal limit when he left the road," the coroner said dryly. "No skid marks up on the pavement. He didn't even try to hit his brakes. Wasn't wearing his seat belt, either."

"How long would you say he's been here?" Cash asked.

Winters shook his head. "Hard to say. My guess is at least a day, maybe more. I'll know more once I get him out of there."

Cash heard the whine of the ambulance siren.

"This has always been a bad curve," Winters said as the siren suddenly stilled, followed by the sound of doors opening and closing from the highway above them. "Looks pretty cut-and-dried. Alcohol-related fatality. Damned shame."

Cash agreed as he stepped back from the pickup, the smell of stale beer and death making him queasy this early in the morning. He turned to go up and help the ambulance crew with the stretcher, remembering the last time he saw Brooks.

The bull rider had been down at the Mint Bar with some of his drinking buddies. He'd been talking rodeo, all he ever talked about. It had been his life. Rodeo and the bulls he'd ridden. Clayton had been bragging about how he never forgot a bull.

As far as Cash knew, he had no family. But Clayton wouldn't be forgotten. The rodeo community would mourn his loss and he would go down in history as a cowboy who had ridden some of the most famous bulls in history during his career. Cash guessed that was more recognition than most people got after they were gone.

Still, it was a shame that Brooks couldn't have died doing what he'd loved instead of missing a curve on some dark stretch of narrow two-lane highway with too many beers under his last winning rodeo belt buckle.

DUSTY MCCALL BIT DOWN on her lower lip, hesitating as she looked toward the cool shaded entrance to the Coltrane Appaloosa Ranch barn.

For a moment, she almost turned around and rode back to her own ranch. But she'd come this far…

The sun was hot on her back. She slipped off her horse and sidled toward the barn door, stopping to peer in. There was still time to change her mind.

She could hear the low murmur of a male voice. Ty Coltrane's. She eased into the cool darkness, aware of something in the air. An electricity like static heat, taut with tension.

"Easy, pretty girl," Ty murmured from one of the horse

stalls. "You're just fine. The first time is always the toughest."

Dusty edged deeper into the barn until she could peer over the top of the stall door. Ty sat on a bed of straw, his back to her and the stall door. In front of him a mare, her belly swollen to enormous proportions, paced in the confined space, her eyes on Ty, her expression worried.

In obvious agitation, the mare turned to her side to look back at her belly as if she felt the foal inside her and was confused by it. She stopped and nickered at Ty as if needing reassurance.

"It's all right," Ty murmured as he watched her. "That's it. Take your time. Nothing to be afraid of."

From experience, Dusty knew that most mares foal between midnight and 3 a.m. for some unknown reason. The fact that this mare was running late didn't bode well.

Dusty wasn't sure how long she stood there listening to Ty's soothing murmur and watching the pregnant mare, worrying that something was wrong.

Suddenly, the mare awkwardly lay down, her legs under her. With a groan, she went to her side.

Ty stroked the mare as he moved into position. From where Dusty stood she could see the foal start to appear. She stared at the purplish white bag covering the foal, trying see the new life inside it.

After a few minutes, she could make out the front hooves and then the head. The foal started out feet first, nose between its front legs as if diving. Then stopped.

Dusty stood transfixed, anxious now for the rest of the foal's body to be expelled. It was taking too long. She could feel Ty's nervousness as well as her own. She bit down on her lower lip, gripping the top of the stall door.

Ty rolled up his sleeves, still quietly encouraging, his hands and voice working to soothe the mare.

Nothing happened.

Dusty chewed at her lip, afraid as she watched him pull gently on the foal each time the mare pushed. It took everything in her not to go into the stall to help, but Ty was doing all that could be done and she didn't want to upset the mare.

Without warning the foal popped out—right into Ty's lap. He let out a surprised relieved laugh as he held the bundle.

Dusty felt her chest swell, tears burned her eyes as she watched Ty carefully brush back the white covering of the sack to let the gawky little thing breathe.

The foal had dark curly wet hair that looked like crushed velvet. As a ranchwoman, she'd seen dozens and dozens of births, but this one felt as if it were the most amazing. She gazed awestruck as Ty toweled the little colt dry, rubbing it gently, clearing away the protective cover, all the time murmuring to both. Talking softly, he rubbed the foal's ears, handled the hooves, flipped him over.

The mare watched. Dusty could feel the trust between the horse and Ty. He drew the foal over so the mare could tenderly nose it, smell it and as Dusty stared into the stall, the foal awkwardly got up on stick-like legs and stumbled to its feet, all legs and big eyes.

Dusty choked back a laugh. The foal nuzzled around the mare until Ty helped him get his first sips from one of the mare's two teats. The mare looked surprised for a moment, then seemed strangely content.

Dusty stared at the two horses standing next to each

other, sensing the instinctive mother-child bond between them. She swallowed back the lump in her throat.

Ty turned, surprised to see Dusty McCall standing at the stall door, watching, her eyes wide and shiny as she stared down at the new foal.

As always, he felt that little flutter in his chest whenever he saw Dusty. He stepped out of the stall, closing the door as the mare began to clean up her new offspring.

"Hi."

Dusty didn't respond, seeming at a loss for words over the birth. He smiled at that. She never ceased to amaze him. After as many livestock as she'd seen birthed, she still got teary-eyed. He knew the feeling.

"It's just so incredible, isn't it?" she said after a moment.

He nodded. He'd seen more foals born than he could count, but he never got over the wonder of it.

He watched her peer into the stall, the expression on her face tender. He couldn't remember the last time she'd just dropped by like this. He had to wonder what she was doing here. Not that he was complaining. He liked her. He'd always liked her. Sometimes, he almost thought they were friends.

"It's just so…cool," she said, peeking over the stall door at the new foal again.

"It is that." He studied her, realizing she must have ridden over here. That's why he hadn't heard her drive up.

She was dressed in her usual: jeans, boots and one of her brother's cast-off western shirts under one of her brother's large cast-off canvas jackets, no makeup, her long blond hair plaited in a single braid down her back, her western straw hat pulled down low.

He had a sudden memory of her standing in the middle of the rodeo corral last night with wild bucking horses pounding around her. What the hell had she been doing there? After watching her ride one of the bucking broncs yesterday morning at the clinic, he wouldn't put anything past her.

"What are you going to name the foal?" she asked, finally looking over at him. She had the palest blue eyes he'd ever seen, peering out of gold dusted lashes.

He wondered what she saw when she looked at him. She usually treated him like one of her brothers—her least favorite, he thought with a wry smile.

"Haven't given a name any thought," he said. "What do you suggest?"

"Miracle," she said without hesitation. "What's his mother's name?"

"Rosie."

"Rosie's Little Miracle."

He laughed. "Great name for a roping horse." He pretended he was a rodeo announcer. "And our next contestant is Big Jim Brady on his horse Rosie's Little Miracle…" He laughed again.

Dusty mugged a face at him.

He headed deeper into the barn, needing to check several other mares that were due to foal. Unlike Rosie, though, those mares were old hands at this and wouldn't need any help. He'd been worried about Rosie. The first time was always the hardest.

Dusty followed him like one of the ranch dogs.

He stopped in front of a stall and she practically plowed into him. She hadn't just dropped by. The girl had something on her mind. He was dying to know what it was. "There something I can do for you, Slim?"

"Last night, did you go straight home from the rodeo?"

He raised a brow, amused. "You asking if I have myself a girlfriend in town?"

She rolled her eyes. "I just wondered, since you left before I did."

"Sorry to disappoint you, but I came straight here." He frowned. His horse ranch was down the county road from the McCalls' Sundown Ranch. "You rode all the way over here this early in the morning to ask me that? What's going on?"

She looked down as she dug the toe of her boot into the dirt and shook her head. "Nothin'."

He'd learned that *nothin'* with Dusty McCall was always *somethin'*. He leaned against the stall and crossed his arms. "Come on, what gives, Slim?"

She made another face at him. "I wish you'd quit calling me that."

He studied her. "Why do you care when I got home?"

She looked away, worrying her lower lip with her teeth the way she did when something was bothering her. "Someone followed me last night from town."

He felt his insides go cold. "What do you mean *someone?*" Last night, he'd seen Boone move through the bucking horses, heard him open the gate. At the time, Ty hadn't understood why Boone had sent the horses back through the empty corral—until Ty had hauled Dusty out a few moments later.

Had Boone known Dusty was in there? Or had he just heard someone and been afraid they'd overheard his argument with Dobbs and Lamar? Maybe Boone thought it was Ty in the corral spying on him. But that didn't explain what Dusty had been doing in there, did it?

"All I know is that whoever followed me was in a dark-colored pickup." She met his gaze. "Whoever was behind the wheel pretty much *chased* me home though."

"You mean like tried to run you off the road?" he asked, his mouth dry as straw.

"I never let him get that close."

Ty sighed, thankful Dusty was one kick-butt girl. "You couldn't tell the make or color of the pickup?"

"It was too dark." She cocked her head at him. "I just thought it might have been you because you're always turning up where I am. Like last night after the rodeo." Her big blue eyes narrowed. "What were you doing there anyway?"

"Well, I wasn't following you, Slim," he said, shoving off the stall door. "I need to get to work, even if you don't." He didn't like hearing that someone had followed her home. Any more than he liked hearing her complain about him always turning up around her.

"Well, you don't have to get mad."

He ground his teeth. Sometimes he wanted to ring Dusty McCall's slim neck. Other times…

It was the other times that had him walking away from her. She was just a kid. Just an annoying, pain-in-the-neck kid.

Dusty trailed after him until he stopped and spun on her. "I told you it wasn't me who followed you home."

"I believe you," she said, looking indignant.

"I could ask you what you were doing there," he said.

"I already told you. Nothing."

"Right. Well, now that we got that cleared up, is there something else I could help you with?"

"If you have to know, I left my bag and went back for it," she said.

He cut his eyes to her. "You left your bag in the horse corrals."

"I found it in the grandstand where I left it and then I wandered down to the horse corral."

He didn't believe a word of it. "Just to see the horses."

"No," she snapped. "I heard arguing. I was curious."

That, he believed. But something was bothering her. "Okay, Slim, spill it. Whatever it is, let's hear it."

She gulped air. "I need to ask your opinion on something." She swallowed and seemed to be having trouble finding her voice. A rare occurrence, considering how many times she'd told him what she thought in no uncertain terms. "It's kind of...personal."

Today he'd seen her wordless *and* choked up, all in the same morning. And now she wanted to ask him something...personal?

She opened her mouth to speak, but closed it as a truck came up the road.

Ty swore under his breath when he recognized the rig. This didn't bode well, he thought, as the dark brown pickup pulled up in the yard and Boone Rasmussen climbed out.

"Stay here," Ty said to Dusty.

She didn't answer. Nor did she move.

As he stepped out of the barn, he glanced back. She was standing right where he'd left her, still as a statue. What the heck was going on with that girl, anyway? She never did what he told her. Hell, she did just the opposite to show him she didn't have to listen to him.

Except for just now.

Rasmussen got out of his truck and sauntered toward

him, his face expressionless. Ty fought the bad feeling in the pit of his stomach.

Rasmussen had never been out to the Coltrane Appaloosa Ranch before. For that matter, he'd never acknowledged Ty, even though they'd met numerous times at rodeos. Every time they'd been introduced, Boone acted as if it had been the first, saying, "Coltrane? You raise… horses?"

Roping horses. Some of the best known in the world, including horses now being ridden by the top ropers in professional rodeo. But Boone Rasmussen knew that. Ty wondered why the man seemed to purposely rub him the wrong way. Or maybe that was just Boone Rasmussen's way. Whatever, Ty hadn't liked him. Didn't trust him. Especially after last night.

"Mornin'," Rasmussen said, glancing toward the barn, his gaze skimming over Dusty who stood silhouetted in the doorway, head down, her straw hat hiding her face. He shifted his dark eyes to Ty again without giving her another glance.

Ty waited, afraid he already knew what was on the cowboy's mind.

"I heard you raise horses," Rasmussen said, shoving back his hat.

"You know damned well I raise Appaloosa ropers."

Rasmussen's brow shot up. He pushed back his hat and smiled. "A little testy this morning, ain't we."

If he thought his good ol' Texas boy routine was going to work, he was sadly mistaken. "What is it you want, Rasmussen?"

"I was looking for a horse." He glanced toward the green pasture dotted with Coltrane Appaloosas.

Ty knew Rasmussen had no need of a roping horse. "You just missed our production sale. You might want to check it out next spring if you're still around. We'll have some yearlings and two-year-olds. The competition is pretty stiff, though."

Buyers came from all over the country. A Coltrane Appaloosa often went for thousands of dollars, especially progeny of one of his more famous roping horses with potential as breeding stock.

"But you're probably looking for a trained horse," Ty added. "Those go even higher and faster at the sale."

"I can train my own horse. And I will be around next spring." Rasmussen's jaw tightened. "You seem to have a burr under your saddle when it comes to me."

"You didn't come out here for a horse. What is it you're really after?"

"I could ask you the same thing." He glanced toward the barn again. Dusty was still standing in the same spot, hat down over her blue eyes, probably straining to hear their conversation. Ty doubted she could from this distance, but he knew she was damned sure watching them from under the brim of her hat. Slim was nothing if not nosy.

Rasmussen pulled off his straw hat and burrowed his fingers through his thick black hair. "What's your interest in my bulls?" he demanded, flicking a look at him.

"Who told you I was interested?" Ty asked, although he knew it was that rough-looking cowboy Rasmussen used in his chutes, Lamar Nichols.

"Doesn't matter. I just wondered why a man who raises roping horses would care about roughstock," Boone said. "You thinking of raising bulls?"

Ty wanted to laugh. Boone Rasmussen knew damned

well that wasn't the case. "There a problem with me checking out your bulls?"

Boone shifted on his feet, looked down at his boots, then back up, the dark gaze boring into him. "Nope. But if you're that interested I'd suggest you come out to the ranch in the daytime. Easier to see when it isn't pitch-dark."

"I just might take you up on that," Ty said. "The last time I saw a show like the one your bull put on last night was in Mexico."

Something dark and threatening flickered in Rasmussen's eyes before he looked away toward the barn. Ty followed his gaze. Dusty was gone.

For no reason he could put his finger on, Ty was relieved. She'd been near the corrals last night after the rodeo and had almost been trampled by the bucking horses, thanks to Rasmussen. Had she been snooping, too? More to the point, had Rasmussen seen her? Someone had followed her home. No, *chased* her home, she'd said.

Ty wanted to confront Rasmussen about opening that corral gate last night, but then that would mean involving Dusty and that was the last thing Ty wanted to do.

When Rasmussen looked at him again, Ty could feel rage coming off him in waves. They were about the same age, Rasmussen a few years older. Ty was a little taller and a little lighter, but he figured he could take Rasmussen in a fair fight. Except he doubted Boone Rasmussen had ever been in a fair fight in his life.

"You got quite the spread here," Rasmussen said, his voice sounding strange as if he were fighting to get some control over that rage. "Must be tough for someone your age. Have to keep your eye on things all the time. Probably don't have time to do much else."

Like snoop around rodeo arenas after dark? Ty heard the jealousy in Boone's tone and what sounded like a threat. He'd been running the Coltrane Appaloosa Ranch since his father's death two years ago. Rasmussen was right about one thing: it didn't leave much time for anything else.

"There a point you're trying to make?" Ty asked as he crossed his arms over his chest.

"Just making conversation."

"Well, if that's all, I've got some mares about to foal and don't really have time for conversation this morning."

Rasmussen flashed a smile that had no chance of reaching his dark eyes and tipped his hat. "I'm sure we'll be seeing each other again."

Count on it, Ty thought as he watched the cowboy get into his pickup and drive off.

Why had he driven all the way up here to begin with? Not for a horse, that was for sure. No, he wanted Ty to know that he knew about last night—knew Ty had been snooping around Devil's Tornado. And he'd come out here to warn him off.

This morning, Ty had half convinced himself that he'd been wrong about Devil's Tornado last night. That there wasn't anything to find out. Hell, hadn't Rasmussen invited him out to see the bulls in the daylight?

If there was something about Devil's Tornado that Rasmussen didn't want him to see, then why make that offer?

It didn't make any sense.

So why was Ty even more convinced that Rasmussen had something to hide? Because he'd seen the cowboy's rage and something more. Boone Rasmussen had a mean streak that made him dangerous to anyone who got in his way.

And Ty had gotten in his way.

As he looked back toward the barn, Ty wondered if Dusty had also gotten in Boone Rasmussen's way.

CHAPTER FIVE

Shelby McCall was waiting for him when Asa came down to breakfast. They hadn't talked yesterday after his ride. He got the feeling she'd been afraid to ask him anything for fear he might tell her.

That wasn't like Shelby.

But one look at her face this morning told him everything he needed to know—even before she pulled the envelope from her apron pocket.

How ironic that his first thought was that he'd rather die than face her right now.

"When were you going to tell me?" Her voice quavered, eyes filling with tears but not falling, as if by her strength of will she could hold back the torrent.

He started to muddy the waters by demanding to know what she thought she was doing going through his things, but she would have seen right through that.

That day he'd gotten the letter, he'd been the one to go down to the mailbox at the end of the road. He'd seen her watching him from the window. He'd had to stuff the letter into his pocket to keep her from seeing it when he entered the house.

He smiled ruefully now. Of course she would have noticed. He couldn't get anything past her. Never could.

"Where did you find the letter?" he asked, stalling.

She gave him an exasperated look. “In your jacket pocket where you put it. Not that it matters where I found it. *Asa.*” The pain in her voice was heart-wrenching, but he could tell she was trying to be strong for him. For the children. “You have to tell them.”

He nodded as he pulled out a chair at the kitchen table and lowered himself into it. He couldn’t remember ever feeling so bone-weary.

“There’s more,” he said, his voice sounding hoarse even to his own ears. He looked up at her.

She straightened to her full height, head going up, that stubborn determined look in her beautiful face as she took the chair across from him. “Tell me.”

“It’s rather a long story.”

“I have time,” she said, then seemed to bite her tongue. One errant tear spilled over her cheek. She hurriedly wiped it away and met his gaze, still refusing to acknowledge something they’d both known for a long time.

He was dying.

The letter only confirmed what he’d suspected. For him, time had run out.

TY FOUND Dusty by Rosie’s stall. She stood on tiptoe, peering in at the new foal she wanted to name Miracle. Her expression was so tender he felt his heart do a slow painful somersault in his chest.

It surprised him she hadn’t come out of the barn when Rasmussen was here. It wasn’t like her. Normally, she would have been right in the middle of the conversation. Strange, she had almost seemed…shy.

He shook his head at such a thought. This was Dusty McCall, he reminded himself. Dusty and shy didn’t go together.

But was it possible she was scared of Rasmussen?

"What did Boone want?" Dusty asked as she glanced toward the barn door. Dust still hung in the air from the trail his pickup had left behind.

"Nothin'," Ty said. She looked pale to him. He watched her burrow down into her jacket. "You all right?"

"I'm fine."

"Any reason you didn't want to see Rasmussen just now?" he asked.

She gave him a surprised, wide-eyed look. "I've never even met him, just know who he is. Anyway, you told me to stay here."

Ty studied her. *She never does what I tell her.* He sighed. "What was it you were going to ask me before he showed up?"

She looked away. "It wasn't important."

"Fine. Whatever." Turning, he headed down between the stalls. He'd never understand that girl. He checked the mares again, mentally noting that he might have to call in a couple of his hands if the mares decided to foal at the same time, just to keep an eye on them in case anything went wrong.

Still no word from Clayton. He was torn between worry and annoyance. Mostly worry. No one seemed to have heard from him for several days.

Ty turned, surprised to find Dusty had followed him. "I thought you left." He didn't know what was bothering her, but she was starting to irritate him. He knew Dusty too well. Something was on her mind and he was getting tired of waiting to hear what it was.

He thought of Rasmussen and was reminded again that Dusty had almost been trampled by the bucking horses last night. Just the thought made his stomach churn. He told himself that Dusty had just been in the wrong place at the wrong time last night. But if he was right about Boone Rasmussen, then he didn't want Dusty anywhere near the man. Or his roughstock.

"Last night after the rodeo, you didn't happen to hear what Boone and his buddies were arguing about, did you?" he asked, thinking that might be the problem.

She shot him a surprised look. "No. Why?"

"Just curious," he said and wished he hadn't said anything. She was giving him that fish-eye look of hers and he could almost see the wheels turning in her head.

"Is that what you were doing there? Trying to hear what they were saying?"

"I stayed around to see one of the bulls." He turned to walk away from her, hoping she dropped it.

But then that wouldn't have been like her.

"Why would you want to see one of Boone's bulls?" she demanded, trailing after him. "The two of you didn't seem all that friendly a few minutes ago."

He spun on her. "Was there some reason you came up here today other than to give me a hard time?"

She seemed to deflate before his eyes. She let out a sigh. "There's something I need to know." She sighed again. "You're a man."

He let out a laugh. "Last time I checked."

She rolled her eyes. "You know what I mean."

He didn't really, but she'd definitely gotten his interest. Where in the world was she headed with this, though? He gave her his full attention as he waited to see.

"Do you think I'm…*cute?*" She practically choked on the word.

"Cute as a button," he said meaning it, relieved beyond words that this was all she wanted to know.

She swallowed and bit her lower lip, lowering her eyes. "I mean do I turn you on?"

"I beg your pardon?"

"Oh, I knew you were the wrong one to ask." She spun around and stalked toward the barn door.

He went after her, grabbing her arm and spinning her around so he could see her face. Damned if she wasn't crying. He let go of her in surprise. "Talk to me, Slim."

She made an angry swipe at her tears. "Do you have any idea what it's like being raised on a ranch far from anything in an all-male family? I've spent my whole life trying not to be different. I just wanted to fit in, and that meant trying to be just like my brothers."

He raised a brow. "I don't think being a tomboy is a bad thing, Slim. Hell, you can ride better than most men and before your brothers Rourke and Brandon started helping, you and J.T. were running the Sundown spread."

She windmilled her arms and let out an exasperated breath. "I'm not saying I don't love ranching. And I never wanted to be one of those prissy girls like you've dated." She made a face. "It isn't about that."

He waited, trying not to comment on her jab about the prissy girls he'd dated.

"It's about *sex,*" she said on a breath and looked down at her boots.

Ty reared back. "Wow. Slim, if this is about the birds and bees, then you should be talking to your mama."

She mugged a face at him. "I've known about sex since I was old enough to peer through the fence at the cattle."

"Then you've lost me," he said just wanting this conversation to be over.

"Lately, I've been having these…*feelings,*" she said, her head down again.

Ty let out a nervous laugh. Oh, brother.

"I should have known you wouldn't help me."

As she started to stomp off, he reluctantly grabbed her arm again. "Look, I'd help you if I could. It's just that this is the kind of thing you discuss with your mother or a friend."

"I can't talk to Shelby about anything."

He knew that Dusty was still having trouble accepting her mother. Shelby McCall had only recently returned after being gone most of her children's lives— all of Dusty's.

"And I thought you *were* my friend," she accused, eyes narrowing.

He took off his hat and shot a hand through his hair. "I was thinking more of a *girl*-type friend."

"Letty?" she cried.

Letty, who was even more of a tomboy than Dusty, probably had less experience with this type of thing than Slim. "You have a point. What about your sisters-in-law?"

"I hardly know them and they're…old."

He smiled at that. Her sisters-in-law were all in their thirties. "Okay," he said before she could take off again. He was five years her senior. Did she see him as "old" too?

He groaned at the thought. The problem was: he'd never seen her like this. Sure, he'd seen her upset. Usually after she'd been bucked from a horse. Or tossed into a mud puddle by one of her brothers when she was younger. But this was different, and he knew he couldn't just let her leave thinking he wasn't taking her seriously.

"Come over here," he said and pulled down a straw bale for her to sit on. He dragged up one for himself and sat facing her. "What brought this on, anyway?"

She bit down on her lower lip, eyes down, then slowly raised her lashes, those blue eyes huge in the cool darkness of the barn and swimming with tears. "I'm *twenty-one.* I'm tired of being treated like a kid."

Twenty-one. He stared at her, realizing it was true. He hadn't even thought about how old she was, even though he'd known her since they were kids. She'd always just been the girl next door—well, the tomboy down the road at the next ranch, anyway. He'd pretty much always thought of her as a kid.

On top of that, she still *looked* like a kid. For starters, she was only about five-five, lean and youthful-looking. But he knew it was more than that. She was the kid sister of the very protective McCall boys. That alone made any man with any sense shy away from her. Just as that alone should have made him nervous about having this conversation with her.

"Have you mentioned this to your brothers?" he asked.

She rolled her eyes and shot to her feet. "Just forget it."

"Hold on," he said, pulling her back down to the straw bale. "I'm not sure I'm the right person," he said, adding quickly before she tried to hightail it again, "but I'll help you if I can."

"You do know *something* about women, don't you?"

He smiled. "Something."

Her blue eyes pleaded with him. "Well, then help me. I want people to see me as a…woman."

Oh, man, Slim. He told himself that she wouldn't be here asking him—of all people—unless she was desperate. "Okay," he said uncomfortably. "Don't take this wrong, but it could be the way you dress."

She looked down at her clothes. "What's wrong with the way I dress?"

"Well, for starters, you look like a boy. You have any of your own clothes? Or is everything you own handed down from your brothers."

Her jaw tightened. "I like roomy shirts."

He nodded. Either she was wearing a tight-fitting sports bra under one of her brother's western shirts and canvas jacket or she had no boobs and didn't even need a bra. "Don't you ever look at magazines? Or try makeup and fixing your hair different?"

"*Of course.* I looked like a streetwalker!" She let out a half sob, half laugh. A couple of big tears shimmered in her blue eyes. She ducked her head again, obviously embarrassed as she made a swipe at them. "I need one of those makeovers like on TV."

He shook his head. "You don't need a makeover. You just need a little help. Look, if you're serious about this—"

"I am."

"—then I'll help you," he said with a groan.

The relief in her face made him smile. Then realization hit him. What did he know about girl stuff? Clearly more than Dusty, which wasn't much. Fortunately, he knew someone he could get to help them, a young woman he'd dated a few times who owned a boutique in Sheridan.

"We'll go down to Sheridan."

She stood as if ready to go right now.

He wondered what the hurry was. "Can you go this afternoon?"

She nodded, looking determined and a little worried.

"I'll pick you up after lunch."

She launched herself at him. He hugged her back in surprise and then she was racing toward the barn door. He smiled, thinking he didn't see any reason for her to change. Personally, he liked her just fine as a tomboy.

Over her shoulder, she called back, "If you tell a soul about this—"

"It will be our little secret," he said, getting up to follow her to the barn door. No chance he was going to tell anyone.

She swung up onto her horse outside the barn and cut her eyes at him. "It had better be our secret, Ty Coltrane, or you will regret the day you ever met me."

No chance of that, he thought as he watched her ride away. He'd never met anyone like Slim. She was one hell of a horsewoman. And she had spunk and something he couldn't put his finger on. Something that had always drawn him to her. Yep, as far as he was concerned, there was nothing about Dusty McCall that needed to be made over.

As she disappeared over the horizon, he turned back to the barn. A bad feeling settled over him as he thought again of Rasmussen's visit and Dusty's.

What *had* Dusty been doing in the corral last night after the rodeo?

ASA HAD KNOWN the day would come when he would have to tell his family. Telling them he was dying seemed easy compared to the really bad news. Telling Shelby took ever ounce of strength he had left in him.

"Remember Charley Rankin?" he asked.

She frowned. “The two of you owned that land together to the north.”

Asa nodded. “Charley helped me buy up some other prime acreage that is now part of the main ranch. I bought the land from him when we dissolved our partnership.”

“That must have been when Charley married and moved back east.”

Asa nodded, realizing not for the first time that Shelby had kept close track of his life and the kids all the years he’d forced her out of their lives. It added to the weight of his guilt to know that she’d been watching them all from the sidelines, staying involved in their lives as much as she could. As much as he’d allowed her.

He met her eyes, wanting desperately to tell her how sorry he was but never able to find words to encompass the extent of that sorrow—of that regret.

Ashamed, he looked away.

“I heard Charley and his wife were both killed when his private plane crashed,” she said when he didn’t go on.

He nodded and plunged in, needing to get the words out before he didn’t have the courage. “When our partnership was dissolved, I didn’t have enough cash to buy him out, so I signed an agreement giving him the mineral rights to the ranch.”

She let out a small gasp, her eyes widening with alarm as the enormity of what he’d done hit her.

“It was collateral, nothing more,” he continued, not wanting to drag it out. “Just before he was killed, I mailed the last of the land payments. Charley had never cashed the checks. He didn’t need the money, so I guess it was his way of helping me out. With the last check, I also sent him a legal form to sign that would void the mineral rights agreement."

He looked at Shelby. He could tell by her expression that she knew what was coming.

"Charley and his wife had a son," she said. "Reese. He must be about twenty-five by now."

Asa nodded, figuring Shelby also knew that Reese had never gotten along with his father and been in trouble since he was young. "He found all the paperwork on the deal after his father's death, including all the uncashed checks and the unsigned document that would have voided the agreement."

"Oh, Asa," she breathed.

He nodded. "Thanks to the discovery of coal-bed methane, the mineral rights on the ranch are worth fifty times what I paid Charley for the land."

"He plans to drill wells on the ranch." Shelby covered her mouth with her hand, eyes welling with tears. She knew better than anyone how much this ranch meant to him.

She pushed herself up from the table and went to the window, her back to him. "There has to be some way to stop him."

"Even if I mortgaged the entire ranch, there wouldn't be enough capital to buy him off. He always resented Charley. Charley's dead. But Charley's best friend is still alive. At least for a while."

She turned from the sink and sat down at the table again. Reaching across the table, she covered his weathered old hand with her still pale pretty one. "Have you told J.T.?"

J.T. was their oldest, the one who had been running the

ranch along with Dusty the past few years. Asa shook his head. "Other than my lawyer, you're the only one who knows."

"You have to tell them."

He turned his hand so hers was enclosed in his rough weathered one. He squeezed it gently as he looked at her. He'd been so angry at her for coming back from the dead the way she had. Breaking their agreement without notice. Just showing up at the door. Giving him no choice but to let her stay because she'd learned about the cancer.

Then when it had gone into remission, she'd stayed, refusing to leave him again. He'd been angry at her, not wanting her pity. Not wanting her to come home only to watch him waste away and die.

Now he wondered what he would have done if she hadn't come back. How he and the children would have gotten through this without her here. How could he ever tell her how much it meant to him? How much she meant to him?

"You have to tell the children," she said again.

He nodded. The cancer was no longer in remission. The letter had only confirmed what he'd already known.

He drew his hand back and stood. His eyes burned at just the thought of leaving her and the children with the mess he'd made. "I need a little more time."

It was so like Shelby not to say that he might not have more time. "Take all you need."

He smiled ruefully at that. He would need another lifetime and even then, he doubted it would be enough time to undo all the mistakes he'd made in this one.

Instead, he had a few weeks. If he was lucky.

CHAPTER SIX

Letty Arnold stared at the caller ID as the phone rang again. She'd been waiting for this call all her life. She just hadn't known it.

Her hand shook as she picked up. She crossed her fingers and closed her eyes. "Hello?"

"Ms. Arnold?"

She held her breath, squeezing her eyes tighter.

"This is Hal Branson with Branson Investigations."

She recognized his voice from the day she'd hired him. The same day she'd found out from the sheriff that she'd been illegally adopted.

The truth about her adoption had only come out because of an investigation involving a local doctor. It seemed he'd taken babies from what he considered unworthy parents, telling them that their infant had died. Then he had given the babies to couples desperately wanting a child, couples he considered more worthy.

The doctor had handled everything, including birth certificates that made it appear the new mother had given birth to the baby. If he hadn't told the sheriff about her in a deathbed confession, she might never have known the truth. "Did you find my birth mother?"

"Maybe," Hal Branson said.

Letty opened her eyes. "*Maybe?*"

"I found a woman who gave birth to a baby at the clinic where the doctor worked on the day you were supposedly born." He seemed to hesitate. "She was an unwed mother." Just the kind of woman the doctor would have considered unworthy. "I don't want to get your hopes up. The only way to be certain of your maternity will be DNA tests."

He'd already told her all of this. Why was he telling her this again?

"Keep in mind that the date of your birth could be incorrect," he continued. "You could have been a home birth. There are just too many factors. And with the doctor not keeping any records of the adoptions—"

"Mr. Branson—"

"Hal." He sounded young and she wondered how old he was. For all she knew, she'd hired a kid. That's what she got for not taking care of this in person. Not that she hadn't checked out Branson Investigations on the Internet to make sure it was licensed, bonded and reputable.

She hadn't wanted anyone in Antelope Flats to know that she was one of the crazy doctor's "babies." And she hadn't had the patience that day to drive clear to Billings to find a P.I. It was also easier to talk about this over the phone rather than in person.

She knew she shouldn't feel this way, but it was embarrassing not knowing who her parents were. Not knowing who *she* was.

And she had to know. She'd always suspected that she didn't really belong to the Arnolds. It wasn't only their advanced ages and the fact that they were more like grandparents. She'd never looked like either of them or acted like them or even really understood them. The Arnolds were quiet, solitary, stable and bland. Both were short and round.

Letty was thin as a stick, with a wide toothy smile, and had been all cowgirl from the time she could walk. Neither of her parents had ever ridden a horse in their lives and didn't like rodeos. And while both of the Arnolds had light brown hair, Letty had a wild mane of hair red as a flame, a face full of freckles and emerald green eyes. Both Arnolds had brown eyes.

The truth? She'd been relieved when they'd retired and left her the motel so they could move to Arizona. Not that they hadn't been good to her. She *loved* them.

That's why she felt guilty about her feelings. They were the only parents she'd known and she felt as if she were disrespecting them by even looking for her birth mother.

"Are you still there?" Hal asked.

"Tell me how I can find this woman you think might be my birth mother." Letty unconsciously glanced toward her reflection in the mirror on the wall. She had to know who she was. No matter the outcome.

"Her name is Florence Hubbard. She goes by Flo."

Letty heard the slight catch in his voice and braced herself.

"She…plays in a rock 'n' roll band," Hal said. "It's called Triple-X-Files. I understand they play some rock, but mostly heavy metal music."

She could hear his distaste and smiled. "What kind of music do you like?"

"What?" He sounded more than surprised, maybe even embarrassed. "Country," he said almost sheepishly.

Her smile widened. "Me, too. So where does this X band play?"

"Well…there's a three-day rock concert next weekend during a fair in Bozeman. Triple-X-Files will be there. If you like, I could e-mail you all the information. You can camp near the concert or stay in one of the local motels."

"Thanks, you've been very thorough."

"It's what you're paying me to do." Again, he sounded embarrassed.

"You'll send me a bill?" she said, thinking this might be the last time they talked if Flo Hubbard really was her mother.

"Ms. Arnold—"

"Letty."

"Letty, if I were you, I wouldn't go to meet this woman alone. Do you have a friend or relative who could go with you?"

She smiled ruefully at the relative part. None who lived nearby, none she was all that close to even before she found out they weren't blood-related. She had no one who could go with her. Except Dusty McCall, her best friend.

But she wasn't ready to tell even Dusty about this yet. Dusty knew something had been bothering her. Letty wished she could confide in her friend. She wasn't even sure what was holding her back. Maybe the need to find out who she was before she told the world that she was one of the babies the doctor had stolen.

"If you would like, I could meet you there," Hal said guardedly. "I mean, I wouldn't mind. In fact, I think it might be good to have someone who isn't involved in the situation there with you."

To her surprise, she heard herself say, "Would you?"

"Of course." He sounded relieved, almost excited, as

if he wanted to see this through to the end. "Just tell me when and where to meet you."

They worked out a plan and she found herself torn between her anxiety at the thought of meeting her possible birth mother and her curiosity about Hal Branson as she hung up.

For a moment, she thought about calling Dusty, telling her the news. She hesitated, feeling guilty. But the truth was, Dusty hadn't been interested in much of anything lately except Boone Rasmussen.

Letty told herself that wasn't fair. She knew Dusty would just think she was jealous. But it was something else that bothered her about Dusty's obsession with Boone. A fear that she might lose her best friend. But not to love.

BOONE RASMUSSEN STORMED into Monte Edgewood's ranch house, letting the door slam behind him. Hadn't he known Coltrane was going to be a problem? The Coltranes of the world were always a problem.

The ten-mile drive from Coltrane's ranch hadn't calmed him in the least. He'd driven too fast on the way to Monte's, reckless from his anger. How dare Coltrane butt into his business?

Coltrane had everything Boone had ever wanted—one hell of a ranch, money, standing in the community—and all of it handed to him on a silver platter when his old man died.

Boone hadn't been so lucky. His father hadn't left him a thing. In fact, he'd had to pay out of his own pocket to have the old son of a bitch cremated. He smiled bitterly at the memory. He should have let the state deal with G.O. Rasmussen's sorry remains.

But Boone had gotten the last laugh. He'd spread that bastard's ashes over the local cow lot. Ashes to ashes, so to speak. It was little consolation for the years his old man had worked him, paying him with biting criticism and the back of his hand, but it was something.

The difference in their lives alone made Boone hate Coltrane. But now the horse rancher was snooping into the wrong cowboy's life. No way was he going to let Coltrane ruin everything he'd worked so hard for.

Monte looked up from the kitchen table. Boone saw the older man's expression and felt his stomach clench. Something *else* had happened. Something to do with Devil's Tornado? Or did this have something to do with Coltrane?

Monte lowered his big head as if in prayer. "I guess you heard about Clayton," he said with a wag of his head.

Boone tried not to let Monte see his relief. So this was only about that ranting old drunk bull rider. He thought for a moment of pretending he hadn't heard, but everyone in town was talking about Clayton's death.

"I heard," Boone said, drawing up a chair at the table and sitting down, trying to mirror Monte's sorrowful expression. "Did you hear what happened?" Monte had more reliable sources than Boone did.

"His body was found in a ravine south of here. Guess he missed a curve," Monte said.

"Probably blind drunk."

Monte gave him a hard look, disappointment shining in his light eyes. "Shouldn't speak ill of the dead, son. Clayton had his share of demons like all of us, but he was a good man." He reached across the table to drop a big palm on Boone's shoulder and gave it a squeeze as he smiled sadly. It was clear to both of them that Boone would never be the man Monte had hoped.

But Monte refused to give up on him.

And that was what Boone was counting on.

With each passing day, though, the stakes got higher and higher. So did the danger of being caught.

Sierra sashayed into the room. "What's going on? You look like you lost your best friend."

Monte gave her an indulgent smile and motioned for her. She stepped into his open arms, stroking his hair as she looked across at Boone.

"A bull rider I admired died in a car accident," Monte told her. "Clayton T. Brooks. He was quite the rodeo star in his day."

"That's too bad," Sierra said, her gaze heating up as her eyes locked with Boone's.

Boone pushed to his feet. "Need anything from town?"

Monte shook his head, dropping his gaze again to the table as Sierra stepped away from him. He looked old and tired, and more upset over Clayton than Boone would have expected. It made Boone wonder how well the two had known each other. And if that was a problem he should be worrying about.

He shoved that worry aside and concentrated on a more immediate one. Judging from her size, it had been a cowgirl he'd seen in the empty corral next to the bucking horses last night after the rodeo. A lucky cowgirl who'd somehow escaped being trampled by the bucking horses.

Coltrane had fished her out of the corral. Boone had seen the two head for the parking lot. Then he'd lost sight of them. At first, Boone had been worried that she'd overheard him and Lamar arguing with Waylon Dobbs. That alone would have been a loose end he couldn't afford.

But he'd seen the cowgirl reach down in the horse corral and pick up something from the ground. His hand had gone to his jacket pocket. The syringe was gone! It must have fallen out of his pocket when he'd climbed over the corral fence earlier.

He'd seen her put it in her purse! It made no sense. Why had she been there in the first place? Why put a used syringe into her purse?

"Pick me up some ice cream if you're going to town," Sierra said.

"I'll buy you some ice cream, sugar," Monte spoke up.

Boone glanced back at Monte, trying to read his expression. Monte met his gaze and for an instant, Boone thought he saw something he didn't like flicker in the older man's gaze. Just his imagination?

Well, there would be plenty of time to deal with Monte later—if it came to that.

And Sierra too, he thought stealing a look at her as he left.

DUSTY PACED on the porch, mentally kicking herself for asking for Ty's help. What had she been thinking? Surely she wasn't *that* desperate.

At first, all she saw was the dust on the county road. Her heart lodged in her throat as Ty turned onto the road to the ranch. She would tell him she'd changed her mind. Didn't women do that all the time?

She groaned, reminding herself why she *was* so desperate for a makeover to begin with. But desperate enough to see this through with Ty, of all people?

He pulled up in the yard and she ran out, jerked open the passenger side door of his pickup and jumped in before she could change her mind—or he could get out.

He looked over at her and slammed his partially opened door.

"What?" she asked seeing his annoyed expression.

"You might have given me a chance to open your door for you," he said.

She rolled her eyes. "You have to be kidding. Does anyone do that anymore?"

"I do when I come by to pick up a woman," he said, sounding indignant.

She cut her eyes at him. "Why?"

"Because it's polite."

"I can open my own door."

"That isn't the point," he said as he shifted the pickup into gear and started out the gate. "Look, think of dating as a game between men and women with certain rituals involved. There are steps a man and woman go through in the relationship. Certain roles each sex plays."

She groaned. "Why does it have to be so complicated? Why can't we just cut to the chase? Be honest? Tell the person how we feel? Have them tell us how they feel? And if we both feel the same…"

Ty laughed and shook his head. "Sorry, Slim, but it doesn't work that way. It's the anticipation, not knowing what's going to happen, that adds to the excitement."

She thought about Boone. She wanted to know what was going to happen. She couldn't stand the suspense.

"It's all part of the mating ritual. You just need to get into your role."

Dusty scoffed. "This role you're talking about. Tell me

it doesn't mean I have to act helpless because I'm never going to be one of *those* women," she informed him haughtily. "So if that's what I have to do, forget it." She could feel him studying her out of the corner of his eye as he drove.

He laughed. "No, you're never going to be one of those. Lucky for you, there are men who actually like strong independent women. But no man may be ready for *you*."

She punched his arm but laughed with him, then turned to gaze out at the countryside. Was Boone ready for her? White billowing clouds scudded through the summer-blue sky overhead, casting pale shadows over the red rock cliffs, the silken ponderosa pines and tall, dark-green grasses. The land stretched to the horizon. McCall land.

Dusty welled with pride, never tiring of the landscape. This was her home. Her mother and father hadn't understood why nothing could dislodge her from the isolated ranch.

A few months ago, Shelby had cornered her, questioning her about her future. "You need to go to college," her mother had insisted. "You need a good education."

"I have a good education," Dusty had snapped. "Not that you would know, but I graduated from high school early and have been taking college courses for years online. I'll have at least two degrees, one in business and another in agriculture by this time next year."

"I'm aware of that," Shelby said tightly. "But it's not the same as actually attending a university, meeting other people your age, broadening your horizons."

Dusty had laughed. "Look at my horizons," she'd said widening her arms to encompass the ranch. "They're plenty broad."

“What do you have to say?” Shelby had asked turning to her husband.

Asa had studied Dusty for a long moment. “Dusty’s always known her own mind. Much like her mother,” he’d added, his gaze shifting to Shelby. “I’ve never been able to change either of your minds. And God knows, I’ve tried.”

Dusty had seen the look that passed between her parents. There was little doubt they had a secret, one she and her brothers obviously weren’t privy to.

She’d never regretted her decision to stay on the ranch. Her father had given her some acreage to the south and told her she could build a house on it someday if she wanted to—now, or when she got married. Unless the man she married wanted to live elsewhere.

She had laughed. “I wouldn’t marry anyone who wanted to leave here. Don’t you know me better than that?”

Her father had frowned. “You haven’t been in love yet. Love changes everything.”

She had scoffed at the idea. But now as she watched the land blur by, she thought of Boone Rasmussen. Was this love? She felt all jittery inside. Her heart beat out of control half the time. And it made her unsure about everything. Especially herself. Was that love?

Ty turned onto the highway. Dusty’s shoulder bag rolled off the seat, hitting the floor with a loud thump.

“What have you got in there? Bricks?”

“Stuff. A bridle I need to get repaired. Books,” Dusty said scooping the heavy bag up from the floor. “Sometimes I want to read when I have to go into town on errands for the ranch. There’s nothing wrong with reading.”

He laughed. “I didn’t say there was.” They passed

through Antelope Flats, the small Montana town quickly disappearing behind them.

Dusty reached over and turned on the radio, not surprised to find it tuned to a country-western station. Leaning back, she watched the willow-choked Tongue River twist its way through the valley as she and Ty wound south toward Wyoming, not wanting to talk. She had a lot on her mind.

"Did you find out who that was who followed you home last night?" Ty said reaching over to turn down the radio.

She shook her head, the memory still making her uneasy. "Just a dark-colored pickup. The driver stopped at the ranch gate and sat there with his headlights out for a while. The next time I looked, he was gone. It was probably nothing." She wished she could believe that.

She saw Ty's concerned expression. The last thing she wanted was Ty Coltrane keeping an eye on her. He'd done that her whole life.

"Any chance it could have been Boone Rasmussen?" he asked.

The question took her by surprise. "Why would *he* follow me?"

Ty looked over at her. "Good question. Maybe because you were spying on him last night in the horse corral. I heard him open that gate. It was no accident that you were almost trampled by those bucking horses."

She stared at him in shock, remembering the sound of the gate latch being pulled back, the gate swinging open.

"That's crazy. Why would Boone want to hurt *me?* He doesn't even know who I am."

Ty lifted a brow. "Maybe. Or maybe he thought you overhead something you shouldn't have last night."

The thought chilled her. "I didn't hear *anything.*"

"But maybe Boone doesn't know that. Just be careful, okay?" His tone was relaxed enough, but she could tell he was anything but. "Stay away from Boone Rasmussen."

She cut her eyes at Ty. Did he know the real reason she was in that corral last night? Was he just trying to keep her away from Boone? A thought struck her. Was it possible Ty was…jealous? She rejected that explanation instantly. No, Ty was just playing big brother like he always had.

"You never told me why *you* were there last night," she said. Did it have something to do with Boone and why Boone had stopped by Ty's ranch this morning?

From the barn, she hadn't been able to hear what the two had been saying to each other, but she could darn well tell by reading their body language that they'd been at odds over something. Could it have been about *her?*

"Well?" she demanded when Ty didn't answer her.

"Settle down, Slim. What do you want me to say? That I saw your truck was still in the lot and figured you were in some kind of trouble, as usual? That when I heard arguing, I just assumed you were at the center of it?"

She angled a look at him. He didn't take his eyes off the road making her suspect there was more to it.

Didn't he realize that trying to keep a secret from her was like throwing a rodeo bullfighter at a bull? Especially since whatever Ty was hiding had something to do with Boone Rasmussen.

Boone wouldn't have purposely opened the corral gate. But she had a flash of memory: the expression on Boone's face when he'd reached through the chute toward Devil's Tornado. She shivered, hugging herself. Ty turned on the heat in the pickup, but this chill went bone-deep.

If Boone had opened that corral gate, then it had been to scare her away. But then she had to wonder what he'd been arguing about with the two other men that he'd feared she'd overheard.

JUST NORTH OF Antelope Flats, Boone Rasmussen turned onto a dirt road that wound down to the Tongue River Reservoir. The beat-up, older model truck and camper were parked next to the water near the dam.

As Boone got out, he saw no sign of life, but a pile of crushed beer cans glinted in the sun outside the camper. He swore under his breath as he pounded on the door and waited. Inside, he could hear rustling. "It's me," he said.

The door opened. Lamar Nichols squinted down at him. He held a Colt .45 at his side. Lamar was almost as wide as he was tall, a burly cowboy with a smoker's gravelly voice, dull brown eyes that could bore a hole through hardwood and hands large and strong enough to throttle a grown man.

"What the hell time is it?" Lamar demanded with a scowl. He wore nothing but a pair of worn jeans, his furry barrel chest bare like his feet.

"Almost two in the damned afternoon," Boone snapped. An odor wafted out of the camper. The damp small space smelled of mold, stale beer and B.O. The last thing Boone wanted was to go inside the camper with Lamar. He motioned to the weathered wooden picnic table outside next to the camper.

"Give me a minute," Lamar said and stepped back inside, closing the door.

Boone took a seat at the table facing the lake. A breeze rippled the silken green surface of the water. A few fish-ing boats bobbed along the edge of the red bluffs on the other side.

"So what's up?" Lamar said behind him.

Boone turned at once, never comfortable with Lamar behind him. "Clayton T. Brooks' body was found in a ravine."

"Where else would you expect a drunk has-been bull rider to end up?" Lamar said, making the picnic table groan under this weight as he sat down across from Boone. He'd put on a flannel shirt and wet down his dark hair—hair the same color as Boone's. Other than hair color, Boone had little else in common with his older half brother.

"That it?" Lamar asked rubbing a hand over his grizzly unshaven jaw, his eyes never leaving Boone's face.

"Monte's taking Devil's Tornado to the Bozeman rodeo."

Lamar nodded. "No big surprise there. He needs that bull. You've got him right where you want him." His beady eyes narrowed to slits. "What about last night?"

"I told you I'd take care of it." He didn't want Lamar going off half-cocked and ruining everything.

"You talk to Coltrane? He tell you what the hell he was doing back by Devil's Tornado's trailer?" Lamar asked.

"Said he was just curious about the bull. But he doesn't know anything." At least Boone hoped to hell that was true.

"You sure about that?" Lamar challenged. "What was he doing nosing around, then?"

Boone looked past him to the lake, his jaw tightening. "Coltrane isn't the only one interested in the bull. Everyone's curious. We just have to be careful."

Lamar cut his eyes at him. "There was someone else there last night. Someone over by the horse corrals."

Boone had hoped that Lamar hadn't seen the cowgirl.

"Coltrane tell you who the cowboy was with him?" Lamar asked.

Lamar thought it was a cowboy in the corral? Obviously he hadn't gotten a good look. Boone tried not to show his relief. Nor did he mention that asking Coltrane about the cowgirl would have been stupid. Lamar had been told too many times in his life he was stupid. He didn't take it well anymore.

Nor was Boone going to tell his half brother that he'd tracked down the drivers of both vehicles that had been in the lot last night after Coltrane left. One led him to the Lariat Motel in Antelope Flats. The other to Asa McCall's Sundown Ranch.

"You don't think it was Monte, do you?" Lamar asked.

Boone sighed. "Trust me, it wasn't Monte."

"Yeah, well, he might think you're the greatest thing since sliced bread, but I wouldn't trust him," Lamar said picking at his ear with a thick finger. Lamar didn't trust anyone.

Boone pushed himself to his feet. "Don't worry about last night. You just take care of your end. We're going to Bozeman. Three-day rodeo. I'm thinking we might throw in a couple more bulls. See how they do."

Lamar gave him a lopsided crooked-tooth grin.

"I just want them to look promising," Boone said. "Nothing like Devil's Tornado. He's our star. But last night in Sheridan… Let's try not to let him be quite that wild, okay?"

Lamar's expression made it clear he thought Boone was making a mistake. "You're the boss."

Boone studied his half brother, hoping he didn't forget that. He didn't need to worry about keeping Lamar in line. He had other worries. Ty Coltrane. And the cowgirl who had something that belonged to him. A syringe he had to get back.

CHAPTER SEVEN

Ty Coltrane looked over at Dusty as he slowed the pickup on the outskirts of Sheridan, Wyoming.

He couldn't help worrying about her, even though he figured she was probably right. Rasmussen hadn't even seemed to notice her this morning at the ranch. He couldn't have known she was in the horse corral last night. Maybe it *had* been an accident. And maybe it hadn't been Rasmussen who'd followed her home last night.

But warning Dusty about Boone Rasmussen was still a good idea. Ty's instincts told him that Rasmussen was dangerous. And up to *something.* He just hoped to hell that it really didn't have anything to do with Dusty.

Ty parked in front of the Sheridan Boutique. Dusty shot a look at the front window and the mannequin outfitted in a skimpy cocktail dress. He could see her already digging in her heels.

"Here's the first rule," he said quickly. "You do as I say, or I take you back to the ranch right now."

She shot him a look. He could see her struggling with the need to tell him what she thought while being forced to bite her tongue.

He grinned at her. "Sit," he ordered and got out to open her door.

She scowled at him, but let him open her door. "Oh, I

get it. Guys want to open your door just so they can look at your butt, huh?"

He laughed as she swayed her hips as she walked away from him. "Now you're starting to get the idea," he called as he slammed the pickup door and turned to find her waiting for him outside the shop.

Her head was tilted back, the western hat on her head no longer shading her lightly freckled face. In that instant, with the sun shining down on her, she looked like a goddess, capable of ruling the world. Certainly capable of stealing a cowboy's heart.

"Okay, let's get this over with," he said shaking off the image. "Go into that dressing room. I'll have clothes brought to you." She gave him a narrowed look. "This was your idea. You wanted my help," he reminded her as they entered the shop.

She clutched at his arm. "Promise you won't make me look silly?" she whispered. Her eyes were big and blue, as clear and sparkling as a Montana summer day.

He would have promised her anything right then. He nodded. "I promise. Now get in there."

The moment she disappeared behind the dressing room curtain, Ty looked around for Angela. She came out of the back, smiling as she recognized him.

"Ty," she said, surprise and what sounded like pleasure in her voice. She was an attractive twenty-five-year-old, tall, slim, with big brown eyes and hair the color of an autumn leaf.

"Hi." He felt a stab of guilt. He liked Angela. They'd dated a few times. He hadn't seen much of her since then, though. He'd been busy at the ranch, but he wished now that he'd called her.

Angela was waiting, no doubt wondering what he was doing in a women's clothing shop if not there to see her.

"How long do I have to wait in here?" came Dusty's plaintive voice from the dressing room.

"Hold your horses," he called back.

Angela glanced toward the closed curtain of the dressing room, then at Ty. Her expression altered, as if it were all suddenly clear. "Your girlfriend?"

Ty hoped to hell Dusty hadn't heard that. He took Angela's arm and led her out of earshot of the dressing room. "I'm just helping out a friend. She needs everything from the ground up. Feminine stuff."

Angela nodded as Dusty stuck her head out and Ty shooed her back into the dressing room.

"It isn't what you think," he said to Angela.

She chuckled. "When a man says that, it's exactly what a woman thinks."

"Not in this case. Dusty's just a neighbor girl."

Angela nodded, clearly not buying a word of it.

"She asked me to help her. She needs some girl clothes and I haven't a clue—"

"Let's have a look at this…*girl*," Angela said, heading for the dressing room. Ty followed her as she drew back the curtain a little and stared at the fully clothed Dusty McCall and smiled, as if relieved. "Hi. I'm Angela. Let me see what I can find for you."

Dusty looked from Angela to Ty, a smug knowing glance that said she knew at once what his relationship was with the saleswoman. He closed the curtain on her look and wandered over to a rack of blouses. He found one the color of Dusty's eyes.

"What do you think about this one?" he asked Angela.

She cocked her head at him. “You have good taste. It matches her eyes.” She pulled out a pair of slacks to go with the blouse. “Dresses?”

He nodded. “Nothing too…” He made a motion with his hand. “She’s just a kid.”

“Right,” Angela said with a note of sarcasm and headed for the dress rack.

“Also, I promised her I’d help with her hair and makeup,” Ty said quietly as he followed Angela to the back of the store.

She shot up an eyebrow.

“Exactly. I know nothing about either. Any suggestions?”

“Maxie next door at the beauty shop.” Angela pulled down a half-dozen dresses and looked over at him. “I suppose she will need lingerie as well.”

Angela moved to the lingerie and held up a black lacy bra and panties. He nodded wondering if he looked as ill at ease as he felt. Dusty in black lace? He didn’t want to think about it any more than he did the red silk teddy Angela held up. This was Slim, the girl he’d teased and tormented, trailed after and picked up from the dirt. Recently.

“Why don’t you go down to the Mint Bar and have a beer,” Angela suggested, seeing his discomfort. “I’ll send her down when she’s done.” His instant relief made Angela laugh. “How did you get roped into this, anyway?”

“Like I said. She’s a friend and I guess there wasn’t anyone else.”

Angela smiled, looking unconvinced.

“I really appreciate this,” he said. “Maybe you and I could have lunch one of these days,” he suggested.

"Maybe," she said, but something in her tone said there was little chance that was going to happen.

Sheepishly, he sneaked out the door as Angela headed for the dressing room and Dusty. He couldn't get out of the place fast enough and he did have some chores he could do before getting the beer.

He was too antsy to sit still, anyway. The way he figured it, if Dusty didn't kill him when she saw the clothes Angela had picked out, then Asa McCall or one of the McCall boys would for sure when they heard about this.

The good news was that Dusty wouldn't ever ask for his help again. That thought stopped him cold. He couldn't imagine not having Slim around.

He told himself that was because he'd always been around to protect her. Like a fifth older brother. And Dusty needed him around. Maybe especially now, he thought, frowning, wondering why she'd suddenly decided she needed a makeover.

LETTY WAS SURPRISED when she heard someone ring the bell in the motel office and realized she hadn't locked the door.

The No Vacancy sign was still up outside. She hadn't had time to take it down yet. The housekeepers were busy cleaning the rooms and since it was pretty early for anyone to be checking in…

If it was anyone she knew, they would have called out to her and then come on back through the narrow hallway that attached the motel office to the house.

She frowned as she stopped what she was doing—packing. Excited and anxious about the coming weekend, she'd already started packing, thinking she might camp out, as Hal Branson had suggested. In case she stayed. Sleeping bag, tent, cooler. She really needed to trade off the VW Beetle her parents had bought her for high school graduation and get herself a pickup truck.

The idea appealed to her, even though she knew it would shock her parents—that is, the Arnolds, she amended, who felt a young woman shouldn't drive a truck.

As she passed the hall mirror, she glanced at her image again. Her bright-red, long, curly, unruly hair was pulled back into a ponytail, her pale skin sprayed with reddish freckles, her eyes green, her mouth too large and filled with too many teeth.

She wondered what kind of car her birth mother drove. Would the woman look like her? Or was this the first of a long line of wild goose chases?

"There is a possibility that you were stolen from your birth mother and might never know the truth," Sheriff Cash McCall had told her when the doctor who'd done the illegal adoptions had confessed that she was one of the babies involved.

Stolen. Or maybe her mother hadn't wanted her. She couldn't help but think about Dusty's mother giving her up to Asa McCall when Dusty was a baby. Letty sighed. Maybe she and Dusty had more in common than either had known.

Letty told herself that she would tell her friend *everything* as soon as Letty herself knew the truth. But first she had to know who her birth parents were, what blood ran through her veins, what relatives she might have out there somewhere. She'd always envied Dusty her four brothers. A brother, or even a sister, would be cool.

Maybe even a mother named Flo who played in a heavy

metal band. She cringed at the thought, glad Hal would be going with her to meet the woman.

The bell in the office rang again. She'd been hoping whoever it was would just go away. No such luck.

As she headed for the office, she knew part of her problem was that she'd resented the fact that her "adoptive" parents had lied to her. She'd argued with them on the phone about it recently, which only made her feel more guilty. But how had her shy, couldn't-tell-a-lie-if-her-life-depended-on-it mother managed to keep such a secret? Or, for that matter, covered up the fact that she was never really pregnant?

By isolating herself from everyone, Letty thought as the bell in the office dinged again. Her adoptive parents had been standoffish, not mixing with the community at large. Now she knew why. All to hide the biggest lie of all—Leticia herself.

As Letty came down the hallway toward the motel office, she saw the broad shoulders of a man standing with his back to the counter. He wore a gray Stetson on his dark head. Even before she saw his face, she felt a premonition quake through, just a flash of danger, fear and ultimately pain.

Boone Rasmussen turned, his dark eyes fixing on her. "Leticia Arnold?"

DUSTY STARED AT the tiny red silk bra in her hand. "You have got to be kidding." She felt like she did the first time she and Letty tried on bras. How humiliating. She'd gotten all wrapped up in the stupid thing and Letty had had to help her out of it.

Angela handed in more clothing. Dusty took it, thanked

her and made sure the curtain was closed all the way before she slipped the sports bra over her head and looped the cool red silk around her, fastening it, then drawing it up over her breasts and slipping the straps over her shoulders.

The effect shocked her. She'd never owned anything but sports bras. They worked better for horseback riding.

She pulled off her boots and jeans and the same style of cotton underwear she'd worn since she was six and drew on the skimpy red silk panties. She was glad Letty wasn't here. She would have been rolling on the floor with laughter.

But the truth was, the cool red silk felt…good. Maybe too good. And she looked…okay. Better than okay. She crossed her arms over her chest, a little embarrassed. The bra made her look stacked! And the thin silk was so *revealing!*

She reached for one of the dresses and slipped it on over her head. The lightweight material dropped over her like a whisper, making her suck in her breath as she looked in the mirror.

She let out a laugh of surprise, quickly covering her mouth. That was *not* her in the mirror. No way. Well, the head was still hers, the face, the hair—but the rest…

Angela slid a couple pairs of high heels under the door and some strappy sandals.

Dusty snatched up the sandals in a pale blue that matched the color of the dress. She slipped them onto her feet—feet that hadn't seen anything but cowboy boots since she was three. Flipping her long braid up and brushing her bangs out of her eyes, she stared at herself in the mirror. The partial transformation left her speechless.

In the mirror, she saw Angela peek through the curtain behind her. "How are you doing?"

Dusty could only nod, filled with a strange mixture of having a lump in the throat and being embarrassed.

"Stunning," Angela said and gave her a smile and thumbs up.

Dusty blushed.

"Maxie next door said to send you over and she'd show you how to do your makeup and your hair," Angela said. "This for a party?"

Dusty shook her head. "I just need a change."

Angela nodded. "Who's the guy? Never mind, I think I already know. Ty Coltrane is a lucky man." She ducked back out before Dusty could set her straight.

Dusty stood in the front of the mirror, hating to take the dress off. She tried on the others, picked three, and put the blue dress back on. "Is it all right if I wear this now?" she asked Angela when the clerk returned. She handed her the extra lingerie, the blue blouse and black slacks and two other dresses. "I'll take these, too, and the sandals. And could you box up my boots and clothing I wore in?"

Dusty took another look in the mirror, hating to admit that Ty might have been right. Maybe it *was* the clothes. She couldn't wait to get the rest of her makeover.

It surprised her, but she was anxious to see Ty's reaction. As soon as she got her makeup and hair done and figured out how to walk in these sandals. If the new her passed the Ty Coltrane test, then she would be ready for Boone. But even as she thought about it, she wondered if she would ever be ready for Boone Rasmussen. Or if she wanted to be. Something about Boone still drew her and at the same time repelled her. If he really had opened that gate last night…

Well, she would find out for herself soon enough.

LETTY STOPPED SHORT of the motel counter as her gaze met Boone Rasmussen's dark one. She didn't like or trust him, and she feared it showed in her expression because his eyes darkened at the mere sight of her.

"Leticia Arnold?" he repeated staring at her as if trying to recognize her.

"Letty," she said out of habit and wished one of the motel housekeepers would come into the office. Both housekeepers were only local high school students, but Letty didn't like being alone with Boone. It was silly. She could see a housekeeper cart just two doors down. If she had to scream—

The thought shocked her. What did she think Boone would do that she would have to scream?

"Have we ever met?" he said looking around the motel office, down the hallway toward her house, then over his shoulder to the empty parking lot. Empty except for his dark green pickup.

She shook her head. "But I know who you are."

He raised a brow. "Really?"

She flushed. "If you're looking to rent a room, check-in isn't until one."

He let out a deep chuckle. "I don't want a motel room." He glanced around again, making her nervous. "I wanted to talk to you about last night. After the rodeo." He looked down the hallway again, toward her house. "Is there some place we could sit down?"

Why would Boone want to talk to *her* about last night?

No way was she going to ask him into her house. "I was just going out to get some lunch." She was a terrible liar and it showed in his expression.

He flashed her a cool smile. "This late? Okay, I could use some lunch."

The last person she wanted to have lunch with was Boone Rasmussen. She'd only said that in hopes that she could cut short whatever he wanted. But clearly, he was determined to talk to her. Better at the café than here.

"We can take my truck," he said, pushing open the motel door and waiting for her. "Don't you need to get your purse?"

She hesitated, then nodded.

"Don't get me wrong," Boone said with that same slick voice. "I'm buying. But most women I know don't go anywhere without their purses."

"I'm not like most women you know," she said without moving.

He chuckled at that. "I'll be in the truck."

This had to be about Dusty. She was doing this for her best friend.

She waited until Boone was behind the wheel of his truck before she went down the hall to her house and grabbed her small leather clutch. As she left, she locked both the house and the office. No one locked their doors in Antelope Flats. But today she was feeling strangely vulnerable.

Boone leaned across the seat as she approached the pickup and shoved open her door. With a sigh, she climbed in and closed the pickup door. *Dusty, you owe me.*

Boone looked over at her, his gaze going to her purse, his lips turning up fractionally before he started the engine.

The older model pickup was covered in mud and manure on the outside, which wasn't that out of the ordinary in a ranch town. But the inside was dirty as well, with dust, a stack of papers on the bench seat between them and empty fast-food containers on the floorboard. The cab interior smelled vaguely of onions and manure. Great combination.

"Sorry about the truck," he said as he glanced over at her again. "The hired help's been using it."

She nodded as he pulled onto the highway and drove through Antelope Flats. She'd expected him to stop at the Longhorn Café, but he drove right past it. She felt her apprehension spike before she realized where he was going. That new In and Out Drive-In outside the city limits, near the soon-to-be completed strip mall.

"Mind if we eat in the truck?" he asked as he pulled into the drive-through. "Sorry, but I don't have a lot of time. Cheeseburger, fries, cola?"

She nodded and he ordered for them both.

The radio was on low. He turned it up. "This is one of my favorites," he said of the country-and-western song playing.

She watched him tap his boot on the floor mat, the palm of his hand keeping time on the steering wheel. He's nervous, she thought. The realization made her even more apprehensive.

They were the only car in line this late. She just wished he'd get to the reason he wanted to talk to her. It certainly hadn't been for her sparkling conversational skills.

Boone took the food shoved through the window and handed her a cola, putting the sack of burgers and fries between them on the stack of papers as he paid, then drove around to the back and parked under a lone tree. They were hidden from the main road, she noted. No one would see them. Was that the idea?

He turned toward her, reached into the sack and handed her a burger and a package of fries. Her fingers trembled as she unwrapped her burger. Not that he seemed to notice. He wolfed down his burger and fries, tapping his boot to the music as if oblivious of her.

She tried to eat, but every bite seemed to grow in her mouth and didn't want to go down.

Boone finished eating and balled up his wrappers. He rolled down his window and took a three-point shot at a fifty-five-gallon barrel garbage can nearby. He missed. Letty tried to hide her smile as he swore and swung open his door, climbing out to pick it up. She bet he would have left it if she hadn't been with him.

She looked down at her food, took another tentative bite and almost jumped out of her skin when her side door suddenly swung open. She recoiled instinctively.

But Boone only moved her purse aside on the dash where she'd put it to grab some junk mail. The purse fell to the floor, spilling what little was in it. "Sorry," he said, and scooped up the contents and handed it to her before gathering up the garbage on the floorboard and taking it over to the barrel. When he slid behind the wheel again, he seemed almost too quiet.

"So what is it you want to talk to me about?" she asked. "If this is about Dusty—"

"Dusty?" he asked.

"Dusty McCall. My best friend."

He raised a brow and seemed more interested. "She was with you the other night at the rodeo?"

Finally. She knew this had to be about Dusty. She nodded. "She's the blonde with the big blue eyes. The cute one."

He nodded and rubbed the side of his jaw. "She was the one driving the pickup?" He sounded surprised by that.

"She's a ranch girl. Rides better than half the men around here. Practically ran the ranch after her dad's heart attack."

Boone smiled over at her. "Your best friend, huh?"

Letty blushed. She hadn't meant to go on so.

"So let me guess," he said glancing at her small leather clutch on the dashboard. "Dusty was the one I saw down by the corrals after the rodeo?"

She wasn't going to admit that her very smart, very capable best friend had been chasing after him. She wasn't even sure she should hint that Dusty had a crush on him. But didn't she owe her friend to at least let him know that Dusty was interested?

"She has four brothers, you know," Letty blurted out. "And they are very protective of their sister."

"I've heard of the McCall boys." Boone smiled a slow unnerving smile. "You're a little protective of her as well, it seems." His gaze shifted to her lap. "You've hardly touched your food. You seemed so anxious to have lunch when we were back at the motel."

Letty blushed again. She looked down at her lap and took a bite of her burger, knowing she'd never be able to swallow it. This had been a terrible mistake.

"I'm curious," Boone said. She could feel his eyes on her. "What exactly was your friend doing wandering around the rodeo grounds so late after the rodeo was over?"

Letty practically choked on her burger. "She was looking for you! You told her to meet you there!"

He drew back in surprise, one eyebrow going up. "Where would she get an idea like that? I don't even know her."

Letty stared at him, all kinds of smart retorts galloping through her brain. She reminded herself that her best friend had a crush on this guy. "I guess there was a misunderstanding," she said feebly. But then Letty added, "She was almost trampled by the bucking horses!"

"That corral gate has a bad latch. She was lucky," he said, the words *this time* seeming to hang in the air.

Letty felt a chill and told herself she was overreacting. What if Boone hadn't been talking to Dusty, hadn't told her to meet him, hadn't had anything to do with the latch on the gate? What if she was dead wrong about him?

"She risked her life to meet you," Letty said.

His brow shot up again and he smiled, this time the humor reaching his eyes. "I'm flattered."

Letty felt her face flame again.

He started the pickup.

She hadn't finished her burger, but he didn't seem to care as he drove her back to the motel.

"Hey," he said when she started to get out. "Why don't you give me Dusty McCall's number? If there was a misunderstanding last night, I'd like to apologize to her."

He took a pencil and a scrap of paper from the glove box and scribbled down the number Letty hesitantly gave him. "Thanks."

"Thank you for lunch," she said, good manners taking over.

As he drove off, Letty stared after him wondering what

that had been about. One thing was clear. Boone Rasmussen hadn't even known Dusty McCall existed.

Well, he did now, thanks to her. Dusty was going to get her wish—a call from Boone Rasmussen.

But Letty wasn't sure she'd done her best friend a favor.

CHAPTER EIGHT

Ty was sitting in the Mint Bar drinking a cold beer, worrying about Dusty when he heard the news.

Clayton T. Brooks had been found—dead.

He took the news hard. He'd liked Clayton. "What happened?"

The bartender, a short stocky man named Eddie, told him that he'd heard that Clayton had been killed when his pickup went off the highway north of town. "He was in here Thursday night. Closed down the place, as usual."

"Do you remember him mentioning anything in particular?" Ty asked.

The bartender laughed. "Kept talking about someone named Little Joe." He shrugged. "Have no idea."

Ty nodded, remembering how Clayton had been that day at work. Now that he thought about it, he did remember Clayton mentioning Little Joe and Devil's Tornado. If only he could remember what exactly had Clayton so worked up.

"Anything specific he said about this Little Joe?" Ty asked.

The bartender shook his head. "You know Clayton. Never shut up." He smiled sheepishly. "You just tuned him out after a while. Sorry."

Ty knew exactly what the man meant. "Any idea what

he was doing north of town?" There was little north of Antelope Flats, and Clayton lived in the opposite direction.

Eddie shrugged and shook his head. "No clue. Not much up that way."

Except for the Edgewood Roughstock Company ranch, Ty thought. And Devil's Tornado. Was it possible the damned fool had been going to see the bull? But who was Little Joe?

The door opened and Ty caught a whiff of perfume, something light, like a spring day, that made him turn toward the entrance for a moment.

Couldn't be Slim. She wouldn't be caught dead wearing perfume. He turned his attention back to his beer. Maybe he shouldn't have deserted her. As if his staying in the boutique would have helped matters. But he hated the thought that she might be mad at him. Might never trust him again.

He caught movement out of the corner of his eye and looked up to see a young woman moving through the series of arches along the bar's entryway. All he caught was a glimpse of her. A flash of blue and short, soft blond curls, but they were enough to hold his attention as she moved in and out of the archways. Flash. Flash. Flash. She was slim and leggy, the blue dress fluttering just above her knees as she moved. The dress the same color as the blouse he'd picked out for Dusty. The same color as Dusty's eyes.

Even when she came around the corner toward the bar, he didn't recognize her at first. True to his gender, he was looking at her curves, not her face. That is, until she stopped just feet from him.

His gaze flicked up to her face and all the breath rushed from him. "Slim?" He tried to get to his feet, practically knocking over his stool. She looked so… different. So not like the tomboy he'd known his whole life.

All he could say was, "You cut your hair!"

Her long braid was gone, her hair now chin-length, the pale blond a cap of loose curls that framed her incredible face. But that wasn't the half of the transformation. Slim had curves! He stared at her, dumbstruck.

She smiled tentatively. "So what do you think?"

When had she grown up? Sometime over the past few years and he hadn't noticed. Probably because she'd hidden it so well under those huge shirts and jackets.

He dropped back on his stool, simply flummoxed. This was Slim. The tomboy from the next ranch, the cowgirl he'd teased and tormented for years. "You're…you're gorgeous."

She cut her eyes at him as she slid onto the stool next to him. Did she think he was kidding? She let out a long sigh, as if she'd been holding her breath. Her eyes shone. She blinked, and he realized she'd been close to tears. Did it matter that much to her what he thought?

"You aren't just saying that, are you?"

He shook his head, unable to quit staring at her. He'd wanted to help her find her girl side. He hadn't expected this kind of transformation. Asa was going to kill him. If Dusty's brothers didn't get to him first.

Eddie gave her an appreciative look, took her order and poured her a cola.

"You're okay with this new look?" Ty asked, watching her pluck up the maraschino cherry Eddie had put on top.

She leaned back her head, holding the cherry over her mouth. She was even wearing lipstick! With perfect white teeth, she nipped the cherry from its stem and took a sip of her drink, dropping the stem on her napkin.

"I feel so…different," she said and shot him a grin, the same grin that had always captivated him.

He couldn't believe this *woman* had been hidden under all that loose western clothing and that tomboy attitude. Worse, he couldn't believe she was his Slim. He felt bowled over—stunned by this change in her, of course, but even more shocked at how it made him feel.

He'd always liked her. But she'd just been a kid. The daughter of Asa McCall. The kid sister to J.T., Rourke, Cash and Brandon McCall. In other words, someone he thought of more as a buddy. A safe thought.

The thoughts he was having now weren't safe.

"Thank you for helping me," she said and took another sip of her cola.

"I think we should keep my part in this our little secret."

He caught her checking out her image in the mirror across the room. As far as he knew, the old Dusty had avoided mirrors, never seeming to care what she looked like. In a way, he missed that. He frowned, suddenly afraid he'd created a monster as she licked her lips and gave him a slow smile, as if she knew exactly the effect she was having on him.

"I can't wait to see—" she ran her finger along the top of her glass "—everyone's reaction."

Everyone? Letty, her brothers, her parents or someone else? He hated to think what effect she was going to have on young, impressionable ranch hands. He was still trying to get over the effect she was having on him.

He cut his eyes at her as a thought struck him. Was it possible she'd done this for some boy she had a crush on?

He caught a gleam in her eye that he'd seen too many times before—usually when she was about to do something either dangerous or crazy, or both.

"What are you up to?" he asked, more than a little worried as he caught a whiff of the perfume he'd smelled earlier. The scent was definitely coming from Slim.

"You're scaring me," he said and meant it.

She laughed and downed the rest of her cola. The look she shot him making it clear she wasn't going to tell him, she said, "Ready?"

He frowned at her. He wasn't ready for this new Dusty, that was for sure.

"Would you drop me off at Letty's?"

"Sure." He was relieved it was Letty she wanted to try her new look on first. That would give him time to hightail it back to his ranch before Asa McCall came looking for him with a shotgun. "Don't forget. My part in this is our little secret."

She nodded distractedly. It seemed she had already forgotten about him. The story of his life.

SHERIFF CASH MCCALL was sitting in a booth at his sister-in-law's Longhorn Café when he saw the coroner come through the door. Cash had just finished a late lunch—bacon cheeseburger, extra homemade fries and a piece of her field berry pie—when Raymond Winters slid into the booth across from him.

Cash took one look at Winters' face and said, "Whatever it is, I don't think I want to hear it."

The coroner dropped his voice and glanced around the nearly empty café. "You're going to think I'm nuts."

"I've never thought you were nuts." Raymond Winters

was the most sane man Cash knew, especially considering what he did for a living.

He dropped his voice even lower. “Clayton was murdered.”

Cash groaned, knowing Winters wouldn’t be saying this unless he had good reason. Cash pushed his plate away. “Okay, let’s hear it.”

“Well, this is where it gets crazy,” Winters said. “I was examining the body and I found abrasions that could only have been made *after* Clayton was dead.”

Cash frowned, trying to understand.

“There appeared to be several blows to the head that caused his death,” Winters continued. “One bled profusely, but when I checked the pickup, there wasn’t the type of blood splatter I would have expected to find, given that he was contained inside the pickup as it rolled. Should have been blood all over the place. Also, the head wounds aren’t consistent with those from a car accident.”

“You’re saying he didn’t die in the pickup.”

Winters nodded. “But that isn’t all.” He looked even more upset. “I found something on the knees of his jeans and on one hand.”

“What?” Cash asked, fear heavy as stones in his belly.

“Fresh bovine dung.”

“I beg your pardon? Why in the hell would he have dung on him?”

Winters shook his head. “Good question. But I think you might want to order an autopsy because I’d wager my right arm that Clayton T. Brooks was murdered in some cow pasture and put in that pickup to make it look like an accident.”

Dusty couldn't wait to see Letty's face. She walked into the motel office and rang the bell rather than go right on in to her friend's attached house as she normally did.

"May I help you?" Letty asked coming out from the back.

"I'd like a room."

Letty looked up at the sound of the familiar voice, her eyes widening in shock. "Dusty?"

Dusty laughed a little embarrassed, practically crossing her fingers in the hopes that Letty wouldn't hate her new look. "What do you think?"

Letty seemed speechless. "What happened to your hair?"

"I cut it. This is the latest style. I had no idea I had naturally curly hair. What about the dress?" She turned in a slow circle and waited for Letty's reaction, a little disappointed in it so far.

"I've never seen you in a dress before."

"Because I've never had one before," she said, wishing she wasn't feeling a little annoyed by Letty's lack of enthusiasm at the change. She'd thought Letty would be as excited as she was.

"Did you do this for Boone?" Letty asked, not sounding pleased about the prospect.

"No," Dusty snapped, although she had and they both knew it. "I just decided it was time I stopped dressing like a boy."

Letty glanced down at her own clothing: jeans, boots, western shirt. The two of them had always dressed the same.

"Not that I won't still wear my jeans and boots most of the time," Dusty added.

"You look nice," Letty said.

Nice? Dusty looked away, not wanting Letty to see how hurt she was. Part of her wanted to just turn and leave in a huff. The other wanted to say something to fix the distance she felt between them. It seemed to be widening lately, and she didn't know how to change that. "So what are you up to?"

"Nothing much."

Past her, Dusty saw what looked like a suitcase by the wall. Beside it was a cooler. A sleeping bag was rolled up on top of it. "Are you going camping?"

Letty glanced back at the suitcase. "Just putting some things away."

"Wanna grab something to eat?" Dusty asked, feeling as if she were clutching at straws.

"Already ate." Letty turned back and met her gaze. "Boone Rasmussen stopped by and took me to lunch."

Dusty couldn't hide her shock. Or avoid that sinking feeling in the pit of her stomach. "He asked you to lunch?"

"He just wanted to talk about you," Letty said quickly.

From sinking, the feeling shot to dizzying. Her stomach came alive with butterflies, her head spinning. Wasn't this what she'd wanted? "What did you tell him?"

"It was a quick lunch. He just asked your name. He saw you back by the corrals after the rodeo."

Dusty groaned. "Did he say anything else about me?"

"I'm sure you'll be hearing from him. He asked for your number. Is that lipstick you're wearing?"

Dusty nodded and fluttered her lashes. "Mascara, too."

Letty let out a long breath. "You look so…different."

"Different good, though, right?"

Her friend nodded, her smile wavering a little.

"Letty, I haven't changed."

Letty's look said she wasn't so sure about that.

ASA FOUND Shelby in the kitchen. She hadn't heard him come in. Her back was to him, ramrod straight, shoulders squared, her head up as she stood at the sink, staring out the window as if lost in thought.

She must have sensed him because she tensed, as if braced for a blow.

He stepped up behind her and, on impulse, wrapped his arms around her, burying his face into the soft sweet spot between her neck and shoulder.

She leaned back against him, a small sound escaping her throat.

He gripped her tighter, wishing he never had to let her go, needing her as he'd never needed her before and hating that even more. She deserved better. She always had.

"I love you," he whispered against her warm skin, words he had uttered too few times to her.

"Oh, Asa," she said, her voice breaking. Her body began to shake. She turned and he drew her close, cradling her head in his hands as she buried her face in his chest.

He stroked her hair, closing his eyes as he filed away the memory of its feel beneath his fingers, just as he had filed away every touch they'd shared so he would never forget.

Past her through the window he could see the warm gold cast of the sun flowing over the land. The land he'd loved so much. More than he'd loved his own wife. Fool's gold, he thought. He would give anything to turn back the clock. To undo his two most unforgivable sins. He'd chosen the ranch over Shelby, sending her away from not only him, but also from her own children.

And then he'd turned around and ransomed the ranch. Betraying his children. In the end, he'd lost what he loved most.

He smiled at the irony. His entire life had been about the ranch. Hadn't he promised his father on his deathbed that he'd make the Sundown Ranch the biggest and best? That he would do whatever it took? Sacrifice everything? Sell his very soul?

If only he could renegotiate his deal with the devil. It wouldn't be to save the ranch. It would be for those wasted years he'd spent apart from this woman in his arms. How could she ever forgive him? He'd taken her home, her life, her children. And still she loved him.

His throat closed at the thought, his chest swelling with an unbearable pain. It wasn't cancer that was eating away at his insides—it was regret.

She pulled back to look up at him, hastily wiping at her tears, as if ashamed to have broken down in front of him. Her eyes met his. He felt her stiffen, as if bracing herself. She had always known him too well.

"I'd hoped this could wait until after Cash and Molly's wedding..." He swallowed, trying not to let her hear the anguish he was feeling, failing miserably.

Her eyes filled with tears. "When do you want me to tell them all to be here?"

"Tonight," Asa said. "It's time."

CHAPTER NINE

By the time Dusty got home, her feet were killing her. The new bra was pinching her and the cool evening breeze had chilled her bare legs.

Letty dropped her off, declining to come in. "It's been a long day."

Her friend had told her a little more about her lunch with Boone. The important thing was that he'd not only asked about her, he'd also taken down her phone number.

Maybe he had already called, she thought as she entered the house, having forgotten about her new look—except for an unconscious eagerness to get into something more comfortable.

"What in the world?" said a familiar deep male voice from the direction of one of the chairs near the fireplace.

Dusty froze as she spotted her oldest brother, J.T., sitting in a chair by the fireplace, a stack of papers in front of him. While J.T. had married and lived on another part of the ranch with his wife Reggie, he still did most of the actual running of the ranch and spent a lot of time at the main house. She'd hoped to just sneak in without being noticed. No such luck.

"I cut my hair," she said defensively.

J.T. grimaced. "I can see that. *Why?*"

"Why not? Anyway, I like it and that's all that matters."

"That's good, because it will take a long time to grow back out."

"Who says I'm going to grow it back out?" She groaned, knowing that she'd have to go through this with all four of her brothers. J.T. was the oldest and married to Reggie. Cash, was the sheriff, and marrying Molly in a few weeks. Rourke worked the ranch with J.T. since getting out of prison and marrying Cassidy. Rourke and Cassidy had one boy and another on the way. Brandon had eloped with Anna, the daughter of the family's worst enemy.

Asa was still fit to be tied over that, since the McCalls and VanHorns had been feuding for years.

"I hope you haven't forgotten that we're taking the herd up to summer pasture tomorrow morning starting at daybreak," J.T. said.

Dusty groaned under her breath. She *had* forgotten. "Of course I hadn't forgotten." No getting out of it, either. "I'll be saddled up and waiting for the rest of you before the sun comes up." She didn't give J.T. a chance to say anything else smart to her and would have stormed up the stairs to her room, but her feet were killing her. She slipped off her high-heeled sandals and, carrying them, limped toward the stairs.

Behind her, she heard her brother chuckle. "Women."

Dusty smiled to herself as she topped the stairs. All her life she'd been called kid or girl. Her oldest brother had just called her a woman. That meant that this makeover had worked. Maybe Ty knew more about women than she'd thought.

Dusty tossed the sandals aside with a sigh of relief and got out of the dress and the silk underthings. With a kind of welcome-home feeling, she pulled on her cotton pants, sports bra, worn jeans and her favorite faded soft flannel shirt, one that had belonged to her brother Brandon.

Glancing in the mirror, she told herself that Letty was wrong. She hadn't changed. But when she saw her image in the glass, she knew better. Haircut aside, she now saw herself differently. She kind of missed her long hair. But there was no going back now. She had changed—and more than just her hair.

She hugged herself, remembering how she'd felt with Ty at the Mint Bar. All tingly and warm. And that was with *Ty*.

What would she feel with Boone? The thought scared her. Boone was the unknown. He was danger. Excitement. Was that why she was attracted to him? Because he was like nothing she'd never known? And only he could fulfill this desire that burned in her?

She jumped at the soft tap on her bedroom door. "*Yes?*" It had better not be J.T. to give her more grief.

Shelby opened the door and peeked in, her eyes widening at the sight of her daughter's short hair. She opened her mouth, closed it, opened it again. "We're all waiting downstairs."

Dusty blinked. "Why?"

Shelby pushed the door all the way open. "I thought one of your brothers had told you. Everyone is here for dinner. At your father's request."

Family dinners were never good news. Her brothers all had their own houses and only came to dinner at the ranch when summoned. They were all expected to attend without question.

It still irked Dusty that Shelby had come back after all

those years and thought she could just step into being the mother. A mother didn't abandon her children.

"I really don't want—"

"Your father has something he wants to tell all of you," Shelby cut in, an edge to her words that brooked no argument.

"Fine. I'll be right down."

Shelby studied her for a moment, reminding Dusty of her makeover, but, to Dusty's relief, said nothing as she closed the door and left.

Dusty turned to look in the mirror. On impulse, she took off Brandon's old shirt and slipped into the blue blouse that Angela had told her Ty picked out. Amazing. As Dusty stared at herself in the mirror, she realized the blue was the same color as her eyes. Not that Ty would have realized that.

She considered putting on the slacks. Even the sandals again, but stuck with the jeans and boots. Fluffing up her short curls, she took one last look at herself in the mirror. Why tonight, of all nights, did she have to face the entire family?

But she knew that wasn't what was bothering her. The moment Shelby told her about the family dinner, worry had begun to gnaw at the pit of her stomach. For months, she'd known something was going on between her parents, ever since during one of these "family dinners" Shelby had come back from the dead.

Dusty feared that whatever her father had to tell them tonight would be even worse.

JUST OFF THE HIGHWAY, not a mile down the road toward the Edgewood Roughstock Company ranch road, Boone

Rasmussen saw the big black car pulled to the side, motor running, and knew the driver had been waiting for him.

He swore as he slowed, telling himself he shouldn't have been surprised. Waylon Dobbs. He'd wondered how soon he would be hearing from the veterinarian.

Pulling his pickup behind the big shiny Lincoln, he cut the engine, leaned back and waited. If Waylon thought he was going to make this easy, he was a bigger fool than Boone had suspected.

From behind the wheel of the Lincoln, Dobbs peered into his rearview mirror. Then, seeming to realize that Boone wasn't going to come to him, he finally opened the car door and got out.

Dobbs looked nervous as hell as he walked toward Boone's pickup. Boone rolled down the window as the rodeo veterinarian came alongside and smiled as if glad to see Dobbs when he was anything but.

Waylon Dobbs was a local veterinarian who volunteered at rodeos to make sure the animals were fit. For volunteering, Dobbs got his name on one of the large signs that ringed the rodeo arena. Nothing like free publicity.

In return, Dobbs—a short, squat, bald fifty-something urban cowboy—did basically nothing, which seemed to suit him just fine—and worked well for Boone. What Dobbs didn't see didn't get him into trouble.

That was until last night's rodeo. Unfortunately, Dobbs had seen something he shouldn't have.

"I wanted to continue our discussion from last night," Dobbs said looking around nervously. He had a high, almost squeaky voice that made Boone want to strangle the life out of him. "I didn't want to take the chance that we might be overheard again."

There wasn't another soul for miles, the land spreading out in rolling hills of grass and silver sage. No one could possibly hear what they had to say, if that was what Dobbs was worried about.

"I thought we'd pretty much settled things last night," Boone said, resenting the hell out of the fact that he'd had to cut Dobbs in.

Dobbs licked at his thin lips. "It's just that I've been thinking."

Boone smiled and slowly shook his head back and forth. "That could be a mistake, Waylon." His gaze cut straight to the older man's gaze, as stark and deadly as a bullet.

Dobbs swallowed and straightened his just-out-of-the-box black Stetson. Boone wondered if the vet was already spending his take. Now that would *really* be a mistake.

"I'm risking a lot going along with this," Dobbs said, shifting from one foot to the other, his gaze traveling up and down the road for a moment before he looked at Boone again. "I have a reputation to worry about."

Boone laughed and moved so fast Dobbs never saw it coming. He swung open his pickup door, catching the vet in the chest. The force sent Dobbs windmilling backward, off balance, seemingly destined to land hard on his backside. The man's eyes were huge, his open mouth gasping like a fish thrown up on the bank.

But before Dobbs could hit the ground, Boone was out of the pickup. He grabbed the lapels of Dobbs's western-cut suit jacket and swung him around, slamming him hard against the side of the pickup.

"*Reputation?*" Boone ground out. "Let's not b.s. each other here, Dobbs. I know why you ended up in Antelope

Flats. You got run out of your practice back east. Something to do with gambling and prostitutes?"

"It was never proved," Dobbs cried. "They didn't have any evidence to—"

Boone twisted the fabric of his jacket, strangling any further denials as he leaned into Dobbs's face. "Don't underestimate my generosity," Boone said quietly. "Or my patience. That would be a mistake." He shoved Dobbs away so he could open his pickup door.

"Are you *threatening* me?" Dobbs said behind him, voice breaking.

Boone looked down at the toes of his boots and closed his eyes for a moment, then turned slowly to face him again. "Let me make this easy for you. You tell anyone what you know and I'll kill you, Waylon."

Dobbs let out a nervous laugh. "You aren't *serious*."

"Want to stake your life on that, Waylon?" Boone asked in a louder voice as he advanced on the man again.

Dobbs stumbled back, his Adam's apple bobbing up and down as he shook his head.

"So we understand each other?"

"No reason to start making threats," Dobbs said in a meek voice. "I just thought we could talk some business, that's all."

"We've talked all the business we're ever going to talk, Waylon," Boone said, feeling unusually tired.

"I understand."

"Do you, Waylon? I'd hate like hell for this to be a problem between us."

"No problem, Boone. No problem at all."

Boone studied him, afraid there was indeed a problem. One he'd have to deal with. "And you wouldn't be stupid enough to take this any further than between the two of us, would you, Waylon?"

"Just forget I even mentioned it."

"I'll try," Boone said.

Dobbs turned and practically ran back to the Lincoln.

Boone leaned against his pickup as Dobbs revved the engine and swung the car around, driving down into the shallow ditch and back up onto the road, leaving deep tracks in the dirt as he hightailed it back toward Antelope Flats.

Dust boiled up behind the Lincoln. Boone closed his eyes, fighting the dull ache behind his eyes. He couldn't trust Dobbs. Hell, the man was a walking time bomb.

With a curse, he turned and started to get into his truck when he saw something that stopped him. A second set of tracks in the ditch on the other side of the road, opposite the ones Dobbs had just made.

Boone felt something give inside him.

Waylon had turned around twice. Just now to leave. And earlier, when he'd parked to wait for yours truly.

Which meant… Boone looked up the road toward the Edgewood Roughstock Company ranch. The stupid son of a— No, Boone told himself, Waylon wasn't stupid enough to go to Monte with this. Or was he?

JUST AS Dusty had feared, all eyes were on her as she walked into the dining room. "I cut my hair," she announced before anyone could say anything. "And I like it!" She took her chair next to her brother Rourke and looked around the table, daring any of them to give her a hard time.

"I like it, too," Shelby said.

Dusty didn't look at her mother. She didn't care if Shelby liked it or not. She took a drink from her water glass, hating that she couldn't forgive Shelby for giving her up all those years ago. It was bad enough that a mother would just turn her four young sons over to their father and leave. But to also give up her only daughter…

The rest of the women, all her brothers' wives, chimed in with complimentary things to say.

Dusty shifted her gaze to the head of the table where her father sat. She was still angry with him for the lie he and Shelby had cooked up. Not just about Shelby's alleged death. Almost twenty-two years ago, the two had met supposedly to discuss matters. The one-night "meeting" had resulted in Dusty's conception.

Later, Asa had brought Dusty back to the ranch, telling everyone he had adopted the infant after her parents had been killed.

She looked so much like her father and brothers that Dusty doubted anyone had believed that story. In fact, her brothers recently told her that they thought she was the result of an affair their father had had. They'd just never dreamed it was with their mother—not when they were putting flowers on her grave at the cemetery.

What a twisted pact her parents had made. All, according to them, because they couldn't live together and refused to get divorced. Dusty still couldn't believe the lies they'd told. Still couldn't forgive either of them. But because she'd always been her father's favorite, it was harder to continue being angry with him.

As she waited for him to comment on her new look, she realized she was holding her breath, desperately wanting his approval.

He reached for his wineglass and raised it in a salute. "You look even more like your mother."

Oh, great. As if she needed a reminder of how much she looked like Shelby.

Her father met her gaze, holding it with a tender one of his own, then looked over at Shelby in the chair to his left.

"Both the most beautiful women I have ever known," he said.

The room fell silent for a long uncomfortable moment at the intimacy of his words.

Fortunately, Martha came in to serve dinner and everyone started in at once, the men talking ranching, the women discussing drapery and wall colors since all of them except Cash and Molly had new houses. Eventually, the women began to talk about Cash's and Molly's wedding.

Dusty's new look was quickly forgotten. She breathed a sigh of relief and listened for the phone, hoping that Letty was right, that Boone would call. And that this was just a family dinner, like normal families had. Not a McCall family dinner that bode anything but well.

"So what is *this* dinner about?" her brother J.T. asked, making Dusty want to hit him. "Going to reveal another big secret?"

Silence dropped like a bucket of cold water over the room. Dusty stole a glance at her brothers. They all looked as worried as she felt, their wives just as uncomfortable and concerned.

"Getting everyone together doesn't have to be about anything," Shelby said, a little too sharply. "We're *family.*" Her voice cracked. "Can't we just eat our dinner in peace?"

No one said anything, but there were sideways glances and Dusty noticed that Shelby seemed to purposely avoid looking at Asa.

But the rest of them were looking at him. Waiting.

He cleared his throat, reached over and covered his wife's hand with his own. "J.T.'s right." She seemed to wince at his touch. Or maybe his words. Slowly she lifted her head, her lips quivering for a moment, eyes shiny.

The phone rang.

Dusty's pulse jumped. Not Boone. Not now. Not when maybe they would finally find out what was going on between her parents. The two had been acting more than weird ever since Shelby's return.

Martha appeared in the doorway. "I'm sorry to interrupt," she said quickly. "But it's the fire chief for Cash. He says it's urgent."

Cash excused himself to take the call on the phone in the hall, returning almost at once to say he had to leave. "There's been a fire at Waylon Dobbs's place tonight. He's dead. He was trapped inside. I'm sorry, but I have to go."

Shelby made a small sound, her hand going to her throat. "Cash, can't it wait for just a few—"

"Cash has to do his job," Asa said patting Shelby's hand. "It's all right. We'll do this another night. Soon."

Shelby's shoulders slumped. She dropped her head. Clearly she had hoped to finish whatever she and Asa had planned tonight.

Dusty was relieved. She'd been on an emotional roller coaster for weeks now. While she would worry and wonder, she could wait. She'd been worrying and wondering ever since Shelby had returned.

"Martha, would you serve dessert," Shelby said, surprising Dusty at how quickly her mother could compose herself.

The conversation around the table resumed with talk of Waylon Dobbs. He hadn't lived in Antelope Flats for long and Dusty hadn't known him. She shuddered at the thought of the man being burned up in his house, though.

Her mind had gone back to niggling her about what her father had been about to announce when something her brother Rourke said caught her attention.

"He had this high-pitched and kind of squeaky voice," Rourke was saying. "Odd-looking little man. Drove a black Lincoln."

Dusty felt herself start. She'd heard that voice last night at the rodeo. That was one of the men Boone Rasmussen had been with by the horse corrals. She frowned, wondering now what they'd been arguing about.

The conversation finally came back to cattle, decorating and wedding plans, but the life felt drained out of it. Everyone seemed to be trying to act normal. As if this family could ever be normal, Dusty thought.

She picked at her dessert. Her parents had both grown exceptionally quiet, especially Shelby. What had their father been about to tell them? Dusty stared down the table at her father, hoping he would look up and that she might see the answer in his eyes. He didn't. He seemed engrossed in the chocolate tart Martha had baked—and nothing else.

But she knew better. Her heart felt heavy. She opened her mouth, desperately needing to get his attention.

He looked up, surprising her. Their eyes locked. And she saw a pleading in his look, as if asking for her forgiveness. Her heart dropped like a stone down a bottomless well as he dragged his gaze away, the set of his jaw making it clear she would learn nothing tonight no matter how hard she pushed him.

She took a bite of her tart. Waiting for the next family dinner would be like waiting for that stone to hit bottom.

Dinner over, the women got up to help clear the dishes. Dusty hesitated, but her father didn't give her a second glance as he excused himself saying he had some business he had to attend to.

Her brothers all wandered into the living room in front of the fireplace.

The phone rang again. Shelby took it in the hall on the way to the kitchen. Dusty watched her mother's expression as she took the call.

She heard Shelby say, "Yes, Dusty is here. May I say who's calling?"

Dusty felt her pulse jump. Was it Boone?

Shelby turned to look back toward the dining room, her grave expression softening. "Oh, I'm sorry, Ty, I didn't recognize your voice. Dusty's right here. No, you didn't interrupt dinner. We'd just finished." She signaled with the phone.

Ty? Disappointment made her body heavy as Dusty put her dishes in the sink and went to take the call. She waited until her mother had returned to the kitchen before saying, "*Yes?*"

"Nice to hear your voice, too, Slim," Ty said. "Why so grumpy?"

"I'm not grumpy. There is probably a good reason you called me?"

Ty sighed on the other end of the line. "I was worried about you, okay? How did the new look go over?"

"Fine. My brothers hate it, my dad said I looked just

like Shelby, then he got all teary-eyed and my mother said she loved it."

"That bad, huh?" He chuckled. "I just wanted to make sure you were okay."

"I'm okay." She glanced in the hall mirror, still surprised by what she saw, and ran a hand through her short blond curls. "Thank you for today."

"No problem."

Suddenly, she felt like crying. She told herself it was because she was worried about her father and disappointed that the call hadn't been Boone. She felt awful for being short with Ty. He'd been so good to her today. "What did you name the foal?"

"What do you think? Miracle."

She smiled. "I'm glad you called."

He chuckled, sounding almost shy. "Sure you are. You take care of yourself, okay, Slim?" He sounded worried about her, as if there was reason to be.

"Thanks," she said and hung up. Up in her room, she threw herself on the bed, feeling so overwhelmed she felt as if she were drowning. What was wrong with her?

Her private line rang. She sat up and reached for it, quickly wiping her tears. As bad as she was feeling, she hoped it would be Letty. She really needed to talk. She snatched up the phone.

"Dusty McCall?" a male voice asked.

Her pulse roared in her ears. She swallowed the lump in her dust-dry throat. "Yes?" she managed to get out.

"It's Boone. Boone Rasmussen."

CHAPTER TEN

Boone sat on the edge of his bed in the bedroom Monte Edgewood had given him on the second floor at the back of the house.

Now that he had her on the line, he wasn't sure what to say. If her friend Letty was telling the truth, Dusty McCall was the one who'd been in the horse corral after the Sheridan rodeo. The one who might have overheard his argument with Waylon Dobbs. The one whom he'd seen pick up something gingerly from the dirt and put it in her bag.

The syringe he'd dropped.

He rubbed a hand over his face. "I got your number from your friend Letty?" he said tentatively. "I hope I have the right person. You were at the rodeo with your friend last night in Sheridan? I think I saw you afterward?" He thought he heard a choking sound.

"I'm Dusty McCall," a young-sounding female voice said. "I was at the rodeo last night."

Boone smiled. "Good. Then you're the one I'm looking for."

Silence.

This was going to be harder than he'd thought. What had he hoped? That she'd blurt out what she'd heard. More important, what she'd not only seen, but also now had in her possession? All day, he'd kept telling himself that maybe she didn't know what the syringe had been used for.

But it came down to only one thing: then why had she picked it up?

"Letty told me that you were almost trampled by the bucking horses when they broke through the corral gate last night," he said, trying a different approach. "I wanted to be sure you were all right."

She let out an audible sigh followed by what could have been a little laugh. "I'm fine." She sounded nervous. Or maybe she was scared. He'd tracked her down. He knew who she was.

"I'm glad to hear you're all right. I would hate for you to get hurt because of me." He waited, hoping she would say something. She didn't and he realized he was going to have to get her alone. He couldn't tell anything over the damned phone. "Letty told me you thought you were supposed to meet me after the rodeo."

A strangled sound.

"I don't think we've ever met, have we?" he asked.

"No." Definitely nervous. What did she know?

He felt his skin crawl with worry. "I apologize if there was a misunderstanding last night. Let me make it up to you. What are you doing tonight?"

"*Tonight?*"

He glanced at the clock on the bedside table and swore under his breath. "Sorry, I didn't realize how late it was." His disappointment was real. "How about tomorrow night?"

A groan. "I'm going to be on a cattle drive with my brothers the rest of the week."

How lucky for her. And unlucky for him. Breaking

into the ranch was out of the question. Far too risky. Hell, she might not even have the syringe anymore. Or it could have fallen to the bottom of her bag and she'd completely forgotten about it.

The one thing he was sure of—she hadn't given it to Ty Coltrane, or the sheriff would already be at Boone's door. "What day will you be back?"

"Friday."

Damn. "Oh, that's too bad, I'll be in Bozeman Friday night at the rodeo." A thought. "You wouldn't be planning to go to the Bozeman rodeo, would you?" Better than seeing her in Antelope Flats. If he could get her away from town, away from her family, away from Ty Coltrane.

"The Bozeman rodeo?" she echoed.

He held his breath.

"Yes, that is, I was thinking about going," she said.

Boone began to relax a little. This might work out better than he'd hoped. "Great, then it's a date."

"Great." She sounded strange.

He thought of Dobbs and hoped he didn't have another blackmailer that he would have to deal with on his hands.

"There's just one thing," he said. "I thought I saw you with Ty Coltrane last night. If the two of you are…involved…"

He heard a gasp on the other end of the line. "No! We've just known each other since we were kids."

"You're not…seeing him then?"

"*No*."

"My mistake. I thought I saw you together last night."

Another strangled sound. "We ran into each other after the rodeo."

With a silent groan, Boone lay back against the headboard and closed his eyes. There was no way he'd told this

Dusty McCall chick to meet him after the rodeo. Then on top of that, Ty Coltrane had been sneaking around Devil's Tornado and then he and Dusty had just happened to hook up.

At least Coltrane had been honest about the fact that he'd been there prying into Boone's business.

What did Dusty McCall want? If she'd given the syringe to anyone, wouldn't they have taken it to the rodeo veterinarian? And Waylon Dobbs would have told Boone today on the road. Dobbs would have used it as leverage for more money to keep his mouth shut.

Boone had feared that Waylon had driven down to the Edgewood Ranch house today, maybe told Monte what he knew, hoping to get even more money.

But fortunately Monte had been the same old Monte, clasping him on the shoulder, calling him son, offering him a cold beer, which meant his only loose end now was Dusty McCall. She either still had the syringe. Or, if he had any luck at all, would have discarded it by now, not realizing what she had in her hot little hands.

Either way, Boone would find out in Bozeman. It was the being patient part that was hard. He couldn't chance the syringe getting into the wrong hands.

"So I guess I'll see you Friday night," he said, trying to keep the frustration out of his voice. "Look me up when you get to the rodeo and we can make plans for later."

"Okay."

"Good. I'm really looking forward to this." He hung up and swore. Dusty McCall was the last thing he needed.

DUSTY HUNG UP and mentally smacked herself for being so tongue-tied on the phone with Boone. She sat for a moment, too stunned to move. Boone had asked her out. Wasn't that what she'd been hoping for?

She picked up the phone and called her best friend.

"Boone called. He asked me out," she blurted, surprised that she was half hoping Letty would try to talk her out of it.

"I figured he would." Letty didn't sound all that happy about it, but didn't put up an argument.

"We're going out Friday after the rodeo in Bozeman. Go with me. Please."

"I can't," Letty said.

"Go. I promise I'll make it up to you. I need you with me," Dusty pleaded.

"I can't. Really. There's something I have to do next weekend."

"Oh."

"I'll tell you about it as soon as I can," Letty said.

Dusty rolled her eyes, pretending it didn't hurt. But it did. "If there is something I've done—"

"No. It's not like that. It's just something I have to take care of."

Sure. Dusty couldn't believe this. "Okay." She bit back a snotty reply, telling herself that Letty was obviously going through something, something big, something she didn't want to share. Dusty wondered if it could have anything to do with part of an argument she'd overheard between Letty and her elderly parents who lived in Arizona.

Whatever it was, Letty hadn't confided in her and that hurt more than she could bear. Letty had been her best friend since grade school and they'd never kept secrets from each other. Until now.

"Well, I guess I'll talk to you when I get back then."

She hung up, feeling even more apprehensive about her date with Boone and sick inside over Letty. She was losing her best friend.

SMOKE DRIFTED UP from the blackened shell of what was left of Waylon Dobbs's house. A few firemen moved around in the debris, putting out spot fires.

Cash parked his patrol car behind the coroner's van and got out. The acrid air burned his throat and eyes as he walked toward where Coroner Raymond Winters stood leaning against a fire truck.

Winters took a drink from a can of root beer, tipping the can at Cash in greeting. "We have to quit meeting like this. You know Waylon?"

"Just to say hello. How about you?"

The coroner shook his head. "This used to be the old Hamilton place. I always liked this house. No other houses close by."

"Morgan know what happened?" Cash asked.

Winters peered at him over the top of his root beer can, but said nothing as he took a drink. Cash was beginning to know the look only too well. Past Winters, Cash saw Fire Chief Jimmy Morgan head his way, face covered in soot, expression grim.

The Antelope Flats Fire Department, like those in a lot of rural towns in Montana, was made up of volunteers, except for the chief and assistant chief.

Morgan pulled off a glove and mopped a hand over his face. "Started at the back of the house. Some kind of accelerant was used. Place went up like a torch."

Cash frowned. "Arson?"

"Won't have a definite on that until the investigators

get here from Billings," Morgan said. "For my money? Arson."

"Fire started at the back of the house?" Cash asked, not liking what he was thinking. "It was too early for Waylon to be sleeping. He would have had time to get out."

"Don't see why not," Morgan said. "There would have been a rush of noise when this baby was set and lots of smoke. No way he could have missed it unless he was passed out."

"Or already dead," Winters said.

Cash shot him a look.

Winters shrugged. "Just a thought."

"Is it possible Waylon started the fire?" Cash asked Morgan.

The fire chief looked doubtful. "Suicide?" He pulled his glove back on slowly, studying it as if thinking about that possibility before he spoke. "I suppose it's possible. Found the body in the first-floor bedroom. On the bed."

"That's not suicide, that's just plain crazy," Winters said. "Start the fire, take off to the bedroom and wait to burn to death?"

"He probably would have died of smoke inhalation before the fire reached him," Morgan said.

It sounded as implausible as hell. But otherwise, why wouldn't Waylon get out? Unless Winters was right and Waylon had already been dead.

"The neighbor up the road there called it in." Morgan pointed a few blocks away. "Remember Miss Rose?" Now retired, she'd taught first grade to most of them. "I'll send you a copy of my report, along with the state fire inspector's. He's on his way from Billings."

One of Morgan's men called to him. He excused himself and went back toward the house.

"We'll need an autopsy," Cash told Winters.

Winters nodded. "I know you're hoping for accidental death here. Or if not, suicide. But if the fire really was arson, then we gotta wonder if we don't have another suspicious death on our hands."

Cash was thinking the same thing. "I'm going to talk to Miss Rose and see if she saw anything, since hers and Waylon's were the only two houses on this road. Go ahead and move the body. Morgan will have photographed everything for his report." First Clayton. Now Waylon.

He walked the few blocks to Miss Rose's house and knocked. Rose Zimmer answered immediately. Clearly she'd been expecting him.

"Hello, Cash," she said in that tone he remembered too well from first grade. Instantly, he felt like her student again.

"I just need to ask you a few questions about the fire."

She had to be eighty if she was a day, but she didn't look it. She motioned him in with an impatient flick of her wrist.

He wiped his feet on the mat and stepped in. Before he could even ask, she succinctly told him what she had witnessed, explaining that she had smelled smoke, gone to the window, seen flames coming from the roof of Waylon Dobbs's house and dialed 911.

Cash jotted it all down in his notebook, taking care not to let her see his penmanship. "Did you see anyone near the house?"

"Not at the time," Rose said. "But after the call, I looked out and saw a dark-colored pickup go by. I'm sorry I didn't get a license plate number for you. It was too muddy. Didn't recognize it or the driver. Too much glare off the windshield with the sunset."

Cash thanked her, not surprised by her thoroughness. The problem was that ninety-percent of the county drove dark-colored pickups.

"He was inside, wasn't he," she said.

"I'm afraid so."

"I saw him come home earlier." She gave a small shake of her head, lips pursed. "He was driving so fast, kicking up way too much dust. I wondered what his big hurry was."

Cash wondered, too. "And he didn't leave again?"

She shook her head.

"Did you know him very well?"

"No one did," she said without having to think about it. "Stayed to himself. I'd see his light on late at night and the flicker of the television screen. I don't think he was much of a reader." Disapproval tainted her tone.

Cash closed his notebook and put it back into his pocket. "Well, thanks again. If you think of anything else, would you please call me?"

She clucked her tongue. "I think you know me well enough, Cash McCall, that you don't have to ask me that."

He smiled. "Good night, Miss Rose."

"Good night, Cash."

As Cash started back toward his patrol car, he saw Ty Coltrane pull in and get out of his pickup.

TY HAD BEEN IN TOWN when he'd heard the fire trucks and seen the smoke. But it was a disturbing rumor that brought him to Waylon Dobbs's place to look for the sheriff.

"Ty," Cash said as he approached.

"Got a minute, Cash?"

"Sure." He motioned toward his patrol car. Ty climbed in as Cash slid behind the wheel. "What's up?" the sheriff asked.

"I just heard that Clayton was murdered. Is that true?"

"I should have known the moment I started asking questions around town, it would hit the grapevine," Cash said with a shake of his head. "Let's just say his death is under investigation."

Ty pulled off his straw hat and raked his fingers through his hair. "I don't know if this has anything to do with anything."

"If you know something Ty, I'd like to hear it."

He shoved the hat back on his head and looked at Cash again. "The day he died, Clayton was all worked up over a bull. I know," Ty hurried on, "Clayton was always worked up over some bull or another, but this bull was Devil's Tornado. I'm wondering if Clayton didn't go out to the Edgewood Roughstock Company ranch the night he died to have another look at the bull."

"This bull, it's one of Monte's?" Cash asked.

Ty shook his head. "No, it's Boone Rasmussen's. I saw the bull perform at the Sheridan, Wyoming, rodeo and I got to tell you, it was acting pretty strange."

"Strange how?" Cash asked.

"Like maybe it had been drugged," Ty said, the words finally out.

"*Drugged?* I don't know anything about rodeo, but is that possible?"

"I've never *heard* of anyone drugging roughstock," Ty agreed. "But I think it's possible. This bull seemed disoriented, confused, I don't know, high on something, something that made it buck like a son of a gun."

"Let's say you're right. Wouldn't the rodeo veterinarian have noticed?"

"Not necessarily. Rodeo vets are volunteers and usually only concerned if an animal appears sick or hurt, or falls down three times in the arena," Ty said.

"So you don't know if the volunteer veterinarian noticed anything unusual about Devil's Tornado at the Sheridan rodeo," Cash said.

"No."

Cash pulled out his notebook. "Well, there is one way to find out. Do you know who the veterinarian was?"

"Waylon Dobbs."

Ty looked toward what was left of Waylon's house. "Is he…?"

"Dead," Cash said.

Ty sighed and shook his head. "Maybe it's nothing, but last night after the rodeo in Sheridan, I heard Waylon arguing with Boone Rasmussen and that cowboy who works for him, Lamar."

"Did you happen to hear what they were arguing over?" Cash asked.

"No. But I'm wondering if Waylon hadn't noticed the same thing I did about the way Devil's Tornado was acting and confronted Boone about it," Ty said.

Cash was wondering the same thing.

BOONE HAD JUST hung up the phone when he heard the soft click of his bedroom door opening. He looked up from where he sat on the bed. The room Monte had given him was in a small addition off the back on the second floor—

fortunately not within hearing distance of the master bedroom Monte shared with his young bride downstairs at the front of the house.

Sierra slipped in, closing the door behind her. She wore a thin white gown that seemed to shimmer in the pale light from the lamp beside Boone's bed. She'd come straight from the shower. Her blond hair was wet and dark against her skin. She smelled of the French soap she liked. Her feet were bare.

He swung his boots up on the bed, stretching out, hands behind his head on the pillow as he watched her, pretending that this didn't scare the hell out of him.

She hadn't moved from just inside the door. Nor had she said a word. She just stood there, looking at him.

It wouldn't take much to send her away. A word. Even a look. He hated that he wanted her. And she knew it.

With a curse, he reached over and turned out the lamp. He could still see her in the faint light that bled through the thin curtains as she walked over to the side of the bed.

He closed his eyes. The bed squeaked softly as she curled up next to him. He felt her fingers in his hair, then her lips at his temple, her breath skittering over his skin.

It wasn't too late to send her away.

"Your shirt smells like smoke," she whispered, pulling back a little.

"Lamar's been smoking in my pickup again." He grabbed her shoulders, shoving her down on the bed as he rolled over on top of her, jerking the flimsy gown up as he unzipped his jeans and took her, driving himself into her again and again. The only sound was the squeak of the bedsprings and his own ragged breath until he finally found release.

Spent, he rolled off and sat on the side of the bed, his back to her. But not before he'd seen her smile up at him. A knowing smile that said she owned him.

He heard the bedsprings squeak once more as she got up and left, closing the door quietly behind her, leaving behind not only her scent on his skin, but also the memory of her still in his blood. He rushed into the bathroom, dropped to his knees and threw up in the toilet, just as he'd done all the other times she'd come to him.

CHAPTER ELEVEN

Boone woke up hung over. He opened one eye a crack. Daylight bled through the thin curtains, the sky outside a pale pink.

Monte was sending him to Texas for a few days to look at some bulls. Boone couldn't shake the feeling that he just wanted to get him out of town. Otherwise why trust him with something this important?

According to Monte, everyone in town was in an uproar because the sheriff was asking a lot of questions about Clayton T. Brooks's death. Rumor had it that Clayton had been murdered.

Boone tried to sit up, but fell back sick to his stomach. He had to catch a late morning flight out of Billings, which meant he had a three-hour drive ahead of him, so he had to get up.

He started to close his eyes, desperately needing more sleep. But he couldn't chance missing the flight.

Lifting his left arm, he squinted at his wristwatch. Maybe he could get in a few more minutes.

Both eyes flew open. Only a white strip shone on his wrist where the watch had been. He sat up, head reeling from the sudden movement. Swiveling around, he looked to the small table beside the bed, trying not to panic.

Monte had bought him the watch after Devil's Tornado's first rodeo. He couldn't have lost it.

But the watch wasn't on the table—just the empty bourbon bottle. He had hit the bourbon hard after Sierra left last night and must have passed out.

Getting up, he searched the small room, finally dropping to his knees to look under the bed.

No watch.

Awkwardly, he got to his feet, his heart beating abnormally fast, his pulse a deafening drum. He gripped his head in both hands, telling himself it was just a watch. Hell, would he really want to keep it when this was over? He could buy his own watch one day. An even more expensive one.

But he knew that wasn't the problem.

He plopped down on the foot of the bed and scrubbed at his face with his hands as he tried to remember the last time he'd seen it. Did he have it on yesterday when he'd stopped to talk to Waylon? He couldn't remember.

It was one thing to lose the watch. It was another to worry about where it would turn up.

Monte had had Boone's damn initials engraved on it.

SHERIFF CASH MCCALL was disappointed when he called Monte Edgewood to find that Boone Rasmussen had flown to Texas and wouldn't be back until Thursday.

But he told Monte he still would drive out; he had a few questions for him. Monte had seemed surprised, but said he would be there.

True to his word, Monte was waiting on the porch. He walked toward the patrol car as Cash parked.

"Howdy, Sheriff." He extended his hand.

Cash had known Monte his whole life. After years of riding saddle broncs, Monte had started the Edgewood Roughstock Company. Cash did a little research and found out that while Monte wasn't one of the top roughstock producers in the country, he was definitely getting a name for himself. Especially in the past six months, when he'd hooked up with Boone Rasmussen and his bulls. The name Cash kept hearing was: Devil's Tornado.

"What can I do for you?" Monte asked. "I get the impression this isn't a social call."

"I need to ask you some questions about Clayton T. Brooks's murder."

Monte drew back in surprise. "Clayton's *murder?* I thought he was killed in an automobile accident."

"It appears his killer just wanted us to believe that," Cash said.

Monte frowned as he rubbed a hand over his jaw. "Clayton murdered. I can't believe it."

"The day Clayton died, all he'd been talking about that day was one of your bulls, Devil's Tornado," Cash said. "It seems Clayton saw the bull at the Billings rodeo."

"Yeah, Devil's Tornado was in rare form that night in Billings, that's for sure," Monte said. "But what does that have to do with Clayton's...death?"

"Maybe nothing. It sounds like your bull is causing quite a *lot* of talk," Cash said. "I understand the more talk, the more money's he's worth."

Monte smiled and nodded. "But you know he's not my bull. He's Boone's. I'm helping him out by using some of his bulls. As it turns out, Devil's Tornado is helping us both."

"What is Boone doing in Texas?" Cash asked.

"Checking out some more bulls for us. He has a good eye. His father was in the roughstock business, you know."

Cash knew. He'd been learning more about rodeo and roughstock than he'd ever wanted to. "When will Boone be back?"

"He's flying in to Billings Friday morning but going straight to Bozeman for a three-day rodeo we're putting on there." Monte seemed to hesitate. "Boone didn't have anything to do with Clayton's death. I've known Boone since he was a boy. He's had his share of troubles, but he's trying to turn his life around."

Cash wanted to warn Monte about Boone. He'd learned a lot about rodeo roughstock—and Boone Rasmussen. Boone had been in trouble since he was fifteen. Nothing that had him behind bars for more than a few months, but the pattern was there.

"As for Devil's Tornado…" Monte pointed toward a bull standing alone in a small pasture. "That's him *right* there."

Cash shaded his eyes, squinting as he walked to the pasture fence, surprised at how ordinary the bull looked. "He's not what I expected."

"Doesn't look like much, does he?" Monte chuckled as he joined him. "But put him in a chute and look out. I've never seen a bull like him. He just keeps coming up with new tricks to throw riders."

"Is there any chance Clayton came out to the ranch the night he died?" Cash asked. "That would have been Thursday, probably after the bars closed."

Monte looked surprised. "Why would Clayton come out here?"

"I don't know. Maybe to see Devil's Tornado."

"We had the bull in the pasture down there." Monte pointed up the road. "But I would have heard a vehicle drive in. Even if it was late. I'm a light sleeper."

"Monte, I'm going to need a sample of Devil's Tornado blood."

Monte drew back. "His blood? You're serious."

Cash studied the docile bull in the pasture. "If I have to, I can get a warrant."

Monte shook his head and gave him a smile weighted with sadness. "That won't be necessary, Cash. I have a contract with Boone to use the bull for rodeos. I can okay any tests you need to run. Especially if it will help you find Clayton's killer. It just upsets me to think that your investigation has led you here."

ALL BOONE WANTED WAS a good night's sleep. But when he parked his pickup in front of the Edgewood house after the long flight from Texas and then the three-hour drive home, he saw that a light was on in the kitchen.

He'd changed his flight at Monte's request so he could come back early rather than meet Monte in Bozeman. Boone was worried about his damned watch, worried about leaving Lamar alone for too long, worried about Dusty McCall and the syringe, just plain worried and anxious.

"Boone, son, could you come in here?" Monte said, the moment Boone stepped inside the house.

Something in Monte's tone warned him. Boone tried to keep his cool as he stepped into the kitchen.

Monte sat at the table alone, a bottle of beer in front of him, several empties off to the side. He'd been there for a while.

The older man looked up and Boone saw at once that whatever had kept Monte up so late wasn't good.

"The trip went really well," Boone said filling in the silence. "I found a couple of bulls that would be great additions to your herd. I'll tell you all about them in the morning. I'm really beat."

"Have a seat, son," Monte said as if he hadn't heard.

Boone stood for a moment, then pulled out a chair. He wondered where Sierra was and how worried he should be.

"The sheriff stopped out while you were gone," Monte said and took a drink of his beer.

Boone held his breath and waited.

"He seems to think Clayton was murdered and that he came out here the night he was killed to look at Devil's Tornado."

Boone tried to show the right amount of surprise and sorrow. He'd never gotten it right. "Why would Clayton be interested in our bull?"

Monte smiled slowly at *our bull,* but the smile fell short of his eyes. "There anything you want to tell me, son?"

Boone gave that some thought, pretty sure Monte was asking about a lot more than just Clayton. What would Monte do if he told him the truth? "I don't know what you want me to say."

Monte seemed disappointed by that answer. Or was it relief? "Cash is going to want to talk to you."

Boone nodded, pretending that didn't worry him. He hated the law and unfortunately had had more than his share of run-ins with police in the past.

"It troubles me that the sheriff's investigation led him to my door," Monte said and took another drink.

Boone could only nod, his mind racing. "I guess you won't want to use Devil's Tornado at the Bozeman rodeo, then."

"Cash had the lab come out and take some blood from the bull," Monte said picking at the label on his almost empty beer bottle. "The sheriff had it in his head that the bull might have been drugged."

Boone couldn't breathe, even if he had dared to take a breath.

"But when I talked to him yesterday, he said he didn't find any drugs." Monte looked up. "Where would he get a fool idea that we were drugging Devil's Tornado?"

Boone forced himself to take a breath. "I'm just glad the sheriff knows there was no truth to it."

Monte nodded, even smiled a little. "You ought to get to bed. You look like you've been rode hard and put to bed wet. We're taking Devil's Tornado to the Bozeman rodeo tomorrow. We'd be fools to pull the bull now, don't you think? He's a star in the making."

Boone got to his feet. Every instinct in him told him to hit the road and not look back. With the sheriff sniffing around asking questions about that damned dead bull rider and Ty Coltrane snooping around Devil's Tornado, the safest thing he could do was sell his bulls to Monte, cut his losses and move on. There would always be other bulls. Unfortunately, there were few marks as easy as Monte Edgewood.

"I suppose you heard the other news," Monte said as Boone started toward the door. "Someone set a fire at Waylon Dobbs's place the night before you left for Texas. Burned to the ground. Poor Dobbs. I guess he couldn't get out."

"That's too bad," Boone managed to say as he glanced back at Monte.

Without getting up, Monte reached into the fridge and snared another bottle of beer from the door. " 'Night, son," Monte said and snapped open the twist-off with his huge paw of a hand.

Boone went upstairs to his bedroom. That night, after everyone was asleep, he told himself he could get up and leave. But he knew he wouldn't. He'd come this far, risked so much; he'd be a fool not to see this through.

If he had to, he'd sell Devil's Tornado and the other bulls after the Bozeman rodeo and leave town.

By then, he would have taken care of the only other loose end he had to worry about now—Dusty McCall. He could only hope that she'd discarded the syringe days ago. But if there was a chance she'd held on to it for any reason…

Tonight, he locked his bedroom door. He thought he heard the soft rattle of the knob sometime during the night, but maybe he'd just imagined it.

Bozeman Rodeo Grounds

TY COLTRANE TOLD HIMSELF he had no business in Bozeman. He had a horse ranch to run. But the talk around Antelope Flats was that Clayton T. Brooks had been murdered—and possibly Waylon Dobbs as well.

First, an old bull rider who had been upset about Devil's Tornado had been found dead on the highway north of town, just miles from the Edgewood Roughstock Company ranch. Then Waylon Dobbs, the veterinarian that Ty had seen arguing with Boone Ras- mussen after the rodeo not a week ago had been killed in a fire.

Both tied to Rasmussen.

Cash had called yesterday to say that the blood sample on Devil's Tornado showed no sign of drugs and while he was still investigating both Clayton's and Waylon's deaths, he had nothing that tied either to Rasmussen.

Ty had been so sure Devil's Tornado had been drugged the night of the rodeo in Sheridan. He'd been around livestock his whole life. He knew when an animal was acting strangely. How could he have been that wrong?

He shook his head.

But Ty knew he hadn't driven five hours because of Boone Rasmussen—or Devil's Tornado. No, he thought, as he parked at the back of the rodeo lot and got out. He wasn't here because of some bull or some roughstock producer. He was here because of Dusty.

And he was late. The rodeo was almost over.

But the truth was: he hadn't been able to get her off his mind. Not the cowgirl who'd peeked over the stall door to watch the birth of the foal, nor the one who'd come into the Mint in that blue dress.

This afternoon when he'd called the McCall ranch and found out that Dusty had gone to Bozeman to the rodeo, he'd had the craziest feeling that she needed him.

Yeah, right.

But hey, look what had happened to her at the last rodeo. She'd almost been trampled by a herd of bucking horses. Then someone had followed her home. There was true cause for concern when it came to her.

And now she'd driven five hours to go to a rodeo in Bozeman? And without Letty, according to Shelby. What was up with that? Dusty and Letty had been attached at the hip since grade school.

As he started toward the rodeo arena, he spotted the Sundown Ranch pickup that Dusty drove. He'd never believed in premonitions, but he couldn't shake the feeling that she was in trouble.

Or maybe that was just an excuse to see her.

Either way, once inside, he scanned the grandstands for Dusty's adorable face, warning himself that she wasn't going to be happy to see him.

LETTY KNEW the moment she saw the man standing in the shade at the entrance to the rock concert that he was Hal Branson. She smiled to herself as she watched him try to smooth down the cowlick in his carrot-orange hair.

Her heart did a little flip inside her chest. She knew it was silly, but the fact that he had red hair struck her as fortuitous.

He wore new jeans and a button-down blue checked shirt. She couldn't help smiling as she neared him, betting with herself whether his eyes would be blue or brown. Blue, she decided.

He spotted her and straightened, his smile tentative. "Leticia?" His gaze went to her hair and she saw his expression almost relax.

She touched her wild mane of red hair, a shade darker than his own. "It seems we have something in common," she said and gave him a shy smile, even though she'd always been self-conscious about her teeth.

His smile broadened, lighting up his blue eyes. Up close she could see a sprinkling of freckles across his nose and cheeks. She knew without having to ask that he'd hated them since kindergarten, just as she had hated hers.

He seemed to study her, his jaw dropping slightly, his eyes wide and intent. He was about her age, maybe a few years older. Her heart beat a little faster and her face flushed warm under his perusal.

He cleared his throat. "Sorry. I didn't mean to stare. It's just…"

She'd only talked to him a couple of times on the phone, but both times she'd liked his voice. It was soft and reassuring.

He was still staring. "We could be twins. We're not," he added quickly. "Related, that is."

She laughed nervously. "I'm glad to hear that."

His eyes locked with hers. He swallowed, as if he had a lump in his throat. "You're probably going to think I'm crazy but do you believe in…fate?"

She smiled, forgetting that she'd always felt her teeth were too big for her mouth. "I'm beginning to.'"

TY WONDERED IF he would ever find Dusty. The grandstands were full. A truck circled the dirt oval dragging a rake as a team prepared the arena for the next event. Loud country music played over the outdoor speakers and a clown told jokes to the crowd.

He caught sight of Lamar by one of Monte Edgewood's semitrucks and trailers. A few cowboys hung around the empty chutes talking. He wondered if he'd get to see Devil's Tornado tonight. No sign of Rasmussen.

And no Dusty.

At least, not in the stands. Maybe she was at one of the concession stands.

He turned. His heart did a two-step at the sight of her

coming toward him. She smiled and waved, and all he could do was stare.

She was dressed in jeans, ones that fit like a glove, and a sleeveless halter top that hugged her curves.

All these years, he'd liked her. But at that moment, he finally admitted it had been a whole lot more than that. He couldn't keep kidding himself. He was wild about her, and always had been.

He stopped walking, frozen in midstep, his breath seizing in his chest as the simple truth of it staggered him.

She was still coming toward him, her grin turning into a dazzling smile as she got closer. She looked a little shy, a little unsure. He knew *that* feeling! He couldn't move. Couldn't speak.

He wasn't sure when he realized that she wasn't looking at *him,* but at someone over his right shoulder.

He glanced back and in that instant, saw whom she was headed for—Boone Rasmussen.

It came to him in a blinding flash. The smile. The wave. The gleam in her blue eyes. The *new* look.

It had all been about *Boone Rasmussen!*

No! Anyone but Rasmussen.

Dusty didn't even seem to notice Ty as she walked right past. Her eyes were only on Rasmussen. And from the way he was looking back at her…

Ty let out a curse. He had to be mistaken. But even before he turned to watch her with Boone, he knew he wasn't.

Dusty shifted one hip and cocked her head, the soft blond curls swaying a little as she leaned toward Rasmussen grinning that devilish grin of hers, blue eyes wide. No mistake. She was flirting! And to make matters worse, Rasmussen was responding. But then, what man wouldn't?

Ty let out another curse. When had this all happened? He frowned as he remembered the morning at his ranch. Rasmussen hadn't even noticed the old Dusty. So why the interest now?

Could it simply be because that Dusty had looked like a cow*boy?* Because this one looked like what she really was: a very desirable woman? Mentally he kicked himself. Slim had been transformed. And what fool had helped with this makeover?

Ty groaned. Or could there be more to Rasmussen's interest in Dusty? Did this go back to the night after the Sheridan rodeo?

He swore. He'd tried to warn Dusty off Rasmussen, but in retrospect he realized that would only have made her more curious about the cowboy. Ty could only blame himself that Dusty was now a Scud Missile—and headed right for Boone Rasmussen. Right for a man that Ty believed capable of anything. Even murder.

CHAPTER TWELVE

It took every ounce of Ty's restraint to keep him from going after Dusty.

All he could do was stand back and watch as Rasmussen ran a finger down Dusty's arm to her hand clutching the top of her leather shoulder bag. Dusty was nervous, something Ty noticed because he knew her so well. What the hell did she think she was doing?

The rodeo announcer called for the last event: bull riding. Rasmussen leaned toward Dusty, whispered something in her ear. Ty swore, desperately wanting to slug the guy.

As she swung around, Ty saw her face. It was flushed. She headed right for him but he could tell she hadn't seen him yet.

He swore under his breath and tried to go back to thinking of her as just the kid next door.

No chance of that.

"Slim," he said as she approached. It didn't matter that the nickname no longer fit her. She was still his Slim. Past her, he saw that Rasmussen had stopped to look back.

"Ty? What are you doing here?" She looked more than surprised. She looked worried. "You're going to mess up everything." She started to walk past him.

"Oh, no you don't," he said grabbing her arm before she could get away. "You and I need to talk."

THE TRIPLE-X-FILES were just coming on stage when Letty and Hal reached the bandstand.

Letty quickly scanned the band members. They were all at least in their fifties, all hippies with long hair, a lot of it gray, wearing ragged shirts and worn jeans. But they appeared to be the real thing, and she found something about that endearing.

There was no sign of Flo Hubbard.

The band broke into a rock introduction and a tall woman with flaming red hair streaked with gray came bounding onto the stage, strumming a guitar. She wore a cutoff western shirt and worn jeans that hugged her slim body. She was barefoot, her toenails painted a rainbow of colors.

Her head was down so all Letty saw at first were her hands—hands that were so much like her own she felt tears burn her eyes. Her heart began to pound louder than the music.

The woman raised her head.

Letty's chest swelled, filling as if with helium. Her joy spilled out in tears. She felt Hal take her hand and squeeze it. She squeezed back, choking on the sobs that rose in her throat.

All those years of desperately needing someone who looked like her. Letty stared at the woman on stage, the face and green eyes so like her own, and felt as if she'd finally come home.

She'd found her birth mother.

BOONE WATCHED Coltrane draw Dusty McCall around the corner of the grandstands, their heads together conspiratorially. Something definitely going on between them. Dusty had lied about how close she and Coltrane were. He could see that just looking at the two of them together.

Why did that surprise him? Just moments ago, she'd been flirting with him. Teasing him. She had the syringe. Of course she did. He recalled now the way she'd had her hand over the top of her shoulder bag.

Women, they were all alike. Hadn't he learned that from his mother, who'd run off and left him with that low-life father of his?

He swore and turned to go back to find out what was going on with little Miss Dusty McCall. Sierra Edgewood stepped in front of him.

"Going somewhere?" she asked as she caressed the collar on his shirt.

He stepped back just out of her reach. Speaking of women… "I don't have time for this right now," he said impatiently. Was the woman crazy? Monte was over by the chutes. He could be watching them at this very moment.

She lifted one finely sculpted brow. "Maybe you'd better *make* time."

Something in her tone brought his attention away from the spot where Coltrane and Dusty had disappeared.

Sierra smiled, but something was different about her. "Now you're listening. That's more like it." She was looking at him as if she knew something. No, as if she had something on him. Even more leverage than just his inability to turn her away from his bed?

"Is this about my watch?"

She frowned. "Your watch?"

"Never mind," he said seeing her confusion. "What is it you want?" He hated being cornered.

"I missed you last night," she said with a nervous laugh.

So she *had* tried his door. He glanced toward the chutes, saw Monte watching them. Monte motioned to him. "I've got to get to work."

"Tonight after the rodeo. And Boone, don't disappoint me." She turned and walked off before he could answer.

Boone looked toward the chutes and saw Monte's eyes following Sierra, the look on his face twisting Boone's insides. Monte loved his wife, trusted her. Trusted everyone. Even Boone Rasmussen. Maybe especially him.

When Boone glanced back toward the grandstands where Coltrane and Dusty had gone, he swore. He should be helping Monte and Lamar with the bull riding. But he had to find out what Coltrane and little Miss McCall were up to first.

CASH AND HIS soon-to-be wife Molly had just finished dinner when State Fire Inspector Jim Ross called.

"Sheriff? I've got the final report on the Waylon Dobbs fire. There's something you need to see."

Cash drove over to what was left of the Dobbs place. Ross was waiting for him in his Chevy Suburban and motioned Cash inside.

"You already know that the fire was intentionally set at the back of the house. It appears the arsonist entered through a window and made his exit through the same window. We found this caught on a nail of the window frame." Ross lifted an evidence bag.

Cash's pulse jumped at the sight of a watch inside. The leather band, now partially burned, appeared to have broken prior to the fire.

Ross nodded. "It gets even better. The back of the watch is engraved with three initials. B. A. R."

Cash took the bag. B.A.R.

"Will that help narrow down your suspect list?" Ross asked.

Cash nodded. When Boone Rasmussen had been arrested in Texas, his full name had been on the paperwork. Boone *Andrew* Rasmussen. B. A. R.

TY DREW Dusty under the grandstands, where it was dark and cool and somewhat quieter. People wandered past to the concessions or the restrooms, but with the rodeo in full swing, no one paid them any mind.

"All right," Dusty said the moment he let go of her. "What?"

"You should have told me that all this—" he waved a hand over her, taking in her new look "—was about *Boone Rasmussen.*"

She frowned. "Excuse me?"

"*Rasmussen?* Dusty, have you lost your mind?"

"Look Ty, I know you don't like Boone—"

"He's up to his neck in something. Have you forgotten that he almost killed you in the horse corral?"

"He said the gate latch was faulty."

"And you believe that?" Ty let out an exasperated sigh. "Slim, I think Boone had something to do with Clayton's murder and Waylon Dobbs's fire and his death."

"That's crazy," she snapped. "Why would Boone want to kill anyone?"

"It's all tied in somehow with Devil's Tornado," Ty said.

She stared at him. "You just don't want me going out with Boone. You're..." Her eyes widened. "You're... *jealous!*"

"*Jealous?*" He practically choked on the word. "This has nothing to do with how I feel about you."

"*Feel* about me?" she echoed.

She was close enough he could smell the light scent of

her perfume. Slim, wearing perfume! Her lashes were dark with mascara, making the blue of her eyes seem bottomless.

This was Slim, he reminded himself. The girl next door whom he'd grown up with, looked out for, teased, tormented, adored. Slim. The pouty red lips, the palest blue eyes he'd ever seen, that adorable face. That body. He groaned. *His* Slim.

And all he wanted to do was throw her over his shoulder and haul her butt back to Antelope Flats. Either that or…kiss her.

He went with the kiss, drawing her to him. She was soft and lush-feeling in his arms. Her eyes lit with surprise in that instant before he dropped his mouth to hers.

He half expected her to pull away. Maybe even cuff him up side the head. That would be like the Dusty he knew and loved. Once he had her in his arms, once his mouth was on hers, he deepened the kiss.

Her reaction was nothing like he'd expected. No kick to the shin. No slugging him. She responded to his kiss. Not at first. But within a split second, her lips parted. Her body melted against his. All with stunning effect.

She let out a soft, almost pleased moan, then slowly, she drew back, eyes wide, her breath coming in short gasps.

He opened his mouth to speak. Nothing came out. He was breathing hard, surprised and delighted and confused by what had just happened. He watched Dusty slowly run her tongue along her upper lip. She was still breathing hard, just like him, her face flushed with heat.

"Ty?" she whispered, staring at him as if she'd never seen him before.

He could only look at her, words lost on him.

"Why did you—" She broke off suddenly, her eyes narrowing. "Was *that*—" she waved an arm through the air "—about *Boone?*"

He scowled at her. "Hell, no. Listen to me, I know it sounds crazy, but I think Boone's drugging Devil's Tornado to make him perform better and I think Clayton and Waylon figured it out and that's why they're dead. Look, I know Cash didn't find any drugs when he tested Devil's Tornado, but don't you see the drug must be one that doesn't stay in the system long. He drugs the bull to work it up for the ride, then must give it something to bring it back down once the ride is over."

"*What?*" She looked shocked as she stepped back, her hand dropping to her shoulder bag.

Behind her, Boone came around the end of the grandstands. Had he been there the whole time listening, watching them?

Following Ty's surprised gaze, Dusty turned to look behind her. "Boone," she said, the name coming out on a surprised gasp.

"Dusty and I are having a private conversation," Ty said starting to step past Dusty to confront Boone, but Dusty grabbed his arm to stop him.

Rasmussen smiled at Dusty, completely ignoring him. "I have a surprise for you." He motioned for her to come with him.

Ty cursed. "Dusty—"

She gave him a warning look and slipped something into his hand. "I'll talk to you later, Ty," she said without looking back at him.

AT THE END of the first song, Flo Hubbard spotted Letty. Letty saw it happen—saw the instant of recognition, then the confusion.

Had her mother known she existed? Or had she been told, as some of the doctor's victims had been, that her baby was stillborn?

Flo turned to the bass guitarist and said something to him. He seemed a little surprised, but swung into another song. Flo looked at Letty, motioned for her to come around to the side of the stage. Leaning her guitar against one of the speakers, she disappeared from view.

Hal let go of Letty's hand.

"Come with me?" she pleaded.

His eyes met hers and locked for a long moment. He took her hand again, and they worked their way through the crowd to the side of the bandstand.

Flo shifted on her bare feet, her hands fluttering in front of her as if she didn't know what to do with them. The band was playing something slow and melodious. Without discussing it, the three stepped away toward the concessionaires until the noise level was such that they would be able to hear each other.

Flo stopped, turning to look at Letty. "You're going to think I'm totally out of my mind…."

Letty shook her head. "I think you're my birth mother."

Flo seemed to slump, as if her bones had suddenly dissolved. She stumbled into a chair under the covered sitting area at a taco concession and sat down heavily, her gaze never leaving Letty's face. "It's not possible," she whispered.

Letty pulled up a chair next to her. Hal took one across from them. "It is possible." She glanced at Hal for help.

"Didn't you give birth twenty years ago on March 9 in Antelope Flats, Montana, at the clinic?"

Flo's green eyes filled with tears as she nodded. "Was that the name of the town? My van ran out of gas just outside of it. I was hitching into town when I went into labor. Just when I thought my luck had really run out, I was picked up by a doctor who worked at the clinic."

"That might not have been so lucky," Hal said.

Flo didn't seem to hear him. She appeared lost in the past as she said, "I was so young and scared, and it wasn't time yet for the baby to be born." She looked up at them. "But the baby was a boy, the doctor said. He was stillborn."

"Did you see your baby?" Hal asked.

She seemed to think for a moment, then shook her head. "The doctor put me out right before the baby was born. He told me something was wrong and wanted to spare me."

As Letty stared at her mother, Hal filled Flo in about the do-gooder doctor. "Let me guess. The doctor took care of everything, right?"

She nodded.

"I'm willing to bet, unless my eyes deceive me, that the doctor stole your baby and gave it to an older couple in town who couldn't have children," Hal continued. "Of course, DNA tests will be required to be absolutely sure…"

Flo let out a sudden laugh. "This is so freaky. I knew. I knew the moment I looked out into the crowd and saw you. I said, 'That's my kid.' I mean, how could I know something like that when I thought there was no way?"

"History has proven that a mother often knows her child on some level that we will never understand," Hal said quietly.

Flo nodded, studying her daughter's face. "You look exactly like I did at your age," she said with a laugh. "Sorry about that, kid."

Almost shyly, she reached out and placed her hand

over her daughter's. Letty intertwined her fingers with her mother's, and the two began to laugh and cry at the same time.

DUSTY FELT Boone slip his arm around her waist and pull her to him, his hand going to her shoulder bag.

Her head was spinning. Ty's kiss had left her weightless, trembling, excited and a little scared. She'd never felt anything like that. Still couldn't believe it. Ty?

She couldn't think. Everything was happening too fast. Ty thought Boone had been drugging Devil's Tornado? Was it possible the syringe she'd found and had just given to Ty had been used on the bull?

She didn't want to believe it of Boone, but she was reminded of his odd behavior at the Sheridan rodeo. She'd seen him jab the bull with something. A syringe? The one that she'd had in her purse all this time?

Boone suddenly stopped and turned her toward him. "You all right?" he asked, eyes narrowing.

"Fine." She forced a smile and added, "Great." Just great. For weeks, all she'd thought about was getting Boone to notice her. In her wildest dreams, he would ask her out and, if she got lucky, kiss her.

As he drew her toward him, she felt his hand part the top of her shoulder bag and his fingers dig inside. He was looking for the syringe! He must have seen her pick it up that night after the rodeo. All he'd ever wanted was the syringe!

He dropped his mouth to hers, his kiss hard and punishing as she felt him dig deeper in her bag.

TY FOUGHT TO BREATHE, the weight on his chest crushing his heart, his lungs, making him sick inside as he watched

Boone kiss Dusty. She was right. He *was* jealous. Jealous as hell. But it was fear and anger that simmered inside him, making him want to do something stupid like bust this up right now. He could see that Boone had his hand in her purse as if looking for something.

Frowning, Ty looked down in his own hand and saw what Dusty had put there. A used syringe. He quickly stuck it into his jacket pocket, his hand shaking. That's what Boone was looking for. But what would Boone do when he didn't find it?

BOONE DREW BACK from the kiss, his dark eyes boring into hers for a long moment, before he shot Ty a look filled both with contempt and a warning as he drew Dusty toward the arena.

"You can watch the bull rides from the chutes with me," Boone said to Dusty, gripping her arm.

Ty saw Dusty wince and started to go after her but at that moment she glanced over her shoulder at him and mouthed, "Call Cash." Her look warned him. "Call Cash," she mouthed again. As she disappeared around the corner of the grandstands, Ty saw her shake off Boone's grip.

Boone looked angry but didn't reach for her again as she went with him willingly.

Oh, hell, what was she up to? Knowing her, she was going to try to get more proof. Where had she gotten the syringe? *When* had she gotten it? Had to have been that night at the Sheridan rodeo.

That look of shock on her face when Ty had told her his suspicions about Boone—it hadn't been because she didn't believe him, but because she *did!*

He took a breath, trying to think. Dusty was safe as

long as she was at the rodeo around other people, right? He had the syringe in his pocket. If a lab could determine the drug inside, it might explain Devil's Tornado's behavior.

Unfortunately, it wouldn't be enough to put Boone Rasmussen behind bars. Not unless Boone drugged the bull again tonight and Ty could get a sample of the bull's blood right after the ride.

But if Boone had overheard Ty's conversation with Dusty, he wouldn't drug Devil's Tornado tonight. Unless it was already too late…

Over the loudspeaker, the final bull ride was being announced. Devil's Tornado in chute three. Ty didn't catch the bull rider's name as he hurried to the arena. Pulling his cell phone from his pocket, he dialed Sheriff Cash McCall's number.

HER LEGS STILL quivering, Dusty climbed up onto the fence, oblivious to the noise, the dust, the action in the arena in front of her.

"You're sure nothing's wrong?" Boone asked. His dark eyes drilled into her as if he could read her thoughts. She tried to smile, tried to act normal, whatever normal had been before today.

"I heard Coltrane warn you to stay clear of me. What is it he thinks he has against me?"

If he had heard Ty warn her about him, then Boone knew exactly what Ty thought he had against him. *"Nothing."*

Boone narrowed his dark eyes, a mocking smile curling his lips.

"It doesn't matter what Ty thinks," she said.

Boone didn't look convinced. "Stay here. "I'll be right back."

It wasn't her nature to stay. Especially when ordered. But she wanted Boone to believe that everything was all right. Ty would have called Cash. The police would come. This would be over soon. She just had to keep pretending that she liked Boone Rasmussen.

That was going to be the hard part.

SHE WATCHED HIM rush over to the chute, saw his intense conversation with Lamar. Clearly, they were arguing. Boone looked furious. And…scared.

She stared at him, wandering what had ever attracted her to him. She touched a finger to her lips, remembering Ty's kiss. The feeling still burned inside. Ty. She smiled, still too surprised to believe it.

Now she knew what Ty had been doing that night after the Sheridan rodeo. She looked across the arena, hoping to see him. By now, he would have called Cash. If her brother could get the local cops down here fast enough…

She didn't see Ty anywhere. Devil's Tornado was kicking up a ruckus inside the chute. Boone and Lamar were hanging over the chute now, the rider trying to get his rope wrapped around his hand.

All these weeks of dreaming about Boone and then Ty Coltrane kissed her and—

Her heart kicked up a beat just at the thought of Ty. She felt her face warm. She smiled and caught her lower lip in her teeth, feeling a little lightheaded. Ty Coltrane. Who would have known?

Suddenly, the chute banged open. Devil's Tornado lunged out, twisting and turning, a blur of movement. The rider tried to stay with him, but was quickly unseated. The pickup riders rode in an attempt to corner the bull. One of the horseback riders managed to get the bucking rope off, but it had little effect on Devil's Tornado.

Dusty stared at the bull as he stopped just feet from the fence where she sat. She could see now what Ty had seen. And Clayton and Waylon, had they seen it too?

Her pulse thundered in her ears. Had Boone killed to keep his secret? He didn't have that much to lose if he got caught drugging the bull, did he? He could just pack up and go somewhere else. Start over again. But murder…

The riders cornered Devil's Tornado, got a rope on him and dragged him out the exit chute.

She looked around for Boone, finally spotting him by Devil's Tornado. Past him, she saw Monte Edgewood climb into his pickup. He seemed to glance around as if looking for someone. His wife Sierra?

Dusty knew Monte Edgewood to say hello to on the street. He'd always seemed nice. She'd heard that he'd married a woman not much older than she was a while back. She'd only seen Sierra Edgewood a few times and felt sorry for her since Dusty knew only too well what it was like to have the whole county talking about you. He glanced at Boone, then slammed the door and drove off.

Because it was a three-day rodeo, the animals would be staying on the rodeo grounds. She could see the bucking horses in an adjacent pasture. The semitrucks and trailers were parked in a line along the back road.

Dusty saw Boone moving Devil's Tornado toward one of the corrals. She thought about when he'd kissed her and how she'd felt him digging in her purse. Looking for the syringe. Did he think she'd discarded it? Did he feel safe, even though he'd overheard Ty voicing his suspicions?

The lights went out, pitching the arena into darkness. In

the distance, she thought she heard the wail of sirens but it was quickly lost in the boom of fireworks as the show got underway and some of the crowd began to wind their way out to their cars to beat the rush.

Dusty rubbed her arms, suddenly chilled at the memory of the anger she'd seen in Boone's eyes. Was it possible this man she'd thought so intriguing was a murderer? She rubbed her arm where he'd grabbed it.

Fireworks burst in bright colors over her head. She looked toward the corral where Boone had been headed just moments ago. He and Devil's Tornado were gone!

Her gaze leaped to the semis parked out back. All three were there. He couldn't have gotten away. He must just have moved the bull to another corral. Or maybe the pasture out back.

She shivered in spite of herself as another volley of fireworks exploded, showering the night sky in blinding white.

Suddenly, she sensed someone behind her. The next instant, two strong hands grabbed her shoulders and hauled her off the fence and back into the shadows.

CHAPTER THIRTEEN

"You're coming with me and don't even try to argue," Ty whispered as he dragged Dusty off the fence and back into the dark shadows of the rodeo grounds as fireworks exploded all around them.

The moment he released her, Dusty swung around to face him. To his shock, she planted a quick kiss on his lips before he could speak again and hugged him fiercely.

Fireworks set the night sky ablaze. The boom reverberated in his chest.

"Why haven't you ever done that before?" she demanded drawing back to look at him.

"Done what?"

"Kissed me."

He quirked a smile at her. "What? And get my head knocked off? No way was I going to chance that."

As fireworks detonated overhead, she smiled at him in the brightly colored light. What he saw in her eyes bowled him over. He never dreamed that he and Slim—

"Who would have known?" they both said in unison, then laughed, instantly sobering at the distinct sound of sirens between bursts of fireworks.

"The police are on their way," he said and drew her closer. He had the syringe in his pocket. Once the police got blood from Devil's Tornado, they'd at least have a motive for Clayton and Waylon's murders.

The fireworks finale began, with one rocket blast of color and noise after another, ending in a thunderous boom.

Sparks drifted down, blinking out in the odd quiet that settled over the arena. Ty heard the distinct sound of a semitrailer door slam shut.

He and Dusty both turned in the direction of the trucks in time to see someone climb into the cab of the last one in line. Ty could make out the large shape of a bull in the back.

"Boone!" Dusty cried. "He's taking off with Devil's Tornado."

As the lights came on in the arena and people began to leave, the truck engine revved.

"We can't let Boone leave with that bull!" Dusty cried and took off running toward the semitruck before Ty could stop her.

He swore as she slipped through the chute fence, running ahead of him. He had to leap the fence, coming down hard in the soft earth.

Ty tried to keep his eye on the semi as Dusty closed the distance on it. On the other side of the truck, he saw boots as a second person moved along the back side of the trailer. The boots stopped at the driver's side door.

Dusty was almost to the semi, Ty right behind her. The motor suddenly revved even louder, but the truck didn't move as Dusty jumped up onto the running board and grabbed for the passenger side door handle.

Ty only got a glimpse of the boots on the other side of the truck before they disappeared as Dusty flung open the door and screamed.

LETTY HAD PARKED in the rodeo grounds parking lot as everyone else was leaving. Dusty had said she was meeting Boone near the concession stands after the rodeo was over, so Letty headed there. She was surprised to hear sirens. They sounded as if they were headed this way.

What kind of trouble had Dusty gotten herself into? Letty joked to herself. With an affectionate smile, she thought of her friend. She couldn't wait to tell Dusty the news. Not just about her birth mother, but about Hal, whom she was meeting later tonight.

The concessions were all boarded up and dark. With a wave of disappointment, Letty looked around but didn't see Dusty. Maybe she'd missed her. Letty chastised herself for not confiding in her friend sooner. But then, Letty hadn't known things would turn out so right.

Hugging herself, she glanced toward the back of the rodeo grounds and spotted a semitruck and trailer parked behind two others. She could hear the truck's motor running. Starting toward the line of semis, she heard the crunch of a boot sole on gravel and saw someone moving along the other side of the trucks.

"Boone?" she called softly. The figure behind the semitruck froze. Her heart kicked up a beat. She licked her lips and took a breath. "Boone?"

Behind her, two police cars came tearing into the parking lot. Several officers jumped out and ran toward a dark-colored pickup parked in the lot. Boone's truck?

At a sound behind her, Letty swung back around. The figure behind the semitruck was gone!

Run! She barely got the thought out before he came out of the dark, his arm locking around her neck so quickly she didn't have time to react. She opened her mouth to scream but his free hand clamped over it.

She struggled, kicking and clawing as he dragged her deeper into the darkness.

"Keep fighting and I'll have to hurt you," a male voice whispered hoarsely in her ear, his breath hot, his arm tightened on her neck, cutting off her air.

She stopped struggling.

DUSTY'S SCREAM was lost in the sound of the sirens.

"Wait!" Ty yelled after her. But that, too, was lost in her scream.

Ty was right behind her, leaping up to grab the edge of the door, afraid the truck would take off and kill them both.

Dusty shoved back against him, her mouth a perfect *O*, her eyes filled with horror in the dash lights of the truck cab.

Ty caught her and held her with one arm as he ducked down to look inside. Lamar's huge shape was behind the wheel, his head lolling back against the seat as if resting, his eyes wide with terror, his throat cut from ear to ear, his shirt crimson with his blood.

"Son of a bitch," Ty said and pulled Dusty from the running board to the ground. She was shaking hard. He wrapped his arms around her, burying his face into the hollow of her neck, his mind racing. He'd seen the killer's boots moving along the back side of the truck.

"I saw Boone arguing with Lamar before Devil's Tornado's ride," Dusty said glancing back at the semi. Boone. Where the hell was he?

"We have to find the cops," Ty said, turning to look

back toward the arena. The grandstands were empty now, smoke from the fireworks show hanging heavy in the air.

"Boone is long gone," Ty said trying to still Dusty's trembling.

She shook her head and stepped from his arms to move along the side of the steel semitrailer. "He wouldn't leave without Devil's Tornado."

Through the narrow slit openings, Ty could see a bull standing inside the trailer.

But Boone and Devil's Tornado were gone.

DUSTY COULDN'T quit shaking. She stared at the bull in the stock trailer. Boone had fooled them! He'd put a different bull in the trailer. He'd made them think he was the one in the semitruck trying to get away with Devil's Tornado, get away with what he'd done. Instead, he'd disappeared with the bull—after he killed Lamar.

She shuddered at the memory of Lamar, his throat cut.

Ty put an arm around her. "Come on, Slim. Let's find the cops."

She snuggled into him. Ty had always been there for her. What about that had she equated with a lack of mystery, no surprises? She'd known him since she was a child, and yet she didn't know him. Not the man who'd kissed her. Not the man who made her quake in his arms. Nor the strong, capable man who held her now.

"How did Boone get the bull out of here without us seeing him?" Dusty asked, turning to stare at the line of semis.

Ty shook his head. She could tell he was wondering the same thing she was. Boone might be a lot of things, but he was no magician. So didn't that mean that he and the bull had to still be here somewhere?

Or maybe he'd left with the crowd, disappearing among

the other cowboy hats. And Devil's Tornado? Where was the bull?

She shivered, chilled to the bone at the thought of what Boone was capable of. Instinctively, she'd known he was dangerous. That had been the attraction. The unknown. Letty had tried to warn her, but Dusty hadn't listened.

They hadn't gone more than a few yards from the trucks when Dusty sensed someone behind them. She saw Ty tense and spin around, pushing her to one side to protect her with his body.

Before Ty could get an arm up, Boone raised a gun and brought the butt end down on the side of Ty's head.

"No!" she cried as Ty crumpled to her feet and Boone Rasmussen grabbed her arm and jerked her to him.

"Where is the syringe?" Boone demanded, grabbing her shoulder bag and dumping it on the ground while keeping a firm grip on Dusty's arm.

"Ty," Dusty cried. He didn't answer, didn't move. She could hear the sirens again, only this time they seemed to be going away from the rodeo grounds.

Boone kicked away the larger objects that had fallen from the bag, then jerked Dusty to him hard. "*Where* is the syringe?"

"I threw it away," she said.

"You're a worse liar than your boyfriend."

He dragged her over to Ty and pulled her down next to him as he quickly went through Ty's pockets.

Questions ran through her mind: why would Boone stay around here after killing Lamar to get the syringe? Was he crazy?

But Dusty quickly forgot Boone as she touched Ty's face. He felt ice-cold. "You bastard, you killed him!"

Boone let out an oath as he found the syringe in Ty's pocket. Clutching it in one hand, he dragged her up with the other. As he tried to stuff the syringe into his own pocket, Dusty launched herself at him. The last thing she remembered was seeing his fist, feeling it connect with her temple just before the earth came up to meet her.

BOONE KNEW he shouldn't have been surprised that things were going so badly. Hell, hadn't he blown every chance he'd ever gotten? Why should this time be any different?

He stared down at Ty Coltrane. Dusty lay beside him, out like a light.

What the hell should he do now? He looked to the road past the rodeo grounds and blinked as he saw his pickup go racing by. Two cop cars were in hot pursuit. What the hell? *Someone had stolen his pickup?*

He felt in his pocket. How was that possible? He had his keys. Who in his right mind would go to the trouble to hot-wire and steal an old pickup?

The sound of the sirens grew fainter and fainter, the flashing lights disappearing in the distance.

How was he supposed to get out of here now?

The arena lights were still on. From this corner of darkness, he couldn't see anyone left around the rodeo grounds. Monte had left earlier. Apparently none of the cops had stayed behind—both police cars were chasing a car thief instead. Lucky for him, except now he had no vehicle to get the hell out of here.

What had the cops been doing here in the first place? All he could assume was that Coltrane had called them, planning to hand over the syringe—and Boone. That would explain why they were hot after his pickup.

Coltrane moaned. He wasn't dead. Boone was surprised at his relief. He couldn't stand the sight of Coltrane. What did he care if he was dead? But his body would be a complication Boone didn't need right now. He had enough complications.

He touched the syringe in his pocket. He had taken Devil's Tornado out to a field a quarter mile from the rodeo grounds. The bull wouldn't be found for a while and by then, there would be nothing *to* find. Hell, what did the cops have on him, anyway?

Nothing. He had the syringe. There was no evidence he'd been drugging the bull. Coltrane might have him jailed for assault, but other than that the cops couldn't prove anything.

Dusty was starting to come around. He knew she would start screaming her head off the moment she did. He didn't want to be around when that happened, he thought, glancing back at the semitruck and trailer.

He wished there was another way as he moved to the hulking shadow of the semi and swung open the driver's side door.

At first, his mind refused to accept what he was seeing. Blood. Lamar. So much blood. His stomach did a slow sickening roll. He stumbled back, fighting to keep from throwing up. His head was reeling. Someone had killed Lamar? Who—

He never saw the tire iron. Or the hand that wielded it. A blinding pain ripped through this skull an instant before the darkness as Boone pitched forward.

DUSTY OPENED HER EYES and was instantly assaulted by the smell, the noise and the jarring movement. She blinked, her head aching. Her hands and ankles were bound with duct tape. Another strip had been put across her mouth, forcing her to breathe through her nose.

The darkness stank of manure and hay, and she couldn't be sure which she was lying in.

Only a little light bled in through the slits along the side of the semitrailer as it rattled down the highway through the dark. At the front of the trailer where she lay was blackness. No headlights from other vehicles on the highway illuminated the interior.

She tried to sit up, but fell over as the semi took a curve. Pushing with her feet, she managed to work her way into the corner and get her back against the walls of the trailer, her eyes finally adjusting to the dizzying darkness.

At the far end of the trailer by the door, she saw a shape. She stared until her eyes burned. The dark shape moved and Dusty let out a muffled cry as she realized it was a bull. Devil's Tornado?

Fear paralyzed her. She could feel the bull looking at her. She'd seen what Devil's Tornado had tried to do to the cowboys in the arena after the bucking rigging had been removed. The bull was a killer. He'd stomp her to death or gore her or—

Devil's Tornado seemed to sway before her eyes, then dropped to his knees, going all the way to the floor of the trailer as he lay down as docile as an old cow.

Closer, Dusty heard another sound. Movement and a low moan. She looked to her left, to the adjacent dark corner of the trailer. Ty?

Her eyes widened in horror!

Letty—her hands bound, her mouth taped, her eyes wide and terrified stared back at her from the darkness!

What was Letty doing here? And where was Ty? She searched the darkness, but quickly realized that she and Letty were alone with a bull in the back of the semi-trailer headed for God only knew where with a killer at the wheel. Where was Boone taking them?

Frantically, Dusty began to work at the tape on her mouth, pushing it with her tongue as she rubbed at the corner with her shoulder along the rough edge of her jacket. She could feel the edge start to peel back. Her skin chafed from the effort, but she had to be able to talk to Letty. To reassure her. To reassure herself that somehow they were going to get out of this.

BLINDED BY the bright light, Ty Coltrane closed his eyes and tried to sit up. "Where's Dusty?"

"Easy," one of the policemen standing over him warned. "You've got quite the knot on your head. We've called for an ambulance. Can you tell us who hit you?"

"Boone Rasmussen. I have to find Dusty," Ty said, pushing to his feet. His gaze went to the spot where the semitrucks and trailers had been. One was missing. "He's got her. He's taken the truck." Ty turned to head for his pickup, but one of the cops grabbed his arm.

"Hold on," the officer said. "You're not going anywhere. We need to ask you some questions."

Ty jerked free and probably would have ended up in jail if he hadn't stopped to watch a helicopter set down in the middle of the arena—and see Sheriff Cash McCall climb out of it.

"Cash!" he called as the sheriff ran toward him. "Rasmussen has Dusty. I think he took her in one of the Edgewood semitrucks. Lamar is dead."

Cash began barking orders, starting with getting an APB out on the semitruck, then turned to the police officers in confusion. "Did you just get here? I called you hours ago."

One of the officers, Sgt. Mike Johnson, stepped forward. "After your call, we came to the rodeo grounds, spotted Boone Rasmussen's pickup, based on the description and plate number you gave us, and pursued the pickup as the driver gave chase."

Ty stared at the cop. "But Rasmussen was here with me and Dusty."

The cop nodded. "We finally forced the driver of the pickup off the road about twelve miles out of town and took her into custody. It wasn't Boone Rasmussen, but a woman by the name of Sierra Edgewood."

"Sierra was driving Rasmussen's pickup?" Ty asked in surprise.

"She'd been drinking," the cop said. "Told us that she thought her husband, Monte Edgewood, had set us on her and that she had kept going out of fear of what her husband would do to her if she was caught and turned over to him." The cop looked to Cash. "Is there any basis for her concerns about her husband?"

"Not that I know of," Cash said. "She had a key to Rasmussen's pickup?"

The cop nodded. "A single key. She said she'd had it made one day when she'd borrowed the pickup. Planned to use it to get away from her abusive husband."

"No way," Ty spoke up. "She was a diversion so Boone could get away." His head ached. He rubbed a hand over his face. "But why would Sierra Edgewood help Boone Rasmussen?"

"Good question," Cash said.

From over by the other two semis, one of the police officers yelled, "I've got a body over here."

"His name is Lamar Nichols," Cash said after taking a look. "If you have any more questions for Mr. Coltrane, they will have to wait. It appears the killer might have my sister. Don't try to apprehend him if you find him. Wait for me." He looked to Ty. "Let's find Dusty."

The two ran to the highway patrol helicopter and buckled up as the chopper took off.

"Boone could be headed in any direction," Cash said. "He's originally from Texas. I'd think he would head south on 191 along the Gallatin River."

Ty tried to calm the panic rising in him as Cash told the pilot to head south toward West Yellowstone and the Idaho border. Had Boone taken Dusty? What would he do to her? Was she even still alive?

Ty stared down at the dark ribbon of highway and river below them. Who knew where Rasmussen would go. Or what he would do. Ty tried to concentrate and not panic.

Would he go back to Texas? Or hide somewhere? "He'll have to get rid of the semi for something less conspicuous," Ty said out loud. But why take Dusty? "She has to be a hostage in case he's cornered and has to bargain his way out."

"We can only hope that's the case," Cash said. "That means he will want to keep her alive."

Cash checked in with the highway patrol and sheriff's departments on the ground. Ty could tell from this side of the conversation that there was still no sign of the semi.

Ty thought about what Cash had told the Bozeman police. It was believed that Rasmussen had killed three people to keep his secret—Clayton T. Brooks, Waylon Dobbs and Lamar Nichols. He was desperate. He could do anything.

Cash took another call on the radio. Ty saw him frown and held his breath, terrified it was news of Dusty. Bad news.

"Is it…?" he asked.

Cash shook his head. "No word on Rasmussen or Dusty."

Cash got another call and took it as Ty watched the highway below them for the semi.

Cash clicked off and Ty could tell from his expression that this call hadn't been good news. "It was one of the roughstock producers in Texas I'd contacted about Rasmussen." Cash frowned. "Did you know that Lamar was Rasmussen's half brother?"

Ty shook his head.

"If Rasmussen had one allegiance, it would be to his own blood, wouldn't you think? And given that he'd brought Lamar up here with him from Texas, given him a job…"

"Unless he killed him to keep him from talking," Ty said.

Cash shook his head as if struggling with the same thing Ty was. If Rasmussen hadn't killed Lamar, then who did that leave?

Cash let out an oath. "You aren't thinking what I'm thinking?"

"That Sierra was a diversion, but not for Boone Rasmussen?" Ty said.

Cash swore again and leaned toward the pilot. "Take us to Antelope Flats as fast as you can get this thing to go."

CHAPTER FOURTEEN

Dusty managed to peel back the edge of the tape on her mouth. She used her tongue to free all but one corner.

"Letty!" she cried as she scooted toward the opposite corner to her friend. Tears shone in Letty's eyes. "Turn around and I'll try to free your hands."

Dusty squirmed around until she had her back to Letty's. She began to work at the tape around Letty's wrists. It was slow going. As she worked, she told Letty everything, about Ty and the kiss, about Boone, about the syringe she'd picked up in the corral that night in Sheridan and had forgotten about. She left out the part about Lamar, not wanting to scare Letty even worse.

She almost had Letty's hands free when the truck slowed, throwing them both off balance. The semi turned onto a bumpy dirt road. Dusty worked her way close to Letty again and tugged faster at the duct tape holding Letty's wrists together.

Dusty could feel time slipping away. The semi moved slowly along the dirt road, giving her the feeling that it wasn't going far. She had to get Letty free and quickly.

As the truck began to slow down even more, the last of the tape pulled free.

Letty reached up and jerked the tape from her mouth with a cry of pain then hurriedly began tugging at the tape on Dusty's wrists. She talked ninety miles an hour, telling Dusty about having been stolen from her birth mother, about meeting Hal Branson, finding her birth mother and coming to the rodeo to tell her best friend.

As Letty freed Dusty's wrists, the two hugged fiercely, both crying in relief and fear, before quickly working to free their ankles.

As the truck rolled to a stop, Devil's Tornado stirred at the rear of the trailer.

A yard light came on. Light cut through the slits in the side of the trailer.

Dusty blinked, seeing something she hadn't been able to earlier. There was something lying on the other side of Devil's Tornado. Ty?

She scrambled to her feet and rushed toward the bull, forgetting about her safety in her fear that she would find Ty lying dead at the back of the semitrailer.

But Devil's Tornado didn't move. Just watched her with a disinterested, almost too calm look. *He's drugged,* Dusty thought, an instant before she saw the cowboy stretched out on the floor next to the bull.

It wasn't Ty, she saw at once. Behind Dusty, Letty let out a small cry. "Boone? If Boone's in here with us, then who—"

Letty didn't get to finish as the door of the trailer clanged open and the two stood staring down at Monte Edgewood—and the gun he held in his hand, the barrel pointed in their direction.

"WELL, AREN'T YOU two clever getting loose," Monte said congenially. "Come on down from there."

"I don't understand what's going on," Dusty said as she

looked from Monte's big open face to the gun in his hand. Everyone in the county liked Monte Edgewood. Some had wondered if he'd lost his mind when he married a woman half his age. No one had ever really liked Sierra. But if anything, they were kinder to Monte because of their dislike for his young wife.

"Come on down, girls," Monte said and motioned with the gun for Dusty to step down first. Letty followed, hanging on to the back of Dusty's jacket.

He herded them toward a small old barn. Dusty could see the moon peeking in and out of the clouds overhead and tried to estimate how long they'd been in the back of the semitrailer. She didn't recognize the barn. It was old and crumbling and could have been located anywhere in Montana, or for that matter, in Idaho or Wyoming.

But she got the feeling that it was on Monte's property as he swung open the door and ushered them both inside. Straw bales were stacked along one wall. An old lantern sat on a bench nearby, the flickering flame lighting the small interior.

Dusty stumbled in with Letty at her side as Monte forced them back against the straw bales. There was little else in the barn. She tried to see past the lantern light to dark corners, looking for something she could use as a weapon. There was no doubt in her mind that Monte Edgewood intended to kill them.

"Where is Ty?" she asked, afraid of the answer. But she had to know.

"At the rodeo, where we left him." Monte patted her shoulder. "Don't worry. He's fine. By now, the police have found him. He'll live."

Dusty felt Letty shudder next to her, the words, *he'll*

live hanging in the air as if to say Ty would live, unlike her and Letty.

"Mr. Edgewood—" Letty began.

"Call me Monte," he said. "You're the Arnolds' girl, right?"

Letty didn't answer. "What are you going to do with us?"

"Not me. Boone." He made a disappointed face. "He was like a son to me. I trusted him. I took him into my home. I taught him about the roughstock business. I would have given him anything." Monte let out a laugh that chilled Dusty to the bone. "Hell, I *did* give him everything." His eyes narrowed, darkened; the hand holding the gun seemed to quiver. "Including my wife."

Dusty took Letty's hand and squeezed it, trying to reassure her when Dusty herself was scared speechless.

Monte looked up at them as if he'd been gone for a moment. He blinked, seemed to refocus. "Boone was such a fool. If he'd just come to me with his plan. Hell, I would have helped him. But he didn't trust me." He shook his head. "Trust. It all comes down to trust, doesn't it?"

Dusty thought about making a run for it with Letty, but she knew Monte would chase them down even if they split up, which Dusty wasn't about to do.

She listened, thought she heard something, a faint hum in the distance. A vehicle? Ty had called her brother. Cash would be looking for her. Only both Ty and Cash would think that Boone had her—not Monte Edgewood.

"It's funny," Monte said more to himself than Dusty and Letty. "You never know what you will do. You think you know yourself. You have this image of the kind of person you are. Then something happens. You have everything you've ever wanted and more, and someone comes along and offers you a chance to be famous. And even though you know it's a false kind of rise to fame, you latch on to the dream because you want so desperately to be a part of it."

Dusty let her gaze scan the barn for a weapon. She had no idea what Monte was talking about. He sounded half-crazy. That scared her as much as the gun. The hum in the air she'd heard earlier seemed to be getting louder. Not a vehicle. More like a plane. Or a helicopter!

She spotted a pitchfork by the door and an old ax handle on the floor in the corner, nothing else. Neither was close enough to get to them before Monte fired the gun.

But the lantern was only a few yards away on the other side of Letty.

Dusty realized that Monte had stopped talking. "What was the dream?" she asked hurriedly, latching on to the only word she could recall.

He frowned. "A bull that would make everyone in the country remember the name Edgewood Roughstock Company. Devil's Tornado."

Everyone will remember that name now, Dusty thought.

Monte had stopped talking again and was listening now, his expression making it clear that he, too, heard the sound of what could have been a helicopter outside, coming closer.

"I'm sorry it has to end like this," he said. "Boone was a bad seed. It was my fault for letting him infect me and my wife. Once he is gone… I'm just sorry that he killed so many people before he was stopped." Monte raised the gun, pointing it at Letty.

Dusty still had hold of her friend's hand. "No!" Dusty

cried, stepping in front of Letty to lunge for the lantern Monte had left on a small bench nearby. She flung the lantern in Monte's direction as she dragged Letty to the barn floor with her.

The deafening sound of a gunshot boomed in the empty barn, sending a flock of pigeons flapping down from the rafters overhead. Dust filled the air an instant after the lantern ricocheted off Monte's arm. Glass exploded as the lantern hit the floor. Fuel and flames skittered up the dry wood wall, setting the straw bales on fire.

Dusty and Letty scrambled to their feet. But Monte was blocking the door, the gun raised as he tried to take aim at them. They dove for the back of the barn, realizing too late there was no way out as flames lapped at the dried wood of the old barn, thick smoke quickly filling the small space.

Dusty's eyes burned as she pulled the corner of her jacket up to cover her mouth and nose. Letty did the same. They were trapped. There was no place to run. No place to hide. Monte raised the gun.

Something moved behind Monte. Dusty felt her heart jump, praying it would be help. Boone Rasmussen materialized in the doorway.

"Monte!" He picked up the pitchfork and called again. "Monte!"

Monte turned slowly, seeming surprised to see Boone, even more surprised to see the pitchfork in his hand. The older man shook his head, as if he knew Boone wouldn't use it. He raised the gun and fired.

Boone stumbled back a step and looked down at the blood pouring out of the bullet hole in his chest. Then he raised the pitchfork and lunged at Monte.

Monte fired again. Through the smoke, Dusty saw Boone fall to his knees. Behind him, Ty appeared like a mirage from out of the darkness in the barn doorway.

The fire crackled all around them, sweeping up the walls, setting the roof on fire.

Dusty called to Ty to watch out as Monte raised the gun to fire at him. She rushed Monte, Letty beside her. They hit him hard from behind. He stumbled and went down.

Ty grabbed Dusty and Letty and dragged them out of the inferno. Dusty caught sight of her brother as Cash pulled Boone's body out as charred timbers began to fall from overhead.

Cash started to go back for Monte, But it was too late. The roof collapsed in a shower of sparks and smoke. Dusty buried her face in Ty's chest as flames engulfed what was left of the barn—and Monte Edgewood.

CHAPTER FIFTEEN

Dusty felt as if she were in a fog as they left the Edgewood ranch and headed for the clinic in town.

Boone had already been pronounced dead at the scene. Parts of the barn still burning. The fire department and coroner had been called.

Cash had the helicopter take Dusty and Letty to the clinic, sending Ty along with them. Although everyone involved in the case seemed to be dead or, in Sierra's case, in jail, Cash wasn't taking any chances.

Cash stopped by the hospital with questions for Dusty and Ty. Dusty told her brother about the night after the rodeo when someone had followed her home.

"It was Boone," Dusty said. "I didn't know it at the time, but he must have seen me pick up the syringe. I stuck it in my purse and forgot all about it."

"I've seen all the stuff you have in that purse, so I can believe that," Cash said. "But why pick it up at all?"

Dusty shot him a duh look. "One of the horses could have stepped on it. Any rancher would pick it up and pocket it."

"Probably why I became a sheriff," he said.

"Sierra is singing like a canary from her jail cell in Bozeman," Cash said. "She said she'd awakened the night Clayton T. Brooks was murdered to see her husband coming in from the far pasture, his shirt and jeans covered in blood. She'd pretended to be asleep as he put the clothes into the washer and showered before returning to bed."

"So she knew," Ty said shaking his head.

"When she'd heard Clayton had been murdered and that Cash thought Clayton had come out to the Edgewood Roughstock Ranch the night he died, Sierra still couldn't believe Monte had killed him," Cash said. "At least that's her story. She said she thought Monte was covering for Boone."

"What about Waylon's murder?" Ty asked.

"Sierra says Waylon had been by the ranch the day he died," Cash said. "She'd seen Waylon and Monte out in the yard arguing."

"So you think Waylon tried to blackmail Monte?"

"Appears that way," Cash said. "According to Sierra, Monte had come into the house upset. Later he left and when he came back, she smelled smoke on him. But she also smelled smoke on Boone later that night when she went to his bed. Boone said it was from Lamar smoking in his truck. We still don't know how Boone's watch ended up in the ashes at Waylon's house if Monte set the fire."

Dusty frowned. "I might. You know that night at the rodeo in Sheridan, the night Boone chased me home? I saw Boone drop something on the ground. At the time I just saw something glitter. It must have been his watch because Monte picked it up and pocketed it."

"Then used the watch to try to frame Boone for Waylon's murder and the fire," Cash said.

"So Sierra really did take Boone's truck to get away from Monte?" Ty asked.

Cash nodded. "She says she realized he knew about her and Boone and that she feared he planned to kill her, too."

"Why?" Letty asked. "Why would someone like Monte Edgewood do this?"

"Greed, pride, the need to be somebody," Cash said. "He saw that Devil's Tornado could make him famous. Once he found out that Boone was drugging the bull, he chose to kill to cover the deception."

"By killing?" Ty asked. "He couldn't possibly think he could get away with it."

"Once he found out about Sierra and Boone, he planned to frame Boone for all the murders," Dusty said, remembering what Monte had said in the barn last night.

"According to Sierra, under the contract Monte had with Boone, if something happened to Boone, Monte would get Devil's Tornado," Cash said. "Except it turns out that Devil's Tornado is really a docile bull named Little Joe."

"What happens to the Edgewood Roughstock Ranch and Little Joe?" Dusty asked.

"Sierra inherits it all," Cash said. "She already has a lawyer looking into selling everything, lock, stock and barrel. I would imagine that will be the last we see of her."

"So it's over," Ty said.

"Seems that way," Cash agreed.

Dr. Taylor Ivers came back into the room to give Letty and Dusty some salve for the slight blistering they'd suffered on their faces. She'd already treated them for smoke inhalation and said they could go.

Dusty thanked the doctor. Taylor was part of the McCall family in an extended way. Everyone had thought Taylor would leave town after everything that had happened, but she seemed determined to stay on at the clinic.

Taylor seemed to be lightening up a little. Dusty had heard that Taylor and her sister Anna Austin VanHorn McCall even had lunch once a week now.

"You need a ride home?" Cash asked Dusty.

"I borrowed a pickup from a friend," Ty said quickly. "I'll take her and Letty home."

Cash smiled and nodded, giving his sister a hug before he left.

When Ty pulled up in front of Letty's motel, Hal Branson was waiting for her.

Hal had been out of his mind when she hadn't shown up for their date and, after talking to the police, had driven clear to Antelope Flats in the middle of the night because he'd been so worried about her. The last time he'd talked to Letty, she was headed for the rodeo to meet Dusty—and Hal had feared she'd met up with more than Dusty.

Dusty couldn't have handpicked a man more perfect for Letty, she thought, when she met Hal. She could just imagine their children. And seeing the joy in both of their faces, Dusty had a feeling marriage and children wouldn't be that far off.

Hal offered to make coffee since the sun would be coming up soon. He and Letty went into the house behind the motel office.

"I'll give you a ride home," Ty offered. "Unless you want to stay here and have coffee."

Dusty shook her head. "Three's a crowd." She reached over and took one of the keys off the board behind the motel desk. "Looks like No. 9 is empty," she said and tossed the key to him.

TY STARED DOWN at the key, then up at Slim. He'd never been so thrown off balance by any woman in his life. His gaze met hers.

"Well?" she asked.

"Slim—"

"I know. It's been one hell of a night. I have no intention of going home and having to tell this story again." Her eyes locked with his. "Nor do I plan to spend what's left of this night alone in my bed." She smiled. "I already told Cash I wouldn't be coming home tonight. You going to try to make a liar out of me?"

"You sure about this, Slim?"

"More sure than I have ever been about anything in my life," she said leaning into him to kiss him. "And you know me."

He chuckled. "Oh, yeah, I know you, Slim." And he was about to get to know her better. "But I have to tell you that I always pictured us married first, me carrying you over the threshold of our new house."

"Really?" She smiled. "How long would it take to build this house?"

"Six months, at least."

"Great," she said, taking the motel room key from his hand. "That will give us plenty of time to get to know each other better. Starting tonight."

She started to walk past him, but he reached out and pulled her to him, kissing her as he took the motel room key.

"It's not the same as our own home, mind you," he said as he swung her up in his arms and shoved open the door. "But for tonight, it will have to do."

DUSTY WAS TREMBLING when he set her down in motel room No. 9. Nine for luck, she thought as she looked up at him. A chill rippled across her skin, an ache in her belly. This was Ty, a boy she'd known all her life.

Only as she looked at him, she realized he wasn't a boy anymore. She was staring into the eyes of a man. A man whom she suspected would continue to surprise her until the day she died.

A shudder quaked through her as he took her in his arms and kissed her, deepening the kiss as he molded his body to hers.

"Ty," she moaned against his wonderful mouth.

His large hands took her shoulders and backed her up until she was pressed against the wall. His mouth dropped to hers again. The sensation was like fireworks exploding through her body.

He rested his hand on the curve of her hip. Snaked his fingers up her rib cage and slipped it under the edge of her bra. A soft sigh escaped her lips as his warm hand cupped her breast. He bent to press his mouth against her throat, sending a shiver of kisses along the rim of her ear. His tongue licked across her warm skin as his hands skimmed over her body, as if he were memorizing every inch, tasting every inch.

Her fingers dug into his muscled back as he carried her over to the bed. "Slim," he whispered, then drew back. "Would you rather I call you Dusty?" he asked, so serious it made her laugh.

She shook her head. She was his Slim and they both knew it.

She didn't remember him taking off her clothes. Or her taking off his. But suddenly they were naked, their bodies melding together as they rolled around on the bed, laughing and kissing, his blue eyes a flame burning over her bare skin, hotter than the fire in the barn.

His mouth dropped to her breast and she thought she would die from the sheer pleasure of it. She buried her hands in his thick hair, moaning as he gently bit down on her hard nipple, arching against him, loving the feel of flesh to flesh. Loving Ty.

He made love to her slowly, gently, with a kind of awe, as if amazed that she had given herself to him so completely. She found even the pain of her first time was pleasurable. They made love again as the sun rose on another day, all the horror of what they'd been through slipping away like clouds after a rainstorm.

In Ty's arms, she found everything she'd dreamed of and more. He fulfilled her every fantasy as if he knew exactly what she wanted. What she needed. Later, she propped herself up on one elbow and looked down at him, surprised that she felt no embarrassment.

"Your father is going to think we're too young to get married," Ty said, running his thumb along her lower lip.

She kissed the rough pad of his thumb and shook her head. "My father will be delighted."

Ty didn't look so sure about that.

"You'll see. I know my father." She fell silent for a moment, thinking about Asa. "Can I tell you something?"

"You can tell me anything, Slim."

"I think he's dying."

Ty sat up in surprise. "Oh, honey."

She nodded and brushed at the tears that blurred her eyes. "I saw something in his expression at the last family dinner. I think he planned to tell us all, but then Cash had to leave." She bit down on her lower lip as Ty pulled her to him, holding her tightly in his arms.

They made love again, slow and sweet. She fell into a deep sleep in Ty's arms, only to be awakened by the phone late the next day.

Ty answered it, listened, then handed it to her, his face set in a grim line that frightened her.

"Dusty?" It was Shelby. What was her mother doing calling her? The only way she would have known where to find her was from Cash—and there was no way he would have told Shelby about what had happened last night.

"What's wrong?" Dusty asked, sitting up, thinking it might be about her father.

"You have to come home," Shelby said.

Dusty was ready to launch into a speech about how she was twenty-one and she didn't have to explain herself when Shelby said, "I wouldn't have called you, Dusty, but it's your father."

Dusty gripped the phone tighter.

"He wants everyone to come out to the ranch," Shelby said. "Rourke, Brandon and J.T. are already here with their wives. Cash and Molly are on their way. You're welcome to bring Ty with you. This concerns everyone who your father—" her voice broke "—loves."

Dusty could hear her mother crying softly.

"We'll be right there."

ONCE EVERYONE WAS SEATED around the large dining room table, Asa McCall stood. It took all the strength he had, but he wanted to do this standing. He didn't want them to see how weak he was. Soon enough, they would know.

"I appreciate you all coming on such short notice," he

said, looking around the table at each of them, his sons and their wives or soon-to-be-wives, Dusty and Ty. He'd always hoped his headstrong daughter would realize that the man of her dreams lived just up the road.

There was so much he wanted to say to them.

To think he'd almost lost Dusty last night. Cash had filled him in, no doubt leaving out many of the more frightening details. The thought that Dusty might not be here with them practically dropped him to his knees.

Shelby reached over and took his hand, squeezed it and smiled reassuringly at him. The love of his life. Strong, just like her daughter. He thanked God for that.

He cleared his throat and began the story about his friend Charley and the land deal, telling the story quickly, simply.

He knew his children would understand the consequences at once. They were too smart not to.

When he'd finished, J.T. had his head in his hands. Everyone looked stricken.

"I don't see how you could have let something like this happen," J.T. said, then shook his head.

"It happened," Rourke cut in. "The question is, what can we do?"

Asa shook his head and suddenly had to sit down. "We haven't enough money or capital to buy him out. The mineral rights are worth more than the land."

"There must be some way to stop this," Cash said. "Have you talked to a lawyer?"

"The contract cannot be broken," Asa said. "I've already tried to buy back the mineral rights. He wouldn't sell to me even if I could raise that much money."

"But we're at the north end of the coal fields," Rourke

said. "There might not even be any coalbed methane gas at this end of the valley. That mineral rights contract might not be worth the paper it's written on."

"It seems Charley's son is willing to take that chance," Asa said.

"It will change the ranch, but we will still own the land," Dusty spoke up, as if waiting for worse news. He'd seen the look in her eyes when she'd come into the room. She knew he was dying. Like her mother, she probably could also see how weak he was and that this was taking every ounce of his strength.

He smiled down the table at her, grateful to have such a daughter.

"There will be roads all over to the gas well heads," Rourke was saying. "Even if they don't find gas, they will drill for months. Maybe even years, putting in roads, ruining the land."

"Yesterday, I received a letter in the mail that Charley's son has sold the mineral rights lease," Asa said and looked down the table at his youngest son. "It was bought up by Mason VanHorn."

He watched Brandon look over at his wife, Anna VanHorn McCall, in surprise. Asa had been trying to come to terms with the fact that Brandon had gone against his wishes and married Anna. He'd feared that the long-standing feud between the McCalls and the VanHorns would end up destroying his son's life. When he'd seen the letter and found out that Mason VanHorn had bought up the mineral rights lease for McCall land, Asa knew his worst fear had come true.

Only Mason VanHorn had the kind of money to buy up

the lease. Asa was thankful he wouldn't live long enough to see a VanHorn drilling on McCall land.

"Is that true?" Brandon asked Anna.

She rose slowly from her seat at the table. She was a beautiful woman, just as her mother had been. Reaching into her pocket, she pulled out a thick envelope of papers and handed them to her husband. "These are for Asa."

Brandon took them and, without looking at them, passed them down the table to Asa.

"It's true, my father purchased the mineral rights lease," Anna said. "It was his wedding present to me and Brandon." She met Asa's gaze. "And a peace offering, so that the children and grandchildren of the McCalls and the VanHorns can finally live in peace."

Asa felt his hands begin to shake as he read the papers, his eyes filling with tears of gratitude as he looked down the table at his daughter-in-law. He could only shake his head in disbelief, his sworn enemy coming to his rescue.

The irony wasn't lost on him. VanHorn had made a fortune in gas wells—something Asa had sworn would never be found on his ranch. And in the end? VanHorn had used that fortune to buy back Asa's soul from the devil. In return, Mason VanHorn asked for nothing. Nothing, after all the years of the bad blood between them.

"Thank you," Asa said. "I look forward to the day when I can thank your father in person."

"But there's more, isn't there?" Cash said. "More you need to tell us."

Asa nodded and looked to Dusty. "But first, I think there is something you'd like to say?"

Dusty got to her feet, all eyes on her. "I'm in love with Ty Coltrane."

Everyone looked at her as if waiting for more.

"Of course you are," Shelby said, smiling, as if she'd known it all along.

"He's asked me to marry him," Dusty continued, her gaze shifting to her father. "It's going to be a small wedding. Just family. Tomorrow."

There were sounds of surprise around the table, but Dusty saw her father nod and Shelby start to cry quietly.

"You sure about this?" J.T. asked, looking around the table in confusion. "This is so sudden. You haven't even *dated.*"

Dusty smiled. "Someone once told me that when you found your true love, you just knew. You didn't have to kiss a lot of frogs. Or a lot of princes. You just had to know in your heart that this was the right person for you. Ty's my true love." Tears rushed to her eyes as she looked at her father, saw him squeeze the hand of his true love. "I want you to give me away," she said to her father.

His jaw tensed, as if he were fighting to keep his face from showing the emotion she saw in his eyes. "It would be my pleasure," he said, voice cracking.

J.T. let out an expletive. The rest of the family had fallen silent. He looked down the table at his father. "How long do you have?"

"Not long enough."

EPILOGUE

Rain fell in a light drizzle on the day of Asa McCall's funeral. Dusty stood on the hillside, her husband Ty beside her, his arm around her as she huddled against the cold and wetness and grief.

Across from her stood her brothers Rourke, Cash and Brandon, next to them their wives, their expressions somber as they stared down at their father's casket.

Brandon's eyes filled with tears. Dusty saw Anna clutch his hand tighter. Mason VanHorn held his daughter's hand as he, too, stood in the rain over his once worst enemy's grave. The two had found peace only at the end of Asa's life, a horrible waste that Dusty knew would haunt Mason to his own grave.

Shelby stood between Dusty and her eldest son J.T., his wife Reggie next him.

The pastor cleared this throat. "As anyone standing here knows, Asa McCall wasn't much of a churchgoer." There was a slight nervous titter from the crowd. "In fact, he didn't hold much patience with a man of the collar." Pastor Grayson smiled. "I remember the first time I met Asa McCall. We got into a discussion about God." He chuckled. "Asa said he had a fine arrangement with God. God tried his patience every day—and Asa tried the Lord's. He said they'd been getting along just fine with that arrangement for years, and he saw no reason to confuse God by acting any different."

A smattering of laughter, then sniffles.

"That strong, sometimes impossible, man is who we are putting to rest here today," the pastor said. "Asa lived life on his terms and took full responsibility for the whole of it. He was a God-fearing man who, like the rest of us, made his share of mistakes." Pastor Grayson looked over at Shelby. "I had the good fortune to speak with Asa before he passed away. He told me of his regrets—the greatest one being not living long enough to see all of his grandchildren."

Dusty blinked back tears. Ty pulled her closer.

"But Asa died knowing that his children and their children would continue the legacy his father had begun so many years ago when he brought the first herd of longhorns to Montana and settled in this valley. That, he told me, was more than he ever could have wanted—to see his lifework continued by his own children and their children."

Pastor Grayson opened the small black Bible in his hands and looked down. "Asa asked me to read this today. It's something he wrote just before he died."

The pastor cleared his voice and began to read, "By the time you hear this, I will be gone from you. Don't mourn my passing. I had a long and fruitful life. Bury me on the hillside with the rest of the McCalls and then get on with your lives. You have a ranch to run and children to make and raise. Don't try to make me into a saint. I was a stubborn jackass. I want my grandchildren to know the man I really was. Maybe it will keep them from making the mistakes I did.

"I ask only one other thing. Take care of your mother.

Don't blame her for my asinine behavior so many years ago. Pushing her from my life is my greatest regret, second only to never telling all of you how much I love you, admire you, respect you. You have all made an old man proud."

Tears streamed down Dusty's face as she looked over at her mother and saw the naked grief in her face. Dusty reached out and took her mother's hand. Her mother seemed surprised, then smiled through her tears and squeezed her daughter's hand.

Slowly, Asa McCall's casket was lowered into the ground on the ranch he'd loved. Dusty looked past the old family cemetery to the view of the Big Horn Mountains and McCall land stretching as far as the eye could see. Her father's view for eternity, she thought as she turned her face into Ty's strong shoulder, felt his arms come around her as she said goodbye to her father.

* * * * *

A single mom puts her life, and the life of her little boy, in the hands of a sexy, protective county prosecutor...

It was well after nine when Dalton finally called Briar to tell her he was coming up the front walkway. She hurried to unlock the door and let him in. "All stitched up?"

He nodded. "Want to see my wound?"

Smiling, she shook her head. "You hungry? Logan and I had chicken soup for dinner. I can heat some up for you."

He caught her hand as she moved toward the kitchen, his fingers warm and firm around hers. "Doyle and I grabbed a burger on the way home."

"How'd that go?" She waited for him to let go of her hand, but he twined his fingers with hers instead, leading her over to the sofa. He sat heavily, tugging her down beside him.

"It went...better than I expected. He wasn't a complete smart-ass, and I tried not to be a defensive jerk. So...progress." He gave her hands a light squeeze. "Logan asleep?"

She looked down at their twined hands, her gaze drawn by the intersection of her fair skin and his tanned fingers. "About thirty minutes ago. We had to read a couple of extra stories, and he was worried that you weren't home yet, but I explained you had to go somewhere with your brother. I also promised you'd look in on him before you go to bed. You don't have to, though. Once he falls asleep, it takes a bulldozer to wake him. He wouldn't know you were there."

HIEXP69753

"I'll know," he said, rolling his head toward her.

She met his gaze, a ripple of pure feminine awareness rolling through her, setting off a dozen tingles along her spine.

But was she woman enough to deal with a man like Dalton? A man who'd lived a life of privilege she couldn't even begin to imagine, much less understand? A man with his own demons that made her day-to-day struggles seem like bumps in the road in comparison?

"Last night," he murmured, "I wanted to kiss you."

She closed her eyes, overwhelmed by his raw honesty. "I know."

"I still do."

HIEXP69753